Dreamland

by

Bryan Roy

Published by New Generation Publishing in 2020

First Edition

ISBN 978-1-80031-640-9

Cover design by David Gallimore

www.newgeneration-publishing.com

New Generation Publishing

1

The State of Iowa USA Present Day

Principal J. Jones Junior, M. A. stood on the thirty-third and top white marble step that led to the Grecian-style colonnade entrance of the Columbia Faculty of Psychic and Paranormal Research at the Iowa State University.

Inside the imposing façade lay the impressive entrance lobby floor. Skillfully manufactured by time-honored craftsmen, who had painstakingly carved and polished the imported marble checks, that generated undulating hypnotic optical patterns, that made a curious viewer's eyes quiver and twitch as they tried to focus on the intricate geometric configurations.

Around the lobby walls hung illuminated gold framed portraits of the many past and present Principals and university benefactors. Some of them, not all, were 'Shriners,' regaled in their finest, Middle-Eastern inspired, fraternal society costumes: hats, sashes, bows and gallant-less medals. Lamb's wool aprons, hard metal set-squares, needle-sharp compasses and pristine coruscating golden trowels. All on public display. Each regaled item portrayed in paint and captured in a timeless brush-stroke gesture, which was both significant and symbolic. The artist's brief clearly defined, his fanciful subjects adorned purposefully and strategically positioned, frozen within their respective glittering frames.

The curious and more observant onlooker would note the hands and feet of the numerous canvass caught subjects, were all stationed at strict right-angles. Honorable postures that emulated the more recognisable, ubiquitous and most eminent Masonic representation of all time. None other than 'dollar bill' George Washington. Captured for all time and for all generations, on stretched and fading canvass. Washington, a man of great virtue and moral standing, being as he was, one of the founding fathers of the United States of America.

Stars and Stripes flags and State University pennants fluttered in the foyer area, dancing in unison each time someone went out the glass fronted lobby, or, beyond the smaller rear doors that led to the rest rooms.

Taking pride of place in the faculty entrance lobby stood a gigantic bronze representation of the Owl of Minerva. A classic historical deity and important symbol for both Greek and later Roman cultures.

The predatory Owl of Minerva, commonly associated with wisdom and knowledge. An icon adopted by educational institutes around the world. Minerva, also identified by many as the virgin goddess of music and poetry. Representative of perspicacity and erudition throughout western history and culture.

The dominant, faculty lobby owl representation, was a wild and powerful image presented to the Iowa State University by one of it's past major patrons.

Concerning the domineering and enduring bird: many of the commonplace, uninitiated students, freshmen and sophomores alike, considered the ornithological exhibit a mere representation of natural history and no more.

However, to the enlightened fraternities of 'Theta Delta Chi' and 'Sigma Alpha Epsilon,' as well as others, such as, the sororities of 'Kappa Kappa Gamma,' the towering effigy held a darker, and perhaps more significant meaning. Plainly speaking Minerva was 'their' goddess, a meaningful emblem of 'their' group and society. Representative to those few who had been inducted and instructed in the three-hundred and twenty-two ways of the 'mystery schools.'

The subject of which was never alluded to in the regular curriculum.

The late morning light was perfect. The sun kissed the white Grecian colonnades of the university buildings, and warmed the high grey tiled roofs of the campus lecture halls. The radiant aura that cascaded through the autumn trees perfectly illuminated the faculty entrance pillars. Named as they were, according to tradition: 'Joachim' and 'Boaz.'

These particular constructs, so some said, were half the size and scale of the original ancient pillars that once stood proudly in the porch of King Solomon's temple in Jerusalem. Boaz to the left and Joachim to the right.

The first temple pillars of course had been torn down and destroyed by one of the numerous marauding-empire-building- conquerors of the ancient world. The original unique pomegranate contoured bronze pillar caps were smashed down and cut up, to make their transportation back east to the smelter's fires easier.

Now, even in the present 'modern era,' these two majestic towering replica pillars still stood superior. Representations, as with the owl in the lobby, that few students understood or had even noticed.

During the previous week a student (and clearly an emerging artist), had spray-painted one of the white stone colonnade replicas with a distorted image of a man sporting a massive erect phallus. One that was dripping with spent semen, that had been conveniently, and no doubt pleasurably, ejaculated over a rather overpowering out-line of a pair of female breasts. Unmistakably an imitation and graphitic representation of two anonymous staff members. Everyone however, without dispute or contention, knew exactly who the subjects were: Principal J. Jones Junior and his ever-loyal secretary, Ms Celia Jones.

Today, graffiti aside, was a momentous occasion, and the clean-shaven and immaculately dressed (in a bespoke silver-grey silk suit and fraternity tie), the now approaching retirement age, Principal J. Jones, was more than proud.

In many ways he could have claimed to be the inspiration behind the forthcoming: (some critics would say), foolhardy, and all together risky, Magnetronic

Research Unit's (MRU) attempt to universally measure the earth's magnetic field.

Mainstream science had for years predicted at some point in the future an inevitable reversal of the earth's magnetic poles. A cataclysmic event that may end life on earth; as humanity knew it. However, speculation as to 'if' this would happen, had now been superseded as to 'when' this freak of nature would take place?

This Iowa University sponsored fact gathering venture would commence here, now, today, in the heartland of the USA. And eventually, over the next decade, would (it was planned), circumnavigate and map the entire globe. Gathering important and crucial data as they went.

A great day indeed. However, in Principal J. Jones' view, there was a short-term more immediate outcome present in his scheming mind. And that was to boost the reputation of the Iowa State University. Thus, appealing to more students to attend an increasing number of science-based courses, and therefore attracting more investment and funding. Whilst, affording 'him' a criminally large pension increase.

As it was, today at least, he would take on a low-key role in the ceremonial proceedings. Therefore, he gave his approval, on this singular occasion, to allow others to take the credit and receive the accolades for what he claimed was 'his' and only 'his' theoretical idea. In the near future he imagined a much coveted 'Nobel Prize' in the offing and rapidly coming his way.

An unexpected September breeze suddenly caught Principal J. Jones' thinning fair hair and he quickly swept his left hand over his scalp to smooth the wayward hairline back into place; whilst taking care not to smudge the foundation make-up he had applied to his face earlier in the morning to cover the blood-red thread veins he had recently noticed invading his cheeks and nose.

Meanwhile, the agitated air continued eddying across the white marble steps, and eventually blustered, in a languid, playful fashion, across the wider concourse below. Painting random Maple leaf patterns as it swirled about in the minds of those who looked on in anticipation and hope that something captivating and entertaining might eventually take place.

However, such wild and abandoned stimulation of the imagination did not occur to Principal J. Jones, who pragmatically thought: 'where are the janitors and gardeners to sweep the concourse?' Whilst others, with more liberated child-like minds, may have contemplated playfully dancing through the dying burnished vegetation; kicking the soggy leaves high into the air, before allowing the storm of plant life to rain down upon their lively animated heads.

Autumn was without doubt here. September-third and soon the next seasonal intake of scholars would gather. All prior to the October graduation ceremony, honours presented to and in aid of, the latest batch of students. Those who had enjoyed three or more hard and long years of supposed 'value free' education. Which naturally was going to put them in good standing for the remainder of their lives. They would all soon pass through the gates of academia into the real world of corporate mind-control.

To the Principal's right, standing so close to him that no daylight passed between them, was Ms Celia Jones (the other victim of the heinous graffiti attack), who had earlier strategically positioned herself in such a prime location. As the Principal's long-standing secretary and (as he considered), 'personal friend,' she had every right to remain shoulder to shoulder with her employer.

On this occasion, as with others, the Principal's brazen right hand took the opportunity to slide down the form of Ms Celia Jones' black pencil skirt, and playfully squeezed her shapely buttocks. Most women would call that: 'sexual harassment in the work place.' However, the middle-aged spinster, Ms Jones, who was the faculty Principal's confidant and eager lover, called it: 'keeping your job!' Maintaining her top flight position on campus was a constant battle. And without doubt, 'keeping her job' took a great deal of work and effort on her part. Hence the diets and visits to the campus gym. She, at all times, had to be on top of her career game, which amounted to ensuring the good Principal J. Jones, not only had eyes for her, but at the same time making certain his eyes did not roam up and down the chequered marble campus corridors in search of the latest and most shapely young bodies to grace his personal academic seat of learning. Therefore, to this end, Ms Jones spent money on breast enhancements, Botox treatments and frequent beauty parlor visits. These feminine activities were coupled with a healthy diet, whilst taking regular exercise to maintain her own shapely, Monroe-like figure.

On several occasion the dedicated secretary, who for the most was taken for granted by the Principal, had saved his 'ass' from litigation and law suits, perhaps even criminal charges. J. Jones, even though in a couple of years he was due to retire, was a serial sexual predator, who blatantly used his power and influence to seduce young female students; if and when he could. His was the classic: 'Hollywood Casting Couch' set-up. He could make or break, or pass or fail any female undergraduate. The future of so many young inexperienced scholars lay in the palm of his abusive grasping hands.

To the left of the cosy couple, also gathered on the top-step, were a group of curiously dressed 'Shriners'. All hailing from the mysterious 'Kaaba Temple', which in 1878 had been, along with much pomp and ceremony, established as a society with secrets in the State of Iowa.

The now global 'Shriner' movement, first conceived in 1870 by Walter M. Fleming and William J. Florence, today boasted three-hundred and fifty-thousand members world-wide. Iowa (once home of the 'Ioway' Indian people), eventually supported two further temples. One in Cedar Rapids and the other at Des Moines, the state capital of Iowa. Concerning which, was officially recognised as a state in 1846. Thanks mainly to the influence of the great-great-great-grandfather of the self-conscious young woman standing on the lonely lower steps below. Thelma Jones, who was deservedly the main object and attention of the day's proceedings.

As it was Thelma knew and cared little concerning her ancestors or current 'Shriner' benefactors. Who were, as far as she was concerned, just another 'all male' fraternity, of which Principal J. Jones was apparently a high-ranking and influential member? They, the 'Shriners,' so it was said, promoted fun and fellowship and above all the Masonic principles of brotherly love. Or that's how the young female Iowa graduate (now with a doctorate to her name), understood them to represent. Privileged she was, so they had said. 'She,' who was about to ascend the white marble steps before her, to a higher, dominant and loftier social position. Where, once at the zenith, she would accept a substantial donation towards her work from the 'Shriners.' The press, TV reporters and other state media representatives, stood on both sides of the pristine polished steps, eagerly awaiting events to unfold.

The 'Shriner' temple members were ultimately, in Thelma's view, on the surface at least, devoted to the community, and were committed to perform good deeds. This clearly afforded them an air of respectability. Philanthropists to the man, who interacted with the community when and wherever they possibly could.

It was of no surprise then that most tutors at the university, as with Principal J. Jones, and many other prominent Iowan citizens, were 'Shriners.' To be received into this illustrious and most erudite of fraternities, a man would need to be at least an accepted Freemason, initiated into either the Scottish or York Rites. All those 'Shriners' present were clearly colleagues of J. Jones the Principal, Thelma concluded. Although she thought them comical and carnivalesque, wearing, as they did, their Egyptian Fez-style hats and bright red uniforms; most of them covered with braid and gleaming medals, awards for no particular act of bravery. The group were heavily inspired by older civilisations, their ideas and eclectic imagery drawn from Arabic culture and mysticism.

Seeing as they, the 'Shriners,' were her sponsors, she felt grateful towards them, and it was clearly her duty to go along with their act of mummer. (Thelma, by the way, had already received the 'Shriner's' donation of one-hundred-thousand dollars, some four-weeks before hand).

A giant banker's check, designed with the press cameras in mind, was in the offing behind the faculty building's glass entrance doors, waiting to be presented to the young, and soon to be, intrepid explorer, Thelma Jones.

An inspiration to women of all ages. A girl whose ancestry dated back to the very founding on the state of Iowa. One of her great-great-great-grandfathers being: The Reverend Selwyn Jones, who had migrated with others to the United States in order to follow his puritanical forebears and establish a new and independent Protestant community in the New World. One free from both Catholic and High-Anglican dogma.

Once the new arrivals had walked through the lush verdant Iowan countryside and seen that the soil was rich and fertile, they decided to stay put. However, what had to be attended to first was the removal of the native Indian 'Ioway' people. A shipment of army rifles and other weaponry was the answer. And with the blessings of their god the Welsh Puritans proceeded to share the love of Jesus and exterminate the native population.

Be that as it may, if the truth be known, and if the so-called historians cared to carefully look deeper into the events of the past, they would see that the good Reverend Jones, and others of his ilk, were in fact 'all' Freemasons. And, along with the other newly burgeoning States of America, Iowa State was not founded on biblical truths and the love of Christ, but rather on the so-called basic principles of Masonic dogma disguised as brotherly love. Available to all new migrants, but clearly not intended for, or extended to, the native population.

The name 'Jones' soon became synonymous with Iowa. Together with wealth and moral values. Whilst conversely Iowa became synonymous with the Jones clan. Whose members rapidly spread abroad and colonised the entire state. Dividing, as they did, the land into counties as they saw fit. Establishing schools and hospitals as the population grew. And above all erecting places of worship in every town they founded and settled in. This was 'Dreamland' in the making, the initial home of the new American dream.

As it was, the Jones dynasty cleverly maintained their wealth, influence and power, by ensuring all financial and domestic matters were kept in the 'family' and not widely shared with outsiders or interlopers. This often-meant cousins marrying and even uncles and nieces being joined in matrimony. All in order to give rise to the next Jones' generation. As society and families grew, nepotism was at the heart of every household. It soon became the norm for every household head to be appointed to a position of power and influence in every institution in the State.

There was a Jones behind every high position or place, from Governor to State Attorney, from the church to the medical profession, from schools, and much later to even the 'Hawkeyes' football team.

Within a generation or two of occupation, Iowa was soon established as the best place to live and raise kids in the new USA. The rich land became the agricultural corn-belt of the nation, the bread-basket of what would become the world's only true 'super power' and food capital of the USA.

However, fertile land aside, its university currently only ranked number thirty-three in the US academic statistics charts. This despite the faculty motto of: 'never afraid to explore new frontiers!'

Outside of main-stream science, the Columbia Faculty of Psychic and Paranormal Research boasted a wide range of collaborative partnerships with some of the Principal institutions in America. Among them being: Google, Microsoft, and of course NASA. This so-called, 'lose affiliation,' allowed the faculty to use NASA maintained satellite links which enabled them to upload information from the field, to any given home-base laboratory. A facility that Thelma Jones was eagerly anticipating testing out.

More so, the wider campus prospectus offered a diverse range of creative and sporting study subjects, whilst maintaining an organic and vibrant alumni-based artistic community. The 'Gallery of fame' located in the main reception building was evidence enough of that. Past graduates who had 'made good' were honoured and praised for the success they had achieved in the world outside academia.

Past university registration documentation demonstrated the unusual, but predictable fact; that over fifty-three percent of all past and present attendees shared the family name of 'Jones.'

And then of course there was Football. The 'Hawkeyes' were big in the leagues with fans filling the Kinnick Stadium every weekend.

Iowa as a State was a compelling attraction and without doubt a 'Dreamland' to behold and enjoy. And its university, under the leadership of Principal J. Jones Junior, was about to be launched to the top of the academic charts, or so he hoped. That would take place only once the findings of this latest: 'never afraid to explore new frontiers' quest, became accepted as mainstream amongst fellow academics across the globe.

* * * * *

Thelma Jones' forthcoming 'Magnetronic' research paper would demonstrate new innovative ideas, principles and practices when looking into and examining the very electro-magnetic heart of the planet.

The pageant was about to get started when it suddenly occurred to Principal J. Jones Junior that there were indeed people, senior lecturers and other staff members, including a selection of specially invited former student graduates, standing behind the safety glass frontage of the science building entrance. And so therefore, could readily see his pincer-like right hand manipulating his secretary's rounded 'ass'. Consequently, he reacted swiftly and lifted his arm and hand upwards, pretending to supportively waive towards where Thelma Jones was patiently standing.

For a moment, the young woman waiting on the bottom step, took it to mean Principal J. Jones was signaling her to ascend the thirty- three treads to the top tier. However, that was not the case, as the local 'Shriner' ensemble was yet to melodically walk past those gathered, playing a medley of popular patriotic march band numbers. All part of the colorful extravagant ceremonial spectacle.

Thelma, nervously hesitated as a consequence of the Principal's feeble semaphore-like efforts to divert attention away from himself, and as a result she took a step backwards, prior to unfortunately losing her balance and slipping on a single autumnal leaf, one that had found its wayward passage onto the sole of her black sneaker-style shoe. All eyes of those gathered were now transfixed upon the forlorn young woman, anticipating as they were, her clambering to the top step to collect her well-earned bounty.

For her part, slightly tubby and frumpy Thelma, was dressed, as she always was, in a dowdy plain fashion. Primarily consisting of dun-colours and dark clashing patterns. The typical non-trend-setting-style of dress, that was typical of a person with higher than average I.Q. One that could not readily be matched. Whilst at the same time, unfortunately possessing no dress sense at all.

The mind of a genius yet, inept.

All adorned with a shock of dark brown hair, that had been cut for convenience and not for the sake of fashion or style.

Her heavy rimmed glasses added to her seemingly lugubrious looks and appeared to unkindly elongate her face to something reminiscent of the equine family.

Those who studied the human genome may have concluded, (and even verbally suggested) this 'look' was a result of long-term Iowan inter-breeding. Others may have more wisely refuted such a notion. Either way, her spectacles hid her deep hazel-brown eyes and horse-like characteristics away from public view. Her general features were, without doubt, passed down through the Jones' family line.

Apparently, Thelma had inherited her strange, yet unforgettable looks, from her great-great-grandmother: Catherine Jones, wife of Senator Thomas Jones. A picture of her hung in one of the many corridors of the sprawling university campus, one closest to the library. Catherine Jones was accredited with having nursed the sick during a past, particularly virulent, decimation of the Iowan population. Caused mainly, as claimed by various physicians, by a deadly derivative of the Bubonic plague. She herself had become its victim and died whilst trying to bring comfort to the sick.

Meanwhile, the gathered 'Shriner' sponsors remained rigid at the sight of the helpless Thelma. Not one man amongst them took the steps required to rectify the poor woman's predicament. All forms of help, aid and assistance appeared to dry up, as Thelma struggled to right herself before sprawling flat out on the lower-step. The expedition, her precious expedition, was about to depart and already they had hit a potential embarrassing impediment. Thelma felt a sense of humiliation and hopelessness as a pain shot around her right ankle, followed by a throbbing sensation that travelled up her right leg.

Suddenly, as if to ensure there was no hiatus in the proceedings, the band, which had been stationed in readiness around the corner of the building, struck up with their rendition of the Star-Spangled Banner. Automatically, Stars and Stripes flags were waved in a flurry of colour, as everyone stood tall and proud.

Shoulders back and arms stiff and straight. All, other than Thelma, felt a sense of patriotic pride and self-satisfaction.

Next, as if she were a white knight on an even whiter charger, Thelma's close colleague and assistant: Diana Rogers, unexpectedly appeared braking through the 'Shriner' ranks. Metaphoric Samurai sword in hand, ready and prepared to slay the dragons of ill-fortune. Beautiful Diana Rogers: graceful pin-up, a sacred feminine beauty, one-time pageant queen as well as being a deadly martial arts practitioner. Sensibly dressed as always, (so she thought) for today's events, in close-fitting gaudy pink jogging attire. She was more than sporty, and as always, the envy of many younger and older females alike. With a toned figure most women would depart this life for. The perfect Wonder Woman matinee idle and object of every red-blooded male's fantasy dreams. Diana's long blonde hair flew in tresses behind her. Whilst the girl's elongated and shapely, karate-kicking-legs, rapidly carried her the short distance between the parked Magnetronic expedition vehicles and the lower tread of the faculty building steps.

"Somebody call 911! An ambulance! Quickly!" Came the lone voice of Diana Rogers. Her voice instantly drowned out by the military music booming from the 'Shriner' band.

This stunning twenty-five-year-old, soon to become a heroine, was a former Iowa graduate, now university alumni, who had been assisting Thelma Jones with the preparatory work of the Magnetronic expedition for over two-years. Diana worked directly with Thelma as her indispensable assistant, and had and was being paid, as was the team leader Thelma, out of the university science department budget.

Despite what could be termed as her 'dumb blonde' looks, Diana was a straight 'A' student and an academic in her own right. She had been a student of and majored in astrophysics.

Regardless of her stunning looks, she had no time for

boyfriends, or any form of socialising. As with Thelma, her life was her work and she studied relentlessly in pursuit of the goals set out by the team leader, and her role model, Thelma Jones.

"An ambulance, someone call 911!" The lone voice repeated. Sill no one stirred, whilst Thelma doubled up in agony. The leg, according to Diana's limited medical experience, was clearly broken albeit an incomplete fracture in two painful parts. She clearly required immediate medical attention.

What had been glaringly odd and amiss, regarding the 'Shriner' led handing-over-the-money-ceremony, was the fact that no members of the Magnetronic Research Unit team, (MRU) other than Thelma, were invited to be included in any aspect of the presentation, including being precluded from all media coverage, such as direct interviews. Or, so the 'Shriners' apparently had insisted.

For some obscure reason the day belonged to 'Thelma Jones' and her alone.

This was nepotism at its worst. And all due to the fact that Thelma was the 'only' Jones family member in the MRU team, and therefore related to most of the 'Shriners' present.

Nonetheless, upon the appearance of Diana Rogers supporting her injured colleague, and regardless of the sponsor's bizarre request to the media representatives present, all the eager news cameras homed in on the arrival of the blonde bombshell, and began to record the bold attempt she was making to save her co-worker and make the best of the impromptu and embarrassing, yet news-worthy, state of affairs. News in the making that was rapidly unfolding before them. Yet, once again as before, not a single man, 'Shriner' or otherwise, moved a muscle to assist Diana get Thelma back on her feet and up the marble steps to accept her prize.

As it turned out though, Thelma required no further outside assistance, other than the now mightily empowered, Diana Rogers, who ultimately seized control of the situation. And, by means of propping her colleague up, she began to clamber alone and unaided up the cold stone flights, whilst dragging, as a child with a rag doll, her co-worker with her.

Initially, the potentially tragic scene had presented itself as being a rather comedic, therefore more than news-worthy, clumsy rescue attempt. But once Diana, with her high cheek bones, curvy body and warm luscious lips, had attained the top-step summit, all cameras, video or otherwise, were focused on her alone. By which time she had skillfully managed to turn the potentially tragic event, around into a sex-charged provocative stroll along a cat-walk model's runway.

2

The State of New Mexico

Both (MRU) Jeep Renegades were fitted with a specialised platform built over the roof to enable two people to recline back and lazily observe the night sky as a diversion away from their real undertaking, which was locate and record electro-magnetic activity through the earth's crust. For now, looking for falling stars to wish by was about all the team had achieved. Unfortunately, Thelma Jones, due to her severely sprained right ankle and fractured shin bone, could not manage to haul herself up onto the observation platform.

Her condition had puzzled the emergency medical staff. Such an unfortunate slip, and on a leaf? It was uncanny as well as inexplicable that so much physical damage could be caused by a simple Maple leaf? For some strange and also inexplicable reason, Thelma had managed, in her prone state, to remove the dastardly injurious leaf from the lower white marble step and continued to grasp the offending piece of vegetation, which would eventually be pressed between two pages of the novel she was currently reading. Which happened to be Dan Brown's latest 'block-busting' work of fiction, a most exciting sacrifice to the ravenous gods of publishing. And she was loving every addictive page of it.

What had also vexed the doctors and medical staff who attended to her 'serious fracture' was the fact that she categorically insisted on discharging herself from hospital as soon as she was able, and further more to carry on as normal with her magnetic mapping expedition. The medical staff talked about weeks to recover. Thelma worked on a recuperation time-scale of literal hours!

As it was, the 'Shriner's' symbolic gift presentation, now some three-days in the past, seemed to Thelma no more than a distant memory, or perhaps nightmare, depending on how, as an individual, you perceived the event. The heroine here being the ravishingly lovely Diana Rogers, who had truly saved the day and consequently ended up being the main focus of the news-starved media. Thelma did not mind that so much. She was out of it anyway, under anaesthetic whilst her broken right limb was being set and put in a walkabout plaster cast.

Thelma had never craved public notoriety and was far happier away from the prying eyes of the press.

Yet, the most undignified, or others may have possibly thought surreal and cartoon-like, part of the grand presentation spectacle was, not Thelma slipping on an out of place leaf, rather when the giant dummy bank cheque was presented by eager 'Shriners' to a grasping Principal Jones and his young substitute for Thelma, Diana, the new heroine of the hour. At that very moment, as if it had been previously destined to do so, an untimely gust of wind caught the sail-like paper prop and took it way into the air, free of its greedy human shackles, beyond the marching band and on-lookers. Later it was discovered by a grounds man somewhere out on the football field, wrapped around a post. No problem really as it held no fiscal value and was only of symbolic importance.

The majority of the gathered presentation day throng eventually retreated back into the faculty foyer for coffee and a finger buffet, whilst Thelma was being driven by ambulance to the county medical centre fracture clinic for x-rays, tests and ultimately plaster casting.

* * * * *

Thelma, with leg truly wrapped in autographed plaster, stretched out in the relative thirty-three-degree coolness of the autumnal New Mexico evening. She struggled to comfortably sit back with her awkward plaster cast and, as it transpired, bandaged sprained right ankle. It was all she could manage to raise the damaged limb up onto a camping chair.

As it was all the experimental equipment had already been set up ready for their first test run. The boys had made camp, just as they had for the past three-nights since leaving Iowa. Now they were at their first investigative stop: Roswell. However, not on the now infamous crash site, which is where the team would have expected to register the most positive magnetic activity, but just around thirty-three miles outside Roswell, and some nine-hundred and ninety-nine miles from their starting point in Iowa. This was the place of convergence between two known and identified magnetic signatures, and therefore the place to start looking.

They were arguably camped out at the most iconic place on the planet as far as people seeing and believing in UFOs were concerned. If you were going to encounter alien activity, then Roswell was apparently the place to go.

The present town was a curious combination of modern concrete and desert scrub. The city boasted a zoo, Bitter Lake wildlife park and the strangely designated: Bottomless Lake State Park. Not forgetting the 'Crash Site Diner,' 'Crash Down Café' and 'Aliens Have Landed' gift emporium. Along with the old abandoned Air Force base, they were all places reflective and reminiscent of a bygone era, all now confined to history and located along 'UFO Alley,' with a host of other 'space invader' related tourist attractions. Not forgetting a museum dedicated singularly to UFOs.

The 1947 Roswell incident was, in Thelma's view, without doubt the world's most famous and exhaustively investigated phenomena. Whilst being one of the most thoroughly debunked mysteries of all time. In ufological circles this place Roswell was 'Mecca.'

The controversial discourse surrounding the weather balloon circus performance had moved the idea of 'green men' from outer-space, from slightly comic obscurity, to obsessive mainstream, quasi-religious belief. As it was, whether the event took place or not, was neither the aim or concern of the Magnetronic expedition. Neither was it of any significance when it came to believing and accepting or not whatever had gone on all those years before. It was what people believed in today, the here and now, that counted, not the facts or fables of whether or not the events actually took place as they were originally reported. The truth may never be encountered by any devoted alien hunter.

As a leading scientists Thelma and her eager Magnetronic team were only concerned with the real facts, and only the real facts. The team limited their research and concern as to how any, if any, proven numinous occurrence had had an impact or effect on the magnetic fields that surrounded the planet?

For every action there is a reaction. Any event, natural or otherwise, leaves a tell tale trail, a foot-print in the sand, as to the nature and make-up of the occurrence. A disturbance in the magnetic field told a thousand tales, and may just point to a clue as to 'when' not 'if' there was going to be a magnetic polar shift anytime soon.

As it was, with regard to UFOs, by the end of the twentieth-century, the vast majority of those interviewed by investigators, who were doggedly still studying the Roswell phenomena, believed that it did happen and more so that alien entities were being held captive, like zoo animals, in a top-secret US military bases.

Mass hysteria was and is a highly potent trigger that generated energy. Power that once released could have a direct effect on not only the human psyche, but the earth's magnetic signature as well. Which was what Thelma believed and held dear to.

Subsequently, if Thelma's theory was correct and true, then the magnetic signature of the land, in and around Roswell, should be humming with electro-magnetic energy. Power generated and released by thousands, perhaps millions of inquiring people from around the world, all searching for answers to questions that pushed and swirled the magnetic energy fields about. Kinetic-like waves pounding against a rock strewn sea shore. Thus, leaving a prominent legacy and powerful magnetic signature.

Such power would be similar to (and Thelma aimed to prove this), the measurable energy levels of ancient sites, such as: the pyramids at Giza, Stonehenge in England, Easter Island, and respective temples in Central America and South East Asia. Places all connected by so-called 'Ley' lines. Although the study of such phenomena may be and was by many, classified as 'pseudo-science,' there was still sufficient interest in and evidence to suggest such connections were real. Furthermore, such crossover points suggested there existed a grid-like formation or pattern surrounding the globe. A form of energy matrix that could be tapped into, and therefore penetrated in such a manner that human energy could enter the matrix and exist within, what possibly could be a fourth, fifth or even tenth-dimension, as some ancient cultures believed and understood.

To sum up: there was a possible correlation between human existence, more specifically their psychic signature, and the planet they lived upon. The earth was and is a living and breathing organism and people, their human energy source, are all a part of that living entity.

The research unit camp, as alluded to, had intentionally been pitched some thirty-three miles north of Roswell, roughly speaking at the same recently disclosed longitude and latitude as the original so-called crash site. Accordingly, now the team were present and set-to-go, they began their first experiment. Which, surprisingly, was to amount to little or nothing!

3

Through the Camera Lens Darkly

The drive down from Iowa had passed without incident. Apart from that was: Thelma's broken right leg, which appeared to become increasingly swollen, as was her sprained right ankle; which was also becoming progressively worse. As it was the hospital had provided her with crutches and pain killers, which all helped to enable her to be somewhat excruciatingly mobile. The medical advice had been to stay off the leg and rest, such a break and strain would require a significant time to heal. Regardless, the ever-stoic young women patient refused all and any medical advice. The show had to go on and on it did go. As soon as Thelma woke up in the hospital recovery ward.

* * * * *

Now under the stars with computer tablet in hand, Thelma tried to settle back, having eaten her meagre ration of bacon and beans. (The boys had insisted on a typical cowboy diet whilst out on the trail). The electronic tablet in Thelma's hands glowed, as a now familiar voice led into an introduction. Thelma was fully prepared once again to watch the recorded footage of the TV interview previously captured with Diana, in Thelma's painful absence. Footage that also included the humorous reportage concerning the wayward flying bank draft handover. Perhaps naively, Thelma had mistakenly expected positive, up-beat and sympathetic news coverage of the event. Particularly as the reporter on site was one: 'Gracie Lin Jones,' a wayward cousin of Thelma's.

'Scheming Gracie' was an apt title the would-be journalist had earned for herself almost throughout the entire

Jones dynasty. When and where ever there was family strife, Gracie Lin, with her strange, retrospective, dress sense and melancholic appearance, was sure to be part of and party to. She would calculatingly play one side of her family off against the other. Some younger members of the wider family considered her to be a witch. A notion commonly reinforced by parents who often, in a threatening manner, used the imagery of 'wicked aunt Gracie' the witch, to try mollify their youngsters. Action which inevitably resulted in having the complete opposite effect. In one sense the wicked witch persona was all part of a strange family tradition, one designed to force the adolescents to tow the apparently 'boogie-man' infested family line.

It was said that in the distant past, two Jones sisters, twins, were hung, then burnt as accused practitioners of witchcraft. A subject kept under the carpet of family historical affairs. After all, the entire family were supposedly, to the man, all staunch puritanical Christians. As well as being dedicated Freemasons and of course devoted 'Shriners'.

Gracie Lin was accused in all quarters as being the very blackest of black sheep in the Jones family dynasty. A rebel, who deliberately went against the ethical grain and generally thought the world and her family owed her a living. She openly shunned and ridiculed the religious aspects and practices of her relatives at every given opportunity. Rather than tow the 'holier than thou' Jones-line, she preferred to go try it alone and become a career journalist. However, she soon discovered that every media outlet in Iowa belonged to the Jones family, one way or another.

Jones women, with the exception of successful scientists such as Thelma, were expected to marry and have babies. That was their traditional given role.

* * * * *

The digital TV footage rolled.

"Here I am," Gracie Lin opened, "at the Iowa State University and have with me Diana Rogers a distinguished scientist and member of the Magnetronic Research Unit."

A microphone appeared bottom left of the screen as reporter on site Gracie Lin, offered up her introduction. Her style was languid, laced with a form of disrespectful indolence. For the camera, and for her friends and followers out there, she wore a white plastic 1960s retro-style Mary Quant Mac', black over-the-knee plastic boots and a black plastic skull cap. Into which her jet-black bobbed hair was tightly concealed. When previously she had been standing inside the lobby, it was difficult to distinguish the plastic retro-woman from the black and white marble tiled floor.

Gracie Lin gathered her thoughts and positioned the microphone to ensure all questions and respective answers could be heard equally.

"Diana, a great day for you and the Iowa State University." Her opening gambit.

"Hi, yes thanks for covering the event." Diana's response.

Gracie Lin moved her Jones family-facial-features closer in to try and get both Diana and herself in frame.

Meanwhile the cameraman: Bud Always-Jones, pulled back to widen the angle. Then zoomed into Diana's torso and cleavage; pretending he was merely routinely focusing the shoulder-mounted digital camera.

"I imagine you are devastated about poor Thelma Jones's little slip-up?" The reporter said the line with a slight hint of mocking amusement in her heavily made-up eyes and glossy black lips.

Diana immediately felt uncomfortable with the manner of the interview, particularly with Gracie Lin's derisive tones.

"Of course," she stoically replied. "But I am sure this will only be a temporary set-back."

"And does this mean you will be taking charge of operations from now on?"

"I doubt it."

"And remind me again, how long have you been working on the project? You must have a very close relationship with Thelma Jones to have to spend so much time working in the same environment?"

Several people, on-lookers, pushed between interviewer and interviewee. Diana resented being jostled.

"As I was saying, how long have you two been 'as one?' Oh! I didn't mean it like that!"

Diana missed the corny suggestive euphemism.

"I bet you became very close hmm … working together as you do, or should I say did?"

Diana ignored the second part of the question and simply replied as off-hand as she could. "Some two-years now almost since I graduated Iowa with a Master's Degree in Astrophysics."

"Very impressive I am sure. But sounds more like a guy's thing to me. And just what are the aims and objective of your research? They sound crazy to me! I mean to say Ley lines? Isn't that some old English countryside fable?" Her tone continued to be derisive and sarcastic.

Diana paused for a moment, slightly phased and intimidated by the number of microphones that were now pointing at her, including Gracie Lin's.

"Well that's not really what we are about." Diana was becoming increasingly defensive, "we merely study the facts."

"Well, what 'are you' about then Ms Rogers?"

The line was delivered through Gracie Lin's sneering lips, that Diana was convinced were turning darker every minute.

Now, to add to the inquisitive throng of eager journalists, came the probing shoulder-mounted camera of Bud Always-Jones. He thought, being an Iowa-alumni, he was entitled to a more privileged front row position amongst the other, lesser known, photo journalists and videographers.

In Bud, there stood a man who Diana vaguely knew of, and had emphatically down as being a total and utter all-round general sleaze-bag. Rumor had it his real forte was producing pornography. A website: 'Always Porn-World' bore testimony to that fact.

The constant movement of his zooming camera lens led Diana to feel he was, layer by layer, striping her naked. Coupled to this the continuous flashing of press cameras were beginning to make her head spin, and unsteady on her footing.

The questioning re-commenced.

"What do you hope to achieve with this expedition?" Another unfamiliar reporter tried to muscle in.

Gracie Lin quickly cut-in and continued with her own line of questioning. "Who funded the expedition?" She lunged forward with her microphone. "What's in it for the university Ms Rogers?" What will the faculty get out of it?"

Diana responded the best she could. "Oh well we had a bursary from the University of Iowa, and then public subscription from interested community groups."

"By that do you mean those creepy 'Shriners'?"

Gracie Lin had nothing in particular against the 'Shriner' fraternity, far from it. As it was, her aim, as usual, was to sow seeds of discord and controversy everywhere she went, as far as she was able.

"Yes sure, and we appreciate their boundless generosity!"

"Well that's nice for you. I guess your daddy was a Shriner too?"

Diana ignored the quip. Her father had been involved with Freemasonry, that much she knew. Beyond that Diana recalled nothing concerning any untoward paternal secret activities.

"And," Gracie Lin continued. "May I ask is this your first major field trip?"

"Goodness no, I already went to Central America to examine and study the Mayan calendar as one of my

25

papers for the degree course."

"I see and what is your role as part of this Magnetronic team?"

"Well all of our jobs crossover, so we are all trained to double up on our designated tasks. One time I may wash up or cook."

Gracie Lin interjected. "Oh, mind those nails!"

Diana missed the feminine cliché "Yeah, I mean, then err, so another time I might set up the recording data gatherers or seismic measuring devices."

"Wow sounds real cosy! Like one big happy family eh? Talking of which, Ms Rogers, it's unusual for the Jones's family to allow outsiders into their fold. How do you feel about all this nepotism going on?"

"What nepotism? I never thought much about that. Anyhow, I just get on with my job and focus on the task before us."

"But here you are playing second fiddle to a Jones, how does that make you feel?"

"I really don't think that discussing such matters is appropriate, this is neither the time or the place."

"Oh, there is always a right time for a good story Ms Rogers!"

Diana felt anger welling up insider her making her feel hot and bothered in her glossy jogging bottoms and gym top.

"Anyhow," she countered. "Surely you are also a Jones?" Referring to Gracie. "Yes, Ms Gracie Lin Jones am I not correct?"

"Jones by name but not by nature Ms Rogers"

Diana continued to feel unsteady and overwhelmed by the throng of press representatives trying to muscle in on the, what was becoming an interrogation, by the acerbic television interviewer Gracie Lin Jones, and her fellow crew member: Bud Always-Jones.

Thankfully at that point Principal J.Jones interjected, sensing Diana Rogers, who in truth he had had his peripatetic eye upon for a number of years, was beginning to fade under the intense pressure of the interview.

Diana gradually felt herself being backed-up into a tight corner. However, the timely and thoughtful interjection by Principal Jones afforded her the opportunity to thank the throng of press representatives, and slip to the back of the foyer, to find a cup of good strong coffee. All under the watchful gaze of an unmistakably huge bronze owl.

* * * * *

Back in the real world, Thelma pressed the tablet's 'off' button and slid the device to one side before rubbing her strained eyes. There was something strange she had noticed concerning the visual imagery of the interview. She had repeatedly scrutinised the footage that was by now on the State TV station's website, for the world to see. The content had been loaded up by Bud Always-Jones to the broadcast channel platform very soon after the presentation. Added to this mainstream version, there had already been six or seven shorter clips posted on Facebook and platforms such as 'YouTube'. Filmed on private individual's mobile phones and other video recording devices.

Meanwhile the boys had been playing about with the decoding equipment and had successfully pinged a sonic-wave across the barren landscape, with no echoing response.

"Watch out for snakes man!" Duncan was as ever nervous concerning reptiles and arthropods. Apparently, his mother had had a 'Solifuge' (also known as a 'Camel Spider'), drop on her face once when she was out in the Middle East as a military medic during the first Iraq invasion debacle. The ten-legged creature was almost a foot long and although not poisonous, could still administer a sharp bite. Added to this, Duncan had once, again when a kid, encounter an incongruous Reticulated Python lazing about in a damp storm drain in Florida.

Apparently back then, as there is today, there was an epidemic of these lurking constrictive reptiles about the Floridian waterways. The result of the legal and illegal exotic pet trade. Folks brought a little worm of a snake home: 'pretty, look how it curls around your arm!' Aha! A harmless pet. Three-years and a ton of live meat later and what you have is one big fucker of a reptilian monsters.

Duncan the kid (Mowgli jungle boy), versus Kaa the killer python.

Fortunately, right at the wrong or right time, a hungry alligator was drifting by the levee and decided to take a chunk from the reticulated cold-blooded beast. There ensued a fight to the death which neither critter won. The serpent bled to death and the 'gator was crushed to death.

A fair draw.

However, since those times Duncan had purposefully stepped away from any potential encounters with reptilians, and if truth were known, all things that crept and crawled.

As if to deliberately add to Duncan's state of paranoia, Frank swiveled the tripod mounted night-vision scope around. Two sweeps and back. Then he clicked on infrared mode. A dozen red blobs appeared through the viewing lens. The signal from which he channeled through the object recognition finder on the main computer monitor. There, fifty-feet away, a snake could clearly be seen and it was in stealthy pursuit of a young rabbit.

"Hey Duncan, thirty-three feet northwest, a rattler!"

Duncan did not hesitate, he picked up a rock and deftly pitched it toward the invisible image. The rock was five-feet short but sufficiently close to turn the snake away, whilst the timid rabbit high-tailed it off. It would live to be eaten another day.

The boys continued to run tests. The magnetic impulses of the earth's shield were registering as normal. Paranormal activity, responded as being well below what would be accepted as being standard. Mass hysteria inducement and hypnotic trance showed no signs of activity what-so-ever. Thelma was both puzzled and disappointed.

With the boys playing some twenty-feet away under the canvass enclosure, which housed and protected the 'live' measuring equipment and devices, Thelma began to relax a little. Diana took the open opportunity and came and sat next to her colleague and team boss. Only the small camping table divided them. Thelma, having gingerly moved her right limb off the camping chair, uneasily tried to ineffectively kick off the cast shoe, before once again lifting her right leg with the intention of slowly lowering the swollen appendage, to rest it down on Diana's waiting and inviting lap. Diana, who was hot and bothered, had earlier pulled off her shimmering jogging bottoms (pants she seemed to have been wearing everyday so far), to reveal a very very small, almost insignificant pair of hip-hugging shorts.

Previously, Frank had nearly expired when seeing the woman, he apparently cared for and he supposed actually loved, wearing such revealing shorts. He wanted Duncan to look away, just in case he got the right, or wrong idea.

Meanwhile, with her leg in a more comforting position, Thelma began to drift blissfully away, due to the overly large dose of co-dydramol pain killers she had previously swallowed. She sat on the edge between dream-state and awakening lurid nightmare. Crossing from one mind-set to the other and back again.

Her disturbing reverie took her back a few days to the presentation at the university that she had unfortunately missed.

She now felt somewhat disembodied, disassociated from her own lifeless body, as if she were out of the frame, looking down on the scene below.

Once back in reality, she saw just a few feet away, that the boys were operating the test equipment, they knew what to do and did not need her assistance. It was a menial task. Diana was there too, close by, yet so far far away, in a pain-killer land that only soporific dreams are made of.

Thelma now saw her dream-self, or the shadow of her dream-self, speaking to those gathered at the presentation, joining in with the narrative, Diana's narrative. Thelma was seeing what Diana had seen, experiencing her every move and utterance. She could whiff the drifting smell of food and coffee, which had predictably roused the other two members of the Magnetronic Research Unit.

As for the boys, she could clearly see them now as they were at the presentation. The 'good old boys': Frank and Duncan who had been patiently waiting the signal to go! Whereupon, they were required to light up their respective gassed-up four-by-four power units and perform a lap of honour at the rear of the continually pacing 'Shriner' music band. As there had been no definitive wave to request the two Jeeps begin their triumphant lap of honour, the team drivers decided hunger overruled all things, and rapidly made their way, abandoning the now silent motors, to leap hungrily up the, what had been painful for Thelma, thirty-three white marble stairs, into the faculty lobby where victuals awaited under the gaze of a giant owl and beneath the overbearing shadows of two white stone pillars.

Thelma was wallowing in past circumstances. Dreamily drifting in a swimming pool without water.

She knew her team members well and had worked with them before on various field and research trips. She had long since psycho-analysed them all, in one way or another.

There he was in the dream, one of the team members: Francis (Frank) Blake, he was a real live character. His fellow football playing jocks would say: 'he was born with a conspiracy theory bible in each hand!' A statement that in real terms was way off target. His 'pretending' to be interested in pseudo-science and conspiracy theories was externally present for one singular reason, and that was to impress the lovely Diana Rogers. And Thelma knew as much.

Frank, as it stood was no academic, albeit he was a supposed straight 'A' student. His area of 'special interest' however lay in sport and his football scholarship. Which led him to success as a first team player with the 'Hawkeyes,' the Iowa State professional football team.

Although he looked the part, no one could or would say he was 'dumb,' far from it. Frank possessed a pure analytical mind, a skill honed on the playing field. A born strategist, who would always find his way out of a tight defensive corner. He often as not out-foxed his opponents and left them high and dry looking for the ball. Yes, Frankie Blake: high school star, university champion and former football scholar, had now turned investigative scientist. Well, perhaps just for this singular trip. Or so Thelma imagined.

Thelma felt relieved that at least he had dressed appropriately for the part: khaki shirt and pants covered his six-foot-three-inch frame. Whilst his feet were sensibly clad in US army, regulation-desert-combat-boots. Over his starched shirt he carried on with the military theme, wearing a camouflaged jerkin, one that looked as if it should have had hand grenades and other military accoutrements dangling from it.

Glass baubles on a Christmas tree.

The only item of clothing that went against his carefully selected martial theme was his 'Hawkeye' baseball cap, which covered his grade-one-army-style-crew-cut, complimented by the three-day old stubble growing out of his rock-like jaw-line.

Thelma continued her dream. Sometimes, so she imagined, Frank happily got the point concerning her calculations and data recording methodology. However, she was fully aware that his unscientific motive for being behind the wheel of a brand-new showroom Jeep, was of course also 'her' object of affection: Diana Rogers. Belle of the high-school prom. The love of his and Thelma's life. His supposed childhood sweetheart and reason he lived and respired fresh Iowan air.

However, regardless of his endless former, and more recent advances, Diana more or less consistently ignored him, much to Thelma's delight, and spurned his every calculated overture. Peppering the hapless man with regular, systematic and well-rehearsed feminine rebuttals. A form of rejection that Thelma, dreaming or not, was pleased to note. She had her own deep-seated designs on Diana Rogers.

However, and Thelma realised this, he was not about to give up on the love of his life without a fight or demonstration of his good-intent. Even to the point of walking away from what was clearly his sporting vocation to follow Diana, and assist her in any way she deemed appropriate and fit for someone of his limited scientific experience.

Frank's main task, other than driving, was to collect and collate data readings on seismic activity, in relation to magnetic strength and intensity. Ultra-sound resonance techniques recorded bounced signals, waves that went back and forth through the upper-part of the earth's crust. The objective of the experiment being: to see how that affected (or not), the magnetic stream that flowed through the planet. A force unseen by the human eye, but nevertheless there. Once detected the readings could be cross-matched with other salient items of information gathered from around the planet. This quasi-geological-numinous-information, would then be filed away once back in the Iowa State lab' and eventually cross-checked with previous pockets of intel' from other global sites. Eventually a complete map would be pieced together showing the relationship between the magnetic fields of planet earth, juxtaposed with other forms of evidence, either collected from mass-hysterical phenomena (such as what had taken place years before at Roswell New Mexico), or other occurrences of high energy paranormal activity.

Such incidents would fall under the heading of: 'unexplained occurrences. Which might amount to any number of simultaneous inexplicable occurrences, witnessed by a small or large number of individual eye-witnesses. Or, any form of paranormal activity that had been placed on record, that previously had some form of 'hysterical' effect on a large or small group of witnesses. Other happenings would also be logged for further study. In particular the simultaneous sighting of aerial phenomena (UFOs), by a group or groups of people, that had left an indelible impact on those eyewitnesses.

A prime example being people mysteriously disappearing (abductees), then reappearing, coupled with a whole host of other strange phenomena. Just as long as these and other similar events could be verified by eye-witnesses (professional people, such as the police, the military and civil aviation pilots). Those whose statements were proven to be reliable, and at the same time scientific and detailed in their approach as to the recording of the event. Even if that meant ultimately there may be some simple basic scientific explanation attached to the incident, such as weather conditions and light refraction.

The point of this exercise, Thelma told herself repeatedly, was that there existed a very serious purpose attached to her theories, which had to be proven, so as to prepare the global community for a potentially catastrophic episode that, according to scientific speculative theory, would take place before the close of the twenty-first-century.

Making comparisons with magnetic activity and the paranormal may have appeared to be a disparate affair and totally unrelated. However, Thelma Jones, dreaming or not, firmly believed that occurrences of psychic phenomena and activity could be used as a metaphoric 'divining rod' to measure magnetic activity. Through which that same magnetic activity could be monitored and comparisons made to gauge alteration in magnetic grid-patterns and potential polar shifts.

Thelma Jones was already an award- winning and accredited scientist, in the fields of the environment and global warming. But this new subject of investigation potentially realised a more impacting problem and a far greater threat to mankind, than she had ever worked on. Thelma Jones, with her dowdy dress sense, had already disclosed to the scientific community that there was nothing on the planet which was a serious a threat as this newly researched subject of magnetic activity. If, as a result, she had discovered, the magnetic fields were to alter in direction, or in some way split and divide, then the results would be totally catastrophic. Firstly, the profile of the landmass would change climatically. North could be south and east be west. Or, worse still would be if north turned into the west and south to the east. Jungles would become deserts, and the ice caps would melt to cause worldwide floods, with much of the landmass going underwater. Furthermore, if there were a severe weakening of the earth's magnetic shield protection, it would ultimately result in the energy of the sun's rays and powerful solar flares hitting the earth. The planet would no longer be able to deflect all of the solar radiation and sun's flames that bombard the planet day in day out. The sea might well boil and the land melt, as if it were molten magma oozing from the heart of a volcanic eruption.

Boiled or fried.

Humanity may take their pick regarding how they wanted to die!

* * * * *

Thelma now clearly saw in her soporific mind's eye, that on the day of the presentation Duncan had left his Jeep and leapt up the marble steps just one pace behind the immaculately dressed Frank.

Duncan Dunkerley. The MRU clown, the stooge, the jester, the wild joker in the pack: his brown hair was long and caught up at the back in a high ponytail. His scruffy purple coloured 'loon' pants were far too tight, whilst his deep red stripped shirt had seen better days, and required an urgent visit to the laundromat. With regard to his personal hygiene and grooming: his thin black beard was unkempt, and Mexican-style moustache, which amounted to a wiry mass drooping over his thin lips, unruly to say the least. His lisping chops struggled to form and shape a sizeable glossary of words. A problem that remained a hangover from when he was a child. Duncan Dunkerley was repeatedly bullied and cajoled at junior-high for his slightly skewed mouth, an impediment that was now clearly covered over, for the better, by upper-lip hair. Tied about his thin scrawny neck was a black Harley Davidson bandana that had never been washed since he first brought it from a cycle catalogue that had arrived through his door several years before. The dark rings around his eyes and gaunt cold expression suggested he stayed up late watching trash movies, and probably just ate and barely survived on a diet of junk food.

Duncan Dunkerley never did graduate from any academic institute. Anyway, not properly and through the normal acceptable channels. He only came along to the graduation day to get his photograph taken. Wearing as he did, a borrowed gown and mortarboard.

The cap of an academic.

In addition, he held in his hand a rolled sheet of velum 'A' four sized paper, crossed over with a red ribbon, looking, to all intents and purposes, like an official certificate of higher education. Yes, he was a fraud, a rogue, but a lovable one at that.

Suddenly, at a most intense moment of her opiate-infused state, Thelma's outlook became blurred as the imaginary images before her soporific eyes wavered. As if some form of outside television interference were affecting what her brilliant scientific brain heard or visualised.

The picture in front of her became dark then blank. Thelma felt trapped, breathless and claustrophobic. She was there, but not there, rather it was Diana! Thelma could now see through the eyes of another.

Diana was at the university interview talking with Thelma's relative, Gracie Lin. Yes, Gracie was her third, or maybe even fourth cousin. No matter, a relative that, for some reason, had hated her for many years, going right back to their childhood.

Was it that Gracie Lin was jealous? She, Thelma, as she recalled, was allowed to do a great deal and get away with so much, whilst Gracie Lin was seemingly being held back, constantly disciplined, by strict puritanical parents. Punished, outcast and ostracized.

Now Thelma, still with Gracie Lin in her drifting hallucinating mind, was aware that she somehow felt as if she were being drawn into the actual body of the digital video news camera. Seeing what Bud Always-Jones could see through his smudged lens. Rightly she slowly began to sense his disingenuous intentions.

Yes, she felt as if she were being drawn into the very mechanics and inner-workings of the video camera. There she was, trapped, yet floating free in a digital sea of an electronic device. In which she was no more than a black smudge, a blot on the obfuscated lens.

Thelma, as suddenly as she had dozed off, awoke from her landscape of dreams. Diana was still sitting there with her, nursing Thelma's swollen right limb and ankle.

"You were dreaming Thelma, what were you dreaming about?" Thelma tried to gradually bring to mind what she, only moments before, could or could not recall. "It's the pain-killers, I may have taken too many? Firstly, in my dream." Thelma spoke softly to Diana, with a slight slur in her voice. "First, there was the bank handover of the cheque and interviews. That much I know. Then there was you Diana, you were so vivid and your voice unmistakable. Then once again your voice and comforting tender hand."

Diana was herself thinking back and trying to fill in the gaps in the chain of events that Thelma missed out on, due to her unfortunate leafy slip-up. As it was, all Thelma could focus upon at that moment was Diana's curvaceous outline: a close-fitting gym top and skin-tight shorts, a perfect figure that moved seductively before her. Consequently, a sleepy tingling sensation ran down Thelma's spine, and regardless of her painful broken limb; crisscrossed between her soft inner-thighs.

Meanwhile, in a moment of wakening reason, the boys appeared, standing there as they were before the two female members of the party. A bunch of blank paper clutched tightly in Frank's hands. Thelma's fantasy immediately dissipated.

"Thelma," Frank sounded off. "It aint no use, we might as well head back home. There's nothing here, not a twitch on any of the screens."

"Yes," Duncan Dunkerley lisped, "look, sorry, maybe we just didn't get all the calibrations right."

Frank agreed.

"Maybe we need extra time to effect more trials?" Duncan added glibly. He for one wanted a juicy hamburger, fries and as shake.

4

Back at Iowa State University

Gracie Lin, lay back, pulled a packet of smokes from her purse and casually lit up. The Principal J. Jones Junior had been easy game for the 'femme fatal.' OK, so he had reminded her they were cousins and kissing cousins were frowned upon and not supposed to be encouraged throughout the family. Somehow Gracie did not feel fourth or fifth cousins really applied to this ruling. OK, perhaps maybe they did share the same great-grandparents, but hey that was then.

As it was, the old boy had been fun. Not surprising, thought Gracie, as he probably took Viagra and enjoyed a great deal of practice with his ever-present secretary. Who he, as was common knowledge, was having a long-term and steamy affair with.

Today however, the ever-faithful Ms Celia Jones, probably yet another cousin, had gone to the Sanctuary Care Home, owned by the Jones dynasty of course, to visit her elderly mother. The Jones private facility was a care home singularly for those of the Jones family, and no others.

Hence, Gracie, in the secretary's absence, had taken the opportunity to call Principal Jones, who she had previously exchanged business cards with at the recent 'Shriner' presentation. Her reason or excuse for meeting him was to get some kind of follow-on-back-story to the donation event, whilst it was fresh in everyone's mind. The vain Principal Jones fell for it hook and line.

She initially suggested meeting at the university golf course for coffee. Or, maybe the campus leisure pool complex? However, the eager predatory Principal Jones suggested, as she thought he would, his opulent apartment, located in a block well out of the way of the main faculty buildings.

He disapproved of her smoking of course, but over-looked the smell on Gracie's breath and clothes. To his joy, her sense of dress left little to the imagination. Consisting, as it did, of a tight-black-mini-skirt, and even tighter fitting black blouse to match the mini-skirt and knee-high boots. All done up for the sake of total sexual stimulation and absolute gratification, as she figured the Principal would be attracted to a certain amount of latex and plastic. Of that she was perfectly correct.

Gracie Lin, as far as Principal Jones was concerned, had been a wild and fortuitous conquest for him. For her part, she had directed all of her energy to making him climax in the most pleasurable way possible. All performed under the guise of answering a few pertinent questions pertaining to the Magnetronic Research Unit. Concerning which, Gracie Lin was certain there was another, 'hidden' agenda floating around. 'Shriners' the expedition sponsors, were not so much of a secret organisation. Rather an association with secrets. And wherever there were secrets, there was certain to be money involved.

Here lay the answer: for whatever reason, the 'Shriners' wanted some form of dirt on Principal Jones, who was as it happened, one of their number. They required some form of 'insurance', a certain security to make sure he towed the official 'Shriner' line.

They had money to part with, and were happy to make some 'special' agreements with Gracie Lin and the inner-lodge members, which boiled down to exchanges of favors. She would serve them in their quest, and they would open doors and provide for her. She, in effect, would be on their pay-role, whilst performing sexual-favors, for those of higher ranking, as and when required. The idea did not shock or trouble Gracie Lin in any way. After all she was used to being sexually abused throughout her adolescent and younger life.

Not one to be out-flanked, Gracie Lin took her own

steps to make certain Principal Jones and his bone headed 'Shriner' buddies towed 'her' line. Consequently, she had Bud Always-Jones fix up a tiny miniature camera onto the strap of her shoulder bag. A lens which she had purposefully ensured pointed towards them whilst they fornicated, like two fecund rabbits, for all it was worth. Now Gracie had Principal J. Jones, her distant cousin, in the palm of her sticky, yet nimble-fingered hand. Whilst at the same time the pornographic video content she possessed could, and she was sure would, later act as a bargaining chip to put into play, if at any time, Principal Jones ever contemplated blowing the whistle on his comrades in arms.

In the meantime, she had no qualms concerning currying at least some small favor with the senior members of the local 'Shriner' temple.

She would not think twice, if required, about laying bare their obscene secrets.

And, as to the revealing footage deviously obtained? It would most certainly be used to her advantage sometime or another in the future.

As it was, Principal J. Jones, whilst on the verge of a well-teased and controlled ejaculation technique, begged the lascivious bitch not to stop, until she reached the point where she forcefully made him scream out the word: 'Gold!'

5

On to Nevada

As it was with the non-eventful drive south from Iowa to
New Mexico, so it was with the dog-leg route to Nevada.
The MRU team's destination and camp site, had been
calculated by the boys to be some sixty-miles south-east
of what was, on the map at least, described as being a
'defunct military air base,' on private government land.

Google Earth satellite pictures of the area were highly
classified and therefore censored, blacked out and
invisible.

Once they had arrived in the area, they would seek to
make camp as close to, but not beyond, the air base
perimeter fence line. As they were funded by the Iowa
University and others, they had to ensure they stayed
within the law at all costs.

The aim was to arrive there on or before Thelma's
birthday. Being the eleventh of September

Stoic, never-say-never-give-up Thelma, refused to
delay the take-off from Roswell, regardless of her ever-
swelling right leg.

Disappointed by the lack of results from their early
measurements, she was anxious to gather some viable
evidence from another, hopefully more rewarding source.
If she did not glean some verification as to her theory in
these initial stages then her career would be in tatters and
funding withdrawn. However, there were and there
remained some clear issues in her mind that were
detracting her from the job to hand.

One was the continual series of narcotic induced
dreams she had repeatedly experienced; even after cutting
back on the opiate-based pain killers she had previously
over-prescribed herself. She had moderated her dosage,
with the help of the ever-watchful eye of Diana.

As a distraction, and as if to pass away the time, Thelma routinely and repeatedly scrutinized the TV footage of the bizarre bank draft handing-over ceremony back at Iowa State. Together with the ensuing painful interview with Diana, conducted by Gracie Lin Jones.

Obsessed with the footage she would pore over it time and time again. And in each viewing instance she clearly saw the black smudge to the upper-left of the screen. That blot she imagined for reasons she was unsure of, was undeniably her. Or more likely, Diana.

But what was the reason for it all?

Thelma had it fixed in her fragmented mind that Diana and her were somehow improbably trapped inside Bud Always-Jones digital camera. Or so it seemed to the expedition leader in her sedated state.

Bizarrely, in her mind's eye, Thelma could also see everything the lens had ever picked up, not just on the occasion of the sponsorship presentation, rather it included all the rewound footage the amateur porn peddler Bud Always-Jones had ever recorded. Which included a recent graphic sexual encounter between her two distant cousins: Grace-Lin and Principal Jones. It all flowed, without effort, passed her eyes. Leaving nothing censored. And what she saw was, in her view, not edifying to say the least.

At this point Thelma had decided not to mention her disturbing findings to any of the other three team members. No, this was something she had to work out for herself. The key to which was clearly in the hands of Gracie Lin Jones, and the camera of porn- monger Bud Always-Jones. It was she, her cousin, who was obviously behind it. Behind what exactly? Just that, what?

'What' was anything that Thelma could not accept or understand as a scientist: fable, fiction, legend, myth, anything that was remotely magical, including the mystical and inexplicable, all that science could not put in a box and label.

It was unthinkable.

If Gracie Lin Jones was party to, whatever it was she was party to, then there was no doubt, anything and everything was possible. Some form of illusion or trickery had to be present. Most magic could easily be explained away as sleight of hand. Hands moving quicker than the eye. Could it be however her cousin was really dabbling in the black arts? Aunty Gracie the wicked witch, as some of the kids of the family called her. An apt sobriquet. Though Thelma found it hard to believe and accept such a proposition. However, neither could she rule such matters out.

A second and subsequent detraction in Thelma's analytical and well-trained mind, was her assistant Diana. Not that the physical presence of Diana was unpleasant. Quite the contrary. For Thelma she was divine, Diana the huntress, a love goddess drawn out of Greco-Roman culture. Smooth as alabaster, a statuette of perfection.

For Thelma this love of Diana from a distance was nothing new. Thelma had been in love with the young female scientists since the first day they began working together. As it was, somehow toiling in a laboratory environment curbed and kept in check Thelma's fantasies and aspirations towards Diana. But here, now, out in the wild arid landscapes of America, it had all changed. Thelma felt liberated and free. She no longer needed to conform or put on an act. Here she could, as it were, 'come out' and confess her undying love for this joyous living work of art. She the artist's model, the Mona Lisa, Helen of Troy, Venus rising from her shell. For Thelma, Diana was everything, and most of all, for a refreshing change, she was not just another ubiquitous Jones clan member.

Yes, this was all new for Thelma, a scenario never previously thought through or physically explored. Far from it. Now however, since embarking on the liberating expedition, and despite her broken leg, her emotions had run away with her. She felt as if she wanted to shout from the peak of a high mountain, to tell the world everything that she was feeling and to send a once and for all clear message to everyone, particularly to the young woman she had already fallen in love with.

* * * * *

The moment Thelma had digested the disappointing outcome of their Roswell tests, she gave the order to the crew to saddled up and head off down highway thirty-three which doglegged north-west to the State of Nevada. With a strict proviso (and for a hundred obvious logical reasons), to bypass Las Vegas in its entirety; for fear they may never be able to drag themselves away from the welcoming lights and star-struck-spangled glamour. No, they would keep going along the fabled: 'Yellow Brick Road'. That in Thelma's fantastic imagination had started in Kansas, and would be heading towards a place that was allegedly, and according to conspiracy theorists, popularly known as: Area 51. The home of the Wizard of Oz, who would continue to lead them on to the location of those illusive red shoes.

The travel plan was as before: to break up the estimated nine-hundred-and-ninety-nine-mile journey, with a single rest day off the road in a decent motel to enjoy a break and shower down. Allowing (once fed and watered), for the team to sleep. The two girls in one twin-bedded room and the guys in another.

For Thelma these arrangements were pure agony. Not just because of her ever-painful leg, but because she was in very close proximity to the object of her desire and affection, namely Diana. And it was even more agonising for her when the audacious Diana stripped off for bed, replacing her hip-hugging shorts for an over-sized white tee-shirt bearing a comical 'pussy cat' motif. Whereas Thelma, with a little help from Diana, struggled to clamber into a set of blue stripped men's pajamas which had been an unwanted Christmas present give to her father by one of the many Jones relatives.

At first light, after an uneventful night and hearty breakfast, the team set off once more, eagerly striking out to their next location. Thelma had insisted they press on. Forgetting and leaving behind New Mexico and Roswell, now heading onwards to Nevada and, as marked on the regional maps, the small town of Rachel.

By means of taking it in turn to drive, they covered the distance from the motel to their next stop in only fifteen-hours flat. This time Diana and Thelma, who had insisted she take a turn at the wheel (it was an automatic which after all helped her cause), took one vehicle. Whilst the boys rode jointly in the second Jeep.

Only stopping for gas and comfort breaks. The boys complained of hunger, Diana complained concerning the increasing heat, and Thelma gritted her teeth in agony, trying to hide the fact that her right ankle and leg throbbed. She had sensibly shied away from further over-use of painkillers, as too many tablets may have adversely affected her driving.

All other emotions besides, Thelma was livid with the laws of 'sod' and 'damnation' that had cruelly inflicted upon her such an evil curse as to break her leg and sprain her ankle at a time that was probably one of the most important moments of her life.

Being a scientist however, she reminded herself, meant she was not in the least superstitious and actually did not believe or accept Sod's or Murphy's nonsensical and illogic laws of probability. Neither did she believe in voodoo spells or witchcraft. However, in a wave of clarity, it came to her: curse! Yes!

A eureka moment.

Just suppose cousin Gracie Lin had placed some form of 'curse' upon her in order to thwart the entire project and send Thelma to academic exile and obscurity? That was not beyond all possibilities. Yet a scenario she just as quickly dismissed, as she had heard that a curse only takes hold of a person 'if' they allow it to, and believe and submit to its controlling power.

6

Back in Iowa

Bud Always-Jones pulled away from The Jones Brothers' rental car lot, with a newly hired Grand Voyager. His boss and task master had text him over her credit card details and told him to pick up a vehicle and pack a bag, as they may be away for several days. He had been told to make sure all his camera kit was checked and stowed.

He never questioned Gracie Lin. Actually, she was his real bread and butter, as the porn industry these days offered little or no return, due to the high-level of free sex-sites available. Therefore, he knuckled down and begrudgingly did as he was told.

The previous day, being the last working day of the week, his female task-master had given him a series of key codes. One for the university's main entrance. Another for the Principal's office door. And a third password to gain access to his PC. Bud had also been ordered to buy a high-end memory stick to download the salient information he was about to purloin, as per Gracie Lin's explicit instructions. He had also been assured that no one would disturb him when he went to the university, as only the janitorial staff would be present.

Principal Jones was, 'indisposed.' He had tickets for the pro-golf tournament. A little surprise that Gracie had generously organised for him. And, as far as Gracie Lin knew, the Principal's private secretary, Ms Celia Jones, would still be visiting her elderly mother in the care home. Gracie Lin easily checked this by putting a call through via a public phone to the care facility asking to speak to Ms C. Jones. Then whilst they paged her (having confirmed she was still present at the home), she hung up.

Gracie Lin's steamy sex session with Principal J. Jones had been very profitable. Not only did she have the revealing word, 'Gold' to fathom, but when the Principal was taking a shower the over-inquisitive reporter found his, 'little-black-book,' in plain sight located in the middle draw of his reproduction antique desk. It was all too easy.

The A6 sized journal contained just about every secret of his life. Gracie got busy with her phone, photographing as much information as she could. The most amusing pages being those contact details for escorts and hookers, of both sexes. Principal J. Jones certainly had an appetite for the women. A hunger she would soon totally assuage.

7

Nevada

The village community of Rachel, Nevada was split in two by the legendary 'Extraterrestrial Highway'.

However, If Roswell, New Mexico, had been a surprising disappointment, then Rachel had that beat hands down. Disenchantment, was the word to use.

What had happened to the once alien- occupied village of Rachel? What had happened to the worn and tired, now full of holes, 'Extraterrestrial Highway?' Each way the MRU team members turned was even more of a disappointment. The once world-famous UFO Diner had seen better days alright. The place was not dissimilar to what they had encountered back in Roswell. Gone the aliens walking in the street. Gone the tourist bus that took folk to the boundary fence of so-called Area 51. Gone the UFO ride for kids, gone the life-sized billboards depicting the little grey men.

If Roswell's once alien encountering streets and alleyways were dead, then Rachel in contrast was even more the worse for wear. The township was all but empty. The once crowded and hectic Extraterrestrial Alley was now tragically littered with ancient takeaway packaging and drink cans. Clearly gone the previous glory years, the former robust economy was now consigned to history. It now appeared that the majority of Rachel's population, wanted to steer the community away from being the butt-end of corny jokes concerning little green men, and to get on with living a normal life in the twenty-first century. And who could blame them? Local people were sick and tired of living in the past, when once endless streams of Asian tourists queued to have their picture taken next to a life-sized grey alien.

Further down the dusty main street there were still to

be found a few shrines to TV and movie characters, drawn from, in particular the Star Trek and Star Wars franchises. Even the movie 'Alien' had its own gift store, devoted entirely to the now classic sci-fi horror movie series.

A stars and stripes flag beat the breeze, there were still a few patriots living in the enclave.

As it was, somewhat ironically, there had never actually been any recorded sightings of alien activity in the small community itself. No Rachelite had ever once caught a glimpse of a real flying saucer, by eye or by camera. And all that despite the fact that every adult and kid these days was running around with a cell phone that had better lens quality than any older high-end professional digital camera. Yet there was nothing to view, other than a few blurred images that, to even the lay person, were clearly faked.

Thelma felt down. She could at the worst of times swing from happy-go-lucky to down in the mouth. A doctor had once suggested she may be 'bi-polar,' a notion she swiftly scotched, and insisted such a statement be expunged from her clinical record.

Had she miscalculated the entire venture? Was this part of the United States the best place to kick start her globally impacting expedition into the unknown? Perhaps she should have commenced the search for magnetic activity in New York? 9/11 for instance had certainly made and extraordinary and undeniable contribution to what could be termed as a 'mass-hysterical event.'

If there were no strange goings on in Roswell or around so-called Area 51, well then where else was there?

Frank, in his often-misplaced wisdom, suggested that there were so many UFO sightings across America that there no longer existed any apparent and clear 'focal points' of activity. The American population, rather than look to the 1947 Roswell event for evidence, knowledge or understanding, of extraterrestrials visitations or sightings, now only had to look out their own backyards to see an accumulation of aerial phenomena.

Furthermore, Frank casually reminded her that the entire region of north Mexico and the south-western states of America were a hot-bed of flying saucer activity. Also, up along the east coast, and even the capitol Washington D.C. had given rise to mass-reports of UFO activity. 'UFOs over the White House' was one such classic event, which joined hundreds of other sightings, many of which were hard to disprove. Now more American citizens believed in the existence of aliens than not. Whilst many more believed in men from outer-space than those who categorically held onto their faith in Jesus Christ!

Finally, and feeling dejected, the team found a run-down diner and once through the creaking old door, they hunkered down around a corner table, feeling conspicuous and wondering if there was going to be any service?

A chair being dragged along the strip-wood floor caused the entire party to jump and swing around to ascertain the source of the incongruous and annoying sound. There in the corner stood a man who was deliberately dragging the legs of a dining chair to create an irritating sound that caused, at least Duncan's lank hair to stand on end. Frank's hair was too short to respond in the same if not similar manner. Whereas Thelma winced and groaned as the pain in her leg stabbed right up from her ankle to her knee joint. Diana had previously noted that Thelma's toes were going purple, which, regardless of any medical opinion, was a bad indication and pointed towards urgent need of medical attention. That would entail driving to Vegas, and probably a cessation in the exploratory expedition.

Finally, the strange elderly man stopped moving the furniture and, without any form of invitation, sat down at the foot of the table with Frank on his left, and Thelma to his right. Diana sat next to Frank whilst Duncan felt trapped in the corner chair.

The man looked intently at the four intrepid members of the Magnetronic Research Unit team, as if he were trying to read their collective minds. He was tall and gangly with deep black eyes and a bush of salt and pepper hair that needed cutting, as it constantly fell in his face. His skin was dark and weather-beaten, as were his claw-like liver-spotted hands. Paws that looked as if it had been sometime since they had been scrubbed clean.

"Clint, Clint Clinton." The stranger introduced himself. What followed was a form Mexican stand-off. Eyes met eyes, eyes read lips, hands trembled nervously, dry throats were cleared, before the strange man turned to his right and shouted, "Hillary git our here you got customers." His accent was southern, deep south, laced with corn and musical chicken gumbo. The air infused with Cajun spice, pork stew slowly boiling on a pot-belly stove, and oiled together with velvet bourbon liquor.

The group remained speechless.

"You kids here huntin' them little folks?"

Thelma desperately looked at her colleagues, as if one of them may propose a response to this mysterious aged gentleman.

Finally, Frank, puffed his football playing chest out and bellowed in this best Hawkeye voice: "No sir, we're here for the fishin'!" Frank had no idea why he had said that. Jitters and nerves had taken hold of him.

Just then Hillary, a woman, of late middle years, entered from a door in the back. She wore her greying hair up, tied by a faded scarf and knotted about her slight waist was a food stained apron. The woman walked with an unnerving stoop, that at first glance made her appear slightly disabled. Once behind the safety of the serving counter however, she stretched and attempted to straighten her back, whilst wiping her hands on her already greasy apron.

Armed now with a blunt pencil and dog-eared order pad she calmly enquired: "Well what you all havin'?"

None of the MRU party had as yet seen any form of menu. There was nothing displayed on the tables that was even a hint of a 'carte du jour.'

Suddenly the old southerner at the foot of the table

laughed out loud. "I gitt ya all, fishin' indeed! There aint much of that goin' on around these parts. Not no more. Well maybe some over the lake: cutthroat trout, big mouth bass, if the nuclear waste aint killed them all..." The old man's face split with a toothless grin. "I can bet you ten-bucks you is out here hunting alright, but it aint no fish you is after!"

"'scuse Clint you folks, he aint been the same since..."

"Since what?" Diana was the first to compose herself. "Mister we are hunting, but not for game, but for seismic activity." Diana's statement was vague but accurate enough. Curiously she had; out of nowhere, adopted a temporary southern twang to her usually perfect American English accent. Surprisingly the old fellow Clint seemed to have understood the word: 'seismic.'

"You mean earthquakes and all?" The man added. "We had some of those. But that's not what killed the trade around these parts."

"What's the reason why there's no one around?" Thelma spoke out as she began to feel more comfortable with the situation. Good old southern hospitality was beginning to kick in.

"It's the towns people," Clint continued. "The local folks, they want to rid themselves of the 'alien' image and clean up the place." Hillary, the would-be waitress spoke with pencil poised. "Ever since that Roswell balloon affair people been comin' here looking for UFO crash sites. And me and Clint here once earned our livin' showing Japs about the place. Now the Japs have their own UFO sites back home. Them UFOs is everywhere, all over the place these days. First started comin' when they lit that bomb up. The dust kicked up for miles around and folks around these parts got sick."

The MRU team were beginning to relax and eager to hear more of this seemingly intriguing couple's story.

"We," the old man continued, "we only came here, me and Hillary here," he gestured toward the woman, "back in the late fifties when the place first started to hum and we already had a diner trailer back in Louisiana and all, so we towed her up here, 'cos this is where the tourists were. Gift shop across the street is, was, ours as well. But she's closed now for the season and will open agin' next spring."

"Maybe?" The woman interrupted.

"But that's if they give us another year on our licence see." The old man Clint butted in.

Thelma, taking the lead, having spotted a 'specials' blackboard behind the counter, assertively ordered for the group: pancakes, she knew her team inside out, coffee black, malt shake, bottled water, toast and eggs over-easy.

"That'll be nine-dollars 'n' eleven cents missy." The would-be waitress spoke as if she were desperate to get her hands on some hard cash. Diana searched through her purse and pulled out ten-dollars. "Keep it."

Meanwhile, Clint had been further enlightening Frank and Duncan. "Sees, folks from all over set themselves up in business around here. There was a church, a store or two, there's still old Carlos at the gas station. People invested time and hard cash in the town, and all for what?"

The boys looked on, mouths open wide, eagerly anticipating fresh coffee and everything else that constituted breakfast.

"But now," Clint continued, "all we've been told is that sooner or later they'll wreck the street and build a mall on the site. This crazy circus has 'Walmart' written all over it."

"So, Mr Clinton," Thelma had a flash of creative inspiration, which was why she was team leader. Clearly this old gentleman Clint, possessed a broad knowledge of the surrounding area, and therefore the team could latch onto some of that home spun familiarity. "Are you able to advise, or even guide us?" Thelma kept her assertive mannerism, but laced it with a hospitable, almost pleading smile.

"That's right, I mean we must be some distance to

where we want to be?" Diana had immediately latched onto Thelma's logic.

"Thirty-three clicks to the perimeter fence at least according to my reckoning." Frank enjoined.

"Not no more he don't." Hillary the now up-right waitress sounded emphatic. She carried the beverage order on an unstable tray and stumbled clumsily towards the table. "He's too old for that malarkey, besides it's too dangerous up there in them mountains. Folk have been up there in the past, saucer huntin', and you aint never seen them agin." Hillary was quite serious and categorical regarding the situation.

"We have dollars, good US currency. We could pay you for your time and trouble. Thelma felt a deal was about to be made. And then, as if she were having second thoughts regarding her proposition, she motioned to the MRU team members to close in for a football- field-style-huddle. "Guys, it's just, well do we actually need a guide? When we can easily drive up to the nearest perimeter point, thirty-three clicks isn't that far."

"I agree, I mean to say were not planning to find ourselves beyond the legal perimeter of the so-called base, now are we? This was discussed before we left. We do nothing to jeopardise our safety." Diana added.

Frank interjected. "At the same time we have to discover our best points to take readings, I mean you professionals," by which he was referring to Diana and Thelma, "do you have any intuitive feelings about this place?"

Duncan quickly joined in. "Yes," he stammered over lisping lips. "I mean to say, like all the water maybe contaminated from radioactive leaching. It's cokes only for me, I aint goanna get cancer and die!"

"So, let's pump the old guy for more information," Frank suggested. "And maybe slip him a few dollars and then let's get going up into the mountains and take some test readings." The smell of fresh coffee and frying eggs enlivened the team.

"I mean we have maps and a sophisticated satellite

navigation system, what possibly could go wrong?" Frank added.

"I expect there are dozens of tourists up there right now clambering over the boulders, trying to catch a good view of more mountains and more rocks." Diana was in.

"We have all seen Google Maps, lots of photographs and amateur video presentations, even TV documentaries about the place. Anyway, we're not here to snoop around any United States Air Force bases, derelict or not." Diana sensibly added.

Thelma cringed when the words: 'amateur video' were bandied about. It reminded her of that 'thing' in Bud Always-Jones' camera, a haunting image that was constantly on her mind as if it were eating away at her.

"Yea but wouldn't it be great to take a real look at what goes on in these places?" Frank mischievously added.

"No! Frank that's dangerous and irresponsible talk. We keep to our brief and don't go wandering off on some wild half-ass tangent." Diana was emphatic.

"Well," teased Frank, "suppose, like they say, that there are aliens up there on what's it called? Groom Lake? Then maybe we should go interview them or something."

"Yeah right on! man" Duncan lisped with a wide grin cross his face. The thought of chasing little grey aliens about the place amused him immensely.

"Yes Diana," Thelma's fawning eyes twinkled, "you are right, we keep to our plan and that's it!" Thelma had the last word, as usual.

The brunch came.

Hillary, the clearly out of practice waitress, spilt a few items and the old man Clint left the group to get on with their meal. He only hoped this particular bunch of kids wouldn't be like all the other ass-holes who came to look around, hoping to see aliens and UFOs to order. People like that had no respect for the law, or the military, because, and he knew, that without that respect you weren't going to survive out there on the open range.

"Here, wait! You kids hold on." Clint unexpectedly reappeared. "Let me show you something, maybe this will change your minds about going up into the mountains?" Clint moved to the front of the diner and opened a door adjacent to the kitchen. He beckoned, and the puzzled group moved inside what appeared to be a small storage area.

"See here, look, this is my lost property store."

The room was lined on each side by shelves and racks. Two units divided the room in half. Crammed in on each shelf, were cases, back-packs, rucksacks, shoulder bags and every other conceivable item of luggage.

"See this all here, lost property," the old man Clint continued. "Tourists mainly. Leaves their bags an go off hiking in the desert scrub. Looking for them aliens, but from here we is thirty-mile or more from the air base perimeter fence, the one that goes right around and around everywhere." Clint gesticulated with his arms as if to illustrate the immense length of the surrounding military boundary markers and enclosures.

Clint carried on with his lost property guided tour. "And from that fence it is thirty or maybe even more miles to the 'so-called' whatever it is. That adds up to more than fifty to sixty-mile, as the crow might fly. All mainly off road, amongst the sage brush, tumble weed and dogwood. Higher up you hit the tree-line where it gets freezing at night. Yep, you name it, it grows here, but just slowly. You got them Yuccas and Agave which is hundreds of years old. And of course, scorpions, and them hairy goddamn spiders, and God-awful rattlers, one bite and these'll kill yer."

A shiver ran down Diana's and Duncan's spines at the mention of spiders. Diana looked around as if she were visually scanning the confined area, possibly for evidence of spiders? But was in fact quickly estimating the number of personal items that had been left in store to gather dust. There had to be fifty or more backpacks and other forms of luggage festooned on the shelving.

"So, where are the people all these bags belong to?" Diana, feeling perplexed, justly posed the question.

Suddenly, from out of the kitchen, Hillary, the out of practice waitress, was standing in the luggage store doorway, boxing them all in. "Too many people are dumb enough to think they can go wandering about on government property." Hillary was laconic and somewhat lugubrious, as if she had lived a life full of regret.

"Tourist types," Clinton continued, also with a melancholy and regretful tone to his quivering voice. "They come up from Vegas on the bus, leave their luggage here, nice 'n' safe, then they aint never seen agin." He shuffled toward the door, as if being in the luggage store was a place he did not want to be. "Happened not so long ago." He spoke as he motioned Hillary out toward the store entrance. "Bunch of 'Euro-peens,' came up from Vegas, never even stopped long at Rachel, went further north, never seen 'em' agin."

"Surely?" Thelma was astonished and short of words to express her feelings, "surely their … their families and loved ones must wonder where they got to?"

"Missin! That's where, just missin'. No police, no nothin'. Just plain missin'. See, one word to the Sheriff's office an they has to do what they is told. That is keep quiet. They said the FBI put out an APB, said they was looking for some psycho-shooter fellah up there in the mountains. But we all knows different."

Hillary shuffled in reverse, allowing clean air to pour into the musty confines of the luggage store. "Now you know why I aint letting Clint go out there up them mountains, cos the next time he does he aint gonna be comin' back! For sure."

8

Off of Highway 33 Nevada

Highway 33, south of the small town known as Rachel, is the route to take when going north up through Nevada. A few miles beyond   Rachel is an unmarked road that forks left off of the highway. Initially the road appears durable and well made up. For those not used to the region, who are unaware of all the twists and turns and inconsistencies in the road, driving there can lead to a certain amount of confusion, and indeed getting hopelessly lost.

On this particular day, just about the time Thelma and her team were set to leave the rundown diner in Rachel, a certain multi-wheeled 'Mack' truck found itself going the wrong way up along Highway 33. And so, the driver, who supposed to himself that he was taking positive action to rectify his mistake, branched off to the left at the next exit. Probably thinking that by some magical means, either he could cross the highway some place, or, that maybe further back there might be a bridge he had previously missed spanning the road where he could crossover and switch direction?

If, buts and maybes however, usually add up to a disaster.

The huge vehicle consequently took a left off the highway and turned back on itself. The confused driver soon realised his error, that was, there was no possible way of crossing the highway from where he was now stranded. He only hoped there would be a turning area ahead where he could spin around and backtrack to the main route, and thus be able to continue on his way.

Ignoring the obvious elevation change and the gradual deterioration of the road condition, the driver still stubbornly remained certain that there had to be a fortuitous turning area further on, one that would be the solution to his directional quandary.

The average four-by-four pick-up truck could easily negotiate such an incline and be comfortable with the width and condition of the road. Be that as it may, the 'Mack' truck continued for several miles, blasting uphill and eventually losing site of the highway below. Whilst all the time getting closer and closer to what was, according to popular hearsay, the nonexistent, so-called, Area 51 perimeter fence. Normally at this distance from the top-secret base, there would be a patrol unit in a marked vehicle skirting the boundary ready to turn overly-inquisitive drivers back. As it was the road ahead led for miles to nowhere of significance or import. There was nothing to see. Just scrub, rocks and further along still pine trees

However, on this particular day, due to a number of unseen and unaccounted for circumstances, the fence patrols had been reduced to a minimum (this was in truth due to lack of staff). One scheduled inspection tour had already gone through, but the next check was not due until later that day, perhaps sunset, or even after dark.

As the road narrowed to what was not much more than a pot-holed trail, the truck driver gradually began to realise that he had made a massive miscalculated mistake. The hapless, now panic-stricken vehicle operative, eventually pulled up where he thought the road was sufficiently wide enough to just about navigate the tractor and loaded trailer around and head back the way he came.

This manoeuvre meant a slow, agonising backward and forwards process. Inching as it were to the edge of the road, which dropped down on one side, and then rocking back to the other side, which was a dirt bank, one that rose up thirty-feet, culminating in a precarious bluff that hung threateningly over the road.

The truck driving man broke out in an uncontrollable sweat, due to his fear-induced state. Regardless of which, employing all of his skills as a driver, he eventually overcame the onerous task (after a twenty or more-point turn), and managed to scrape the truck around to point back in the direction he had come from.

However, in the process of doing so, the rear of the truck, it's fender to be precise, snagged the fence surrounding the restricted-nonexistent-government-owned -prohibited-area, known only as 'so-called' Area 51. (Not that this particular driver had any such inclination regarding secret government bases, as he was a native Mexican and did not normally travel this particular road north.)

At this particular proximity the fence was around six-feet high, and consisted of four strands of razor wire, together with signs and warning notices regarding the punishment on offer for trespassing on United States Government land.

Death!

Regardless of the entanglement, the mighty 'Mack' threw into gear and the happy and much relieved Mexican driver picked up speed and started his decent back to the highway.

Clearly, in his relieved state, he was oblivious to his predicament and certainly did not realise he was pulling the government- owned enclosure fence up by its metal posts as he rapidly dropped to safer and better made up roads. After a mile or more of kicking up clouds of choking dust, the luckless driver realised his destructive mistake and pulled up where the trail levelled out. Consequently, he took out a large set of bolt croppers and jumping down from his cab he rapidly freed himself, snip by hurried snip from his self-induced predicament. Seemingly no one the wiser, he went on his way leaving a coil of razor wire over a mile long on the road behind him.

The truck driver felt certain he had covered his tracks and covered them well. However, what he was unaware of was that the latest top-secret addition to the arsenal of surveillance gadgetry made available to the USAF and the private security contractor: Five Star Security, all in order to ward-off unwanted strangers from a location or locations that officially did not exist, was a squadron of nonexistent state-of-the-art aerial drones.

A regular nonexistent secret and well-timed drone flight path over the lower road area, identified the damaged perimeter fence, by way of its on-board, top-secret, up-to-date visual systems, which picked up every wave length of the visual spectrum. From hot red to cool ultra violet. Ultimately relaying the information back to it's hard-standing home base (code named: 'Paradise Ranch'), command and control centre. Which was located off the main nonexistent, even possibly disused 'Homey' landing strip up in the distant nonexistent Groom Lake top-secret facility.

Consequently, as and when its Air Force controllers picked-up this type of, or, any other similar suspicious images, they then immediately forwarded the information to 'Five Star Security,' the private-sector run safety and security contractors for the fully operational base. Who were also the official fence maintenance service providers, and in turn and along with protocol, should have immediately dispatched a couple of standby emergency operatives, both engineers, to survey the damaged fence.

By this time, on this singular occasion, as it was approaching late afternoon and the probability of any public traffic incursions, that was, people in four-by-fours coming up the dirt track to snoop around the restricted area, was slim.

As it was, due to the staff shortage, the two-man engineering team was already stretched to its limit, and had to divert from their normal routine, to drive back thirty-miles or more around the mountains to take care of the current, more urgent, damaged fence problem.

All they could hope to do at this stage was to assess the perimeter damage and then drag the wire off the road and allow it to tumble down the incline out of harm's way. This they promptly attended to, and took their timely leave with a view to continue their normal routine inspection rounds later.

However, clearing the razor-wire fence was one thing, but did not account for the fact that this now left a legacy of a mile-long hiatus in the perimeter defences. In as much as there was a great open expanse of land on the supposed nonexistent-top-secret-government- site. One that did not display any form of warning notice as to the fact that trespasses maybe shot dead if they came snooping around.

9

Gracie Lin

Gracie Lin sat in the back of the rented Chrysler Voyager MPV. Making her face up and giving herself a manicure. Her ever-faithful slave, Bud Always-Jones was as 'always' at the wheel. He, was, 'always' there for her, no one else was, and she felt a certain sense of security being in his company. Despite the fact she actually loathed him and the feeling was reciprocal.

Her current mood was one of self-satisfaction, content that she had not only put her perverse warped plan into action, but surprisingly had been successful in doing so.

She, from now on, could rightfully view and accept herself as being the quintessential; 'femme fatale'. A role she enjoyed playing, particularly the adrenaline rush of blatant deception and risk taking. She was also delighted with her raw instinct and knowledge of the predictable habits and desires of men. They were so easy and gullible, falling at the feet of a woman with a glimpse of leg, a revealing cleavage, or just by drinking in the redolence of her exotic perfume. Or, so she had accurately surmised.

Screwing the Iowa State University Principal had been enjoyable, to a certain extent. A clear means to an interesting end, no doubt. But would not compare with amusingly pleasant sight of him squirming on a hook, as the worm he was.

Yes, once Bud had uploaded the video recording, she had made of their steamy love session, all hell and damnation would be let lose. Utilising a spot of creative editing by Bud, 'her' features were totally masked out, leaving the viewer no doubt or speculation as to 'who' was clearly on top.

Principal Jones' 'Shriner' friends, now felt happier that potentially they held something tasteless and vulgar concerning him. He was, after all said and done, in the context of this latest endeavour; simply their puppet to control as they pleased. Regardless, they still craved a further guarantee, just in case he decided to take the initiative and 'go-it-alone,' so to speak.

Gracie Lin had been correct in assuming he, Principal Jones, held a secret diary of events, including names, addresses, times and places. A typical naughty little black book, hidden in plain sight, as if he wanted the world to see it, in his dresser draw. Everything of importance to him was there, tucked away in his bedroom furnishings. Watches, passport, legal documents, passwords and access codes. The lot. All waiting to be stolen, or used in some way against him.

Perhaps the most puzzling and unpalatable aspect of Gracie Lin's personal plan relating to the matter, was the fact that she had no real justifiable reason or motive in wanting to ruin Principal J. Jones Junior's life. They were distant blood relatives after all, and she had nothing specific against him. But then he was a man, and so probably, like all men, deserved to be punished and totally ruined.

Gracie Lin had also, for a change, been mildly impressed by Bud's Always-Jones' performance. He had demonstrated his stealthy cat-burgling skills and fearless ability to, without question, enter private property, unlock the access code of a computer, download all the salient information and brining it all safely back to his mistress for her to work through and analyses. He was not it appeared an entirely stupid ape, or so it emerged. Clearly, he could rise to the occasion, if pushed sufficiently hard.

For that he deserved a morsel of approval and token of thanks. Consequently, she was contemplating giving him an out of character blow-job one night over the course of the trip's duration. But then she came to her senses after working through the complications that having sex with a minion would give rise to, therefore decided a six-pack of beer would be sufficient reward.

She, after all, did not want to get too intimate with him, as he might work things out for himself and conclude he had a vested interest in, and a right to at least, half of the gold that Gracie was now fully convinced was somewhere out there, just waiting for her to discover. It would be unearthed, with of course a little help from her divine, butter-would-not-melt cousin, Thelma Jones, heroine of the moment but not for long.

10

MRU Team go up the mountain

The routine was the same as before when they had camped up a few miles outside Roswell. The boys set out the equipment, connecting all the systems up with the electrical power supply that came from heavy duty industrial cells located in each four-by-four vehicle. Whilst driving the power-packs charged, and then released that stored energy when parked up. This energy was needed to power the computer systems and other seismic and echo-sounding measuring devices used by the team.

The only difference this time was that all the team members felt optimistic. Certainly the conditions appeared to be suitable and they could all tangibly sense the electro-magnetic static in the air.

Prior to arriving at this particular perfect spot, the team vehicles had driven up Highway 33 and switched left at a fork, that was not shown on any map. It was the old fellow Clint who confirmed to them that the road was there.

The MRU team had imagined the existence of this particular route time and time again. There was plenty of documented evidence to be seen on the internet to suggest that there were numerous hidden access trails leading up into the mountains. Tracks that lead up to the so-called Area 51 perimeter fence; with its dozens of warning signs discouraging people not to even consider entering whatever it was up there that was kept so secret and hidden from public view. Threatening notices such as: *'Trespassers will be shot on site.'* Or, *'enter under pain of death.'*

Strange that the government should discourage people from entering a plot of land that they actually denied existed?!

Apparently, these *'Restricted Area'* notification signs

were hung up all along the wire to reinforce the deadly message aimed at alerting unwelcome visitors, advising them not to enter the prohibited area.

'*Violators will vanish without a trace.*' Was by far the most outrageous warning sign.

That and: '*use of deadly force authorised.*' Thelma wondered just who '*authorised*' the shooting of, or, disappearance of American citizens without a trace?

As it was, two-years of meticulous planning had been invested into the MRU project, so the team should have known in advance, and been cognisant with, exactly where they were going. The plan being, in this location anyway, to avoid trespassing on government property at all costs.

Frank, once off the highway and on the rugged dirt road, took the lead drive. Whilst Duncan, mono-scope in hand, stood on the back seat, goggles on, reconnoitering the landscape for potential set down spots. Eventually, after some distance driving up the incline, Duncan flagged the two-car convoy down to a stop. Through his high-powered scope he could see before him a wide-open section of arid scrubland, where the nonexistent-top-secret, so-called Area 51 perimeter fence seemingly disappeared. Rather, it appeared as if it had abruptly stopped. The sector was open for at least a mile and there were numerous signs of surface disturbance that suggested traffic, probably campers, had recently driven along the road and up toward the tree-line. Which was around a half-mile away. The overall location seemed ideal; it had all the characteristics of being a proper regular public camp site.

Subsequently they continued on for a few more minutes before Duncan gleefully jumped out of his crow's nest and ushered both vehicles to reverse up into a flat area where the north-eastern ridge dropped down to the level of the road, thus creating a cosy niche where an encampment was begging to be set-up.

Once parked, the base camp pitched and systems up

and running, the team enjoyed their beans and bacon and settled down to begin the process of interrogating the data that was coming through in 'tsunami sized' waves. In complete and utter contrast to Roswell, where no activity had been picked up at all. This site was awash with data. The magnitude of the magnetic field in this spot was the strongest Thelma had ever recorded. She lay back with relief, leg propped up in her uncomfortable camping chair, and digested the findings.

However, her mind went around in circles. Energy had to go someplace once released and here was hard evidence of its existence, or so she hoped. Obviously, the Roswell site had now spent much of its energy. The alledged UFO crash landing event had been back in 1947. Roswell had clearly lost its mass appeal over a short period of time. People, outside of diehard ufologist circles, no longer visited the over-researched Roswell location. Now as global public interest and awareness grew, there were it appeared, numerous UFO infested hot-spots around the world. Just as Frank and Duncan had previously alluded to.

However, in respect of UFO phenomena and general sightings, there now existed a paradoxical 'chicken before the egg' scenario. In as much as: was there a dramatic increase in sighting because more and more people were becoming aware and believed in the existence of UFOs and extraterrestrial life forms? Or, was there an increase in the presence of UFOs because more alien life forms were paying the earth a visit? Or, perhaps it was because just about every citizen of planet earth possessed a cell phone which included a high definition digital camera? Hence more recorded sightings?

A very fluid situation that could neither be proved or disproved.

Either way, and in complete glaring contrast (thought the still in serious pain, team leader), as she unwittingly perched herself on the fringes of the nonexistent-top-secret-so-called Area 51, where there apparently existed a mass of magnetic activity that, if she had been a gambling woman, she would have wagered that if there had been any potential sightings of unidentified flying objects in the area (which there had not been), then they must have originated locally from the numerous top-secret USAF fighter and bomber aircraft development programmes that she supposed were currently taking place over the mountains many miles from where she and her team were camped.

Whatever was going on in and around this restricted arena of aerial activity, it was producing a very big signature, that really had to be explored and assessed, one way or another.

Meanwhile the research team's computers whirled and clicked, opening and closing files, whilst disseminating the figures and data. By means of global positioning and NASA satellite technology the data gathered was supposedly catalogued and broadcast back to Thelma's lab' in Iowa State University, ready for further future analysis when the clearly successful team returned from this seminal expedition.

For some time, all appeared well. Night had fallen, the temperature began to drop, Diana was clearing the dishes, Frank and Duncan were looking at the readouts, whilst still bouncing out seismic signals, which were designed to penetrate the natural landscape and assess the composition of the surrounding bedrock. All in order to create a computer generate image of the general topography. Added to which a map of the magnetic energy grid would be overlaid. This would indicate what influence the composition of the ground had upon localised magnetic activity and vice versa.

All was going along smoothly until suddenly Frank, looking out toward the south-south-east, beyond Rachel, towards Las Vegas, which was to be found some eighty or more miles from their current position, told everyone to grab cameras and keep quiet. As, in the distance were two, no four, identical lights, that were slowly approaching their current location.

Duncan fumbled with his phone and dropped it. Diana was having more luck as her digital SLR went to work snapping everything in sight. Before that was, to everyone's utter horror, the tented cover protecting the equipment flew up into the air and disappeared into the distant ever-darkening sky.

The noise that followed was deafening.

The ground literally shook as tainted hot aviation-fuel air blasted out of the rear of what was clearly a pair of fighter jets, landing gear deployed, seemingly preparing to touch down. Frank fell on his back with the force of the blast, as Duncan was tossed against the side of one of the team vehicles.

What happened next however was uncanny and beyond credibility: trailing behind the fighter jets came a dark triangular shaped object, which in contrast to the fighter jets, floated silently through the ether. Whatever it was had three to five coloured lights flashing on it's under belly. The craft tilted from side to side as it followed the two jets, keeping as low as possible, tracing as it was, the contours of the land, heading toward the north-west.

* * * * *

Frank tried to remind himself of his bearings and assess the situation. Where they were currently camped out was almost certainly slap in the middle of a number of active USAF bases. In fact, most of Nevada was occupied by the USAF.

As far as Frank knew, the numerous sections of the Nellis Air Force base and its firing and testing ranges, lay to the north-west, whilst the old nuclear test site lay over one-hundred miles to the south-west. These firing and bombing ranges covered thousands of square miles.

The still radioactive Nevada nuclear testing range, had been and always would be, out of bounds, due to its radioactive signature.

In the middle of all this was whatever the government were diligently trying to keep secret. Such assiduous covert behaviour though, clearly suggested there was something to hide amongst the rocky outcrops. Or, so Frank imagined.

He had no idea in reality. All and any of the information he possessed regarding this extensive secret plot of land had been derived from the internet and numerous popular amateur conspiracy theorist's video clips.

Sections and sub-sections innocuously designated: 'Groom Lake,' or 'Homey,' 'Dreamland' or 'Paradise Ranch.' Places that were perhaps no more than a whimsical fantasy for pseudo scientists to consume. People wanted mysteries, and so therefore mysteries is what they got.

Regardless, here they were, stuck on the periphery of what were massive tracts of government land. From where the landscape rose dramatically to some four-and-a-half-thousand-feet above sea level, before plunging down into a man-made basin out of human sight.

* * * * *

The floating triangle drifted on in dark foreboding silence, but the calm was to be short-lived and broken, as the still air was yet to be agitated further.

As Frank and the bewildered team looked up into the star-strewn night sky, they heard the monotonous sound of powerful gyrating rotors, accompanied by yet another series of lights, all rapidly approaching their position. Soon the aerial monsters arrived, seemingly no more than a few feet above their exposed heads. Now they could be plainly seen: two strike helicopters, one of which hovered directly overhead. And, from its under-belly, came clouds of mist, a toxic vapor that was disturbed further by the air-thrashing gyratory rotors.

And then all went black.

11

Las Vegas

Gracie Lin poured herself another gin. The motel had an ice machine at the end of the hall so she helped herself to the free and plentiful supply. Once back in her room and off the dusty roads, she had decided to shower and dress down into something more comfortable.

The temptation to drop by Las Vegas was too great for both Gracie and Bud. It had been a couple of years since she had visited these parts. Bud, her camera man, apparently was a frequent caller to the play capital of the world:

'Welcome to fabulous Las Vegas!' The Hotel New York, The Eiffel Tower, The Bellagio Fountain, Luxor, The Coca Cola Store, The Rat Pack in concert, Fremont Street, and the Stratosphere Tower. The entire world at your finger tips. So much to see and do, yet so little time to do it! The wide avenues, the endless strings of light, the sound of money pinging through the air and smell of sizzling steaks, choked the already hot and dusty air. All these fantasy images permanently remained in the minds of any sightseeing tourist.

Upon arrival at the mid-town low-budget motel, Bud had gone directly to his room. Then, after showering, he quickly left in a cab to go downtown.

To where?

The devil only knew: no doubt to some sleazy pole-dancing club that he was acquainted with from a previous visit. Apparently, girls in Vegas 'got-off' performing in front of the cameras, for a few bucks that was. Only tonight he had no camera. Why? He enquired of himself. Because his boss wanted it. What the hell for? He asked himself over and over. But only Gracie knew. And Gracie would not tell him or anyone else.

In the first instance Bud should have kicked himself for allowing her to look at the copy of the university presentation footage. Even though it was only on the miniscule digital camera viewfinder, therefore making the image far too small; but nevertheless, of a sufficient quality that the casual observer could just about garner a good idea of what was going on.

OK! Dig it! It was 'his' footage! He possessed the 'master tape,' and would not let go of that at any price. But then his mistress, insisted he hand over at least a copy. Then having initially viewed the tape she complained over the fact there was a distortion of the image, and part of frame was little more than a fluid black smudge.

As it was Bud refuted that fact, he saw nothing and had no idea what Gracie Lin was carping on about. An argument ensued. Gracie questioned Bud's professionalism. Hence Bud's urgency to go downtown as fast as possible, to escape her critical comments and general 'Gracie Lin' self-righteous blame- everyone-else-dogma.

Apparently, according to his mistress, there was a strange image that crept in from the bottom left corner of the view finder. Then edged its way up the screen. It was a ghostly silhouette according to Gracie Lin. He still could not see it.

If there was something out of order, such as a distortion of the raw footage, it could only be explained as being just that, a breakdown in the digital image.

That was it.

OK so his camera was old, past its best, there were gremlins and ghosts in the machine.

According to Gracie Lin; the footage was ruined. Bud had deliberately done something to destroy the tape. Her career was over, it was his fault. He was a fool, a dullard, she had been humiliated by him. She refused to accept any other view or explanation.

And this despite the fact that Bud had already, a few

days back, uploaded the footage onto his editing suite and examined the frames on a much higher resolution monitor screen. There had been nothing then, and there was nothing untoward now. So confident was Bud that he had already emailed out the new footage files for syndication. News rooms, once they had the full interviews in their possession, would then edit the piece down and screen any particular given section of the footage for public consumption as they deemed fit and appropriate. That was always how it was done. Now however it was old news, the past, no one cared, no one bothered.

Let's move on…

But no! All that concerned Gracie Lin was the quality of that miserable presentation piece shot at the university.

And why?

He had no idea.

A copy should have been sufficient for her, for anyone else.

But no, it had to be the original, played back on the same camera. She had no use for DVD screening copies, or mini dv back-up copies. No, the actual master copy was the only one she would contemplate viewing.

Something was clearly going on. Even Bud Always-Jones could work that one out. And what the heck were they doing anyway? Hiring costly vehicles on credit cards and driving half-way across America for what? What was she chasing? Who was she trying to follow? What was she so desperately looking for?

* * * * *

Sitting in the back of an air-con' cab Bud Always-Jones let out a sigh of relief. The passing Las Vegas streets were peaceful and tranquil compared to being in the presence of Gracie Lin. If he had not thought better of it, he would definitely say she was a woman possessed.

Naturally he was aware of her reputation amongst her direct family members. After all they, Gracie and himself, were cousins of sorts. Back in the early 1990s, a progressive thinking male member of the Jones clan had married outside of the family. He wed for the sake of love, not for money or power. His bride a young woman from the 'Always' family originating from across the state line. This was frowned upon, no one had heard the like. She, the new bride, was headstrong and independently minded. It would never do. But it did, it stuck, and the double-barreled Always-Jones name came to being out of the disapproved of union. Bud was only a half Jones. His parents had gone against tradition. As far as the elders of the family were concerned this was akin to a mixed-race union. But as it was, the thought and notion of it was, like so many other issues, brushed away under a rug, not to be spoken of again. Here then lay the possible reason of how it was that the outcast Bud and Gracie Lin were somehow mystically drawn together. Birds of a feather etc. A love-hate-hate-hate kind of relationship.

* * * * *

What was it with this camera? Bud continued in his angry and frustrated frame of mind. Gracie had said something unusual to the effect of: *'it would only work for her if she had the same camera.'* What exactly was it that was bothering her to such an extent? Was it to do with the MRU expedition and following them to wherever it was they were going? If so she had been right concerning their whereabouts thus far. What Bud could make of the non-existent image and what his mistress could catch sight of, through the same digital camera view finder, were entirely different images. Bud, who saw nothing, once again asked himself the question as to why she needed the digital device? And how was it that she required to be alone and in quiet environment each time she looked at the captured footage?

* * * * *

Gazing into a crystal ball or 'scrying' was the answer Bud was so desperately looking for. Gracie Lin Jones had never attempted this occult exercise before and was not entirely satisfied that it worked. The image she could see through the camera view-finder was obviously not that of Thelma Jones, due to the fact she had broken her leg and was never interviewed on the day of the presentation. Rather it was Diana Rogers, who filled the frame for the interview.

But it mattered not. The messenger was not of any importance, rather it was the message she so desperately craved. The message telling her in which direction to go.

Scrying, was a mystical form of seeing or peeping. Looking through a suitable transparent medium in the hope of detecting a specific message or vision. This could then be used for prophesy, for revelation, or for divination. A crystal ball was not always required as a window, any visual or light refractive device would do: a mirror, a glass, a telescope, a digital or other form of camera, all mediums would work equally as well.

Gracie recalled a saying from her grandmother on her mother's side, one of the singular individuals that understood the pubescent Gracie: *'on Halloween look in the glass, your future husband's face will pass.'* From that day on, every 31st of October she peered into the glass, and saw nothing.

Regardless, although nothing was there to be seen, she became increasingly 'aware' and began to know and see a hidden truth. What lay beyond?

On this seminal attempt at unusually peeping at life through the lens of a camera, the process had surprisingly worked well, and immediately pointed Gracie towards the whereabouts of Diana Rogers and the Magnetronic Research Unit.

After the team had quietly left Iowa State, once Thelma was out of the fracture clinic, and the pageantry of the occasion confined to history, Gracie Lin already knew concerning which way they were going and where they were ultimately headed to. She knew, thanks to the information gleaned from Principal Jones' computer files, where they planned to go. Passed and beyond Kansas City. And then they were going to camp out in Roswell New Mexico. After that the aim was to carry onto Nevada. Exactly where in the State? She had not gleaned that information as yet. However, Vegas aside she would locate Thelma Jones and her team, and find out exactly what they were up to and involved in.

Her money-lusting suspicions told her it was 'gold' they were seeking. Gold in them there Nevadan hills. And why not? Back in the 1800s the area had been mined for copper, lead and silver. Therefore, according to Gracie and her 'Shriner' task masters, it made sense that gold was also there in abundance. Just because no one as yet had unearthed a find, that did not negate the fact that precious metals were there in profusion.

* * * * *

Gracie sashayed about the room, gin bottle in one hand, a cigarette in the other, feeling pleased with herself in her see-through-retro-style-baby-doll-nightdress and matching pom-pom mules. Seeing her own, sometimes sharp, and occasionally drawn, reflection was somehow highly erotic for her, writhing as she was before a full-length mirror. Her dyed jet-black hair, as ever, cut back into a Mary Quant style bob.

Gracie held as a maxim one of Quant's more provocative statements: *'Good taste is death, vulgarity is life!'* How true. If only Gracie had been born those few years earlier, she would, she could, have been a true Quant aficionado. Hot pants, mini dresses, micro dresses and platform soles. Quant was the high priestess of sixties fashion, and the young American reporter idolised her.

Setting the gin bottle down and balancing her burning cigarette in the hotel room ash tray, she squeezed her exposed breasts and tweaked her now erect nipples. This was her way of invoking sex-magic. Then, as if it were a phallic extension of her own body, she picked up Bud's precious camera and stroked and caressed its metal body, before eagerly peering through the eye piece.

And all she saw was black!

12

So-called Area 51

Former US Marine Captain K.K. Kruger was the Nellis Air Force Base on-site manager for the private safety and protection firm: 'Five Star Security.' A company with headquarters on three-two-two Main and Berkley Avenue, New York. A business that, it was rumored, was owned by the Bush Brothers out of Texas. This concern handled the protective requirements of the Department of Defence, relating to, in this instance, the Nellis and other connected Air Force Bases, including the entire Las Vegas municipality, the fun capital of the world (all of which were located within the vast Nevada Test and Training Range). The highly efficient and award-winning service offered by the Five Star corporation was tailor made for and on behalf of The United States Air Force, and other understated clandestine agencies.

Each individual section of the entire Nellis region was labelled as being - 'unofficial.' But none more so than the so-called - * * * * * * *.

A site that had only once ever been disclosed as actually existing by the CIA; the most secret of secret agencies simply stating that it was merely a vicinity of - 'special interest and concern,' and no more.

The above-top-secret region was, and had also been, unofficially known by the censors and redactors as - * * * * * Airport, * * * * * Lake, * * * * * land and * * * * * * * *. Amongst other more native nicknames and handles.

The site was and had been designated top secret since the Vietnam War, when it was unofficially branded - '* * * * * *' - by means of (some say), a clerical error. A name no one singular agency ever gave credence to, or even accepted the partial existence of.

However, the official popular line was that the term

'Area 51,' was probably coined from a geographical nuclear agency test site map, that divided the overall region into separate areas: 51.52.53 etc., And no more.

This was in order that the pollution from nuclear test blasts, all seven-hundred and thirty-nine of them, could be measured in terms of fallout and radioactive hot-spots. In such a manner contaminant could be relatively easy to monitor with a systematic approach.

Which understandably was a huge relief for the unfortunate cancer-ridden population living, and more so, dying in and around the surrounding area. The residents faced a dramatic increase in radioactivity levels that slowly diminished the further east the Geiger counters went to collect data. Drinking water readings from radioactive fallout, that predictably leached into the water table, demonstrated the most telling facts surrounding nuclear testing.

It was insanity.

Save for, given sufficient propaganda to influence the opinions of the local population living in Lincoln County, then the government could do and say anything they liked. People in general would accept any untruth once they got used to the notion.

All told this non-existent piece of land, designated as so-called Area 51 was unofficially, 'the' vast Nevada test ranges, and amounted to, unofficially, a rectangle stretching approximately one-hundred unofficial miles by more than one-hundred unofficial miles. Surrounded by unofficial mountain ranges on three asides stretching the boundaries even further. Central to this vast ten-thousand square mile piece of real estate was the Groom Lake six-mile landing strip which in total occupied around six-hundred and seventy-five square miles of mining dross, salt-flats and wild inhospitable desert.

All of which was designated as being 'special use airspace.' Which meant it was a wholly restricted area. A licensed private pilot out of Vegas could not fly over it, or even get close.

And it fell upon Five Star Security to keep hikers, backpackers and other curious people out.

As it was, (so it has been alledged by conspiracy theorists), inside the base proper, there existed an entire city made up of thousands of military personnel, together with private and other vetted contractors. The HR inventory included government paid scientists, and experts in their particular field.

Judging by the very few and rare satellite pictures that had been officially or unofficially released for military or other purposes, the base was multi-functional and, on the surface, consisted of a number of very large hangers and industrial-sized warehousing units.

All connected by well-made roads that crossed the site leading south to the nuclear testing ground enclave of Mercury, via Frenchman and Yucca Lakes. North to Bald Mountain and west across the Belted range.

Inside the restricted area, the well-maintained Groom Lake road, (not reproduced on any existing map of the region) ran south-east through a rugged pass in the hills, which terminated at one of the site's main checkpoints. From there the road continued east to the valley floor, passed the 'Black Mail Box,' deliberately skirting the Bald Mountain range and Coyote Summit, passing several small, little used, or completely deserted ranches on the way. Before, that was, converging with State Highway 33. Also known as: 'The Extraterrestrial Highway.'

Coyote Summit was where in the past the tour busses came in their droves, together with any number of small off-road vehicles carrying sight-seeing tourist. Trips which were conducted from and to the public viewing sites on a regular basis. Asian tourists would stand right up by the fence, or next to one of the warning signs, and have their pictures taken- typical modern oriental selfies.

* * * * *

And all of the security for the world's most secretive

place was the responsibility of one Captain K.K. Kruger, ex-Marine and former special forces operative. Although hailing from South Africa, he was a naturalised US Citizen, and was proud to have served his country.

Under his guidance and command, he had a contingent of some three-hundred men. All ex-service employees who he had personally recruited. This small army was currently divided into three shifts, each with one-hundred men on board. Each shift ran to seventy-five percent capacity to allow for vacations and other absenteeism.

All Five Star shift workers, of whatever designation, were officially not permitted to enter the base they protected (other than under certain clearly defined circumstances). Their authorized task was to keep people out, and therefore the patrols they managed were mainly outside, on, or, about, the perimeter confines. Those clearly defined circumstances included shift changes, which were normally undertaken outside the USAF manned gatehouses that controlled and monitored access by those cleared to enter the base (no one), for whatever business they may be conducting.

Members of the public were never permitted onto any part of the base proper, under any circumstances.

As it was, this restrictive procedure undertaken by Five Star employees was clumsy and the operational system almost impossible to adhere to.

There were however numerous 'exceptions' to the rule. And so therefore there had to be some form of compromise reached. One problem being the location of the Five Star 'Camo' sharp shooters. No one ever knew where they might be located at any given time. As it was, they were permitted to carry out their missions from inside or outside the wire.

Whilst Five Star vehicle patrols were permitted to cross over the inner-perimeter fence, only if and when in pursuit of trespassers.

At any one time there may be up to a maximum of fifty patrol vehicles in positions around the base. This appeared to be an over-kill, but with an outside perimeter of several hundred miles it was a hell of a stretch to police.

Then came the advent of the drones. Clearly, having drone patrols overhead saved everyone time money and effort. It was decided to locate the Air Force funded drone squadron on the 'Paradise Ranch' takeoff and landing hardstand. The site was once used to park-up trailers for Air Force families, before they built more permanent housing. That was prior to the recorded levels of radioactive contamination encouraged them to rapidly move out.

The zone also played host to the 'stand-by' helicopter back-up and support team. The choppers were on standby 24/7 and the Five Star team could summon their support at any time day or night. This then became the perfect marriage between manned and unmanned aerial attack and support roles. The Air Force big-wigs were reluctant to take-over the task of managing drone border patrol duties, as it lay beyond their brief. It was not their responsibility to police the boundary fence, and deal with civilians, that belonged to Five Star and Five Star alone. The solution was simple: to allow a special concession to permit Five Star operatives to manage helicopter dispatching and drone deployment. In exchange, to save money, they could in the future reduce the pick-up patrols down to the level of four six-hour shifts per day.

Shift patterns would remain the same on a one team off, three teams on basis, as far as that was vehicle patrols were concerned.

Rather than drive out to a trouble spot, they could now send out a drone to complete the task in a fraction of the time, with minimal flight costs.

Shift access was normally conducted via the existing gatehouse facilities. 'Off' teams could go back via the gatehouses to Vegas or to wherever they domiciled.

The only proviso to this beneficial arrangement was that Five Star operatives were not permitted to enter any restricted building or hanger on the wider-site. Unless in pursuit of interlopers, fugitives, or trespassers. Access to the 'drone zone' being the only exception. Five Star staff could also utilise the bunkhouse facilities, which included a mess hall and other amenities.

From the 'Paradise Ranch' location, it was impossible to clearly see any other part of the wider-base. It worked and existed in isolation. The only disturbance being the coming and going of aircraft taking off and landing over on 'Groom Lake' and 'Homey,' runways, which were no more than a distant mirage away on any given sun-drenched day.

As for other workers, they were brought in and taken out of the base via, what appeared to be, ordinary commercial aircraft. The only anomaly being their blacked-out windows and the glaring absence of flight markings. Aircraft took off from the 'Homey' airport runway and touched down, so it was generally understood, at McCarran Airport, Las Vegas.

The unregistered aircraft parked up at a reserved area known as: 'Janet's Hub.' Or, in other words: Just Another Non-Existent Terminal. The building was fabricated, (as with the air traffic) with blacked out windows and secured doors, through which the passengers were conveyed onto their aircraft from the private and secure terminal, also managed by Five Star security personnel.

Those workers destined for so-called non-existent Area 51 or Groom Lake were bussed up to the standing aircraft and entered the plane through a series of covered walkways that ensured no one from the terminal proper could photograph, spot or recognise the passengers boarding the aircraft.

Other essential workers, such as cleaners, cooks, domestic staff and so forth, were in the main, drawn from a bank staff of ill-educated Mexican workers who were flown into the base in a similar manner. They had no idea where they were going in the USA. Whilst it was not unusual for pilots to extend their flight time by means of circling. Thus, confusing anyone who might try and calculate where they were headed, based on flight times.

Every worker was under strict and continual surveillance, watched and listened to at all times. No one, from when they entered the private terminal facility, to after they had arrived at their destination, was permitted to talk or communicate, in any way or manner, with any of their fellow workers. Work related communication aside, anyone breaking protocol would be instantly dismissed.

Fortunately for Captain K.K. Kruger, he did not have to police internal workings of the base, with its multi-faceted issues, and the huge number of problems associated with keeping watch over hundreds of busy workers. That was the job of the United States Air Force and the CIA. All he had to do was to keep people, inquisitive strangers out of the base.

Assisting in this matter were his 'Camo' sharp-shooter teams, who were always on the lookout down toward the access roads from vantage points located in the rugged mountainous landscape. They saw you but you never saw them. You only heard their warning shots whistling over your exceedingly curious head.

Meanwhile, a vast network of CCTV cameras and their operatives constantly scanned the entire perimeter.

Thankfully, the more recent deployment of drones had made the Captain's life considerably easier. As did the marked reduction of interfering foreign visitors. But the security team still had to face the hardened conspiracy theorists - 'know it all' high rollers, 'geeks' who liked to play cat and mouse with the security teams, as a kind of display of male bravado fueled by testosterone!

From the Paradise Ranch hard-stand up to ten drones could or would be, in the future, simultaneously released, flying in a grid pattern, all guided by newly trained Five Star operatives. The drones, once dispatched, picked up movement and infra-red signatures. When locked-on to a target the drone could pinpoint the offending object using lasers. The geostatic image could then be relayed to a 'Camo' shooter if required, who then brought down the target from the ground.

Shoot first was always the motto.

If a sniper was not in range then the drone could strafe any given area. Intruder survival chances stood at less than nil.

The legality of such action was of course questionable. However, seeing as the base did not exist, according to many, or indeed any, governmental departments, then no one could ever be accused of any crime, or brought to justice for what may amount to plain and simple murder.

* * * * *

Generally speaking, Kruger was not liked around the base. He was terse and abrupt in manner, whilst being totally uncompromising. Limited in stature, yet keen and muscular, he made up for his lack of height often by shouting and generally throwing his weight around. There was also something cruel and harsh about his eyes and square jaw-line, capped by almost white razor-cropped hair. His overall soldierly style tended further to put people off of him. And, despite no longer being a military man, he invariably insisted on still acting as if he was. All the while he kept his official Five Star uniform pressed and starched as if he were on parade.

Kruger generally considered himself to be above and beyond legal jurisdiction. As a former ruthless government paid operative, he had no qualms what-so-ever concerning shooting any trespassers who tried to enter the base dead on the spot.

Any terminations resulting from his 'trigger-happy' exploits were quickly transported to the 'Yucca Lake' nuclear waste depository, some hundred miles south of Groom Lake. Once cast into the bubbling mire any cadaver would bask peacefully in radioactive slime for the next thousand odd years.

Currently there was a marked downturn in on-or-off base intrusions. Much of, if not all the sightseer excursions to the base out of Vegas, had in recent times been curtailed. There was too much for visitors to see up and around Vegas without going beyond the municipal boundaries. And the new moneyed Chinese tourist cared little of conspiracy theories, he or she simply wanted to take 'selfies' and play on the tables or the slots.

People's attitudes change, what was once 'hot' had now become little more than tepid. Global interest in the life of a secret non-existent military base had clearly waned, as much of the experimental and development programmes that had once been carried out on those bases, were now being consigned, so rumour had it, externally to private contractors. Such as: Lockheed Martin at their 'Skunk Works' California location.

The USA no longer needed high-flying spy planes to see what the Soviets were up to. Satellites meant both Super Powers could keep an eye on each other at all times. Nuclear testing was now almost a thing of the past, thanks to the various non-proliferation and testing bans in place. Too many people were protesting against it and it was no longer a patriotic vote winner in the USA.

Besides, much of America's Industrial and Military Complex had moved its external borders and boundaries outwards. Resulting in an increasingly growing American global empire, consisting of some one-hundred and sixty military bases planet wide. Any and all of which, could be designated as being: 'experimental,' or, 'Top-Secret,' by design or nature.

Be that as it may, it was of some surprise to the Captain that he had been summoned, via his internal radio, to the gatehouse located some miles off of the Highway 33 entrance to the base that did not exist. Where it was apparent that a long section of fencing had been torn down by unknown persons or personnel, driving a multi-wheeled trailer. Which had (according to the report), clearly been deliberately hooked onto the wire fence resulting in a mile-long section being torn out. Whereupon, after an initial aerial examination, the said visible sections of fence had been pushed to the side of the road by someone known or unknown.

Subsequent to the fence removal, a group of four would-be political agitators (who were obviously a security threat and clear danger to the base), had encamped upon the now exposed section of government restricted land.

It had happened before in the past, when protesters literally attempted to physically push the perimeter boundaries back.

Apparently, on that particular occasion, the perpetrators had been rendered harmless by use of Z33 nerve gas. A powerful and toxic agent which had been deployed from a helicopter for maxim effect.

It appeared that a similar situation had now arisen, one that would once again warrant the deployment of Z33. And, once the suspect terrorists had been rendered unconscious and consequently no longer a threat, an Air Force unit, together with Five Star operatives, would remove the fanatical activists, to the temporary holding facility, which was located a short distance inside the perimeter, beyond the innocuous looking gatehouse.

An area not officially accessible to Kruger or any Five Star operatives, unless there was a threat to the on-going security of the base.

This holding area was underground and not visible from the gatehouse. The crude bunker-like facility consisted of a dozen cells, full services and a com's room.

Anyone unfortunate enough to be caught on government restricted land, would or could be swiftly hoodwinked and taken to the holding provision, until such times as it was ascertained who they were and why they were trespassing on government land that was not officially there?

At which point, if suspected of being a terrorist an individual could be taken outside and shot dead by means of an executioner's bullet to the back of the head.

However, the four characters, now held in the holding pens, were not the average activist- come-trespasser who tried to enter the base. Their credentials checked out, which Kruger soon disseminated once he arrived on the scene. And seeing as there were no senior Air Force staff present, he took it upon himself to begin the interrogation process.

The four penned up it transpired, were part of a research team, and at least two of them, the females, were highly regarded scientists sponsored by the Iowan 'Shriners,' a clandestine society known by Kruger and most men across wider America for their benevolence and good works. A society who also supported and sponsored the Iowa State University.

The lead person in the now detained group being a 'Professor Thelma Jones,' with a whole bunch of letters after her name.

Legally speaking Kruger found himself in a contradictory and potentially compromising situation. The group held in custody had clearly illegally entered government property. However, the designated line between public and private property wasn't visible, due to the fence being down. Therefore, the accusation of trespass would not stand. Besides, Kruger had already earlier in the day been made aware that the said fence was down and had sent a team to clear the road of the obstruction. Prior to which no vehicles had been previously sighted along the road in question, other than a rapidly retreating truck. The presence of which had been picked up by base surveillance cameras. In Kruger's opinion it was highly unlikely that the group in custody had anything to do with the destruction of the perimeter fence and probably had no idea they were camped out on private government property.

In Kruger's logic: no boundary, meant no crossing the boundary, meant no trespass. No case.

Let them go?

The former military service man sat back alone in the com's room.

There was a further complication. Not that it was in his

area of jurisdiction. Other than, prior to the Z33 chemical spraying chopper flyover and land team arrest of the four now detained subjects, a top-secret and highly classified aerial vehicle had flown low over where the potential trespassers were camped out. The mere fact that this party had seen the over-passing craft (the nature of which Kruger had no idea concerning, as such matters were well above his clearance and pay grade), if they had unfortunately witnessed as much (and it was more than likely they had), then they could be seen as being a threat to national security, and arrested and put on trial.

Although no court had ever convicted anyone for trespassing, or any other crime, on this particular strip of land, as the restricted terrain they were trespassing upon did not actually exist. And so therefore no act of trespass or any other offence could have been willfully committed. If found guilty however, an individual or group may face the firing squad or life imprisonment. Regardless of their status or contacts.

Consequently, he put in a call to the only other person who could assist him in ascertaining what course of action to take. And that was Colonel K. Kernel.

13

So-called Area 51

In contrast to Kruger's job description; being to keep people out of so-called Area 51, Colonel K. Kernel's job was to ensure no one, once on the base, never got back out of the base. Also, whilst Kruger was a private contractor, Colonel Kernel worked directly for the United States Air Force, and had done so all of his working life.

Most men joining the services wanted to be fly-boys, or ground crew operatives. But the African American Colonel had never seated himself in the cockpit of an F35 fighter, or Apache chopper. He had no desire to fly or fight.

The Colonel's ideal war would not be fought in the sky, but in the minds and imaginations of the opposing factions. Psychological warfare could be fought on many fronts. Propaganda being one of the essential tools. Along with mind-control techniques that, concerning which, the lay person had little notion.

The Colonel's personal advancement in the psy-ops field, and use of mass-mind- manipulation, had been made realisable through the work of one singular individual. A man whose father had been scooped up by the American Military Industrial Complex at the end of WWII as part of 'Operation Paper Clip.' It was all to do with the US Government's desperate requirement to exercise power, not un-like the Nazis, over the people. Those weaker than themselves. All by means of curious mind-altering techniques…

* * * * *

Heading this strand of research, on behalf of the US military, was one singular, almost indispensable man, known only as: 'Der gute Doktor,' or in English: 'The Good Doctor.' A designation first awarded to his grandfather and thereafter his father.

German scientists, many of who had previously worked for the war time Nazi military machine, were rounded up and brought back to the USA, post 1945. They were given homes, jobs and a new start as patriotic flag waving Americans. This was all part of a pre-planned scenario and outcome, ordained by those really in control: the 'Deep State' who were the ones drawing up the post-war-global-geo-political-economic-map.

The Nazis never actually lost the war, but rather they simply moved to the other side of the Atlantic Ocean and took control of the Americas. Hitler, some say, escaped from the Berlin bunker and found his way to Argentina where he spent his last days.

The original 'Good Doctor,' had been doggedly working in a particular esoteric pseudo-scientific field since the early 1930s. This, up to that point, never previously studied branch of research, involved a mix of science, religion, alchemy and the paranormal.

A field of study that was as much to do with mass-hysteria and the employment of propaganda, as a way to control entire populations, as anything else. All mainly via the use and application of mind-altering drugs.

Two generations later and the process had finally been perfected.

Almost to a fine art.

All of this past and now present research work had taken place in one of the many United States Government's secret scientific research facilities. Places that officially did not exist and could not be found printed on any road-map of the most powerful and influential country in the world.

Of the dozens of known or unknown US military underground bases, there was one that had captured the imagination of, not only the America people, but of conspiracy theorists and other interested parties from across the world. A place located in the State of Nevada, was commonly known as so-called Area 51.

Lost amidst the country-sized Nevada's nuclear testing, bombing and firing ranges, so-called Area 51 had over the years been integral to the hard development of a number of experimental aircraft and items of nuclear weaponry. As well as soft developments in the field of a whole range of mind control techniques.

The final results and analysis of which were, in scientific terms, quite simple. The now proven techniques operated on the basis of altering the reality of a subject's mind by use of chemical alteration of brain function. Whilst simultaneously using hypnotic techniques to tell the subject who they were, where they were, or just what they were doing. Key, or trigger words or phrases, could be imbedded in a person's mind. Once released, the subject's trigger word, would prompt an appropriate reaction, according to programming. To which the subject would respond accordingly, and in a manner that they had previously been programmed to react in.

This very system had for some time been physically deployed throughout the entire workforce of the so-called Area 51 complex. All subject to and dependent upon clearance levels. The higher the clearance, the less exposure to mind control programmes were required to pacify and control a particular section of the work force. Or, that was what the data showed. Each sector had imposed upon them a particular drug regime which they were oblivious to. Selected drug formulas were easily administered via the water supply, or though aerosols, via the air conditioning systems.

Airborne chemical delivery often as not took place during the unmarked aircraft flights to and from the Groom Lake landing facility. These brief shuttle trips were cunningly deployed to disseminate information and instructions to the on-board passengers.

Take for example a Mexican outside contract cleaner. He or she would happily accept entering the aircraft, it's the way they go to work. Prior to take off the cabin would be dowsed with a chemical aerosol. Concerning which they, the passengers, are told is an insect repellent, used to kill mosquitoes. Not an unreasonable proposition. (Even the flight crew believed and accept this necessary procedure.)

Meanwhile, once in the air the passengers were routinely exposed to a number of subliminal words or phrases that would potentially trigger off in them a certain mind-set or construct of existing and non-existing reality.

For instance, flying inbound they were told they worked in a hospital, and they have to obey the instructions given to them by their superiors, all in order to maximise productivity, so as to get the job done. To them their environment and space they worked in ostensibly appeared to be a hospital set-up.

Outbound, on the homeward trip, the same group were told they are going home. Once back to their dwellings with their families, they are at liberty to share what their make-believe shift at the hospital had been like. Easy? Hard? What kind of a day did they have etc.?

And that's all.

By employing such a technique an operative could further relate information or anecdotes that are or were total constructs of their imagination, regarding patients, other staff members, accidents and emergencies and so forth.

If asked by an outsider what they did for living they would simply and honestly say that they worked at a private hospital as part of the janitorial team. One well-timed and placed trigger word could potentially alter their perception of their real-time scenario or physical surroundings at the whim of their controllers.

One shift session they maybe in a hospital, the next an office block.

As an example of the technique in action, using one particular 'test' male worker, a scenario had been constructed whereabouts the subject was directed to be in love with a counterpart female worker. And furthermore, that they were having a rampant on-going sexual affair outback in a janitorial storage area. The mutual feeling shared between the male and female subjects of the experiment, were entirely constructed in their minds. They really thought they were having sex together. However, once away from their respective jobs, at the shift's end, they went home to their families as normal, with no notion they were having an affair. The idea and memory completely diminished and forgotten, until their next shift.

The method was so effective that both parties swapped secret love notes to one another whilst at work. (A practice normally banned as part of their contracts.) Regardless, both parties totally ignored the potential risk to losing their jobs. Furthermore, when the hand writing samples used on the notes were respectively examined and compared to previous samples of their handwriting, it was clear that in both cases the handwriting was entirely different. And even a handwriting expert proffered they were from two different people!

Consequently, the individual members demonstrated affection to one another every time their path's crossed at work, but outside of work they did not pay each other any attention.

Taking this peculiar logic one step further; an entire nation could be manipulated in the same manner. The Nazis had used less sophisticated methods to force their helpless victims accept the fact they were just going to take a shower, rather than going to their death in the gas chambers. The masses remained compliant and docile, as lambs all the way to the slaughter. The mass Nuremberg rallies were all part of that process, whereupon thousands of people were mesmerised in one gargantuan session.

The American and other western allied powers were known to be employing these very same techniques subtly against their own people. All to ensure that there would not be any civil unrest when eventually and inevitably the banks close down people's accounts to leave them penniless and starving. At which point they would be, or will be, directed to special facilities where they will be told food and shelter is waiting and available. Once there, behind razor wire fences, they, without cursory thought, will happily go to the guillotine and have their heads swiftly removed, as part of the global population reduction process. Hundreds of people across the country could be exterminated every few seconds in such a manner. The homeless and destitute being the starting point, working through most of the impoverished population: African Americans, homosexuals, the terminally ill, drug addicts, the list goes on. Mass graves, so the 'Agenda 33 Theory' goes, are to be dug to bury the headless cadavers. Or, as an alternative to dumping bodies, there was another macabre scenario that could easily be employed. In as much as the dead corpses could be rendered down to make feed from human remains to fatten beef cattle to produce juicy steaks for the wealthy blood-lusting elite.

* * * * *

Colonel K. Kernel was on his way across the base, in the dark, having been dragged away from the floodlit Groom Lake golf range. A leisure facility located adjacent to the Dreamland cocktail lounge bar and restaurant. The journey would take him at least an hour, maybe more, even if there was no other traffic or activities going on at surface level.

Technically still-on-duty, he grabbed an Air Force jeep from the motor pool and put his foot down hard.

At forty-five the Colonel was probably on top of his game. There were no more positions for him to advance to, there were no higher ranks in the psy-ops division of so-called Area 51. He was it. Being a type and form of regimental 'shrink' allowed him to be slightly more self-expressive than the average officer. He did not have brigades of men to consider, or even squads to look to him for orders. His was an army of one and as such he happily got by.

This particular evening was not dissimilar to any other. The laid-back African American Colonel believed in copious amounts of R and R, and keeping himself generally amused. Hence, his one hour on the golf driving range, a swim and maybe half-hour in the gym prior to slipping into the Dreamland cocktail lounge bar for a few welcome, yet lonely drinks. Then it would be back to his billet, a space typical of officer's quarters across the US military. Here he would stay before visiting the Officer's Mess for what was alleged 'chow.'

Regardless of so-called Area 51 and its component parts being: ultra-top-secret, there was no reason why the daily routine and normal functions of a service man should differ from any other military establishment. A man only needed to shit, shower and shave. Then eat. Maybe relieve himself in other ways? Socialise and have a few drinks with the guys, just the same as anyone else.

And that was just the problem. The Colonel was a loner on the base, there were no 'guys' to shoot pool with. Here was a cold isolated place, where communication between (buddies), members of the military was not encouraged. There was of course a substantial contingent of female Air Force personnel posted across the vast Nellis Air Force facility. However, they did not often wander his way, into the good old Groom Lake facility. They were more at home at the other Vegas side of the Nellis base.

Sometimes a group of 'dames' came along to the Dreamland cocktail lounge. But it was always just out of curiosity, like going back in time. After all, said and done the leisure facilities at Dreamland were not up to the standard of amenities on offer at the Air Force base proper. The Nellis general headquarters boasted its own shopping mall, markets, fashion stores, takeaways, movie theatres, everything you would expect to find in a small town. And then of course you had the actual real Vegas on your doorstep!

The US military was required to offer diversions for its staff to stop them going crazy. And that was how many of the higher-ranking officers viewed Colonel Kernel. As being crazy. His dress sense did little to help. On most days, as he was this particular evening, he would dress in a Hawaiian shirt, bearing large pink hibiscus flowers, Bermuda shorts, that reached the knee, which were emblazoned with Mako shark motifs. On his feet were usually to be found white and tan golfing shoes, all topped off by a baseball cap supporting a 'Playboy' motif. One which served to hide the growing bald patch he felt at the back of his head. Denzel Washington looks aside, he did not give the impression of being, or even appearing to be, in any shape or form, military officer material.

There was however always time for him to shape up, he still had three-years left in the brigade, one-thousand and ninety-five days of not being the commander of a regiment. But only the commander of one. All before going back to his Montana dream: the imaginary family home.

Home?

His parents were both deceased and his brother, now with two kids, had not been in touch for some months.

14

Inside so-called Area 51 holding pen

Thelma Jones did not know where she was. All she knew was she had a splitting headache that thumped across her forehead. The throbbing was excruciating and only served to add to the pain she was already suffering from her broken tibia. She was cold, dehydrated, frightened out of her wits, and totally desperate for answers. How was it one minute she was conscious sitting in her uncomfortable camping chair and the next she was inside some lonely cold and dark place? A sack over her head, or so she surmised. Freezing and dejected, and above all, she needed to use the rest room.

Nonetheless, the woman remained stoic using her indomitable will to keep body and soul together. At least she was in America where the law still ruled, or so she hoped and prayed. Yes, she prayed as she had never prayed before.

15

So-called Area 51 Colonel Kernel cont....

What went on out of sight at the lower levels of what was popularly termed: so-called Area 51, had no connection to what regularly took place on the surface. Even after two-years of his twenty-five-year posting, the Colonel had still yet to go lower than Level 2. He didn't really care to find out what went on down there. All he knew is that some of the most effective and highly technologically advanced weapons systems in the world were being perfected, or had been perfected, on this site in the past.

Well before his time, spy planes had been designed and built. All manner of crazy alternative-looking aircraft had been tested. Everything was all before his time. Prototypes, most of which never flew, before his time. Other aircraft were more successful, before his time. Some had beaten world record flying speeds and altitudes, before he joined the Air Force. Aircraft were built that flew so high they bordered on the edges of space. All had been perfected before his time at Groom Lake, and the other connected areas. Yes, all before his time. And that was it.

The Russians of course had similar facilities deep in Siberia, so Uncle Sam had to keep up with them.

A colossal amount of money had been wasted, squandered on creating sophisticated weapons designed to kill more and more people. All the cloak and dagger secrecy and heavy security was obviously needed as former Soviet, or Russian Federation spies were apparently everywhere, and looking to penetrate the base and others like it, one way or another. Maybe they should just look it all up on-line? These days just about everything was on the internet.

Just Google it!

And this was where he, Colonel Kernel, slotted into the game. With the help of his colleague: 'Der gute Doktor,' it was possible, by using his latest mind-control techniques, to simply make a man say anything you wanted him to say. There was no requirement this day and age for water-boarding spies, or administering electric shock treatment, or just plain beatings.

Drugs could do it all.

Unfortunately, certain branches of the security services seemed not to want to give the brutal old-fashioned methods a miss. Clearly some operatives and assets liked seeing blood, suffering and pain.

The Colonel would say: 'give me a man and I will make him confess to JFK's assassination in around ten-minutes!' The human mind was complex but easy to manipulate and control.

To that end, between them, the Colonel and the Doctor, had formulated a command and control lexicon, a verbal key. The files of which the Colonel kept well away from everyone's view. It was classified; 'for his eyes alone.' Only three people in the world knew this programme existed. Himself, 'Der gute Doktor' and the head of the CIA. Who, although aware of its existence would not be able to decipher the lexicon's coded content. There were many 'key' words and expressions used in the process. Such as: Red Shoes - Yellow Brick Road - The Hippy and the Soldier - The Lesbian and the Whore. And newly integrated: Midsummer Night's Dream as well as Orion's Belt.

Numbers also played a major roll, perfect numbers, the perfect proportions in art, mathematics, sacred architecture and the natural world. All fitted together in a mathematical matrix of 'down the rabbit hole' puzzles and questions, all connected to psychological states of being.

Experiments concerning a wide-range of esoteric and mystical disciplines were conducted and put into practice by the psychological operations team. Exercises covering subjects such as: the examination of parapsychology, mind reading, telepathy, black-magic, spoon bending, clairvoyance, alchemy and even turning water into wine! Or, the very biggest of cheese burgers - turning lead into gold!

Not as easy as everyone thought.

* * * * *

Colonel Kernel eventually arrived at the gatehouse prison-like holding facility. He had already put a call through to 'The Good Doctor,' to get him over as fast as possible, from whichever med-lab he was employing his sordid trade.

When not assisting the Colonel creating new ways to control and manipulate the varied workforce who travelled to the top-secret location every working day, 'Der gute Doktor' was engaged in a wide range of classified experiments, which commanded an even higher level of clearance.

The Colonel enjoyed a similar status, but never displayed any desire or interest in discovering for himself, or posing the question; just what really went on at the subterranean levels? All he knew was the 'Der gute Doktor' spent his entire life underground, like some demented mole. He never went outside, took a break, or even had a weekend off. His was 24/7 work, whilst keeping himself alive on a cocktail of chemicals which he had formulated. He only consumed what his body required for a perfectly balanced diet. A measured combination of sugar's, proteins, carbohydrates and other essential minerals and vitamins. All mainly shot directly into his arm.

A further fifty-minutes passed before 'Der gute Doktor' appeared, accompanied by a petite female Air Force paramedic, 'AFW' Reagan Jones wearing full military fatigues. She appeared stern and remained quiet, submissively keeping her hands behind her back 'at ease', whilst her eyes looked down towards the cold concrete floor.

The time lapse prior to Colonel Kernel and the 'Der gute Doktor' arriving afforded Kruger sufficient opportunity to discover all he now knew concerning the four captives held in front of him. Imprisoned as they were in the Air Force paid for concrete confinement facility. He did this whilst sitting in the observation room where each captive could be individually observed and interrogated through CCTV cameras.

Once the Colonel appeared, Kruger pressed on relentlessly, dogmatic, bombastic and anxious as he was, to clarify with the Colonel the legal aspect of the situation.

"You see technically speaking, as far as Five Star is concerned, no crime has been committed, as there has not been a breach in the fence, because the fence is not there to be breached. You cannot be prosecuted for trespass if you have not trespassed. On the other hand, these four detainees I believe saw something."

"Something being?" The Colonel was quite used to this: 'round the houses' evasive method of communicating with the former Captain Kruger. Who invariably acted in such a manner as to ensure his back was fully protected and his company's reputation kept intact, as far as possible. "I can't say what something is because I am not supposed to communicate with you concerning matters above my clearance." Kruger was emphatic.

"Therefore, you can't say; 'they' saw 'nothing,' because nothing does not exist, you can't see what is not there. Hence, how come they saw 'something,' which in fact was nothing?" The Colonel remained vexed concerning the situation.

"That's a matter for the Air Force and I can't comment because I am a civilian contractor, not an ass-wipe military man, (he was referring to the Colonel) and not privy to any details as to what is taking place on this or any other military base or establishment. The Air Force manage internal security and affairs and we at Five Star merely patrol the perimeter fence, and that's all!"

The Colonel let the ass-wipe comment go. He knew Kruger despised him for reasons of what? Pay scale perhaps? Usually these bouts of petty jealousy went far deeper than money alone. Kruger's comments were often as not racially loaded.

Kruger spoke whilst virtually goose-stepping up and down the hard-concrete floor. At the same time as slapping his thigh now and then like a principal boy in a pantomime, all to emphasis a point. "As it was some of my men also reported, (off the record of course) that they saw 'something' which of course was nothing."

"We can make them forget that they saw nothing and make them think they saw something and nothing." 'Der gute Doktor' made his opening gambit, he had well and truly 'arrived' and reminded those gathered that he was very much present and party to the conversation.

"However," Kruger was still hogging the floor, "as they, my employees, were headed down to the spot where the fence is missing, where these 'geeks' were camped out," he gestured toward the holding pens, "something they should not have seen went by, cruising low over their supposed camp site. It was followed by a couple of escort fighters and a chopper."

"I guess you ultimately used Z33?" 'Der gute Doktor' interjected.

"Of course," Kruger continued, "that is standard procedure. If we can't apprehend some fugitives due to the rough terrain, then we can dust, and the Air Force chopper we lease from the Air Force is on continual stand-by to do just that. As it stands, I have no idea at this juncture who the fly-boy was piloting the chopper, until that is I look at the manifest.

"We can solve all of that for you Captain Kruger." It was once more the voice of 'Der gute Doktor' now barbed with a slight note of impatience.

Of all the people on the base Kruger only warmed to 'Der gute Doktor' not the man himself, but more so concerning his reputation. As it was their paths seldom crossed. There was no need, and besides the Doctor was an underground dweller and Kruger did not have the clearance required to get into the lower levels of the base proper. The holding pens by the gates were as far as he went, likewise his men. Any mutual respect between Kruger and 'Der gute Doktor' came from their shared 'closet' political ideology. Kruger, all be he Afrikaans by birth and not German, was by his own volition very right-wing on the political scale. He firmly believed Germany had won the war, and the evidence to support this supposition was now common knowledge, that was, amongst those theorists who supported and pursued an 'alternative' in-depth account of modern history. According to some commentators, Hitler died in Argentina in the 1960s. An event that 'Der gute Doktor' quietly celebrated in his own Teutonic way. He was clearly proud of his ancestry and ancient Germanic roots. The Queen of England was German after all, and naturally 'Der gute Doktor' had several pictures of her stuck to his bunk-room wall.

Before he elaborated upon his solution to contain the situation, 'Der gute Doktor' laid out his ominous tools of the torturer's trade on the top of an unused desk. His face was gaunt and skin cold and pallid. Underneath his white lab-coat he wore a scruffy hand-knitted sweater, probably made by his mother and given to him as a belated Christmas present. His face was framed by large round wire-rimmed glasses. And on his head, hidden by a pristine white surgical cap, his hair was nothing more than a few thinning comb-over wisps. Somehow his head appeared out of proportion compared to his body. Which was a gangling six-feet in height, affording him the impression of being a female praying mantis who was just about to consume its mate.

"As I was saying," the Doctor continued,

"I know you are all probably aware, that we possess a method whereupon we can clear the minds of everyone we chose to, including these people involved in this err…, shall we say blunder?"

"Well hang on, Five Star had nothing to do with any 'blunder,' plus we have no comment to make on what was and was not seen. Besides, it was the Air Force who steered their little bird too close to the wind. And you just wait, hundreds of people will have made reports, it will be in the Lincoln County and Vegas press. Quote: 'yet another strange sighting at so-called (by conspiracy theorists), Area 51!'" Kruger concluded.

"Just what I am apparently employed to ensure does not happen!" Colonel Kernel picked up the verbal baton. "Recently we, here on the base, have enjoyed a certain status quo with the media hereabouts. I did all I could to keep a number of unfortunate incidents securely covered up. Obviously for fear of creating a panic or public outcry. It was only natural that the friends and family of the Danish party that went missing wanted clear and positive answers. I gave them those answers and if nothing else stalled them, and others, for sometime."

Kruger was fully aware what Colonel Kernel was talking about. It was one of his staff: some months before, a 'Camo shooter' went 'crazy loco' and let off a few well-sighted rounds in the direction of a party of unknown people, who were well within the perimeter wire. Despite the fact that a mobile patrol had previously ushered them away from restricted government land.

Regardless of all warnings, they returned and audaciously cut through the razor wire and amiss any fear or trepidation marched right up the pine strewn incline, thinking no doubt the brush would give them some form of cover. The 'Camo dude,' all according to procedure, initially used the bull-horn, the party ignored the warning: once, twice, third time backed up by bullets.

The bodies were removed and all traces of them wiped-out forever. Fortunately, the group had not visited or made themselves known in Rachel town, or in the vicinity along the Extraterrestrial Highway.

Apparently, the theory was that they were looking to bust into so-called Area 51, then go back to Rachel and boast about what they had seen and done.

This incident pulled in the FBI who doggedly searched the civilian side of the wire for a maniac with a gun, a kind of wild man of Nevada who went around killing tourists. Unfortunately, the political machinery on Capitol Hill got wind of the event. They in turn had to be pacified and reassured that the so-called non-existent Area 51 did not exist and was certainly not a risk to the public, and that the military staff there on the base, the one that did not exist, were competent and were carrying out their duties to the highest degree possible. And were not, not (as some Congressmen claimed), 'suitable for purpose.'

As it was, the truth being - because the restricted so-called Area 51 did not exist, then no crime could have been committed, as there was no one and nothing there to possibly commit any criminal act.

"If the folks on the hill get wind of all this," Colonel Kernel continued, "and conclude we are a risk to national security, and a sore-thumb liability, then it's good-bye to all of our pensions!"

* * * * *

So-called Area 51 cont....

Thelma could not hold onto her bladder any longer. Consequently, a warm stream of urine flowed from her female parts, down her plaster-cast restricted right leg and onto the cold floor below. At which point, the former stoicism left her entirely, and she began to sob uncontrollably. She had no idea where she was, what was happening to her, or where the other members of her group were. Out of desperation she called out, pleading for someone, anyone to assist her.

Inside the observation booth, the military representatives and civilian contractor were still debating the ins and outs of the predicament that faced them. The Colonel looked up at one of the monitors, he could see the person before the camera shaking and jerking. Thinking she might be experiencing some form of seizure; he motioned to the Air Force medic to go and assist the troubled woman.

"Who are these people anyway Kruger?" The Colonel had completely forgotten to ascertain who his captives were, and whether or not they actually 'were' 'his' captives or did they come under Kruger's deadly jurisdiction?

"Well they are a team of sorts, called: Magnetic Research Unit. This one here with the busted leg, who has by the way just peed her panties, well she is out of Iowa State and has a professorship from there. Professor Thelma Jones…"

At the mention of 'Thelma Jones,' 'Der gute Doktor' and the attendant Air Force medic raised a single eyebrow and no more.

The name was familiar.

'Der gute Doktor', recalled having seen some kind of TV comedy programme a few days back when making a very rare visit to the mess hall. A comic news item that had been syndicated via Fox across the USA was on screen. The woman in the clip made a pratfall negotiating a set of steps. And then a bunch of old men had marched up and down and a giant fake bank draft had blown away, taken by the wind.

Yes, that was the same Thelma Jones, it had to be!

It was on one of those shows where people send in footage for money. Anything, crashes, falls or something gets busted up, just as long as it was remotely amusing. For the moment 'Der gute Doktor' kept the fact that he had recognised the hapless woman to himself.

"Yes, I have already looked all of them up. They have their own web site and have thousands of followers on social media. All their identifications match up - Iowa driving licence, all but one alumni. They all are, well the women are, highly educated."

Kruger directed his gaze toward the monitor screen framing Diana. "Then we have this one here, a woman to die for! Look at her shapely body Colonel." He gestured a double curve with his hands. "Now you wouldn't say 'no' to her at any time, now would you?"

Kruger was straying, thinking with his dick as men seem to always do.

"Now, believe it or not, regardless of her looking like a dumb blonde, she just happens to be the alluring sexy brains on legs assistant to Jones here."

"What about the others? The men?" The Colonel enquired.

"The big guy is a football pro'." Kruger pointed to the closed-circuit monitor; Frank's chiseled image filled the fuzzy screen. "Plays Quarterback for the Hawkeyes. And the other guy? Well don't have much on him, he kind of seems to be along for the ride, keeping a low profile, overshadowed by the others I would guess. But, hey! Anyway, none of them have so much as a parking ticket between them, they pay their taxes and are more or less good citizens."

"Now hang on there."

"And maybe you think we should just drag them out and put a bullet in the back of their heads? Like with that party of Danes!" The Colonel, playing the devil's advocate, as he tended to, was over-dramatising the situation.

There were it seemed, some case similarities between this party currently under surveillance, and the intrusive party of Danish nationals who had previously defied the security cordon and entered the base.

Shooting people in the head was always the easy option, far less paperwork. "Now hang on there," Kruger

111

retorted angrily his finger pointing at the Colonel. "I didn't say that at any single one time! No sir! No one here has mention 'ghosting' them out to 'sleepy valley.'"

'Sleepy Valley' was what Kruger called 'Yucca Lake.' A toxic waste dump off the Nevada nuclear test facility.

'Der gute Doktor' interjected. "May I conclude gentlemen? Time is marching on, as it does, and we have to come up with a rapid solution to this dilemma. Allow me to make a suggestion." 'Der gute Doktor' was wearying of all this deliberation. He had other more pressing matters to attend to down on Level 2.

"First our guests here," 'Der gute Doktor' motioned to the monitor screens that showed three detainees, the fourth one being attended to by the Air Force medic out back in the rest room. "They will all have suffered from the effects on the nerve gas, Z33, that they have been exposed to. I can initially reverse that. Afterwards, and when they feel able, we will administer a further shot, which will consist of a mild, yet highly toxic classified and controlled hallucinogenic concoction of my own making. This will relax them, as well as induce a dream-like state. Once in that condition we will tell them whatever it is we want them to remember, forget or understand."

"As in what we do already Doc'?" The Colonel added.

"Exactly what we do to everyone at this facility." The Colonel and 'Der gute Doktor' inappropriately let a classified slice of information slip. The Colonel kicked himself and swiped a sideways glance toward the Doctor. Kruger, being a civilian was not, or should not have been, aware of such a deceitful practice. Clearly however, mind-control activities did not apply to him or his three-hundred strong Five Star security crew. Thankfully the comments appeared to have passed unnoticed.

"I suggest that you Colonel take them, our trespassers, on a guided tour of the base. Give them the VIP treatment, show them 'Dreamland,' give them a late dinner or early breakfast at the lounge, it's open 24/7 these days, so I am told, even though there's no one much around." Anyone would have thought the Doctor was trying to sell a piece of real-estate as he gesticulated, waving his long spindly arms around, like the sails on a Spanish windmill.

He enthusiastically continued, "show them all the wonderful facilities here: swim pool, the gym, movie theatre. You can tell them the hangers are only there to store old aircraft and that there are plans to turn the site into an aviation museum for the public. A family destination to treat the kids. They will absorb all of this information and will repeat it when required. Also, we will give them all a series of what's known as 'trigger' words or phrases. These can be employed at any time to control the individual or group. Bring them back in line if they ever deviate away from our intended course. We can always re-set their minds if needs be." The Doctor finally concluded.

Kruger pretended to be blasé and unfortunately for the Colonel, in the know concerning what he was hearing, as if he were party to such schemes on a regular basis.

"You then take them back to where you found them," the Doctor was keen to wrap up and finish off what he was doing. "When they come round and regain consciousness, they will have little or no recognition as to what has just happened to them. They will then begin to construct their own realities regarding what actually occurred. These opinions will, or may be, in conflict with one another. They will be confused. If you want them to steer clear of the media you can do that. If you want them to 'go' to the media to say there is nothing actively happening here on the base, or anything else you might conceive of, they will also say and do whatever you ask of them. Trigger words can be sent as texts directly to their cell phones."

"By the way," Kruger was looking to score some points with the Doctor. "We, as a matter of course interrogated their cell phones. Absolutely zilch. We still have no idea what they were doing on government land.

Anyhow, nothing incriminating or of interest on any of their devices. In fact, they have hardly made any calls over the past few days, and neither have any of them sent or received any messages. Odd for what are after all 'young' people?" Kruger generally liked to have the last word. But not on this occasion.

"One last word before we proceed, I take it we are going to move forward on this?" The Doctor looked alternately towards Kruger and the Colonel. "Good, yes one final, what could be amusing addition - there is another concoction I have developed that if administered may add some further entertainment and interest in this particular sorry set of circumstances. I can dispense a compound via the nasal passage that, once awake from their ordeal, who or whatever they first see before them will cause them to have an uncontrollable hormonal reaction. They will in fact have amorous feelings for the first person they interact with! Even if they are of the same gender group!"

For a moment, 'Der gute Doktor' cracked a rare, but somewhat perverse smile. "Ensure they keep their cell-phones switched on and close by, they need to be functioning as we will use text or voicemail to convey the command code triggers, we will implant in their young minds.

Kruger, for some bizarre reason, thought about the 'Truman Show' movie.

"Once we have had our fun, we will get onto the more serious business of how we use and deploy these young people."

There was a brief silence as those present contemplated what use the MRU group from Iowa could be to them.

"As a key phrase I am suggesting we initially use: Midsummer Night's Dream. Once we have had our amusement we implement 'Orion's Belt' as our trigger. Do you agree Colonel?" The Colonel nodded his approval.

* * * * *

The Truman Show ... The Truman Show... The Truman Show, the ultimate voyeur's experience. Kruger could think of nothing else. He had experienced an uncommon eureka moment. Imagine, an outside audience looking in at a subject under constant scrutiny. Like a game show where celebrities are taken to the jungle and then observed until the relentless heat and ferocious insects get to them. If you were looking for entertainment for the mind-less masses.

Yes, this was it.

Without doubt this was it, his way out of Five Star Security. And Kruger could genuinely see such a concept working. Yes, Kruger convinced himself this could just be like the real 'Truman Show.' It could go viral? He could make some money? After all, once off the base, these university clowns could be his to own. Particularly now he had knowledge of what the mind-manipulation key text words were, starting with: 'A Midsummer Night's Dream,' followed by: 'Orion's Belt.'

* * * * *

Going back to the first console located in the observation booth, Kruger quickly scanned the area where the unfortunate trespasser's camp-site had been, and where the fence had been torn out. He then checked out the positioning of CCTV cameras, and buried motion sensors. There were at least two cams operational within five-yards of the now partially wrecked camp-site. Regardless, there was no reason why the unsuspecting captives could not go back there. It would be more than interesting to observe at firsthand just what they would do and how they would react given their predicament.

* * * * *

Ten-minutes later Thelma was dressed in an orange coverall that had the right leg section slit up the seam to compensate for her plaster cast. The others were also dressed in bright orange coveralls. This made them look like proper detainees, a bunch of terrorists under the jurisdiction of the Air Force. As it was, to attempt to walk around any top-secret base dressed as civilians, was tantamount to suicide. They would be stopped immediately by the Air Force base internal security.

The Colonel however could and did get away with not conforming to standard dress-code rules. He always dressed as wildly as he was on this particular night. Because everyone knew and recognised him as being the only amusing African American dressed like a golfing professional.

Tiger Woods sprung to mind. The Colonel's dress sense: eccentric, insane perhaps? But that was far from the truth.

16

So-called Area 51 perimeter fence camp-site

Thelma was first to wake to the chiming of her cell-phone. The call was rapidly repeated throughout the group.

The sun was up but not ferociously hot as yet. The former camp site was all but ruined. Everything they had been working on gone. No external tents or canopies, the equipment with strewn about the arid dusty ground or missing. The food supply had been raided and torn apart by probably a wild animal, and there before her, laid out in the passenger seat of the Jeep was the gorgeous Adonis Frank. How she loved him, how she had always loved him. How she wanted him. Her hand reached out to touch his cheek just as Duncan appeared from nowhere and whose face was square onto Frank's as the football Quarterback first opened his tired eyes. Frank sat bolt-upright ignoring Thelma. Frank only had eyes for Duncan. However, Diana, without warning placed her hands over Duncan's eyes and gave him the opportunity to see 'her' before anyone else. But it was not Duncan who caught Diana's gaze, it was Thelma, who, had now clambered into the driver's position next to Frank. She went to kiss him but he struggled away.

Immediately Diana's hungry lips homed in on Thelma. Meanwhile Frank was engaged in some heavy, way out of character, petting with Duncan. Whilst Thelma was developing a jealous rage over Frank, and was determined to split up the two lover boys. The feisty team leader eventually prised the two young men apart, whilst pushing away the advances of Diana. An act she would have never dreamt of carrying out under normal circumstances. The guys kissed once more, before Thelma again spurned the advances of Diana. Doing to Diana exactly what Diana had been doing to Frank for years.

As the group writhed and groped one another on the dirt ground, an environment only punctuated by drifting sage brush and sedge, a cacophony of cell phones rang through the air. Each member of the group ceased their orgiastic activity to earnestly locate their cell phones. Four phones rang, four calls were answered. A deep mechanical voice spoke clearly through each earpiece:

"Midsummer Night's Dream." That was all. Then the phones went dead. The group stopped their romantic foreplay and they looked about, feeling dazed and confused.

"What the hell was that?" Duncan had spoken first.

17

Colonel Kernel

Colonel Kernel tried to grab a few hours sleep. It had been a tough night, now he needed to rest. He assumed the plan 'Der gute Doktor' had come up with had worked. The idea of using the story plot of 'Midsummer Night's Dream' as a trigger code was amusing in its self. Shakespeare's comedy was one of the Colonel's favourite theatre productions, and to use the title as a 'key' phrase was sublime as far as he was concerned.

He imagined the chaos at the camp site.

Nonetheless, he felt he had to draw a halt to its continuance. Mainly due to the fact that potentially the group's mental and psychological capacity would be fully stretched about now. There was the possibility of a brain function overload, followed by severe mental breakdown.

The treatments the detainees had been put through were traumatic to say the least. The process involved taking hold of their minds and making the consciousness of each individual yours to do with as you pleased. Putty in the hands, puppets on a string. The Doctor had made it absolutely clear that it was perfectly possible that subjecting a person to the level of psychic manipulation they had undergone, could and would lead to a total mental collapse - go 'kaput' in his words. Or worse still, brain stem failure. It was akin to overloading an electrical circuit. Too much power and energy flowing through the circuit and boom the circuits are blown, fuses gone forever.

Subsequently, it pleased the Colonel to release the group from his clutches as soon as possible, if only to observe them to see what it was, they would do next.

Conversely, it did not please Captain K.K. Kruger, who was now fully aware of the 'key codes' that would trigger anomalies in the group's behaviour. 'Careless talk' and all of that. The Colonel and 'Der gute Doktor' had said more than they should, and they knew full well that the very walls have ears.

18

So-called Area 51 perimeter fence camp-site

"What the hell was that?" Frank asked the same question Duncan, in his usual laid-back manner, was about to propose. Why were his pants strangely too tight? Whilst Duncan's strides fell down to his knees. Why was it then they wearing each other's trousers? What happened to the bright orange coveralls they were given to wear?

Intending to lend a hand to help Thelma stand up, Diana went over to her team leader who was sitting lost in thought on the dry desert ground. Yet, she was beaten to it by a freshly invigorated and sprightly Thelma, who took to her feet with ease.

It was then Diana noticed. "Thelma, your leg, I mean trousers, where, what happened to the plaster cast?"

"I don't know, all I remember is we, all of us, were wearing orange coveralls."

Thelma then traced her right hand down the seam of the clothes she was wearing. They were obviously not hers, as the line of stitching was visibly intact. Therefore, not able to allow room for her plaster cast.

As if in a quandary, Thelma dropped her pants and stood with exposed legs. The right one showed no sign of swelling, redness, poor circulation, or weakness. It appeared to be a normal leg that had never been broken, coupled with a now no longer swollen sprained ankle.

Diana instinctively stretched out her hand and ran her fingers and palm up the inside of Thelma's leg. "My God, Thelma, this is not possible. Yesterday I was going to drag you kicking and screaming, if needs be, to the hospital in Vegas. Now look, not a mark, or scratch. Nothing!"

Now the boys were becoming curious and the three

team members gathered around Thelma for a closer inspection.

"Geeze, I have never seen anything like this! Not that I have ever had any experience in medical matters." Duncan commented through his now no longer obviously lisping lips.

Diana commented further, "well I don't know, it must have happened last night. I mean somehow we must have lost our clothes or something."

Frank added thoughtfully, "and then that is why Duncan is wearing my pants? What in God's eternal and mighty name has been going on?"

Frank visibly appeared worried.

Psychic phenomena and strange mumbo-jumbo spooky stuff was not his favourite leisure pursuit. He preferred a straightforward game of football.

"Look everyone," Thelma pulled the group together. "Let's go round one at a time and share just what we remember from last night."

"OK, shot-gun I go first please me, me!"

Duncan, in contrast to Frank was mildly excited about sharing. However, his comments disappointingly amounted to - "well nothing really!"

"Come on quit screwing around Duncan or you'll have to wait until last." Diana set her companion straight.

"Well, we were here, and had set up and oh, by the way, yeah, Thelma, you needn't worry about the data. I can see the hard drives have gone astray, but I up-loaded them onto our uni' NASA satellite platform and they should all be on your desktop for when we get back. That's if we get a decent signal out here any time soon."

Duncan's good news came as music to Thelma's ears, despite the caveat. This meant all the data gathered from this location anyway, was saved and safe. "Yes!" Thelma triumphantly punched the air.

"Go on." Diana encouraged Duncan.

"Well then I don't remember much, nothing in fact. Nothing."

Thelma completed going around the group and ended up with her own final observations. Basically, none of them remembered anything concerning the previous night. Frank however had signs of bruising on his forearm which was conducive of having either blood taken from his arm, via a cannula, or it having been injected with something or another. The others were about to develop similar traces of bruising in the hours to come.

However, the exercise in self-interrogation came to an abrupt halt, as down the dirt road a column of dust swirled in the air signaling a vehicle of sorts was tracing its way up the incline and toward their position.

As team leader Thelma, with her newly miraculously healed right leg, barked an order. "Retreat!"

Immediately all hands packed what was left of their camp site in the rear of their 4X4s, leaving behind what non-essentials they could not easily fit in their respective trunks.

19

Las Vegas

Gracie Lin, tore off her slumber inducing eye shade, it had not helped her sleep. She was still fuming from the fact that Bud Always-Jones's camera had not worked for her and therefore she could not do what she had intended to do. A pint or more of gin did not help either the clarity of her head, or loss of sleep. Of course, she had called Bud, who should have been in his room, in the event of her needing his assistance, in matters she had no desire or cause to share with him. But no, he was gone, gone like a vampire in the sultry night air, mixing it no doubt with the plethora of mindless tourists from the world over. All looking to spend-spend-spend, money they probably did not have to spend. And here was she, queen Gracie Lin Jones, soon to be rich-rich-rich beyond belief, if that was, Bud Always-Jones had not deserted his post.

Gracie had a knack of blaming everyone around her for the problems she normally created for herself. In the main the woman was entirely toxic with numerous psychopathic tendencies. And, like so many other disturbed people in the world, she should be handled with care, or better still, avoided at all costs.

The camera lay on the floor where she had thrown it in an earlier fit of rage.

Now, partly out of boredom, using her lap-top, she looked through the myriad of electronic Word files and documentation that belonged to Principal J. Jones Junior, now saved for her on a USB Flash Drive. The files she had ordered Bud to steal, Bud her little thieving magpie.

Page by tedious page had to be gone through. Dozens of saved files, all conveniently numerically coded.

The increasingly drunk, would-be reporter, come investigative journalist, trawled through university accounts, staff background checks, qualifications and interpersonal information. Student years came and went.

'Scrying,' so she thought, was oh so much simpler and quicker. Applied cosmic energy went directly to the point and got you what you wanted. But at what price? Gracie Lin would find out sooner or later.

Eventually, after three cups of black coffee, a file appeared designated as 369. She instinctively opened the document with some degree of excited trepidation. There was some relative significance in the number which she could not quite place her finger on. Three plus six is equal to nine. So what? Two nines make eighteen and eighteen divided by three is six: six, six.

Regardless of any numerical significance, Gracie plundered on and opened the first file in the series. It contained a long and wordy document. A thesis on polar shift and the earth's magnetic field. It was attributed to Professor Thelma Jones, but at the end of the document it was also attributed to J.Jones Junior Principal of Iowa State University. There was no telling which of the two was the actual bona fide author.

A further document, also with ambiguous penmanship, went on to describe the methods of testing and protocols relating to such a cataclysmic episode as a polar shift. It was clear, according to the data from past research, that any shift in the earth's magnetic field would and could signal the end of life as people living on planet earth knew it.

A cataclysmic extinction event.

'What a story that would make!' Concluded Gracie Lin. 'Definitely syndicated material and worth hundreds maybe even thousands of dollars!'

The next paper laid out the methods to be used to gather data in respect of measuring magnetic activity and how that was related to energy manifested by and through human beings.

The theory suggested that, where there was a high-level of magnetic activity, there was, or had been in the past, a high-level of human psychic power present. An example being: how much of the energy created by the Nuremberg political rallies in pre-war Nazi Germany, had increased the magnetic activity of the area? And furthermore had it left a clear magnetic signature behind? This being the case, would it be possible to use focused psychic powers to influence magnetic activity and therefore reverse any potential future polar shift?

A further statement proposed that magnetic activity can decrease once the source of psychic energy is removed. Quite a plausible theory and even Gracie Lin, in her still hung-over state, half understood the basic principle.

In the next file there followed a list of some thousand potential sites across the globe, all ripe for testing and exploration. Starting with the USA and broadening out across the entire world. All this eye-opening information, the basis of a great story, was all well and good. Other than not being exactly what she wanted, or was desperate to find amongst the documentation before her.

What Gracie Lin initially wanted to be on familiar terms with, was, exactly where the Magnetronic Research Unit was located and where it was going next? If there was a story to be had, then she wanted to be the one who scooped it.

'Was there some form of traceable itinerary to be discovered amongst the files that she could follow?' Gracie Lin mused.

'Might it be possible to get ahead of the game and pre-empt her cousin's next destination?' Yes, it had to be possible!'

A further anxious and tedious half-hour shuffling through the documentation slipped by.

Then, in a concluding paragraph: the reference she had been told about, what she had been charged to find, and hoped to see. A clear and precise summery stated that in some high-intensity areas, where magnetic activity was or had been excessive, certain metals exposed to this powerful magnetic phenomenon, could in theory alter in molecular structure. A process which suggested that under the right conditions magnetic intervention could and would literally turn lead into gold!

Eureka!

20

So-called Area 51 perimeter

It did not take long for the Magnetronic Research Unit to pack-up what was left of their expedition equipment and leave the camp site. They headed down the same scrub and pot-holed punctuated road that they had previously traversed.

In front of them a dust-devil whipped up the parched and barren soil which curiously danced about in a convoluted and somewhat threatening manner.

The two research unit Jeeps soon drew level with the assorted on-coming vehicles. A convoy which consisted of two white pick-up trucks, crested with a Five State Securities logo, and a small open top flat-bed trailer, hauled by a tractor. Two more security vehicles were further back, together with a crew bus. Already a team of men were removing the fence wire which had been rolled down the incline, being diligent not to totally impeded the road. Hi-Viz waist coats and hard-hats made it plain and obvious to see these men were no more than contractors maintaining the perimeter fence.

Moments later, as far as the team were concerned, the contractors, and the MRU team's make-shift camp site, were confined to history.

The overriding question being - where to go next? And secondly, just exactly where had they been?

The MRU team members were not even partly aware of having been taken on a partial tour around, what was a highly classified government restricted parcel of arid land, bigger than England, so-called Area 51. They possessed no recollection or clue as to what that excursion entailed, and what events had taken place there during the previous night.

Now, what memories remained between them

amounted to nothing more than a form of closure, and end to what had been. Or, what they imagined had been, or so they imagined. A nightmare occurrence? Perhaps? However, they all imagined imagining what took place. If they could only recall what that experience was?

Confusion ruled supreme.

Frank drove the first jeep, Diana the second and they soon escaped the dusty made-up road and hit Highway 33. At the next proper interchange, they spun about face and drove directly back to Rachel.

As they rolled on down Highway 33 it became blatantly obvious that one of the Five Star Security's pick-up trucks, they had just encountered was trailing them, all be it away back. Yet, close enough to be noticeable in the Jeep's wing mirrors. Frank dismissed any notions of personal paranoia, telling himself that they, in the truck back behind them, were probably going to town to gather some supplies for the contractor guys working on the distant hills out in the burning sun.

As the team approached Rachel (their plan was to go back to the diner), the tension between the confused team members became palpable. Right up to that was until the moment they arrived at the ramshackle eatery. At which point the white pick-up truck's reflection could no longer be seen in their mirrors.

Curiously Clint and Hillary were waiting unwearyingly outside on the swing-out porch, as if they had never moved and were anticipating the Magnetronic Research Unit's immanent arrival. Neither of the old couple flinched when Frank pulled up sharp, kicking dust up and causing everyone to cover their eyes and noses. Moments later they were all sitting inside, cold Cokes all round and brunch sizzling away, this time on the house!

"So, you is back?" Clint opened up what he thought was going to be some form of informative account.

"Sure are!" Frank was somewhat tongue in cheek regarding the matter.

"Still alive then?" Hillary bellowed from the kitchen.

"How did yer find yer-self?"

"Oh, easy old fellah just put one foot in front of the other and there we were, lost and we can't remember a goddamn thing between us!"

Frank was erroneously relieved they were no longer being followed, and, so he concluded, that the Five Star truck driver and passenger had no interest in them the MRU team.

Duncan was not going to be left behind on this occasion. "Only we all got these." He lisped slightly as he thrust out his right arm showing the bruised spot and demonstrated a needle slipping into his vein.

Frank butted in. "We also had the wrong pants on, Duncan and me."

"Oh, and I got this Clint." Thelma raised up her right leg, now covered by her camouflaged print cargo-pants, the leg being obviously healed and fully mobile. Where the orange coveralls went, they had no idea.

Clint remained silent and devoid of any comment. Rather he coldly looked out into the distance, as if he could see or could imagine something preternatural out there. As if something drastic or extreme had already, or was about to, occur.

"Memory loss, aint unusual. Folks have been known to lose sight of who they are and what they were supposed to be doin'. They get sprayed by choppers, they come over, shower the folks who are trespassing, then leave 'em out there, maybe to die in the sun, I don't know. And then sometimes the spray drifts with the wind down the valleys. And those times, when the dry wind is gusting our way, if the wind direction is just right, the people here in Rachel have before now simply passed out. Dropped like stones to the dirt floor. Then they wake-up with a head the size of a water melon, not knowing even what their goddamn names were."

"Well, we can all vouch for that, the headaches that is." Diana interjected.

"Like we were kicking back one minute," Frank

continued, "and then nothing, blank, zilch, zippo, until this morning when everyone went crazy on each other, and yeah…"

"Ok I don't suppose Clint wants to hear all of that! I mean, my plaster cast dropping off, who knows where and how? But I know that's something for real." Thelma was desperate for answers and felt Clint could furnish her with a few more.

"Aint never heard such a thing. In fact I said to Hillary before you left: 'That girl needs a hospital for that leg, it looks as if it's fixing to burst."

"Right you were, it was infected. But there is something I need to tell you all. I know we said none of us could remember anything about last night, well …" Thelma was cut across by the appearance of freshly cooked food.

"Well please do let us know Thelma, you are the dark horse." Frank chided.

"No, it's not that important, nothing really."

"Well spill the beans do." Duncan passed toast around the table and, as they were famished, everyone bolted down the bacon steaks and hash-browns and beans and eggs over-easy. However, Thelma carried on talking with her mouth half-full of hash-browns. "It's just, I peed myself, couldn't wait to go," Both boys smirked at the notion. "I was sitting in a chair" she continued, "with some kind of sack over my head, it was silent all around me. So, then I peed, that's all."

Thelma hesitated … "And then something in my head, kind of cracked. You know just like an egg, you crack it, like these eggs," she looked down at her now almost consumed breakfast over-easy eggs. "And, all the white and yolk comes pouring out. Well I felt that, a crack and suddenly I could see, I was looking into the darkness, then something came out of that darkness. Like a kind of weird person strangely dressed, it was not a man, but neither was it a woman. Androgynous, and it leant forward and kissed me right smack in the middle of my forehead."

Thelma pointed to a spot between her eyebrows. "Then it went, and I could see more, shapes and colours, swirling around."

The group were momentarily silent.

"Do you think that maybe we all got dosed up on some hallucinogenic shit? God! I hope so!" As ever Duncan tried to make light of the situation.

"But hang on, did anyone else see or feel anything like this?" There was a joint emphatic no!

"So, I have no idea where we were, or how long we were there for, or who was even keeping us there."

The group pondered, digging deep into their collective memory.

"Then," Thelma continued in a thoughtful and pensive manner, "just one more thing. I could hear someone speaking. Not whoever it was who tied us up. We were tied up? Did any of you realise that? Were we all bound and gagged and cuffed to a chair?"

The group were silent.

"It wasn't whoever was keeping us locked up. I never heard them speak, whoever they were. No, it was a distant voice, a painful voice, pleading."

"Pleading for what Thelma?" Diana was seriously unnerved.

"It just said: 'Help me, help me, help me…'"

"And what else?" Frank enquired, feeling that hearing voices was unlikely, and probably no more than a passing daydream.

"Well that's it, only, just that my right leg stopped hurting, and then the pain transferred to my left leg…"

"And then what?" The group chimed in unison.

"It just went away and I suddenly felt light and free, then everything went dark again."

"It had to be LSD, no doubt about it, or that DMT shit that all those New Age dudes are always raving about." Duncan as ever had his own personal chilled-out theory.

"Now wait we can't jump to conclusions." Diana warned. "There are no such drugs that can mend a broken leg and remove the plaster cast it was wrapped up in. It can take weeks for a tibia to heal fully, even your incomplete fracture Thelma, and even with your walking cast, it should still take six to eight weeks. There has to be another logical answer to this."

The group were silent once more as they finished their meal. Then Diana looked at her watch, which was one of those: all singing and dancing, everything packed into one, and made someplace in Europe, or more likely China, models. She looked and took a double take. Turning to Hillary she enquired "What's the date today Hillary?"

"Why young lady it's September the eleventh. I do believe"

"My birthday…" Thelma piped up wearing a wide emoji smile.

"Oh Jeeze, we, I mean I forgot Thelma, sorry." Frank was genuinely concerned. Whilst Duncan, also feeling sheepish, pushed a small vase of faded dried flowers (a table decoration courtesy of the diner), in Thelma's direction. It was the thought that counted.

"No wait, everyone what times and date do you have?"

Frank was first to respond, "well I have near enough twelve midnight on September eighth, but my watch has stopped."

"Mine too," Thelma added, "same time and date as well."

Duncan did not wear a wrist watch so he simply shrugged his shoulders.

"We have lost a couple or more days, don't you see?"

The group pondered the situation.

"Are you saying somewhere, somehow, two or three-days have passed us by? That's clear, it has to be, watches don't lie." Diana was weary of all the guessing games, she just wanted to shower then go to sleep in a comfortable bed.

Thelma briefly fell silent. In truth she was slightly hurt that no one had remembered her birthday. However, setting those negative thoughts aside she continued evaluating the present situation. The team had actually left Iowa State university 'after' the parade, and after Thelma had been discharged from hospital. That was late on the fourth of September. And it had taken a day or so to meander down to Kansas, where they stayed for a while to freshen up in a motel before pressing on to Roswell. After breaking camp, they arrived at the Rachel diner on the eighth of September around midday. However, Hillary's time piece verified the date was now the eleventh, which suggested that there were two-to-three days lost and unaccounted for: from the late evening of the eighth, ninth, and tenth.

"Clinton, how many days have we been away?" Thelma posed the question.

"Well you signed out on the afternoon of the eighth, to go up the mountain. And I don't know what you have been doin' but the way I see it is that you should have been back on the ninth. Whereas you are here on the eleventh!" Clinton continued on a lighter note. "Maybe you would like some birthday pie? Hillary come on girl slice up some of your apple pie now!"

21

Kruger at the so-called Area 51 Gatehouse

Captain K.K. Kruger was not going to allow these four college kids fly the nest. No, they were going to be 'his' little future 'nest egg.' His one-way ticket out of this crazy god-forsaken hell hole.

True, he played the game alright. He knew the score OK. Yes, he was acutely aware that if were not for people such as himself, the entire air base would come to a grinding halt.

The proverbial writing was on the back of his Five Star contract. He had read the small print. And each year the font size shrunk smaller and smaller until no human eye could possibly read it without the use of a microscope. Or, that is how he felt concerning the matter.

Nevertheless, leviathan that he was, he would still continue to kick the ball up and down the park.

For now, anyway.

To say his present security squad were 'over-stretched' would be an understatement. Most of his team, those who had turned up for their shift, were engaged in lending a hand with the final stages of replacing the perimeter wire.

Here existed yet another paradoxical situation.

His security team were technically only permitted to station themselves outside the government restricted wire barriers. Kruger himself was not officially cleared to go beyond any of the few gatehouses that were strategically placed around the vast ranges that constituted the Nellis Air Force base and bombing ranges. Unless of course in pursuit of trespassers, or to gain access to the 'Paradise Ranch' command and control centre.

Neither was he cleared to go down into the holding pens where the MRU team were being held for a couple of days to 'cool' off.

With regard to other aspects of security, Five Star had installed cameras all over the base perimeters, but were not permitted to 'officially' view any content recorded by those same cameras. And, regardless of the fact that Kruger had overseen the security surrounding the construction of the concrete bunkers that lay unseen beneath the shifting arid and barren landscape, he was not officially permitted to enter those same bunkers.

As far as recruitment was concerned, any person who was seeking employment with the Five Star Corporation, would be required to go through a series of physical challenges and psychological tests.

The posts, when advertised, were plain enough: *Private security operatives required. Working for America's leading security corporation. Ex-service men, women, and former police officers welcome to apply.*

This class of disciplined workers knew the drill. Which was: *'Keep your mouth shut, obey the rules, stick to the script.'*

Once passed the suitability evaluation tests, a complex indoctrination process took place. Courtesy of 'The Good Doctor's' extensive pharmacology team. Successful candidates would never be the same person again.

This form of play-acting was beyond Kruger, or so he had decided. Despite that fact that he had undergone a similar procedure when he had been offered and accepted his current posting.

He was the most senior ranking civilian operative across the entire Nellis Air Force base. And therefore, held a high level of clearance, for a civilian that was.

And he knew it.

His personal indoctrination was for him no more than a distant memory, a mist that fogged over him from time to time, sending him into a miasmic, almost robotic Metropolis-like world. He ticked over but no more.

What Kruger and his dedicated security team did not realise was that they all, to a man, or woman, were being surreptitiously drugged on a daily basis. Thus, rendering them, along with everyone else working on the base, totally controlled. Their moves were scrutinised, analysed, measured and weighed up. Assessed for chinks in the armour, holes in the dyke walls, that if not plugged may open up the flood doors, and the embankments of truth would not be able to contain the deluge.

Regardless and currently semi-oblivious to all matters to hand, Kruger seconded two of his loyal operatives to go, 'under cover' as it were, and tail the two Jeeps belonging to the so-called Magnetronic Research Unit crew. He had already seen to it that GPS tracking devices were securely attached to the underside of each of their vehicles.

In spite of what they, Colonel Kernel and 'Der gute Doktor' were planning to do concerning the college kids, he had 'his' own strategy and agenda regarding what 'he' was going to do with them. He was certain to make money from this crew of intellectual idealists, now they had been brain-washed and brought to heel.

Kruger had made certain that his Five Star closed circuit tapes were rolling during the entire MRU team brain-washing process, and that duplicates were promptly recorded.

That way, whatever information or key codes that were concocted by Colonel Kernel to control the group, he would be privy to them all. For now, he had the codes: 'A Midsummer Night's Dream,' and 'Orion's Belt.'

And, he had already witnessed, via his external CCTV systems coverage, just what the results were of turning them into a simple single coded statement such as: 'A Midsummer Night's Dream.'

22

Las Vegas Motel

Nearly noon, Gracie Lin was dressed and showered, waiting, waiting, waiting. Bud Always-Jones was nowhere to be seen. Not in his room or answering his phone.

She had tried almost all avenues of approach. What was remaining, and as a last resort, was the old-fashioned detective's 'shoe leather' strategy.

In order to trace her wayward cameraman, she initially required to locate the cab company that gave him the ride into town he apparently so desperately needed. There were almost too many taxis to note.

Next, Gracie Lin attempted to find the driver of that cab and ask him where he dropped his fare?

No good, it was just on a random street corner. The driver could not help her.

Then she Googled the intersection and looked up and down at CCTV footage captured the evening before. This was not the main-drag, so less people. Vegas Fremont Street? Or the New York Hotel?

This was not Bud's style; Gracie Lin knew him well enough. He would not frequent a tourist trap. No, he would hangout where the hundreds of foreign workers came to R and R. The clip joints, the cheap bars, the discretely disguised brothels. All waiting for Bud the dumb-ass, and others like him, to blow his pay-packet.

Call it feminine gum-shoe intuition. Gracie Lin could almost imagine her servant, curled up in a night club, laid out in a curved booth, his shoes off, pockets empty, phone broken or stolen, not even a dollar left. His head pounding, his nose red raw from plying his nasal passages with cheap cut cocaine. Keys to his motel room and the hire car also gone.

He rises at last; a janitor threatens to call the cops if he does not leave the bar immediately.

Not an unfamiliar story.

And all of this Gracie-Lin saw through the motel's rest room mirror. An adept such as her did not require a crystal ball, nor a digital camera to see, only skill, patients and esoteric knowledge.

23

The Diner Rachel Nevada

The pie was fine and just like mamma's home cooking. It took Thelma back to when there was a time, she enjoyed life. When she was a child, gifted yes, intelligent yes. But then you grow up and things are no longer fun, you have to play the game and conform to the system. And just as everyone else, she had to kowtow to the University of Iowa's systems and particular methods of using and abusing students, graduates and alumni alike. It makes little difference. You give them something, they give you something back in exchange.

The Principal. J. Jones Junior. Yes, he was her cousin, in as much as they shared a common great grandfather. A man who was terrifyingly reproductive and had (or so it was said across the family), nine wives at differing stages of his life. He was a baby machine and his sole aim in life seemed to be impregnating young females. Like he was a bull steer, out to stud on the farm. How many off-spring had he sired? No one knew, as he also had a string of children out of wedlock. It also appeared that some, or much of his sexual antics had trickled down through the generations and had in particular taken root in the life of J. Jones Junior. His father being obviously J. Jones Senior. Also, a womaniser par-excellence. A man who had sons and daughters, younger than many of his grandchildren.

* * * * *

There was a time Thelma recalled, when the Principal J. Jones Junior took her young self aside, and, although he did not, and had not, made any direct sexual advances toward her, she sensed the desire was there, ever present and ingrained in the serial womaniser.

Wisely, Thelma adopted and maintained a modest sense of dress, and consciously kept up with her frumpy, 'old before your time' look. Concerning which she was certain had saved her on numerous occasions from misplaced male advances.

No, Thelma was very much aware of what the Principal J. Jones wanted from her - and that was her brain and to control her analytical aptitude. She was clearly a genius. He wanted to tap into that cognitive mind of hers and draw more and more out of her, bleeding her dry of information. All with the promise of bursaries galore, a lab to work in, a paid assistant and now external funding. It was Thelma's intellectual capacity that he primarily desired. She knew it, he knew it. And it was Thelma alone who held the key to understanding her theories. It was she who had written the ground-breaking papers. She had come up with the hypothesis concerning magnetic pole alignment and shift, together with a series of other relative theories.

However, he, for reasons of personal ego-boosting-ambition, gain and possibly sexual allure, craved it all. He insisted that it would be his name on the papers. He would take the credit, accept the Nobel Prize, receive the endless streams of funding from across the globe. He would address the United Nations; his name alone would go down in history as the man who single-handed saved the world. Or, that was how she, Thelma Jones, imagined he, Principal Jones, viewed the situation.

Except, as with most circumstances in life there is always more to it than the individual can initially imagine. There was always more to consider, a bigger picture to contemplate. And Thelma was totally conscious as to the fact that he, Principal Jones, was aware that she the genius knew, that he knew that she was aware she was on the cusp of discovering something far more dramatic than aimlessly measuring the earth's magnetic field. She potentially held the key to unlocking the metaphoric treasure chest.

* * * * *

The 'Shriners' they say were a society who held onto any number of secrets. He, the Principal knew this, as he was one of their number. However, there was one singular alchemic secret that they, and the rest of blind mankind, had been unsuccessfully pursuing for hundreds of years. And now this girl from Iowa had more or less unwittingly stumbled upon the answer - electro-magnetism.

24

The Diner Rachel Nevada continued ...

"You know we were followed here?"

Thelma addressed no one in particular. While Frank disagreed. "We don't know that; I mean where is the white pick-up now?" He gestured looking out of the window.

"White you say eh?" The old man clearly understood more than he let on to the Research Unit members.

"Belongs to Five Star, they handle security up there, keep the tourists out. I mean folks come up here, or used to come up here to the diner, before driving up the mountain to deliberately try make fools of them fellahs." Hillary added to the conversation as she cleared the table. "Heard there was some kind of accident up there a couple of days back."

Old man Clint continued in a reluctant labored fashion. "Truck got stuck or something and tore the fence out. That's what Carlos at the gas station was telling folks. 'Mack' truck going in the wrong way stopped for gas here in the town. There is a turn point further on as I guess you know by now. Your vehicles could easy spin around in the space, but no way a 'Mack' truck. Rear end was all scratched up. Driver must have been loco."

"And what do these Five Star people do?" Frank enquired.

"Police the entire Nellis range boundaries, miles of it, can't walk around, too long, too many mountains in the way. A man, no man could clamber up there."

"Only that Jap gentleman." Hillary added.

"Japanese?" Diana questioned.

"Some years back, called in, left his bags, just needed some climbing gear. I said we was too far away for him to make the perimeter in one day. So, he paid me up, one-hundred dollars, cash for me to give him a ride, not where you was, but further, much further north. You have to skirt the main Nellis base, which is easy. Then you go round back by the Nellis range. Quartzite mountain, then Wheelbarrow peak, over eight-thousand feet of it. Too high to scale if you 're askin' me."

"Dangerous place to be, maybe radioactive, contaminated, who knows?" Hillary speculated.

"No tourist trips out there these days." Clint despondently reminisced. "Still he paid his money and I dropped him off at Warm Springs, t' other side of any place. A week went by and he turns up right back here at the door. Thought we would never see him agin' but he made it."

Hillary spoke once more. "He made himself some kind of Camouflage outfit, so he said, and wormed his way all through the ranges and ending up along the edge of Groom Lake and its six-mile runway."

"Longest on the planet they say. Got right up to Hell's door." Clint added.

"What the Hell's Hell's door?" Frank was curious.

"Just a figure of speech young man, a figure of speech…" Hillary longed to bring a conclusion to the conversation.

However, Frank sensed there was more to tell.

"He reckons he went all the way unseen by them Five Star patrols. Yep, unseen, and managed to get all the way back, once again, unseen." The old man stood back as if he were spent, before continuing, "interesting point he made, not about the range or the lake, but the fact that in the mountains there were a bunch of air vents, sucking in fresh and blowin' out the old. Now if a man could bust into one of them then they could get access to the Groom Lake base, maybe get into the hangers and see what they got up there." Clint bit his tongue, he felt reluctant to give away any further information, as if 'he' were sitting on a great big secret. Regardless of the fact that the entire town of Rachel stood as a living testament to the fact that somewhere up in the surrounding hills and mountains there were certain strange and inexplicable occurrences taking place that deserved further investigation and a fuller explanation. Over and above that was the bland propaganda the government attempted to put out concerning anything that took place in a certain curious location that according to them did not and never had existed.

"So," enjoined Thelma, feeling increasingly suspicious concerning the direction and content of the current conversation, "are you saying this err...Japanese gentleman found his way into some kind of the base up there?"

"No, I aint saying nothin." Clint rapidly retorted. "Real truth, as far as I can tell, was he just spent a night on the side of the Cactus flats, and then the next few days he spent lost trying to find his way back to Rachel!" Clint held no such belief, but thought such a statement might add some credence to his fabricated observation.

"Oh, well, I mean what happened to him? Did he say anything else?"

"Nope!"

"So, we're none the wiser eh!" Diana shrugged her shoulders.

Regardless, the old man's story was plausible. Maybe the Japanese man had managed to get passed the security and had taken a closer look at what was going on over the mountains?

"What we need is a decent map" Duncan stated the obvious. However, any maps they had, along with other paperwork and equipment, were now strewn across the arid prairies of Nevada.

"Look, that's a great story, weird secret bases and all, but does not help us find our lost days." Diana brought the group back to reality. "Now someone at some time has been messing with us, I have no idea who, or why, but what I do know is we can't carry on with our lives until we have a solution to all of this." Diana displayed some true leadership. Frank nodded in partial agreement.

At that moment the cell phones of the research unit team began to simultaneously ring.

"Wait!" Thelma flapped her hands in semi-panic whilst the other three scrambled to locate their communication devices. "Wait, Don't!" Thelma sensibly advised.

"Don't answer! Remember what happened last time?" It seemed to her only moments before they had been duped into performing some bizarre form of orgiastic sex-feast prompted by the ringing tones of their individual cell-phones.

"We got to!" Frank butted in."

"No, wait! Duncan, you answer your phone."

"No!"

"Do it man Jesus!" Frank went to grab the device, he opened the case and pinged the message up, before backing away.

Thelma and Diana briefly ignored the calls to their cells. So, the apparent message was unheard and unseen.

Then, after Duncan pushed his phone aside, part in anger, part fear, part feeling used. The other devices rang again. This time Thelma and Diana responded and accepted their respective incoming calls.

"Don't answer, you know you don't have to!" Hillary pleaded.

"Here, stop, wait-up" Clint's deep gravely voice interjected. But it was too late.

Thelma and Diana were suddenly inexplicably arguing with each other concerning the leadership of the expedition. Diana held a table knife in her hand and was wildly gesticulating mimicking throat cutting movements, before Hillary split them up and sat them back down. Duncan had curled up foetal-like in the corner seat of one of the diner's tables. He was in tears and began to moan incessantly. Frank meanwhile was pacing back and forth until he suddenly grabbed a water melon perched on the counter and smashed it down on the wooden floor of the diner.

The four phones rang again, this time all parties ignored the tones.

For a moment chaos ruled and as Frank looked up from the melon splattered floor, he saw a white pick-up parked-up outside the diner. In the cab were two men, both with cell phones pressed against their ears.

25

Iowa State University

Principal J. Jones Junior, was no fool. He was however, one of those people who possess compulsive and fanatical tendencies and desires. Two of his many vices were: tidiness and order. Clearly, he anticipated some form of disturbance in the bedroom and bathroom when he had entertained a sex-crazed woman in his apartment. On this surprising occasion she had more than made her mark with leaving her cigarette butts floating in a coffee cup, and mascara streaks on his fine linen pillows. No, on this occasion it was not the bedroom that concerned him so much, but rather it was the intrusion into his office back on campus. The deep button swivel chair he sat in daily had been moved, not much, perhaps six-inches out of alignment, as if someone had purposefully pushed it back to position themselves in front of his white encased computer monitor screen. The key board had been pushed to the left, as if, when whoever had placed themselves in his chair, had sat back up and moved away, but had not positioned the key board back where it should be. The desk lamp was slightly askew, and over and above these obvious signs, there was a palpable odour of tobacco smoke circulating around the desk-top arrangement. And, worse of all, minute flakes of dandruff had snowed down and about the inlaid mahogany antique desk top. Sufficient evidence to suggest someone had been at his desk, and he suspected whoever it might have been had downloaded a number of sensitive files. Who? Who? Who? Well, he did not have to be a genius to work that one out. Looking at private business files was one thing; he was not so bothered about that. But what concerned him the most was someone discovering the thousands of pornographic pictures stored on his computer hard-drive.

The subject of which being mainly young children.

26

The Diner Rachel Nevada

"Me? Why me?" Duncan bemoaned, "It's always me, me the dumb one, me the joker, the clown, the fall-guy…" He had previously imagined his lisp had all but faded away. Now however, his speech impediment seemed to increase the more stressed and upset he became.

"No come on Dunc' Now you know that's not true, we love yah guy!" Frank did his utmost to calm his colleague down.

"OK, all of us," Thelma tried to gather everyone to their senses. "There is a white pick-up out front, it's hood pointing up the Extraterrestrial Highway. I suggest we lie-low."

27

Colonel Kernel so-called Area 51

Colonel K. Kernel, was back on duty. Fighting the good fight, as all patriotic African American's should do. Keeping America safe from Russians, Chinese and North Korean spies. Or, so he imagined, as he pulled up to the much to be desired Groom Lake guard post. The box-shaped timber building was in dire need of a paint job and the Air Force sentry looked as if he had been at his post for far too long.

This route into the so-called Area 51 was still the 'official' historically popular way in, as far as civilian sightseers were concerned. Not that any curious tourists would ever pass through its gates.

The tumbledown guardhouse was deliberately designed to look ramshackle and unimpressive. On first glance it would appear that nothing, no traffic, ever crossed the line into the non-existent base. Therefore, there was probably nothing there to see.

Thirty or more miles further in however, beyond the sentry station, was to be found Groom Lake, and some of the other facilities.

Having left the sentry post and the so-called-nonexistent Area 51 base behind him, the Colonel continued methodically along the little-used track down towards the highway, until a left turn appeared at the iconic 'Black Mail Box' cross-road. Just a few yards along this fork, hiding amongst the pine woods, was a very special place for believers in UFO myths. This was where anyone crazy enough could leave messages and post them to fictitious and fanciful alien visitors. No one it seemed knew who originally established the mail box, or what happened to the letters that were posted there.

Be that as it may, continuing down the track for a few

more miles the Colonel passed the point where apparently an eighteen-wheeler had recently got itself jammed, having taken that notorious wrong left turn off the highway, the one that is not on any map of the district.

Today, so the Colonel had noted, the most anyone had left up along the track was fly-tipped garbage. Including take-out cartons that had once contained an 'alien burger,' whatever that consisted of? The Colonel had no idea. Amongst the drive-thru dross were non-biodegradable: 'solar-system' shake cups, 'flying saucer' ice cream cones and 'solar system' carryout fries. All packaged in plastic with a half-life of a thousand years. Longer than radioactive fall-out.

The Colonel recalled from time to time, flatbed trucks had tipped out their entire loads of garbage on the side of the track, and further up by the 'Black Mail Box.' Beds, tables, chairs, clothes, rubble and kitchen items, everything you could imagine. Left for Lincoln Country Refuse Department to come and clear up.

What must the spacemen think of the human race? The Colonel pondered. Not much. Nevertheless, he had noted that today a new shrine had been erected by the 'Black Mail Box.' The original mail slot had been stolen several times in the past, probably by tourists. When that occurred a new mail box always mysteriously appeared to take the stolen item's place. No one knew who replaced the iconic alien monument.

Today it appeared someone had made an interesting addition to the original mail box memorial, which consisted of a heart-shaped pile of rocks, with a vague sort of alien-looking face centred in the middle, made up from pine-cones.

Very touching.

Today however, it was business as usual and he had already started by checking the gatehouse manifest to see who had been calling and just who might be calling later. More specifically he was keen to ensure at this stage no members of the press, legitimate or otherwise, was or had called up at the base.

The events from a few nights back had rapidly made news reportage headlines and now questions were being asked. This despite a genuine effort on his part to deny and logically explain away, to the Lincoln County Press and other publication's, his usual fabricated media statements. However, no one from the papers, not even the intern who made the coffee and fetched the dough-nuts was wearing it. The wild irresponsible press had all gone for front-page coverage with another - 'Lights in the Sky' sensational headline story.

Which was why, according to his methodical manner of lateral thinking, Colonel K. Kernel needed a fresh-faced new kid on the block-type-individual to head-up a press conference he was reluctant to organise and front-up. He had long-since lost all his credibility as far as local and state-wide press were concerned. He had acted out too many radio and TV interviews. (Peter had cried 'wolf' too many times already.) He had concocted so many misrepresentations of the truth that he now no longer knew himself what was fact and what was fiction. He had begun to believe his own lies.

Now however he had stumbled upon the ideal face of credibility and sincerity. The highly qualified professor woman - Thelma Jones, an ideal candidate to speak out on behalf of the USAF, even if she was not 'official' so to speak. It would only be just a one-off occurrence. She was already primed to verify the fact that there were no UFOs about at present, nor had there been at any other time in history. Neither was there any Air Force secret test aircraft currently hidden away on the so-called nonexistent Area 51 base, at this time, nor had there been before or after the cessation of the 'Cold War'. And furthermore, if the facility did exist, which it did not, it was nothing more than a storage museum that housed U2 spy planes and other 'pre-Cold War' heaps of junk.

'Nothing to see here people! So, move along,' were the tactics of the day.

* * * * *

The United States' Air Force had in the past learnt some serious lessons concerning dealing with people and the public at large. More specifically the press and general media, particularly since the 1947 Roswell debacle. At that time the initial sensational UFO headline went out in the Roswell Daily Record. An unidentified flying object had apparently crashed on a ranch in the Roswell region. The ranch site, which amounted to some extensive acreage, was of some great distance from the Roswell town limits.

However, prior to anyone coming up with an official conclusive and laudable explanation, the conspiracy theories were already born. Mainly thanks to the Air Force's own military blabber mouths, who had sent out erroneous reports of: *'captured flying discs, crashed flying saucers found and alien bodies recovered.'* All fueling the fire before the USAF could get a handle on what actually happened.

The media can be compared to a whirlwind: 'whoosh!' and it's out of control. And that was why Colonel K. Kernel had a job, to douse the flames of speculation. And with that post came the onerous task of making certain the military personnel, and other civilian workers in the many departments that constituted the Groom Lake facility, kept quiet, said nothing to nobody, never, ever, for fear of losing one's job, or life.

And what made the Colonel's life easier and what kept the facility and military staff under control was - 'The Good Doctor'. And between them they were having a fascinating time trying out new mind-altering drug regimes on unwitting service men, and outside contractors for that matter. Who were all mere experimental guinea pigs, upon which they could conduct their vampire-like research, at any given time of the day or night. Magic potions were mixed in with the water they drank, and with the air they breathed. Everyone on the Groom Lake site was doped up. 'Dreamland' was exactly what it was, 'Dreamland' by name and by nature. The place could be likened to a massive opium den of clueless people chasing mind-altering dragons each day of the week.

Today, as far as the Colonel was concerned, there was nothing to report, and there had not been any reported visits from reporters, which was music to the Colonel's ears. All that could be reported was the fact that it had been reported by someone that the contractors were almost done working on the perimeter fence, some twenty-miles further out and down the line from the gatehouse, where he had originally stopped to check that no reports or reporters had encroached upon the gatehouse and disturbed the tranquility of the current despondent and lonely guard, who was all alone guarding the gatehouse gate the one that never opened, as it led to the non-existent so-called Area 51.

The same journey in reverse had now to be undertaken by the Colonel. A journey that he, the Colonel, would now have to travel in reverse. Back to the 'lab' where 'Der gute Doktor' was waiting to be updated on any progress that hopefully had been made on the four MRU lose canons who were out there now. And as a priority had to be brought to heal

* * * * *

In the first instance the Colonel did not understand why the second command code had not brought the MRU party back to the base. However, the initial 'Midsummer Night's Dream' key code was only intended to be an aside. A test and singular moment of amusement for the Colonel and the Doctor, to see if they could introduce some of the words Shakespeare had written, hundreds of years in the past, as one of their trigger codes. The comedy entitled: 'A Midsummer Night's Dream,' featured four Athenian star-crossed lovers. A perfect scenario to work with.

The initial trial text code clearly spelt out as: 'Midsummer Night's Dream', had already been infused into the individual and collective MRU team psyche. A process that had taken place during the time they were held captive in the Air Force security holding pens, close to where they had originally been detained.

Once released, after being 'processed' and psychologically 'activated,' via a cell-phone call, the entire party should have been thrown into confusion regarding their sexual preferences and desires, which they were.

To be precise their gender identification markers should have been mixed up, boys would have preferred boys whilst girls would have desired other girls. However, the event was not recorded on video, which was a missed opportunity and total oversight made by both the Doctor and the Colonel.

Be that as it may, 'Midsummer' remained just a joke, a trial run for the Doctor to test to establish whether or not 'gender preferencing' was potentially possible.

There was still some extremist out there who held onto the erroneous understanding that 'homosexuality' was no more than an illness and so consequently could be 'cured'.

A potential multi-million-dollar golden pot. The Doctor all set to patent the chemical formula, and once trials had been completed, it was to be marketed as: 'Gaygone'. Creating a substantial capital windfall for all parties involved.

The release of the second and subsequent command code should have normalised the MRU's situation and psychological condition, and as a result direct the group back to the ramshackle gatehouse through which they had originally, without knowing, passed through to enter the base (the one that did not exist).

Except, that had not occurred.

Such a non-compliance event, although rare, suggested to the Colonel that perhaps a rogue command had somehow entered into the matrix? The result of which would have been similar to delivering to an individual mixed contradictory instruction. One said go left, the other go right. Panic and confusion was a real and possible result of such an inconsistency. The ensuing outcome could and would be dangerous to those participating in the experiment and to anyone who came into contact with a controlled individual.

Potentially 'Pandora's box' may have been opened, releasing mayhem all around. This being the case, at this particular juncture, the experiment's controller could issue a third counter message, and then a fourth and so on, until a favorable and manageable response had been engineered. Any and all codes issued should have immediately halted any unfavorable psychoactive behaviour.

It was possible to send these subsequent command codes directly, as had occurred, to the subject's cell-phone, or any similar communication device. The issuing of other verbal or written commands should take the subjects out of their initial state of confused euphoria and bring them back down-to-earth with a resounding bump!

However, what the Colonel and Good Doctor were amiss, as previously noted, was any first hand visual accounts of how the MRU team had reacted to the chemical and psychological stimulation they had undergone, and just what situation their mind-states were in.

The highly concerned Doctor required at this stage some bona-fide documented evidence of how the guinea pigs were performing. This evidence was simply not there and having prematurely released their captives, they now required to bring them back as a matter of some urgency.

A potential additional and possible alternative test-case situation, would be to attempt to engineer another similar scenario with other additional subjects to further test 'Der gute Doktor's' new anti-gay formula.

As it was neither the Doctor or Colonel had a clue as to

the MRU team's current collective mental state, or physical condition. Neither were they remotely aware of their present location. Consequently, they had to be found, and brought back onto the base to be re-augmented.

The next progressive code - 'Orion's Belt', was ready to be delivered. Whereupon each MRU team member could potentially be pre-programmed to go out as an individual to carry out any given order at any time and independently from his or her colleagues. Or, they could work in cooperation with one another as an effective team.

The Colonel was desperate to have Thelma Jones interface with the press. As he had previously considered, her credibility would impress upon a news hungry public that there were 'no' UFOs circling above and about Nevada. Neither were there any USAF experimental aircraft buzzing around in the ether. Such statements would clearly sound more credible and plausible coming from an independent party, say a civilian academic, rather than an old USAF public relations has-been. To this end, before even locating the MRU team, the Colonel had issued a standard USAF statement, to the eager press corps, concerning the dozens of aerial phenomena reported over the last few days floating in the night sky across the state of Nevada.

As was the current protocol, the statement was issued to all regional newspapers, radio stations and TV broadcast platforms. This mutual beneficial directive had been laid down some time ago and had worked for all parties concerned for a number of years. (UFO reports sold newspapers.) This had been achieved by way of careful negotiation and afforded the USAF the power to issue a total reporter's blackout concerning any news-worthy item they thought unfit for circulation. He, the Colonel, had the power and influence, for reasons of national security, to action such drastic measures. Which at present he did not intend to do.

Nevertheless, by means of coded communication with

the media, using those same protocols that had previously been laid down, it was possible to call an 'all media' press conference. Which was exactly what Colonel Kernel did. The 'all media press conference' would be rapidly organised to discuss the recent aerial phenomena sightings. The meeting was planned to go down in a few hours' time and he, as yet, had not found the star of his show - Professor Thelma Jones. Then again, he had some other means of locating and communicating with her at his disposal, which he would be employing as soon as he possibly could.

28

So-called Area 51

'The Good Doctor,' was not one to idly reminisce and bring to mind what was past. The former glories, the bygone values and what may have been? Had history worked out differently.

However, for some reason, on this particular day, he was overcome with waves of nostalgia as he contemplated why he found himself in the position he was currently in at present. Other than a few stray nostalgic emotions his thought process was, these days, often clouded by a certain level of collective guilt. He was so immersed in his work that he all too often failed to pull back to calculate the 'bigger picture' and the singular consequences of his lonely actions.

He held the balance of power of life and death over the entire two-thousand or more members of staff that worked across several restricted complexes run by the so-called: 'plastic government.' (By which he meant; 'The White House' who knew nothing.)

The recent programme development that occupied so much of his time went under the code name: Mega 1-90. Which, when completed, would ultimately demonstrate and illustrate 90 effective ways to kill human beings without firing an expensive bullet.

* * * * *

Since before WWI, both the German and allied military war machines were working on chemical warfare weapons and ways of delivering poisonous gas to kill thousands of front-line soldiers. 'The Good Doctor's' grandfather, as a research chemist, played a significant role in perfecting such weapons of mass mayhem and murder.

However, it was only after WWII that the application of various chemicals and drugs were considered as legitimate tools, not just to kill enemy soldiers in the face of battle, but also to torture prisoners in order to make them divulge secret information. The object being to force the individual by means of 'mind control' into confessing or divulging information. A subject matter close to the heart of the German high-command and Hitler himself. They, the Nazis were obsessed by the thought of the use of mind control and how to develop psychic powers. And other related ways to manipulate the masses, mainly through the use of propaganda and chemical compounds that would render victims powerless, weak and helpless.

So it was, 'The Good Doctor's' father played a significant role in the development of such chemicals and also perfected the deployment of hypnotherapy techniques, sleep deprivation and isolation. Along with physical abuse and torture.

With the cessation of WWII and 'Operation Paperclip', The Good Doctors' father was, as with other Nazi party members, scooped up by the victorious USA, before the Soviets got a look in, and spirited them all away to America and a new life. Whereupon, the father of 'The Good Doctor,' also known as 'The Good Doctor,' commenced work at a newly developed site close to where they had first tested and were continuing to test nuclear weapons.

The Nevada testing range relatively close to Groom Lake.

A nuclear test site is a good place for people engaged in clandestine projects to work.

Unseen by the covert government agencies who pay the bills.

The notion of uncontrollable radioactive pollution in the air ensured busy bodies from Congress, and other governmental departments, would think twice about snooping around the base. Radioactive fallout figures were falsified to make it appear Groom Lake and the test station at Mercury were a frying pan of cancer-inducing spent nuclear waste.

Like father like son.

The former work of 'Der gute Doktor' was passed down the intergenerational line. Such avenues can move a man upwards with the smell of success. Or, if a failure, he can easily be flung to the side. No one is expendable, but some are more expendable than others.

* * * * *

In his Spartan bunk room 'Der gute Doktor 'had two photographs: one of his grandfather, faded and dog-eared. The other of his mother and father together. He had imagined that one day his picture gallery might be added to by a wife of his own, and maybe even a next generation of Good Doctors? An unlikely scenario that he had resigned himself to. The chances of meeting a woman on the facility were very slim indeed. The Air Force girls all wanted to date the handsome fly-boys. And besides, working under the conditions he performed in had taken its toll. He was prematurely aging, and a routine medical, conducted by 'The Good Doctor's' own personal physician, had revealed some cancerous cells around his testicular area. The situation could be controlled using drugs, other than that surgery to remove his testicles was the only option. Facts that 'Der gute Doktor' was already aware of. Ultimately the choice was his, have his testicles removed or die.

* * * * *

At the present time none of the past or future aspirations he might have or had were of any consequence. It was the past and the past is consigned to history. What did matter was today and the legacy left behind concerning the Mega 1-90 project proper, which actually came into being, thanks to his father, in the early 1950s.

It was generally supposed that the operation had been underwritten by the CIA. Assisted by 'Special Op's' and the 'Army Chemical Corps.'

Official sanctioning and funding came through in 1953. However, due to a number of serious violations concerning the unwitting and illegal testing upon unsuspecting African Americans, prison inmates, mental patients and for some unaccounted-for reason - Canadian citizens, the activities of the project were somewhat curtailed.

An additional reduction in the project's performance condensed its field of operations further in 1964. Which was followed by further cut backs in the midst of additional controversy in 1967.

Punitive action was taken in the courts, which ultimately ended in law suits brought against the CIA, by those who had been afflicted or made seriously ill due to the agencies clandestine activities.

Victims basically.

At the time it was stated that the Mega 1-90 project was: *'concerned with the research and development of chemical, biological and radiological materials capable of deployment in covert operations to control human behaviour'.*

By then the project (in typical CIA black-operations methodology), had been reproduced and spread out across some one-hundred and forty-five contractors, none of whom knew what the other contractors were engaged in. This way no one single entity had the full picture at his or her disposal. These sub-projects were proliferated out across some eighty academic institutions, and over one-hundred and eighty research facilities, in the USA, Canada and exclusively in the UK, through an agency known only as: 'The Tavistock Institute.' Many, if not all of the contractors used, had no notion they were being funded and controlled by the CIA.

As far as legal action was concerned, the CIA always,

not surprisingly, won their cases, which were, as a matter of course, thrown out by the respective presiding judges.

Hardly unforeseen.

However, one court ruling did acknowledge the CIA had, for some forty-years, performed illegal and undercover experimentation on civilians and military personnel alike. All supposedly to merely assess their behaviour when fed psychotropic substances. All source names were redacted for their own protection.

Public opinion ultimately rose up against such secretive undercover activities and finally in 1975 these practices, that President Kennedy had spoken out about, were brought to the attention of the public when a congressional committee commissioned a full investigation into the activities of the CIA on US soil.

As it was, the then Director of the CIA, pre-empted any investigations by destroying all filed documentation with regards to the Mega 1-90 project. Leaving only a very small number of papers that survived the destruction process.

However, a further cache of papers were discovered by means of disclosure through the 'Freedom of Information Act.'

Always ahead of the game, the CIA thereafter condemned its own activities as being: 'un-American' and stating the project had been ill-conceived and a waste of government funding. Whilst all along the work continued in up to forty-four American colleges and universities, as well as big pharmaceutical companies, research facilities, hospital for the insane and prisons.

Groom Lake and other military faculties were an ideal spawning ground for these and other similar 'black' operations. Budgets and funding could be hidden, experimentation on willing or unsuspecting guinea pigs could carry on under the nose of congressional committees and the judiciary. As no one, not even the President of the United States could gain access to certain parts of the facility. In a vast complex such as Groom

Lake, which was part of so-called Area 51, and the related Air Force amenities surrounding this 'non-existent' piece of real-estate, anything, absolutely anything could be going on.

29

The Diner Rachel Nevada

"Here!" Clint thumped down hard on the table. Don't you see!? I can read all the text messages you like, I aint effected by it, nor is Hillary here."

Thelma drunk in the words and immediately understood. Clint and Hillary were not party to this psychological mumbo-jumbo form of communicating, and therefore the couple could mediate and interpret any information coming through. Either verbally, by text, or voice-mail.

"Pass me them phones over here!"

Clint extended his hand out to take Thelma's cell-phone.

"Wait! Don't read it out loud!" Diana declared from the background.

The old man fumbled around getting the phone where he could see it in the dimly lit diner. Once prepared he assiduously read the text message with a nod of his head. "Mmm, give me them other phones." The exercise was repeated. Clint nodded his head once more, before rubbing his hand over four-day-old stubble. "How many incoming messages do you think you have had on these here cell-phones?" He set out each of the four phones side by side.

"One, I mean maybe two? Three? I don't know." Thelma felt dizzy and confused.

"I think it's a couple, maybe three." Diana chipped in, but was unsure of her answer.

"I lost count!" Duncan probably had not even considered the matter.

"Does it matter?" Frank was thinking he had not signed up for this.

"Well, according to my reckoning you have had three."

Clint was emphatic.

"Three?" Thelma automatically questioned.

"Sure, three and they aint the same."

"What do you mean, not the same?" Diana was unsure of the entire idea, phones, messages, cloak and dagger machinations, what the hell was going on? She nervously shifted from side to side.

"I mean twice you have had a message that says the same, but the spelling's wrong on one." Clint spoke with composure.

"Wrong?" Thelma again questioned.

"I aint no high-school scholar, but I kin count 'n' spell a little, and if you is asking me I would say there's been three similar messages, but not from the same person, whoever it was sent them. One spells it right twice, the other gets it wrong." To add to the drama, as if he were engaged in a full-on battle of chess, Clint moved two of the phones away from the other two. "There's a few missed-calls," he determinedly continued, "maybe due to the weak signal we have in these parts, and some calls when your lines were somehow engaged."

"I wish I could read them!" Thelma bit her thumb.

"No, it's too risky," Diana always the cautious one.

Other than it was Frank who came up with the most brilliant of solutions. "I tell you what, draw up a code, a simple one: a is one, b is two etc. Then we read the numbers back using the code." The typical strategist's football mind came into play. However, his idea had one flaw.

"Yeah," Diana waded in like a scolding mother. "But you're still going to end up with a literal message that is too dangerous to read for ourselves." Diana wisely pointed out.

"Then split the message," Frank continued, "Clint does half, Hillary half, and then we between us read half the message, which should not have any effect on us." Frank was out on a limb. When all said and done, he had no idea if it would come back on them or not.

However, it did not take the collective group long,

with Clint's assistance, to fathom out the messages they had received, which ultimately only served to create more confusion. (Silent Charades was a game they all could play.)

Apparently, the messages that came down to them about the time they were still at their decimated campsite twice read: 'Midsummer Night's Dream.' Plain and simple. A third and subsequent message however, one they were now convinced was from a different source, read: 'a midsummer nights dream.' Same message, but far from being identical punctuation.

Moving on from 'Shakespearian' references, a fourth, further dissimilar message, had been sent much later from the same source as the previous correct communication.

Over and above that however, according to the cell-phone time and date counters, several erroneous text messages came through at the same time. One, or however many must have flagged up as being engaged.

"Virgin Media" Clint closed lugubriously, thinking cell-phones were one of man's worst inventions. "don't reach this far into the slopes of the Nevada desert."

Whoever it was originating these voice- mails and texts clearly did not have the idea fully worked out. The system was flawed.

30

Las Vegas

Gracie Lin, decided to revert back to the very basics of news reportage networking. Here she was not far from the offices of the Las Vegas Weekly, the Las Vegas Sun and Lincoln County Nevada News. Not forgetting the radio and TV station platforms, that served one of the most famous and well-visited places in the world. All she needed to do was to grab a few favours, maybe pull some stings, see how much goodwill was floating around. Not that she knew anyone in town. She was a stranger (without Bud the camera operator). in an equally strange land. He being her missing technician who had to be found urgently.

To that end, Gracie Lin, the 'Femme Fatale' singularly driven by pure greed and avarice, was aware of the old newspaper reporting networks that once existed in many American cities. News gathering by way of the ground-up, so to speak.

Once-upon-a-time, according to good old Uncle Sam tradition, news reporters not only reported on the news, but in many ways actually created it. How it worked was simply this: paper-boys would start early, in a town like Vegas, the kids would work downtown and went to the news stands before dawn and then biked around the commercial centres dropping papers at business establishments, hotels, bars and any number of commercial outlets alike. As they went about their business, they picked up items of news from other paper boys, which they then passed around. The system worked very well and became a blue-print for news gathering across the major cities of America. If there was a murder downtown the kids knew about it and passed the information back to the news stand operatives, who then called it in to the news desks. If there was a robbery downtown the boys on bikes became the first on the spot, even before the cops. Their eye-witness accounts had even been used in courts of law.

Except that was the past. Gracie had no idea if the same or a similar system worked for missing persons. Other than it was worth a try, seeing as she had no other means at her disposal. She supposed that in the present-day news events and images could all be captured on cell-phones.

As it was, she checked out where the nearest news stand was, bearing in mind she had opted to stay in a motel outside of the main Vegas strip. There was a nearby news stand that she discovered by reading the motel information pack. It was sighted along Paradise Road. Which she could reach using the monorail from Sahara Avenue.

The weather was fine, so she rummaged through her case and found a suitable Mary Quant blouse, over which she strung a pair of black hot-pants, pulled a white plastic peaked cap over her forehead, and grabbing a black and white check purse she eventually made it out the door. Fixing her loud make-up along the way, all in search of her drunken ass-hole of a camera operator.

31

The Diner Rachel Nevada

Thelma was in a dilemma and she had no idea why? Split between two distinct options: one to more or less stay where she was. The other alternative was motivated by the inner-compulsion she continually felt prompting her to venture into Vegas and by some unknown means throw herself at the media. Given the fact that she had never visited Vegas before, she had a very definite address lodged in her memory banks. It was a broadcast studio in one of the main hotel complexes which doubled up as a convention centre.

When she arrived there, she was to comment on the now old news concerning the almost universal reportage of aerial sightings experienced by, what it appeared was, most of Lincoln County. Except that was several nights ago and try as she may she could not fathom out exactly when. Besides, nothing had been reported since.

Apparently, the country as a whole had experienced a number of very loud 'sonic booms,' reported across the nation, all on the very same night. No answer to what they were was forthcoming from any quarter.

Stone wall.

The papers had already gone to town on the subject of -'lights in the sky,' and other Unidentified Aerial Phenomena. Initially it had been phone-ins on the night. One hundred people had called the various TV and radio platforms to tell of strange lights in the sky. Then there were the eye-witness accounts that came in the following day from people who needed to think twice before telling the world they had seen a UFO, and by doing so would be branded as being insane.

And, by day-two, so-called experts, mainly drawn from the military, had given their hollow opinions on the matter.

Now the next and final stage: the media were in denial of all the first-hand sightings, dismissing them all as - 'crank callers' reporting tricks of the light.

Finally, to create some form of closure, even more brainless experts added to the debate, refuting all other eye-witness claims and reports. And this is where Thelma was about to step in. She was to be the final nail that put to rest all forms of speculation. She apparently was the last word on the matter and was in fact more than delighted to carry out such a task. She could of course have simply called any number of newspaper offices, and TV broadcast studios herself from her cell-phone. (Which under the circumstances she was reluctant to use.)

It seems that there was a large gathering of press representatives waiting for her at a specific predetermined location. For some unearthly reason she was being pressurized by some mysterious compulsive force to attend this particular, what she believed to be, news conference. This she had to do in person. Coerced by a little dark voice in the back of her head that kept on and on telling her to drive into the entertainment capital of the world, some eighty-miles away.

On the other hand, that second voice, her inner-Thelma voice, was telling her to stay well away from Vegas, and concentrate on finding out what had taken place a few nights before and to go back to wherever the hell it was, or what it was, or when it was, or how it was and to find out what the heck was going on. And moreover, to unearth the source of the quiet 'pleas for help' that she continually, like the on-set of a migraine, experienced.

"Well, I am for one not going anywhere until whatever has hold of us lets go."

Diana was adamant, she was full to the brim of being screwed around by some obviously weird and sick people. "And we stink!" She scornfully stated.

Duncan smelt his underarms and nodded his head in agreement. He was still wearing the same incongruous hippy-style shirt and pants he wore the day they left Iowa state. "Yep we do." He lisped.

"Maybe they have a shower out back?" Frank enjoined. He still looked somewhat crisp and neat compared to Duncan, with his slightly crumpled, US army fatigues. Although his once pristine tee' was now caked in dust and sweat.

Diana looked down at herself with a gaze of dismay. Her former sharp track suit was now a creased mess and torn in several places.

She made no comment.

Whilst Thelma, wrestling with her conscience, still had no idea whose cargo-pants she was wearing. Clearly not hers. They did fit however, just, maybe a tad long in the leg.

"Hey, do you have a Laundromat around these parts, Thelma hopefully enquired of Hillary.

Hillary quickly responded. "Why one right here child, back of the kitchen. I have a machine, let me help you all out."

The elderly lady could clearly see the group were in need of washing and cleaning themselves up. A towel came Thelma's way as she modestly removed her pants of dubious ownership. Hillary collected up the items for washing which the group offered to the gods of detergent, and collectively looked about for a shower unit.

"Out back here lady" The old man Clint showed Diana the way as something caught Thelma's eye whilst she was surrendering her grubby pants. It was a laundry label. Common enough. There it was, a label with a numerical code: 217217. A label with a name embroidered into it: R. Jones USAF.

"Guys, wait, just hang on, take a look at this."

The now half-dressed party, gathered about Thelma who was still modestly seated around the corner table.

"Sown into my cargo-pants: a name, R. Jones, USAF and a laundry number."

"Jones! Well it would be!" Frank sounded off with a

sarcastic tone in his voice.

"Don't you see, this opens a big door, as in: whoever had us imprisoned for a couple of days must have provided me with clean pants after my little accident. These are the pants which are clearly USAF issue. We have it, this is our big clue. It must have been the US military, or the more specifically the Air Force no less. Who locked us up?"

"Yeah, but what does that prove? Anything? Anyone could have pants like that." Frank was cynical.

"They're clearly for a woman, look at the cut. Diana held the garment up before inquisitively riffling the button-down pockets. A hairgrip, a piece of candy, sticky and out of sell-by date. The striking woman enthusiastically continued. Down the leg pocket, left and right until she felt a small piece of paper screwed up at the bottom of the righthand pocket. Diana unfolded the slip of lined paper, as a message eventually manifested itself. It simply stated: 'call me …' followed by a strange, what looked like to be, coded cell phone number: 237237237237.

"Eureka! We have struck gold people, struck gold!" Diana shouted out excitedly whilst almost breaking into a twerking-style dance, except with the old man looking on, she thought twice about exhibiting herself.

32

Las Vegas

News spreads like wildfire. All Gracie Lin had to do was to talk to the first news vendor on the street and describe Bud Always-Jones to him, as being a: 'missing Jack-ass loser,' and word came back from the street within minutes. In Vegas everyone is a potential Jack-ass loser, and today was no exception. You could tell them a mile off, this one had no shoes and was nursing his head, sitting as he was, in the nearby park area round the Riviera, off Convention Centre Drive, and had been for some hour or so.

* * * * *

Gracie held Bud Always-Jones by the ear, and threw him in the back of a cab. In fifteen- minutes they were inside their respective motel rooms and Bud was taking a much-needed shower. She felt sheepish (although her contemptuous pride forbade her to demonstrate such emotions.) Bud had picked the digital HD camera up from the floor, and explained to Gracie concerning the battery life, and 'when the cell was out of juice you had to power it up again, using a wall socket and the charger provided.'

Without another word Gracie Lin opened up the view finder, having plugged the device into the wall power socket. Now she would practice her 'scrying' powers and look deep into the mirrored soul of the, 'made in China', video camera. And she clearly saw what she wanted to see: a vehicle, parked up outside of a diner. Not in Vegas, away off, along a highway. Which one? 99/66/33...?

And then it appeared, filling the view finder, an image of a person, a silhouette of Diana Rogers no less, the pageant queen, belle of the ball. It all made perfect sense.

176

33

The Diner Rachel Nevada

It took a while but eventually Thelma was scrubbed up and wearing clean pants. Now she looked more the part of a military person, with her Camo' Air Force fatigues and harsh pulled-back hair. All she was missing was a dog-tag around her neck.

* * * * *

It was patently impossible to be in two locations simultaneously, therefore the Magnetronic Research Unit team decided to split into two groups. Thelma and Frank reluctantly being one. Whilst Duncan and Diana constituted the other. Thelma and Frank would put their phones on silent, in order not to be caught out by answering incoming calls, messages or texts. And then they planned to make their way to Vegas and the press conference, the location of which Thelma still inexplicably insisted she knew.

Meanwhile, Diana and Duncan would hang around the diner and try calling the person whose contact details had been clearly written on the slip of paper found in the side pocket of the Air Force issue cargo pants. They would call the number, and also see if they could locate this probably female Air Force person; R. Jones. At the same time, they would log any incoming text or voice-mail communications, using Clint and Hillary to initially view the commands and coded messages.

However, Thelma was still caught in a dilemma concerning driving to Vegas, or trying to work out where the group's lost days went. And just how many communications had been delivered to them via their mobile cell-phones? First there had been a message that made them crazy for each other. Then something that immediately stopped them making fools of themselves. This was followed up by a slightly different message, that when added to the previous communication sent them into a state of utter confusion. This message apparently had been sent several times; however, Clint and Hillary were now censoring each disturbing delivery.

Then something else, another message, exclusively directed at her, penetrated Thelma's conscious mind. A command of sorts that emphatically convinced Thelma to go to Vegas to the press conference. This message was more subliminal in nature than previous communications. It had not reached her via her cell phone, rather felt like it had been beamed directly into her head. Just like something out of a crazy old science fiction 'B' movie.

How it was done she had no idea, but rather thought she would keep quiet about the episode and not tell the others, but to wait and see if they volunteered anything of a similar nature.

Other than subliminal instructions being broadcast directly into her head, Thelma had to deal with the strange anomalous 'pleas for help' that bombarded her brain cells. Thelma had never considered herself telepathic in any way shape or form. She even had some doubt as to the credibility of telepathy. It had never really been proven to be possible. Being a scientist, she would need to test such a theory in the laboratory.

However, now was not the time to consider such matters, her mind was fixed on leaving for the bright lights of Vegas and therefore deferring all else. Discovering the source of unaccountable subliminal messages would have to be a job for another day.

* * * * *

Diana sat down waiting for her jog suite to fully dry, whilst pondering over the general situation. It seemed logical for the group to split, but she still had a good number of questions and reservations concerning the move.

A further particular irksome point she was bewildered over, was the fact that there had been no contact with the Research Unit's lab back in Iowa.

The least Principal Jones or the admin' team could have done was to call them for an update and maybe even to encourage them a little, just to rally them round.

They must, she questioned, have received the satellite downloads (which were not reliant on mobile phone networks), from the Rachel camp site. But nothing from anyone since they had left the university campus.

Not that they, the team, had reported back to the university faculty. Mainly because, up until now, there was little or nothing to report back.

Another nagging question which continued to haunt Diana was the fact that for some inexplicable reason their watches had been disabled. Diana surmised that they had possibly been 'fried' using some form of electro-magnetic pulse. Which, although feasible, such devices were not widely used, as the practical working mechanics of delivering a pulse had yet to catch up with the theoretical side of the equation. She should know, as it was within her field of expertise. As it was, a major aspect of the MRU expedition was to try to increase the understanding and significance of electro-magnetic energy. A science that was, as far as she was concerned, in its infancy.

Electro-magnetic energy waves are freed when an atomic device is detonated. The emission released literally melts all circuitry within a given radius, whilst everything mechanical ceases to function.

As it was, conversely, the team's cell-phones clearly continued to function normally.

Diana's hand cautiously moved towards her own cell-phone. Once again, she examined the slip of paper discovered in Thelma's pants pocket. 'Call me?' A love note? The owner of the army-style pants a woman? Whoever wrote the note desperately wanted her to call.

He must be a male admirer, for certain. An Air Force man no doubt. Perhaps one of the unknown men, or women for that matter, who had held the Magnetronic group captive?

Her fingers twitched, itching over the odd coded cell number. Until finally she gave in and plucking up the courage, she pressed the digits: 237237237237. One number at a time, taking care not to falter.

Voice message?

A non-human response mechanically stating-the person you are calling is not available at this moment. So please leave a message.' Diana let the answer phone run before cutting it off. She would try again later.

* * * * *

Not having hers or anyone else's laptop, or access to the internet, was a major issue for the entire MRU team. However, Diana reluctantly, using her cell-phone, Googled USAF. Nellis. Personnel. Jones R. (F)

The little blue circle went round and around before a message came over her screen - 'Access denied!' 'Cleared operatives only. Do not search for this information. Classified and authorised persons only.'

Then the screen flickered off.

34

So-called Area 51 Perimeter Fence

Captain K. Kruger's hands were tied. The perimeter fence replacement had not ultimately gone to plan. Just as the team saw the end in sight, the stockists ran out of the materials required. They were short of one-hundred yards of round gauge, and light of at least one-hundred up-rights. This meant more costs, more time, more men. His men would demand paid overtime, as would the contractors, who were currently being paid for sitting under an impromptu man-made sun shade.

When it came to outside contractors working in or around the base, they, as everyone else who worked on the Groom Lake facility, had to be monitored round the clock. Their every step overseen and a careful eye kept on their movements. Anyone of them could be an activist, a crazy conspiratorial fanatic, or an anti-establishment psycho. The die-hard uncompromising types, without anything better to do. Everyone who came to Nevada wanted to bust into the non-existent so-called Area 51, to take pictures of aliens that did not exist either.

Every foreign tourist must have got the message by now? No one at home! As far as Kruger was concerned there was no Area 51, neither was there any Roswell UFO crash, or alien autopsies, nothing. If there had of been the US government would have told the public by now. And as for dead alien bodies? Well, Der gute Doktor' would have known, because it would have probably been his father who was the one to have opened the creature up.

As far as former Captain Kruger was concerned, what was more pressing for him, was his latest scam using the 'geeks' that 'he' had picked up and handed over to be brainwashed by 'Der gute Doktor' and ass-wipe Colonel Kernel. Just a few nights before.

He, Kruger, currently knew where both the 'geek' Jeeps were, thanks to the GPS trackers one of his crew members had placed on each of the vehicles. One was parked up in the town of Rachel Nevada. And two of his crew members had followed them there. The other vehicle was currently speeding down Highway 33 toward Vegas. And all he, former Captain K. Kruger needed to do, to truly screw the 'geeks' up, was to send them another simple text message. But not now, he wasn't ready as yet. He had to have a record of their responses to the 'treatment' they had undergone. Plus, the effects thereof, filmed on video tape, so he could then send a clip off to a guy he knew in Los Angeles, who knew a guy, who knew a guy, who worked for the Fox Network and produced comedy programmes such as: *'You are on camera!'* And: *'You have been screwed big-time.'* Both peak-time viewing.

As it was, being the boss on the ground of Five Star Securities, he had to keep a tight handle on what was going down with the fence repairs, and did not have the time or luxury of being able to drop everything and go to Vegas, or anywhere else for that matter, unlike some others.

Besides this, he was also concerned with what had been going on back in Rachel. And specifically, just what interest did the old couple who ran the broken-down diner have in the matter?

Once-upon-a-time the Five Star crews would frequent the now tired, aging eating house, which was in effect closed down, due to lack of passing trade. Whereas, in the past, folk would drive through and park-up alongside the main road, that in effect cut Rachel in half. Now, they kept on going straight along Highway 33. And if they needed the restroom, they would call in at the gas station and 'Little Ale Inn' diner outside on the edge of town.

Be that as it may, Kruger was convinced something was not right with the entire set-up, something was wrong, nothing made sense anymore. Why were these kids, having been brainwashed, still hanging around? The obvious reason being exactly that, they were brainwashed! And now under the control of a particular top-secret Mega 1-90 programme, the existence of which he was not privy too, it was way way above his pay scale.

As it happened, rule-bending Kruger had not spent the last few years on the wrong side of the security cordon for nothing. He was always wide-eyed and paid attention to everything that went on around him.

OK, so yes, he had done his job and taken out a few too many over-inquisitive tourists, possibly erroneously. But that was what he was paid to do. And most of the time Colonel Kernel knew about his business of keeping people out. Just as Kruger mistakenly thought he knew somewhat concerning the Colonel's main task of keeping people in.

But what was it they: 'Der gute Doktor' and the ass-wipe Colonel Kernel, were up to? Clearly these 'geek' kids were all part of one of his experiments, he was using them to test one or another of his wacky theories no doubt. Whilst it appeared that what they had in mind was the establishment of a new series of operating command codes relating to: 'the big' mind control programme.

Concerning which, he now had in his possession a CCTV video copy of the entire process, including full audio commentary. All of which he had taken during the interrogation of the four 'geeks' they had held captive. And they had remained locked up until the process had been perfected.

Then suddenly they released them!

Why?

Unfathomable.

Not though until frying each of their wrist watches.

Question why? Answer-in order to encourage them to look at the time on their wrist watches, rather than their cell-phones? That being perhaps one subconscious way of delivering a command message directly to each of the individuals.

Whatever the reasoning it was in many ways beyond Kruger's basic understanding, and not a subject he was remotely interested in.

He only cared for that which was prefixed by a dollar sign.

If discovered, he, Kruger would certainly serve a life-term prison sentence. Even simply knowing about such programmes was a treasonable offence, subject to the death penalty.

As it was, Kruger kept his perceptive grey eyes open and his radar ears pinned right back, enabling him to diligently absorbed all that was going on around him. It was not his fault they left the sweet shop door open. As it was, 'Der gute Doktor' and the African American ass-wipe Colonel talked too much. Again, not his slip-up.

And now Kruger was, whether he liked it or not, inadvertently party to whatever was going on. Classified or not, Kruger was fully aware of everything, well almost everything. Or, so he thought.

He also imagined he had Colonel K. Kernel, exactly where he wanted him to be, and soon, after a couple of years of trying, he might, he just might, find out what exactly was going on down in so-called Area 51? And if it were at all possible, could he make any money out of it?

35

En Route to Vegas

Frank and Thelma were gone in a cloud of dust. Frank at the wheel of the Jeep. Driving mainly because of Thelma's inability to take the controls of the vehicle, due to the increasing pain she felt in the centre of her forehead. Post that was, whatever had happened to them, had happened, to them.

Initially, all of the team members suffered headaches caused they guessed by the gas they assumed they had been exposed to.

For Thelma however, there was something else going on. The others had quickly overcome any pains they had post 'the event.' Their headaches apparently soon faded away. But not hers. Now she felt as if shards of broken glass were floating around her cranium, cutting, slashing and tearing at her brain.

36

With the Colonel

Colonel K. Kernel, had, out of desperation as much as anything else, issued the 'Orion's Belt' command code. Save for, he had no idea if the instruction he had broadcast had been received and acted upon.

It was his own fault; he had not given himself sufficient time to contemplate just how he wanted the experiment with the MRU team and their cell-phone communicated triggers to pan out.

He had eventually decided that sending text messages to his target group was not an efficient way to communicate, as it relied on the individual to allow the message to come though, and ultimately read its contents.

Electro-magnetic-conductive-micro-wave- transmitters were already being pioneered at Groom Lake as one of 'The Good Doctor's' multitude of live projects.

Here then, or so he previously thought, with four captives conveniently held in the gatehouse pens, it was an ideal opportunity to make a test run with a live individual.

Whilst Thelma was lying unconscious down in the pen, as a result of exposure to Z33 gas, 'The Good Doctor' had inserted an implant in the base of her skull. In theory, a message could now be sent directly, via an electro-magnetic-impulse-transmitter (hopefully minus any unwanted interference), directly to the chip implant lodged in the target's skull.

The procedure was of high-risk and would only be deployed as a last resort if all other means failed.

* * * * *

The Colonel had been impatient and anxious to visually

see the compact impulse-transmitter in action. Consequently, he had the four MRU team members located in one pen, whilst the Doctor released upon them, via something similar to a satellite TV dish, an ultra-low-wattage-impulse, to verify that the transmitter device was functioning properly.

Team leader Thelma, having been chipped, whilst the other three team members not. The ensuing result was the melting of all the candidate's wrist watches, which had been anticipated. Whilst the group showed no detrimental physical effects from the micro-second experience.

Regarding surreptitiously chipping the other members of the group the Colonel decided not to go ahead, not as yet, the others he would leave to chance.

If the MRU team leader felt any untoward discomfort, it would be suggested to her that her headache was caused by some natural phenomena and would eventually pass.

As it was, once the 'Orion's belt code was released absolutely anything could be suggested to her and established in her mind, or so the Colonel surmised. Just as long as it suited the Doctor's and Colonel's nefarious ambitions

Whatever that might be...

Either way, ultimately, she would be primed and ready for the press conference.

* * * * *

The official line under the current political regime, concerning unexplained flying or other objects, was (according to the boys upstairs in the Pentagon), as always- *'if in doubt and boxed in by the press, instigate an all-out across the board media shut down. Keep quiet at all times, under all and every set of circumstances,'* was the rule.

However, the faceless people on Capitol Hill generally adopted the 'over-kill' policy. As in-a guy on the streets brandishing a knife would warrant the National Guard to be deployed, in order to blast the probably, deranged individual with mental health issues, to hell and back. The United States (land of the free), was more akin these days to a Nazi Police State than a country that prided itself on free speech and equality.

The warning signs around the non-existent so-called Area 51 base were an obvious testament to that. It was the government, not the Air Force, or any other part of the military, that posted perimeter signs up stating: *'violators will be shot!'* Together with-*deadly force will be used if you or anyone else dare take one step onto this secret government land, that does not exist.*

This was good American soil, fertile earth that could be scooped up in a man's hand and allowed to trickle through his fingers. That's how real it all was.

Conversely, the government said it was not there, just like Peter Pan's Never Land. There was of course good reason for all this secrecy and security. Quite what that reason was, nobody in particular knew.

* * * * *

The Colonel, being on the ground, so to speak, saw circumstances as either being useful or useless. If useless then he had no interest in whatever happened to anyone who crossed the wire. That was the obvious racist Kruger's murky domain. Particularly if they were trespassing on restricted government land.

If useful, then he would use them, often as not as guinea pigs to be experimented upon by 'The Good Doctor.' Who, was also clearly, no so much a racist, but rather a white supremacist, interested in eugenics and all that entailed. He had no qualms concerning messing with the heads of migrant Mexican workers. Sub-humans, Untermensch who he would programme to further his own dark ends.

* * * * *

Across the world the United States 'Black Operations' had countless assets hidden away. People who were drawn from all nationalities that could be called upon at any given point to carry out a deed or task. Naturally for the good and benefit of the American people.

The list of sleepers was of course ultra-ultra-top-secret. And perhaps such a list could never in total be accessed by anyone.

Why?

Because nobody knew these assets existed, as their files were buried beneath decades of more files and censored paper pages. Records that now in the twenty-first century had been logged and saved as documents on computer files. Countless names of men and women, still on government payrolls, who no longer were alive. As they had been redacted, wiped out, deleted, expunged, their names crossed out in thick black ink.

An 'asset's' call to action scenario could potentially go something like this: you are a happily married man with kids. One day the telephone rings. You answer. A voice says something like; 'Orion's Belt'. You are fully aware of the trigger code. How you don't know. You get in your car, go to a particular designated railway station locker. Inside there is money, a hand-gun, pictures, passport, other instructions. You drive to some place, say Vegas, there is a top-of-the-bill act performing. Does not matter who that target is.

You go back stage.

After the show the target top-billing artist leaves from the back. Regardless of his body guards, you confront him in the ally, you pull the trigger of the hand-gun and shoot the person in the chest two, three times. The now dead man's body guards (who are also armed), shoot you dead. The press and media are sent a script regarding 'you' the deceased perpetrator. He/you were insane, depressed, on drugs, an alcoholic, a wife beater, a rapist, a terrorist, whatever it takes to defame him or 'you' for that matter.

End of.

Another outspoken enemy of the state taken out (John Lennon 8th December 1980.)

Welcome to Colonel Kernel's 4th of July patriotic world. Drawn out of a plethora of fictional characters dressed up wearing a hibiscus print Hawaiian shirt, surf-board pants and golfing shoes. An African American man living the dream. A man whose life was dedicated to enhance and improve the security shield that encompassed the USAF. And remember, nobody knows nothing. And that was exactly what he wanted and had more-or-less made happen right across, so-called Area 51. Not only Groom Lake, but also Paradise Ranch, the Nellis Firing Range and Nellis Air Force Base, the radioactive Nevada testing ground and not forgetting Homey and 'Dreamland.'

* * * * *

'Dreamland,' the promise of a better life, was exactly that. A place where dreams were made (but did they ever come true)?

Yes, back in the 1950s, when trailers were first parked up on Paradise Ranch to accommodate the new influx of base employees and other military personnel. People who, earnestly and in good faith, transported their own; 'American BBQ Dream' and brought their families in to live with them on the base. A pool was constructed, a market fully stocked, bars opened 24/7, a bowling alley, a baseball diamond and football field. Everything the modern American family could desire. From trailers to brick-built houses and condominiums. Only hitch was the original trailer park site was downwind of the Nevada testing ground, a place created in hell by Satan himself.

Women living on the 'Paradise Ranch' facility suffered from cervical cancer, men prostate cancer, babies were born with strange defects. People were generally sick. It was covered up of course.

Now the trailers were gone, confined to history, but their legacy remained. Meantime, in the short-term, a series of aircraft hangers were rapidly constructed over the former blissful domestic site.

However, according to some rogue commentators and conspiracy theorists, the mighty military industrial complex and its corporate financiers, had over the years opened up the old lead mines and excavated further millions more tons of rock and dirt; creating a labyrinth of numerous below ground levels, underneath the former accommodation units, to create an interconnected network of tunnels and cavernous storage spaces across the base.

All prepared and ready to?

Ready for what?

Some sincerely thought the mass storage areas were constructed to house part of the USAF stockpile of nuclear warheads that had built up during the infamous 'cold war.'

However, what did the employees on the base think they were working on? Now and then a few crumbs of information fell off the table of abject secrecy, landing on the already murky floor of propaganda fueled reality and reason. Such titbits continued to increase speculation and therefore diverted the inquisitive eye away from what was really going on.

Press leaks were a rare occurrence, thanks to Colonel Kernel and his tight-lip-tight-ship policy. One of subterfuge and counter subterfuge. *'Keep the truth wrapped up in mystery and imagination.'*

As it was, everyone working in the upper-levels, the low-grade employees, civilian or otherwise, could be and were being totally controlled and manipulated by 'der gute Doktor' and his team of brilliant scientific minds. All under the direct command of, some would agree, the eccentric Colonel K. Kernel, a man with level G33 clearance.

The thought never crossed the minds of either men that 'they,' the controllers, were in reality being manipulated and controlled by other outside, but equally dark, forces. Other clandestine agencies were up and running, functioning in a manner that they, concerning which, had no idea existed.

To sum up: the spies were spying on the spies, who also spied upon the spies. In truth no one knew who was spying on who or why they were spending time and money on spying on each other? The enemy, according to some, was 'within.' No one singular individual knew or understood or had ever seen the 'bigger picture.' because it did not exist. There was no 'bigger picture' and mention of it was purely an abstract notion.

The initial key to keeping these two, the Doctor and Colonel (and other senior officials,) on stream was to place them in competitive situations, environments and scenarios. Comparative pay-scales being the obvious starting block. Neither man was fully clear as to which one of them enjoyed the fatter pay check The Colonel actually did not give a damn, outwardly speaking, and the Doc' kept his cards close to his concave chest. In a moment of crisis, which man would step up to take control? The situation had thankfully never arisen.

Step two was always to keep all parties in the dark concerning the other parties. What exactly 'Der gute Doktor' developed or gained from his research work, Colonel Kernel did not have the faintest idea. He only knew what 'his' own personal motives were. And that was to get out of the military as soon as he could, and go find his own 'Dreamland,' where he would live out his days in peace. Sadly however, he knew that was never going to come to pass. As, above all others, 'he' clearly understood what happened to people, military or otherwise, who came to the end of their useful lives. They simply vanished. And he knew and partly accepted this is what his fate would be, as he had inflicted as much and even more upon dozens of good men working on and in the Groom Lake and wider facility, over the course of his tiresome dreary posting.

Besides, as a G33 operative in general, he knew too much. For instance, he was fully aware concerning the many false-flag operations the US government had been engaged in. Most of them were politically loaded, but others were pure shock tactics. Such as the concept of global invasions by hordes of blood-sucking aliens. Such were the strategies deliberated upon and put into action by the CIA and upper-echelons of the 'shadow government.' Who were primarily concerned with promoting fear, social unrest and disorder. Wherever 'chaos' reigned supreme, the CIA were more than likely behind it.

Social media had made the dissemination of such false information and fake news stories even easier to spread. As did the staunch and sincere beliefs of the many conspiratory theorists who had recently sprung to life and even created their own broadcast platforms, from which they could easily reach hundreds of thousands, maybe be even millions of people. Sheep who were happy to bleat whilst consuming any and all fake news fodder that came their way. So-long as there were questions that could not be answered, there would always be people who would move heaven and earth to try dig up the truth in response to those questions.

Hence the fake alien abduction stories and phoney flying machine sightings and everything else that was branded as being a UFO.

The former 'Majestic' programme, that had some years before evolved into the ultra-secret; 'Mega 1-90' project, had opened the way forward to release the mystical force of Pandora's Box some years before.

One cleverly devised plan hatched by the 'Doctor was for aliens with electro-magnetic weapons to kill millions of humans. Like a movie, where earth fights for its 'Independence Day.' People would be abducted, knocked out by chemical agents such as Z33, brainwashed and let go. The entire press-corps could and would be manipulated to report anything they were told to report. CGI images of flying saucers would be used to shock people from all around the world. Like the movie - 'Mars Attacks', every broadcast image could be produced on computers by the Disney Corporation. Even so-called world leaders would no longer know what was real and what was a hoax.

Fake news. It was all relative anyhow.

Who or what is fake? What is real? What is the nature of reality? Had they all lost their tiny minds?

* * * * *

These thoughts aside, the Colonel placed a call to a certain Airwoman R. Jones. He had previously messaged her and was going to invite her out one evening to the aptly named 'Dreamland Lounge' for cocktails. A strange and incongruous joint which was in truth no more than a rough shabby little frequented mess hall. Located, as it was, in one of the numerous vast above-ground hangers that constituted the Groom Lake base proper. A place to relax and enjoy lousy food and warm beer.

Every individual patron visiting the facility apparently perceived the salubrious watering-hole slightly differently. That was, according to 'The Good Doctor,' due to a number of complex factors. To the Colonel, that was as good as it needed to get in so-called Area 51.

As it was, Airwomen R. Jones had disappointingly failed to respond the Colonel's clear and obvious advances. Therefore, having been spurned, he now 'ordered' her to pick up a Lincoln Continental from the Nellis Motor pool. Yes, a beautiful Air Force Lincoln Continental staff car. Sprayed dark olive green. Military colours of course; and as a matter of urgency come pick him up at Hangar 2, at Groom Lake. Her orders were to drive him to Las Vegas, as quickly as possible, concerning an issue of national security.

Whilst issuing his remit he commanded the Airwoman to source and bring with her a number of potentially beneficial items that may, in the event of trouble, come in useful.

37

The Magnetronic Research Unit

The MRU team had split, Frank and Thelma were en route to Vegas, as they moved off from the diner a white pick-up truck appeared from nowhere, and immediately began to follow them at a respectable distance. Just out of the sight in the Jeep's rear-view mirror.

38

Kruger

Kruger called through to his men who had been parked up in a white company pick-up by the old diner in Rachel. As he supposed they were about to tail the 'geeky' woman professor and the college boy back down to Vegas. However, mid-stream, former Captain Kruger changed his mind. He was the one who should tail them back to Vegas to see just what they were up to and where they were going. It was his call, he was in charge, and would take full responsibility for anything that took place.

His two men, now engaged in tailing the MRU Jeep, were ordered to about-turn and go back to the old rundown diner to find out whatever they could regarding the old couple who ran the place. And furthermore, just what the 'geeks' had told them concerning the events surrounding their arrest and incarceration.

Kruger was now behind on the rat-run race to Vegas trail. The Highway, unlike love, however was straight and true and he could put his pedal to the floor and play catch up.

39

Colonel Kernel

Colonel K. Kernel United States Air Force, to give him his full and complete title, slid across the rear seats of the sprawling Lincoln Continental and ordered - 'Step on it!"

In the driver's seat, almost dwarfed by the steering wheel and controls, one Airwoman R. Jones. Medic, seconded to base security commanding officer; Colonel K. Kernel USAF.

The very same medic who had given up a pair of her Air Force cargo pants for the benefit of a woman of around her size and age, who had accidentally peed her own pants whilst in the care and custody of a man who she considered at the best of times to be half-crazy. He being, Colonel Kernel, a high-ranking officer who was desperately trying to date her. So desperate was he that he had previously slipped his classified cell phone number into her pocket, in the hope that she would find it and give him a call. Then he would chat some and proposition her. A weekend in Vegas when they both had a couple of days down-time? What girl could say no? However, apart from thinking to himself he was a red-hot-lover aside, he was a consummate professional and would not allow his work to be jeopardised for the sake of a mere date. He would at all times treat her as a subordinate and maintain a psychological distance between them.

What Airwomen Jones did not know at this juncture was the fact that her Air Force issue combat pants were, having been washed and repaired, currently being worn by Professor Thelma Jones, of Iowa State University. Who was (although she was not aware of this fact), her third cousin.

40

Gracie Lin

Gracie Lin, had immediately responded to the images she saw when 'scrying' through the camera lens of the digital video camera belonging to Bud Always-Jones. What she saw was a shack. With a female, her first name, Rachel. A rundown almost derelict diner with a broken sign outside.

Empty.

No customers.

Only a road: Highway 33. That was all she needed to kick her camera operator into action.

Budd had fortunately found the keys to the Voyager and the pair were soon cruising the eighty-odd-miles towards the town of Rachel off Highway 33. What the ill-fated phoney reporter did not know was she was heading away from the regional centre of local news reportage, thus missing all the action. And, as she thrashed down the road, a vehicle passed her, a Jeep going equally as fast, but in the opposite direction towards Vegas.

41

Diana

Diana once again looked at the note she had found in Thelma's loaned Air Force pants. The number written on a scrap of paper was also stored in her phone, but she was reluctant to look at the screen or pick-up any messages, for fear of being mesmerised once again. First it was: 'Midsummer Night's Dream.' And now: 'Orion's Belt' which rattled though her mind over and over again. And she had no real idea of what either statements meant.

The pretty young woman from Iowa State didn't pretend she had all the answers concerning exactly what was going on, but felt she was getting close to a few of them. It seemed to her the entire mission was in total array and the wider objectives? All but forgotten. Every single aspect of the venture had gone wrong from the moment Thelma slipped and broke her leg. Since that occurrence in time, it felt as if there were some influential and mysterious force controlling their joint destinies. What that was and how it came about, she had no logical idea. It was insane, all of it crazy and she was having trouble keeping her normally lucid thought process together.

Regardless of the risks involved in making a call using her cell, she nevertheless did. The number she had gleaned from the note found in the cargo pants, rang a few times and then went dead, as if it were blocked.

Suddenly she felt strangely cold and sensed she was utterly alone. Clint was no longer there, neither was Hillary. And Duncan? She had not seen him for some few trance-induced minutes. She cautiously looked over toward the corner booth where he had previously seconded himself. No, he was gone.

Puzzled, Diana, unsure of her senses and rational state, nevertheless called the cell number again: 237237237237

This time there was a rejoinder. "Kernel!" The response was barked, rather than answered.

"Kernel?" Diana sat bolt upright; phone pressed hard to the side of her face. "Kernel!?"

She enquired, "Kernel who?"

"Please get off this line, you are calling a classified cell phone which is strictly off-limits…"

Unseen by Diana, Colonel K. Kernel, fancy vacation shirt and pants aside, was now dressed in his appropriate USAF formal uniform, accompanied by a cream coloured silk cravat, and a braided cap screwed uncomfortably tight down upon his already hot head. The type of dress-code an officer wore for his or her passing-out parade. Or more likely, at a presentation during which medals are awarded. Even more likely however, at a flag-folding funeral, when a kid comes home a hero to his family in a black body-bag.

The Colonel's nametag and G33 pay scale security code hung around his neck by means of his official lanyard; Colonel K. Kernel. United States Air Force. Propaganda and Media Unit. This pass opened up many many doors for him at the Pentagon and upon Capitol Hill. Being in an African American minority equated to 'inclusion.' As the only black man in the room, that meant you got all the attention, otherwise you could always pull the 'race' card and name and shame the Klansmen in the assembly.

Most other medal-bearing officers of his rank, who had seen active service, would not even care to consider the clandestine nature of his appointment. They really did not want to know just what the Colonel's role and function amounted to.

The delicately balanced relationship he endured with his fellow officers shared similarities to the equally onerous relationships held between the military and party activists of the former Soviet Union. Whereupon a 'party member' in charge of political indoctrination and promotion of the said party line, was more senior than any high-ranking, say, Submarine Captain. The immovable politicians sat in the driver's seat with fingers poised over the button, willing to destroy the world for communistic idealism.

The real honourable members of the military quite rightly despised the men from the politburo. Fighting men have codes of honour, reputation and mutual respect. Whereas politicians are consummate liars and cheating murderers. No matter the geographical location, or political ideology in place.

As for Colonel K. Kernel, his bottom-line job was to keep people within the confines of so-called nonexistent Area 51 happy and blissfully content. Whilst sending out disinformation and fake news, as a matter of routine, to keep the world's media at bay.

These onerous tasks were carried out behind the scenes, on an 'at all costs,' 'dead or alive,' basis. Whilst at the same time convincing people that all was well with the world, which also entailed keeping the clueless conspiratorial theorists on the hook feeding them with juicy worms of false information and fake news feeds.

Just exactly who, as an Air Force man, he was answerable to, was a mystery in its self. He was clearly a loner, who kept himself to himself, yet had an unimaginable network of human resources at his command. Whoever paid his salary was obviously desperate not to allow any real information to leak out to an unsuspecting, yet suspicious world, regarding the real nature of so-called Area 51 and what its true purposed was.

"Who is this? Clear the line immediately." The Colonel thought on his feet and considered tracking the call from its source. Ironically, the very phone being used to call him was one of the very same four phones he had his technical team previously 'doctor' to use as tools in his attempt to control the mental capacity of the four 'green' college kids he had had previously incarcerated, and was rapidly wishing he had not released them back into the outside world.

He played an intuitive hunch.

"I know this voice! I know who you are!"

"Diana considered throwing the cell phone to the floor and stamping on it.

"You are one of those kids that security picked up a couple or more nights ago. You were camping out, I recognise your voice. What do you remember about that night? Any recollections?"

It was vital that the Colonel assessed the situation and quickly, with a view to sending out another general command code via an electromagnetic-conductive-microwave amplifier. A method that did not rely upon a cellphone to convey the message. After all a single word could be spoken or simply shown to a person under Mega 1-90 control, to make them respond as required.

Experiments using this broadcast method had been going on for some years since the days of the Vietnam conflict. Out there US troops had been inveigled to 'hate' their enemy, the indigenous people, calling them: gooks, slit-eye, Charlie, VC, and many other more derogative tags.

'Hate thine enemy.'

"I want to know where my two-days went?"

The Colonel checked himself for a moment. He had to glean as much information from the person on the other end of his cell phone conversation, without letting go too much information from his side.

"Two-days? Sorry I don't know what you mean?"

"I am guessing, but I think you must be one of the people who kept us locked up! What kind of Colonel are you? Are you an American even? You know we have rights, as America citizens we have constitutional rights, and you have violated those rights!"

The Colonel baulked. If only the voice over the cell phone knew exactly what rights and privileges the people of America really enjoyed. That being absolute zero.

"I am a Colonel in the United States Air Force!"

The Colonel thought that by establishing his credentials he just frighten the kid off.

He moved to hang up, there was no point in continuing the conversation as he quickly punched in a text which carried a code, which in turn activated a command: 'Orion's Belt.'

Diana, too slow to react, almost immediately absorbed the code. She could not avoid its creeping tentacles, fibres that crawl around the hollow spaces in a person's mind and force them to see the world from a very different point of view.

The phone fell limply out of her trembling hand and onto the floor, a second before a large US army issue desert boot came crunching down upon the now defunct device. The presence of two men, both wearing dusty off-white sports shirts, appeared to fill the room. The man who had crushed Diana's phone brandished a gun, and motioned to the main doors, whereupon Duncan, Clint and Hillary all appeared from outside. They had, moments before, been jumped on and thrown to the ground by the two strange angry assailants - whoever they were.

Diana could see the old man was cut about the face and was doubled up in pain. Duncan, in his usual inert way was gibbering like a demented fool, whilst being totally tremulous in his shoes. He was most likely contemplating leaving by the closest exit.

Hillary, on the other hand, knew full well who the men were, not so much as identifiable individuals, but she recognised the uniforms worn by those who had attacked Clint and herself. They, as were many other former clients at the diner, Five Star security team employees. Who, once-upon-a-distant-dream had regularly come by for coffee and doughnuts, often joking that: *'Ma Hillary's pie was better than what they served up in the Las Vegas 'Dairy-Bell drive thru!'*

They were similar men to the ones they used to know and serve, but there again, total strangers. The uniforms remained the same, but the man wearing them were a different, more ruthless breed.

42

Gracie Lin

Gracie Lin approached Rachel; Bud was as ever in the hire-car driver's seat following orders.

There were a small number of people on the street. Clearly these days not much traffic passed through the 'single horse' town. Parking was by means of central bays, whereupon visitors could just cruise on in and park up for as long and they wanted.

Gracie, still dressed in her incongruous retro-fashion designer clothes, felt very much out of place. She was not used to dusty, dirt-blown streets, in a town that looked on one side to be populated by cowboys, and other, overrun by small grey aliens.

43

Diana

Diana could not think straight, neither could she hear or speak. The command code 'Orion's Belt' triggered a bunch of neurons in her already over-loaded brain. Out-of-place chemicals raced through her nervous system, like so many Amtrak trains heading for Chattanooga and beyond.

A great rush of natural fight or flight adrenaline, pumped through her heart and surged through her body.

Her long, elegant, 'crouching tiger' limbs carried her through the air and behind the counter of the diner. As she was fully aware, there were knives and an array of potentially lethal kitchen accoutrements to be found there. Taking the longest knife from the block the brave young woman, now apparently seething with anger, lunged at the gun-toting man who had stomped on her phone. He retracted his arm to avoid the strike, but in doing so dropped the handgun he had been wielding in a threatening manner.

A neat 'round-house' martial arts kick, skilfully delivered by Diana, hit the man square in his chest, sending him reeling over. The next moment Hillary was there and taking a frying pan from off of a hook in the wall, struck the same man squarely on the top of his head. Rendering him, at least momentarily unconscious.

The second assailant found and targeted Duncan, who had already given his phone up for dead, and allowed it to be torn apart by, what was the bigger of the two Five Star operatives. Clint went to grab hold of Hillary's side and was clearly unstable and about to collapse. Diana was by now, psychologically speaking - 'out of control.' The scent of death filled her nostrils and murderous martial arts inspired words were hanging upon her lips. She spoke, cried out and screamed but, no sound came from her mouth. Regardless, by now, just about all the kitchen implements were airborne, deployed and heading for the second man, who sensibly, not wanting to die, grabbed his limp partner and dragged him towards the open and beckoning diner doors.

As he left in haste, a strange, incongruously dressed woman, appeared at the same threshold. With a her, a disheveled man, crowned with unkempt, lank and greasy hair, together with several days growth of beard. On his shoulder he had mounted a digital video camera which he constantly adjusted, consequently missing most of the dramatic action.

The rush of adrenaline-pumped-action subsided, just as quickly as it had manifest itself. Now Diana stood stock still whilst suffering a camera pointing in her direction. Which, in turn, triggered in Diana the most powerful sensation of 'dé ja vù' she had ever experienced.

44

Thelma Las Vegas Press Conference

The Colonel, having sent the command text to Diana, decided he may as well message Thelma, with the 'Orion's Belt' code, just for good measure. The electromagnetic broadcast method was good, but there were some side-effects. Among them - having your brain fried permanently.

The code went through at around the same moment she entered the press conference auditorium, at which point her still functioning cell-phone sounded off.

Moments before, at almost the same time, Diana, a hundred miles away, had just lost control of her entire faculties.

Once in the auditorium, the ever-attentive Frank, went to divert his expedition leader from reacting to her classical ring tone. But he was too late. Out of sheer habit and instant reflexes, Thelma looked at the phone and saw the text message on the screen. Immediately her blood pressure rose beyond danger levels. And, as if propelled by some unknown, almost demonic force, the brilliant and gifted woman strode up to the podium and grasped hold of one of the numerous microphones located along the edge of the lectern.

"Ladies and gentlemen of the press, I am Professor Thelma Jones of the Iowa State University. And I am in attendance here in this the wonderful town of Las Vegas to tell you all, quite categorically…"

At that very moment, Colonel K. Kernel, in his impressive full military dress uniform, also strode confidently into the arena. Behind him, eying up Thelma's familiar 'Camo' cargo-fatigues, a female Air Force person, carrying a substantial briefcase. Which was in fact almost empty and certainly devoid of paperwork…

Thelma, unaware of who this military man was, continued. "Members of the press, I can categorically inform you that up on the wild ranges of Nevada are places you and I are forbidden to step foot upon."

A lone cheer went up from the audience, probably originating from a whacko UFO hunter, or similar breed of obsessive geek-like individual.

The Colonel and his female aid exchanged glances as they found themselves a place to stand, as it was, by an emergency exit, left of the podium and now just out of Thelma's line of sight.

"Why?" Thelma continued, "because these places hold some very very dark secrets.

The reason why everything is so secret up there in the mountains is because, or so they say, that the Russians and now Chinese and North Koreans need to be kept well away. It's top-secret and no one must know about what is happening, just in case the USA falls behind in the global arms race..."

Thelma caught her breathe for a moment before continuing. "Espionage is a word no one likes to hear, something the Industrial Military Complex does not like to happen to them. So they design and build more and more increasingly fast and high flying aircraft and satellites to 'spy' on their potential enemies. Whilst both sides of the divide copy the other and buy and sell technology in and across the 'black market.' To some folks' war equates to money. Trillions of dollars worth. And those who profit from war are the arms industries, the banks of course, and sometimes government representatives. Or, even speculative politicians, who have shares in all these death-promoting agencies."

The Colonel was becoming agitated. This was not his script. This is not the reaction the speaker should be having after the command code 'Orion's Belt' had been administered. Right now, the Iowa based professor on the platform should be praising the Air Force and denying anything untoward was going on behind the locked gates of so-called Area 51. Anyway, it was due to be turned into an aviation museum, a popular notion unofficially promoted by all parties. Something was wrong, but this was not the time for analysing the pros and cons. He would deal with that after he had stopped Thelma Jones from spilling any more bogus US military secrets to the world media. In fact the world media needed to be securely gagged so that nothing left the auditorium under any circumstances, At all costs, dead or alive. This was a protocol which had to be followed. Consequently, the Colonel took out his phone, a military issue device, unlike any run-of-the-mill domestic cell phone. This was 'his' special piece of equipment with the caller number of: 237237237237. He punched in a few carefully selected high priority numbers, whilst his female aid (and as far as he was concerned, would-be potential lover), kept her eye on the increasingly agitated, several hundred strong, audience. She scanned the lines of cameras, the clutches of microphones and the luminous faces of the press corps, whose eyes were all fixed on the podium.

"This is how it works." Thelma happily continued. "Politicians declare war, the arms industry sells a lot of weapons to the government, who have to borrow from the banks to pay for it all. Now who ultimately picks up the tab for all this? You of course! You poor tax payers who keep on having to go further into debt because your government wants to kill woman and babies in a far-off excuse for a country."

An audible cheer of support hummed through the auditorium, where the evening before the 'Rat Pack' tribute band had played to a full capacity house.

"The political situation," Thelma continued, "in the western world has become surreal. Our great nation is run by faceless people who are nothing more than controlling power-grabbing racketeers. Our supposed democratically elected politicians can only be likened to some kind of diversionary side-show, a mere comedy programme to distract us all away from what is really going on. Sports, music, movies, all there to dumb your minds down so you no longer think for yourselves. Why they even dowse you with toxic aluminum chemicals sprayed directly into your once clear blue sky. And no one admits to anything. Why? Because 'they' don't even know what is going on. Because it's a big secret. People who work on these so-called clandestine black projects, in these so-called secret facilities, have long since lost the ability to differentiate between what is fictional and fake, and that which is actual and real. Today, 'all' news is fake news."

45

Las Vegas Military Garrison

A few miles south of the auditorium where Thelma was preaching her - 'Gospel of conspiracy' - lies the McCarran airport facility. Adjacent to this public aerodrome, at the private 'Janet' Hub, were stationed, as usual, a squad of US Marines.

A long way from water? But stationed there none-the-less. The squad was responsible for 24/7 coverage of the military facility to ensure its continuing integrity. The on-base team packed a formidable array of weaponry, including the chemical nerve agent; Z33. Which could be deployed against activists and enemies of the state, in the advent of social unrest.

The duty squad numbers fluctuated from just three personnel, to, in excess of twenty armed soldiers.

Colonel Kernel was lucky today as there was about to be a squad rotation. Which ultimately meant double figures of standing soldiers on duty for at least another couple of hours.

Each of the squad team member were fully prepared: armed with stun grenades, gas canisters and masks, as well as all the standard US Army issue firepower.

The squad duty sergeant, in the absence of any higher-ranking officer, picked up an incoming directive on his satellite communication handset.

Having read the brief message, he quickly contacted his command centre to verify the coded instructions and furthermore, to ascertain how exactly to act upon them. There was no response.

Maybe out to lunch?

Regardless, he had no choice, other than to take command and follow through with appropriate responsive action.

The same urgent communiqué message picked up by the duty sergeant, was relayed to the wider Las Vegas Police Department, as part of the previously agreed and arranged protocol, set up between the State Police, Municipal Police, and if needs must, the National Guard.

In certain circumstances if there were US citizens involved, it was mandatory the State or Municipal Police took control and command. If it were a foreign invading army, they were dealing with then the military took authority and control. The National Guard stepped in if there was large-scale civil unrest amongst US citizens, rioting and the such like.

Within a few minutes the team of Marines were mounted up and ready to move out in four jeeps and two canvass-topped trucks. The heavily armed combat group left the airport escorted by four police cars and two outriders. The convoy headed north, parallel to Highway 15. Turning right into Twain, and then left into Paradise. Which directly led to the rear exit and parking lot of the convention centre, where Colonel Kernel was asking himself just what exactly had he done?

Part of the Nellis Air Force Base was to the north and an armed Air Force squad could have been drawn from there. However, because the Vegas section of Nellis was a closed facility, and not much more than a parking lot for transport aircraft, they did not have the military fire power stationed there, in comparison to the armed military presence stationed at McCarran.

Five Star Security held the contract to keep all the Nellis and the other Nevada located Air Force bases secure. However, the coverage and manpower seconded to the overall security of Nellis proper was a fraction compared to other sections of the base, such as that of the Groom Lake facility.

* * * * *

Oblivious to what was about to happen, Thelma continued

violating whatever official secrets acts she was breaking, probably enough to put her behind bars for life. However, the Colonel was going to make certain her current life expectancy was reduced to a few minutes.

"Now," Thelma continued through gritted teeth, "official sources will always deny the existence of any odd or clandestine events occurring or taking place. They publish information that throws the local press in a spin, so as to inveigle and obfuscate just about every goddamn journalist they can. Well, over the last few days your local newspapers have had thousands of UFO sightings reported. Be they unidentified fakes or foreign objects, tricks of the light, or even flying circus phenomena. Discs have been seen flying in the sky, and not forgetting their latest top-secret 'stealth' flying war machines, which, as many commentators will tell you, the Air Force are both building and testing out on the flats of the ultra-top-secret Groom Lake facility."

Thelma was soaked in sweat and beginning to feel exhausted. Regardless, she being ultra-stoic, continued.

"Then, they are going tell you there is only old junkyard planes waiting to be scrapped up there at Groom Lake, and there is going to be a museum dedicated to all the work people have done in the past to protect this great country of ours. I hand it to them; their media propaganda has improved dramatically since the 1947 Roswell incident."

The audience were captivated. Whatever the Colonel was going to do to intervene probably was not going to work out well.

"But, let me tell you," Thelma gritted her teeth once more, "making spy-planes is only one little slice of the big 'Dreamland' pie they have going on…"

The Colonel looked at his watch, then back to his female aid, then back to Thelma, and was thinking to himself that he was going to have to go up there and strangle the woman before she mentioned anything about the 'big Enchilada' they had under wraps. Not that he had ever seen as much, being as, back on the base, he only ever dropped down to Level 2, and never further.

What the Colonel did not specifically know at this particular juncture, was that his high-caliber Marines rescue column was stuck in a traffic jam on Twain, where road works were taking place and a truck had got its rear axle caught down a trench and the vehicle and associated traffic looked as if were going no place fast.

Meanwhile, "Now." Thelma continued, "I am going to level with you all, and many writers and theorists will agree with me, that there are, or maybe, here in Nevada, held up in prison-like facilities, creatures, beings of sorts, that are from another dimension, from other worlds, and these creatures have been there for a long long time."

The Colonel screamed out internally: 'not the aliens please!' before swiping his decorative cap from his head, as sweat began to trickle down his forehead and into his rapidly blearing eyes. Meanwhile his faithful aid looked on.

"And let me tell you about Roswell. First the Air Force said it was a crashed UFO, then it was a weather balloon. But the truth of the matter is that this weather balloon was not launched to tell you when it was next going to rain. It was meant to take pictures from just above the mushroom cloud that is created when a nuclear weapon is deployed... And see here, due to the Electromagnetic pulse produced, as a result of a nuclear detonation, no mechanical instrumentation works, the circuits get melted. Consequently, only an old-style camera sent up moments after the mushroom cloud forms can take images looking down toward the top of that cloud. And it was this so-called weather balloon that tangled up with, and brought down, what most of us would call a UFO. As a result, both counts were correct. It 'was' a weather balloon, and it also 'was' a UFO. But the USAF never took the time or had the inclination to set the record straight. They just let it hang unanswered for years instead of scotching the myth. Until back in the seventies, experts and conspiracy theorists alike resurrected the past to create an urban legend: called Roswell. Fake or fact?"

Colonel K. Kernel had had enough.

Thelma, on the other hand, was getting overheated. "Because of my so-called expert's status, they wanted my highly-valued opinion. They craved my insight. They wanted my professional and therefore credible point of view, concerning the matter. So, I was told, no coerced, by means of mind-altering drugs, to stand up here and totally refute the existence of either UFO's, or cutting-edge fighter technology the Air Force might be deploying. I have even been told to deny the existence of little grey men! Can you credit it?"

The Colonel was becoming unbearably agitated and his young female wing-person motioned towards the briefcase she was still carrying. Of course, he was aware of what she was intimating. Inside the case was a primed and cocked sidearm, standard issue, point and shoot. If the Colonel or preferably his assistant, could reach the podium and discreetly position the firearm in front of Thelma, she would then in all probability, use it. 'Orion's Belt' was the trigger for her to become ultra-ultra-violent.

And it was working.

If the female professor started shooting people then she would obviously be shot herself. Or arrested, to be held in custody and labelled as insane. After all that is how the process worked and that was how 'they' killed Lee Harvey Oswald, before he could tell his tale. And in turn Jack Ruby.

Airwoman R. Jones required no prompting from her superior. It had all previously been discussed. All it necessitated was a mere facial expression on his part to put the plan into action.

Reagan Jones, herself a victim of mind control techniques, was devoid of fear or emotion when she determinedly clambered on-stage and moved like an unstoppable locomotive toward the podium, where she positioned the open briefcase and set it down on the lectern out of sight of the audience, but in full view of Thelma.

Backing off, the Airwoman and her superior inched discretely away before the 4th of July fireworks went off.

As it was, Colonel Kernel, was totally baffled by the fact that Professor Thelma Jones appeared generally to know more concerning the function and current activities taking place around the area known as so-called 51, than he did! She certainly was aware of a wide range of classified projects that she should have been totally unmindful of.

It occurred to the Colonel that it may be possible, during any command and control programme application, that information, subliminal or not, may seep over into the target individual's memory banks. It was like a leak of information trickling through the synaptic functioning of the brain.

Whilst at the same time it was obvious that she possessed a clear overall picture of how, and by whom, the world was currently being run? Not that the Colonel or even the Doctor knew all the idiosyncrasies concerning the mechanics of how the planet was being controlled.

A scant few open minded individuals however called it - 'The Dark State.'

Perhaps Thelma must have been staying up late tuned into 'YouTube!'

Though, in the final analysis, most of what she was repeating was the staple diet of any regular conspiracy theorist. And he, the Colonel, figured that any mildly discerning newspaper reporter would know just as much. Nonetheless, what was more troublesome to the Colonel was the fact that Thelma Jones had completely defied and resisted the mind control techniques placed upon her by himself, and his colleague, 'The Good Doctor.'

This non-response was unprecedented, having never to have occurred since he had become involved with the programme some years before. No one had ever resisted or acted contrary to any programme of mind control they had so far worked upon and experimented with.

If he hadn't known better, he would have conjectured that there was another entity playing in the game. Another unknown performer manipulating an additional metaphoric hand-set. An operator who was somehow jumbling up directives and therefore rendering the asset potentially useless. Probably before abandoning them entirely.

It momentarily occurred to the Colonel, just how little he actually did know and understand regarding the state of the world. After all he kept himself to himself, never or rarely picked up upon the 'word on the street,' which was a major part of his job description.

He was, if nothing else, ill-informed and struggled to discern the difference between fake or fact. He had for some time had faith in and believed upon his own lies.

Still, what he did know was on the evening when the team from Iowa University were picked up, they had witnessed a phenomena that they were not supposed to see. The Air Force's latest 'gravity defying' aerial marvel: code name 'Aurora,' a new generation of stealth fighter, that not only rendered the aircraft invisible to radar, but also, due to the speed it flew (Mach 6 or four-thousand miles per hour, thereabouts), could in full flight barely be seen by the human eye.

This particular test flight had originated out of Edwards USAF base in California, and had gone horribly wrong. The 'Aurora' guidance system had failed. The escorts had to fly low in case the Aurora craft hit the dirt and their intervention was required.

The crazy fly-boys had an idea and that was to somehow try under-pin the experimental aeroplane, before it grounded, and lift it just high enough, and long enough, to pitch it down inside the perimeter of what some people identified as so-called Area 51.

It was a ridiculous plan which would never have worked. Plus, by flying in low, the strange airborne anomaly had caused public alarm along a straight line running over Vegas and up towards Nellis. Before veering off to come down on Groom Lake, located over 100-miles to the west.

Now this black-black-black experimental aircraft was safely tucked up in the same hanger it had started its life on the drawing board, twenty-years before.

* * * * *

Be that as it may, there were other factors concerning Thelma's insight that they, the Colonel and she, the university professor, were not fully aware of.

Firstly, neither party was conscious of the fact that Thelma's pineal gland had been disturbed by 'The Good Doctor's' implant and was now very slowly becoming decalcified. A process which eventually would lead to it perform as all human pineal glands should.

Sodium fluoride added to tooth paste and global water supplies had been and still was, for decades gradually poisoning human beings, steering them away from their real potential. Just one of the many ways of dumbing down the human race. Fluoride, at the end of the day was cheap and plentiful, being no more than an industrial waste bi-product used in fertiliser.

The fully performing pineal gland helped to produced and regulate natural melanin, which assists with sleep patterns. Whilst at the same time enhancing human perception. When the gland was regulating at its full potential, the perspicacity of the person with an active functioning 'third eye' was increased a hundred-fold. Extra clarity was there, sensitivity increased, precognition and an understanding of deep esoteric knowledge were merely normal experiences.

Secondly, a further key attribute and benefit of possessing a working 'third eye' was that chemicals, such as fluoride, used to control or confuse the brain, no longer took any significant or lasting effect. Ultimately, no form of hypnosis practiced on a 'free' individual would have the desired outcome. The brain could potentially be released from all manner of manipulation.

* * * * * .

Meanwhile, in the Las Vegas auditorium questions directed at Thelma came in a wave of what were clearly mixed opinions and emotions. Some people cheered; others jeered. The Colonel, disregarding the gun, tried to take the podium over to use the question period to deflect most of what Thelma had said.

"It's OK folks, calm down, most of you know me, if you don't then you are about to be introduced: Colonel Kernel, Press Officer, United States Air Force, here at Nellis base. Happy to field your questions from the floor."

As the Colonel tried to intervene Thelma more or less automatically took the pistol hidden in the briefcase, behind the lectern and held it in the air before gently squeezing the trigger. The report of which caused mass panic and pandemonium around the auditorium.

Meanwhile outside, taking the gun shot as some form of signal to attack, the Marines, having now escaped the traffic hold up, broke into the building from the back door. Stun grenades sounded off and several canisters of Z33 sprayed their deadly mixture into the auditorium.

At that point Frank took hold of Thelma, whilst the Colonel had already tried to grab the gun from her. The six-foot plus footballer mentality finally kicked in and the younger and fitter Frank landed a blow to the side of the Colonel's head. This was followed swiftly by a second blow to the other side of his head, causing a short spell of concussion.

The Airwoman Jones read the situation well and tried to lead her superior towards the side emergency exit. Dragging the half crawling Colonel along behind her, she crashed out of the emergency exit door into the light of day. Behind her wisps of toxic Z33 gas filled the auditorium, where the press and other media representatives alike were falling like flies.

Having hold of the gun Thelma levelled it at the two Air Force uniformed personnel. Moments later they were sitting in the USAF Lincoln. Airwoman Jones in the driving seat, attentively following her captor's lucid driving directions. Frank had already settled down in the front next to the pretty chauffeur. Thelma sat comfortably in the rear seats with the gun pointed at the Colonel's broad chest. They moved quickly, despite the presence of military and police vehicles, their passage aided by the Lincoln's military Camo' paint job.

Without any form of hindrance, they sailed straight out of the car lot and headed to Main, where they picked up Highway 18 to North Vegas. And then eventually turning north-west onto 93, before some miles further up the road connecting to Highway 33 and the town of Rachel Nevada. Which was the only enclave for a thousand-miles that Thelma could think of going to.

Meanwhile, Colonel K. Kernel in a mild state of shock, found it impossible to settle back, particularly since there was a gun pointed in his direction. He sensed on the other hand, that he could seize the gun from the woman without much effort and at any time. Except, he decided not to take any chances or punitive action, because he was intrigued as to exactly what she would do next under the influence of the chemical cocktail that had previously been dispensed to her. She was under his control anyway, or so he thought.

Having given her the challenge and the freedom to make the decisions he would be happy to go with her to wherever it was she wanted to go.

For now.

* * * * *

The Vegas press conference event turned out to be the worst and most outrageous terrorist attack on US soil since 9/11. According to that was the media. It was a debacle that eclipsed all previous terrorist related incidents. At least that was what it felt like.

Left to pick up the pieces? A Marine Corp Sergeant and his squad. Reinforcements were eventually pulled in from any place the military could find them. At least forty news reporters and associated personnel were hospitalised having been rendered unconscious, by a chemical agent the nature of which and source remained unknown.

Be that as it may, the same Marine Sergeant, relishing the opportunity to be in the news, spoke to what media was left standing in the car-lot outside. He announced before any clearance was given, that an Islamic terror cell had attacked members of the press during an address by an official Air Force spokesperson. Who had, by all understanding of the situation, been kidnapped by the same terror faction along with an Air Force Colonel. The fanatics may still be at large in the local vicinity, he sternly warned.

It was assumed that the terror group known as: 'SISI' were involved and were generally thought to be the most likely perpetrators of the atrocity.

Or, that was the overriding opinion amongst the members of the public who were randomly interviewed for the cameras by a Vegas cable news station.

Before that was, the act of terrorism being rapidly called into question by the so-called experts that randomly appeared in news rooms across America to offer their priceless opinions.

There being scant evidence to suggest such a terror group was involved. Conversely, the same so-called experts later admitted the act of violence 'had' been perpetrated by radical Muslims. Apparently, three terrorists had been shot and killed and surprisingly, their Iranian and Syrian passports had (conveniently), been discovered at the scene.

The CIA soon made their mark and took control. A so-called 'Shadow Team' appeared from seemingly nowhere, as did two conspicuous 'Men in Black.' Just in case there 'was' an alien connection.

Meanwhile, amongst the utter confusion, all those caught up in the event and unfortunately in attendance at the Air Force sponsored press event were required by Home Land Security (who invoked anti-terror legislation and powers), to hand over to the security forces any and all video or audio footage and any written dialogue or texts pertaining to the tragic incident. Also, everyone had to surrender to the military and or the local Sheriff's department to be searched and interrogated. Groups of journalists were gradually rounded up and taken away to be grilled. Four arrest were made from among the Press Corp, for possession of various 'Class B' drugs, including marijuana. It appeared 'Gonzo Journalism' was still alive the US of A. Other than that, no one was allowed to leave the scene.

The response to Colonel Kernel's coded emergency signal had been expertly and professionally responded to, proving the USA was ready for anything the Muslim terrorists could throw at them.

Local heroes emerged; their praises sung from every quarter. Eye-witness accounts spoke of seeing terrorists shooting and running into the conference building then out the other side, across the car-lot and into a mall. Footage taken on a mobile phone showed confused people fleeing for their lives and terrorists randomly firing automatic weapons into the hapless crowds.

Fortunately, and as was to be anticipated, the FBI were soon there. As it happened all three American security agencies had field offices in Vegas. Not surprising as the entire Nevada entertainment enclave was and is owned by corporate giants who consider themselves to be, and are, above the law. And of course, not forgetting the Mafia criminal fraternities.

A high-ranking White House official was about to draw up a statement, and the President of the United States of America would address the nation on prime-time and reassure the country that they were safe, and that he would retaliate and punish those who had attacked Americans on American soil.

Within the hour US missile cruisers in the Mediterranean Sea released a hail of Tomahawk cruise missiles in the direction of Syria and Iran

46

Headlines

Las Vegas and Nevada press, radio and television stations:

'WWIII starts in Vegas - Rat Pack concert will go ahead.'

'The Aliens Have Landed' - casino boss welcomes them to the gaming tables.

Terror cell exposed - plan to rob casino - three aliens admit involvement.

National Headlines-

Iowa University faculty involved in terror-plot.
FBI investigates.

University Magnetronic Research Unit exposed - cover-up for alien invasion of the planet.

Missing University Principal Jones wanted for questioning on foiled espionage plot.

Iowa State University Professor, and Air Force official spokesperson Thelma Jones, makes contact with alien visitors - insists they're friendly!

Air Force official spokesperson states according to his understanding of the situation, a university professor had been kidnapped, along with a high-ranking Air Force Colonel, by the terrorist cell.

National and International Headlines -

Mid-East Conflict triggered by Terror Attack.

US Navy let loose cruise missiles.

USAF Leak existence of Secret New Fighter.

Mach 6 stealth bombers deployed.

USAF Admit they are probable cause of UFO Nevada sightings.

Alternative 'free media' -

'I was right all along' states British conspiracy theorist.

Alien prisoners held as hostages.

Roswell - the answer to decades old mystery.

The speculation continued ...

47

Principal J. Jones Junior goes to Vegas

Principal J. Jones Junior felt it best to hire a helicopter: Trump Air Taxi Service, (TATS) paid for by the university, of course. It was a matter of urgency and utmost importance to get him to Las Vegas, which is where he suspected Gracie Lin Jones, thief and potential blackmail artist, to be holed up. It was a mere process of deduction. The itinerary file for the Magnetronic Research Unit had been opened on his computer terminal and not closed. A big over-site made by his thieving burglar friends.

Her partner in crime? Obviously, the camera operator Gracie Lin had been using at the presentation event.

The chopper would put him down on the roof of one of the main hotels along the Vegas strip. He had booked it all using the faculty Amex credit card. Now he was, he supposed, a notorious and sort after VIP, he decided he might as well fully enjoy himself whilst he was there in the town where the lights never went down, and booked a show: 'The New Rat Pack.'

He also went on line - 'Adult Services USA' and browsed a few adult escort sites and eventually, after a great deal of scrutiny, engaged for himself; 'Suzy Cream Cheese,' a leggy blonde, to come visit him in room 217 for a full massage, with all the seductive trimmings and of course a 'happy ending.'

His hand luggage did not amount to much, after all he was not planning to stay for too long. Just an overnight wash-bag and a '.45' hand-gun. His '.45' Licensed, legitimate and kept ready and waiting, just in case someone ever broke into his apartment and he had to defend himself.

48

The Getaway

"Just exactly what is it you know Professor Jones?"

"Know?"

"Yes, Know, and please do you have to keep pointing that gun at me? I mean to say if we happen to hit a dip in the road it might go off, scattering my brains across the back seat, and of course yourself."

Thelma paused for a moment's reflection.   "I promise," the Colonel gave a mock scouting salute, "I promise I will be good."

"Good? Is that possible?" Frank Quipped from the front seat.

The Air Force woman driving, looked at her rear view and tilted it so that she could see Thelma clearly.

"Look, you are in a very difficult and dangerous situation. We all are in our different ways."

"So, how's that whoever you are?" Frank was thinking back to his double ear-buster that he had afflicted upon the Colonel. It was a move he had learnt from his MMA (Mixed Martial Arts) classes back at college. Hit a guy hard enough on the ear and it would ring forever.

"I am Colonel Kernel USAF at your disposal, or should I say service? Of course, we have all met before. But I doubt you recall."

"I do, yes I do recall," Thelma spoke with pain in her voice. "Something, well not all of what you did."

"And there are two more of us, the others." Added Frank. Who, as he spoke, could not help but mentally undress the female Air Force driver. He was after all a typical testosterone fuelled male.

"Yes, I am aware that there are two more of you. Where, please tell, might they be at this moment in time?"

"Back at the old diner I guess," Thelma suddenly realised she did not fully know exactly where the diner was to be located. She looked out of the rear passenger windows for signs, anything familiar land-marks that might jog her memory and lead them out of the city limits and away from the chaos she seemed to have instigated.

"Yes, they are waiting for us and we need to get back to them. They are in Rachel, a little town, on 33."

"I know it, I know where you mean." Retorted the Air Force driver. They were headed in the right direction

Meanwhile Thelma cautiously tightened her grip on the gun. Whilst the Colonel swallowed hard.

"Ah well it will be an interesting reunion." The Colonel added with a resigned intonation in his voice.

Thelma decided to open up to this anomalous military man, who although he wore the appropriate customary uniform, it did not quite fit him. Not in the meaning of size and cut, but rather in the sense of belonging. The evidently African American Colonel simply did not appear comfortable dressed up in a typical military-style uniform.

Thelma thought for a while before concluded that she did recall some of the details concerning when and where she had first encountered the Colonel's presence.

On that evening he was dressed in the type of clothes you would wear when going on vacation. Together with a plus-sized pair of hand-stitched golfing shoes. Very out of place for the military, and not something Thelma was going to misremember in a while.

Be that as it may, Thelma continued to mentally recount what else she could remember from the previous nights. An overbearing image of a Blackbird spy-plane was etched into her mind. Such beauty, such fine design. Yet so deadly, like the world's most poisonous snake.

Then she recalled there were many flashing orange warning lights, accompanied by alarms sounding off.

The glitter and glamour of a stage show. Then more flashing lights added to the spectacular Vegas-style illumination show. Could it have been Vegas? The main strip? Thelma had never been. Or, perhaps not, just the insides of an aging aircraft hanger and no more.

She further recounted another light source, brighter than all else. A luminosity that appeared to flow out from the furthest corner of the vast dusty hanger.

That was it.

There was nothing else stored in Thelma's memory-bank that she could recall, apart from whatever had occurred the next morning. A dawn that actually was not the next morning, but another unknown lost morning. One with no rhyme or reason, only to its waking, as if from a dream, driven and motivated by desire. Lusting after one another like crazed vampires at sunset. All triggered by a wild and extreme phone message about …?

She deliberately stopped herself before even thinking about insane trigger codes. Commands that were still swimming around in her head. Thoughts and feelings, she initially had no control over.

Though now, that was slowly all beginning to change.

"And," Thelma concluded, "what I can't expunge from my mind, are the 'pleading' voices I distinctly keep hearing in my head."

Thelma spoke as if she were addressing no one in particular. Her words aimlessly broadcast, released into the ether, as if someone or something may latch onto them and explain what they meant.

As she continued to reflect further concerning the 'voices,' Thelma, seemingly as a form of concession toward the Colonel, slowly and calculatingly lowered the gun somewhat. The barrel was now aimed at the Colonel's vulnerable groin area.

"What were, or who were, or where did those voices come from?"

The Colonel tightened his lip. He could, so he thought, at this juncture tell the over-eager professor anything she wanted to hear. Of that form of approach, he was a seasoned expert. Whatever the requests and needs might be. Spin them a yarn or two, tell them what they want to hear and then perhaps they will shut the fuck up! Or, that's what he supposed. In truth he had little or no idea what she was talking about? Strange voices-indeed!

"I actually have no idea what any voices you may have allegedly heard could have originated from." The Colonel announced. "No one on the entire Nellis base that I know of, has ever referred to voices coming from any one of the hangers."

A form of embarrassing silence clouded over the group. The Airwoman driver was latching on to every word. She would have dearly loved to enjoin the conversation, but had to keep at least one eye on the road.

"Let me explain." Thelma tried to make herself comfortable just as the speeding Lincoln hit a hole in the road, causing those in the back to roll around a little. The gun jabbed the military man awkwardly and he winced in anticipation of the gun firing and ending his love-life.

"The point being that we are 'all' now in trouble. You Miss Jones have broken every single one of the official secrets acts available to humankind. Enough to send you away for life. And your muscle-bound friend here, will also go down as an accomplice."

Frank had never considered as much, that he might be put on trial and imprisoned as a traitor, which in some states carried the death penalty. More than ever he wished he was back home at a practice match with a gal by his side. Perhaps the Air Force missy? But then he recalled the slip of paper and the phone number, and it occurred to him these two, now their prisoners, might have something going on between them. The testosterone fuelled football Jock felt a tinge of jealousy.

"Guantanamo bay for you fellah with all the real terrorists." The Colonel remarked, pointing towards Frank glibly.

"May I ask you something Miss, err Jones?"

Thelma looked up toward the rear view and caught the Air Force woman's eye.

"What?"

The lady driving faltered for a moment. Thinking

Thelma was distracted, the Colonel half-moved to grab the gun, but Thelma had seen it coming and thrust the gun barrel up under the Air Force man's chin. "Nice try, but you need to get up early if you going to mess with me."

Even Frank quaked in his shoes.

Right now, no sensible person needed to be fooling around with Thelma Jones. She acted as if she were possessed. Despite the fact she thought she had at least partially gained her sanity back. Truth was though, her aggression was due to the fact that Thelma, regardless of her steadily healing pineal gland, still had the chemical-induced killer-instinct drugs frothing away inside of her. Her out of character actions were all normal signs post a Mega 1-90 procedure.

Nevertheless, it was always possible that once triggered, the mind control procedure, and the harsh consequences of the programme, might never fade away.

"No, I mean, it, we, I want, I need to ask you a question." The Airwoman driver sounded sincere.

"No more funny tricks eh?" Thelma addressed both her prisoners.

"I can't do anything from here, I am driving."

Thelma gave her some leeway.

"I err Miss, I mean Thelma."

"Go on then what is it?" Thelma was surprised to be called 'Thelma' by a person she did not really know.

"Well it's kind of personal."

"Please, let me leave the room why not!?" Frank was already tiring of the convoluted dialogue.

"OK, here goes…Who was your great-grandfather on your father's side of the Jones clan?"

Thelma was taken by surprise. A family tree? What the hell was that to do with anything? Regardless Thelma mentally pondered, counting the generations backwards. "Great-great-grandfather you say?"

"Yeah, great-great-grandfather." The Airwoman driver possessed an excited edge to her voice.

"You mean: 'Iowa Jones,' the guy who helped

233

establish the State of Iowa?" Thelma was guessing out loud, this was not her area of expertise.

But it was the vehicle driver's.

"No, here wait, 1838, that was your great-great-great-great grandfather. The 'Indian Killer' they called him. Now he had children, lots of them, one was Jack, Jack George Jones, He helped establish the state as part of the Union, founded in 1846. After Jack there was …"

"How much longer is this question going to take … Miss err?" Thelma had no time for guessing games.

"Jones."

"Jones?"

"Yes, that's my point, we share a common ancestry. We have the same great-great-great -great, or maybe just great-great-great grandfather. We are cousins Miss Jones, from both our mother's and father's sides of the Jones line from Iowa."

"So how come you are in Nevada playing army games?" Thelma was disinterested and skeptical.

"Well, like a lot of Jones people, I had to get out. Iowa was too small a state for me to get lost in. So, I left home."

Thelma understood such reasoning, the Jones family were an oppressive bunch at the best of times.

"It's such a vast family. My great-grandmother must have been your great-great aunt?"

Thelma had no idea. She snatched a deep breathe and relaxed her hand momentarily from the gun. Much to the Colonel's relief. It was beginning to make her arm ache anyway.

"And what's the point you are making eh? What's your name anyhow?"

"It's Reagan!"

"Jesus!"

Despite Thelma's lack of knowledge when it came to genealogy, the name 'Reagan' rang an ancestral bell. "Are you my great-uncle John Paul's daughter?"

There was clearly a family resemblance. The nose and

234

overall equine facial shape were similar, Regan's hair, part hidden beneath her Air Force head-gear, was however much darker than Thelma's.

"Granddaughter!" Reagan corrected. "I haven't seen you since we were in kindergarten!"

Thelma was aware that John Paul Jones Junior had previously served in the Iowa State administration. He had been Governor for a spell, and was one of the main patrons of the Iowa State University, whilst also during his life-time been a well-known 'Shriner.'

"So, we are sort of cousins then, second or third?"

"I don't know, Thelma replied, "I mean now is hardly the time to talk family business!" Ever careful Thelma suspected some form of diversionary rues was about to take place.

The Air Force driver thought differently. She was helping pass the time, with a view to further along down the line, disarming Thelma. By doing so she might just be able to redeem herself, as she well knew the Colonel would ultimately tear her apart and feed her to the hungry Congressional wolves, that would set up a committee to investigate just what had happened and more significantly who was to blame for what had taken place at the press conference.

To save his own skin, the Colonel would undoubtedly tilt the onus her way and she would be the one to lose her pension and end her life in a military stockade. Therefore, relative or not, if she could be seen as the heroine of the piece then let it be so.

Meanwhile Frank had been keeping a close eye on the lady Air Force driver. Under the Camo' outfit she was keen, a good figure, curvy hips, but slim with it. A woman he would definitely want to date sometime in the future. Who was he kidding? What future?

49

Kruger goes to Vegas

Kruger, was now making his way back to Rachel where he had previously lost contact with his men. To cap it all, the phones belonging to at least two of the 'geeks' had now gone dead.

He had arrived in Las Vegas in good time. Following as he did the GPS trackers, he had previously fixed to the 'geek's' Jeep.

After turning off 93 onto 15 he continued along the road that split Nellis AFB in half. The small arms range to the north, and base proper to the south. He drove along the road that passed the famous: 'Vegas Speedway track.'

Once in town along 15 he could see the situation was not right and was soon forced to grind to a halt at a Highway Patrol check point. Apparently the centre of Vegas was closed down due to a terrorist attack. He, as with everyone else, was ordered to go back and take the diversion round Henderson and Boulder City.

Tired and partially confused, he turned around feeling dejected before heading back toward Rachel along 15. Only stopping over for coffee at a truck stop. Whereupon, he saw, on the top of the hour news, a video clip and still pictures of the ass-wipe Colonel Kernel holding onto a lectern, whilst unsuccessfully trying to shout a great number of people down. At the same time as wrestling a gun from? Could it be true? From one of the 'geek' crew that he had apprehended a couple of nights before! Who incidentally he had been trying to restrain and manipulate using the mind-control process that he had picked up, or rather stolen, from the strange, but highly respected, 'Good Doctor' Who, as far as Kruger was concerned, was the 'atypical' Nazi type. A quality he liked and valued in the otherwise poor excuse of a man.

Kruger could not contain himself and broke into a belly laugh like no other in recorded history.

50

Principal J. Jones hits Vegas

Principal J. Jones wasted no time. He had no conclusive idea whatsoever concerning how to find Gracie Lin Jones. The woman his loaded .45 sidearm was intended for. If, that is, she did not cooperate.

What he was not aware of was the fact that Bud Always-Jones, had already been instructed by his 'boss' to edit out a slice of their bedroom action and post it up on the University of Iowa face-book page. The clip clearly showed the sad old Principal 'dogging' a woman who was wearing nothing other than black and white plastic over-the-knee boots and matching peak cap. All energetically acted out across a plush bed, accompanied by an additional voiceover and special visual effects, which Bud had edited in for good measure.

The additional audio went something like: *'fuck me big boy.' 'Come on give it to me harder! Harder! Harder!'* Plus, a great deal of moaning. All in all, it lasted seventy-five seconds which was sufficient for it to be entertaining and easily consumed by mindless students. Therefore, the clip went viral, with over a million hits in just a few hours.

Ignorance they say is bliss and in the first instance the Principal of Iowa State had no idea why this distant female cousin of his would want to seduce him. Other than she wanted to steal highly sensitive files that belonged to him, of which he alone knew of their existence and importance.

It eventually dawned on the man of letters that 'she' 'must' have been aware of the significance of the documented information he had filed away, and reasons for him wanting to keep such records strictly private and confidential. How was that possible? Only a few highly respected, upright and honourable men of integrity shared the 'knowledge' with J. Jones. All of who were his fellow 'Shriners.'

Could it be that Gracie Lin had already 'worked' on other 'Iowan' 'Shriners?' A notion that was far from being in the realms of impossibility. If so, then which one of the 'Inner-Shrine' members had been 'got-at?'

However, placing all reasonable speculation aside for now, his instincts told him she and her film making friend would be found where the news was being made. According to the American Tabloid Press WWIII was about to take place, with Russia now being accused of plotting the recent terrible terror attack on Las Vegas, sacred American soil.

Too busy with other problems on his mind, Principal J. Jones had not taken the time to fully review the latest press, radio and TV broadcasts.

Consequently, as he meandered by a news stand, he stopped for a moment, before an ice-cold sweat crept down his spine. There in front of him, taking up half a front page, in black and white was Professor Jones, 'his' Professor Thelma Jones. The picture had caught her in an out of character aggressive stance, holding a gun in the air, whilst standing behind a speaker's lectern in what appeared to be some form of auditorium.

The Principal had to look twice and rub his already weary eyes. Yes, it was her, standing large as life right before him. Captioned as: *'Professor Jones' from Iowa State science faculty.*

'His' University.

The worst was yet to come, in the left-hand bottom columns of the front page was another picture.

It was him!

Below what was an old press photograph of the Principal, was the bi-line: *'Terror Mastermind'* ... *Principal J. Jones Junior of Iowa State University.*

His life and career floated by him.

The Principal quickly fished into his pocket and came

out with loose change, with which he paid for several papers and retreated with them into a globally branded coffee shop.

51

Gracie Jones arrives at Rachel

Gracie Lin Jones lit another cigarette and looked disparagingly about the run-down diner.

The place was empty.

Other than a ripped pool table, dusty floor, fused neon sign outside. This place had not seen a customer for months maybe longer.

Unlike the 'Little Ale Inn' out on the highway, which caught all the passing trade. On Highway 33 there was the gas station, the Rachel library and information centre, and gift shop; with its giant alien figurine standing by the entrance, a sight no one could possibly miss. On the town sign by the highway were hundreds of stickers and notes wishing the alien visitors well. Whilst inside the emporium you could just about buy anything branded as being alien you could imagine. Including Star Trek and Star Wars model figures. Tee shirts celebrating and commemorating the X-Files, Close Encounters, Lost in Space, Cowboys v Aliens, Men in Black and more. All being figments of someone's imagination. These were all images of fictitious characters, no more that representations of little grey men, reptilians and Nordics types. Nothing however was real, but rather generated by a script writer's pen. The myth however must be perpetuated, the merchandise must keep being churned out. The movies had to continually earn more and more money from prequels, sequels, and sequel-prequels.

Tell the people what they want to hear.

It was obvious to Gracie Lin that someone was making a shit-load of cash out of this little circus act. Clearly, she thought to herself, the idea of men from outer-space running around was both pertinent and relevant to the needs and objectives of the United States government. A

241

thought that she had been reflecting on for a few days. Wikipedia had told her everything she needed to know about little grey men from Mars and conspiracy theories in general. There must have been a logical reason (gold?), why 'they' wanted to keep people off of a country-sized piece of mountainous Nevadan wasteland. Or, was all the cloak and dagger secret stuff just to ensure the same curious folks would keep on coming back to see for themselves, and consequently spend more money in the gift-shop? Was it all simply part of the Disney corporation?

They came to look at nothing, thinking it was something, when it never was, and never had been and never would be anything. All the time this kept prying conspiratorial eyes off the ball. Looking at the wrong game meant they were not looking at the real game. Or, so she supposed.

* * * * *

Meanwhile, wistful thoughts aside, in the diner before her, Gracie Lin observed an old couple who were consoling each other behind what was once probably a busy service counter. At a table towards the corner of the room, she noted, what she supposed was a man, sitting bent and hunched up, head in hands. On the floor a mobile cell phone with broken screen asked to be picked up and placed on another rickety table, where, to Gracie Lin's surprise, Diana Rogers (who she knew well), sat wearing a pained and somewhat, lugubrious expression. The attractive young woman was still wearing the same, now crumpled and dusty, once brightly coloured jogging suit she had previously worn at the university send-off. (How remiss of her!) She looked out of place dressed as she was, in mainly pink. Particularly when compared to the dark grey, browns and black interior decoration and atmosphere of the crumbling diner.

Gracie needed a leak, so without speaking she located

the cobweb infested rest room and, still smoking, disappeared behind the outer-door, and into one of the two vacant cubicles.

52

Thelma et al En Route to Rachel

"There is so much you don't know or understand." The Colonel coldly stated.

"Look, we came here in good faith, just to start our research project, that's all. Not to spy, to snoop, to commit acts of terrorism and above all not to be fugitives." Thelma was not acting her normal, good-natured composed 'spinsterish' lady-self. A woman who would not dream of performing in an aggressive manner. And would certainly never speak out of turn.

"Now this is what 'you' need to understand Colonel! So! Here's what we're going to do and that is: drop 'you' off someplace in the middle of the scrub and then we're going to find my team members and then we're going to drive as far and as fast as we can away from all this insanity."

Natural reaction thought Colonel Kernel, she wanted to find her compatriots, quite what would be expected of her.

Conversely, this was never going to happen. By his estimation they had another fifty-sixty-miles to go before route 33 and the road to Rachel, fondly known as: 'The Extraterrestrial Highway.' He should know as he had made this two-hour or longer round trip on far too many occasions.

As it was, to relieve the stress and pressure of having a gun levelled at him, he tried to think of everything he could recall regarding the town of Rachel. A place he had not visited in a long while. First time around it was fascinating, then after a few visits the gift shop became stale, mundane and prosaic.

He did eventually recall to himself, that Rachel was an enclave with a sad history. A little girl, Rachel Jones had died, this was way back. Her father was a miner, up out there in the mountains, where they once used to mine Borax, Arsenic, Silver, Lead, and a mess of other heavy metals. Most, if not all, were toxic to human beings and animal life in general.

The girl's father got sick and they moved out. But still, even after the mines were all closed down, they (the 'Atomic Energy Commission'), were mysteriously continuing to monitor the region. Thanks to the mining the area was already foul, the water, the dirt, the air all unclean. So why not use the facility to test H Bombs?

Seems logical!

So, they did, not in the immediate vicinity of where the truck-stop of a town Rachel still continues (just about), to stand today. But miles deeper in, where the old mines once were, high up in the mountains south-west of what was to become Highway 33.

Subsequently the town was dedicated to the memory of the little girl, who, like her father, contracted and died of a cancer-based illness.

The government never paid out a cent in compensation, and had never done so to anyone since.

The way the government was able to legally wriggle out of its honourable duty to compensate its tax-paying citizens, was by way of legal gobbledygook and bull-shit, delivered by hot-shot-over-paid lawyers acting for the government. Who callously stated: *'you cannot pay compensation to people who have died or been made sick by contamination from sources known or unknown, if there was no source of contamination there in the first instance.'*

According to the government and it's lawyers at the time, the now so-called 'Mercury' nuclear testing sites did not exist.

Therefore no one could possibly come into contact with any radioactive contamination, if there were no sites where bombs had been detonated. Thus, releasing contamination. According to all official sources, there never was any nuclear testing ground in Nevada. Just as there was no such place as so-called Area 51, and the Colonel could happily live with that.

Simple.

And, as it was, the Colonel based all of his fake press-releases and contradictory news broadcasts using the exact same principles of denying, and then denying that you have denied anything in the first instance.

There never was any 'Mercury' testing ground, therefore no base equates to no bombs. No bombs meant no contamination by radioactive substances. All adds up to no grounds for lawsuits and compensation payouts.

Sweet.

Keep the contradictions flowing and make no comment outside of an outright denial. That's the key to keeping secrets.

All despite the fact that Yucca Lake and Papoose Lake were polluted back then, and still are to this day. Mere toxic waste dumps, not that anyone official could or would verify such a statement. These places weren't there, so no point in looking out for them.

Life around Rachel was quiet, once-upon-a-small-mining-town-time. Then the Roswell myth kicked off just after the cessation of WWII. The USA had a new enemy, the Soviet Union and the rise of global communism. But that was insufficient. The Soviets simply did not cut the mustard. The USA had to help them develop their nuclear programme in order to keep-up with the USA, who even allowed them to take the lead in rocket propulsion technology. First man in Space, Uri Gagarin a Russian Cosmonaut!

No, what was required was a more dangerous and provocative otherworldly threat, and that came via the movies, with Hollywood churning out a glut of low-budget 'hammy' flicks that scared women and encourage young men to enlist to fight the hidden enemy in their midst. Korea was next up, which would be closely followed by Vietnam. Proxy wars that no one actually won or lost. War for the sake of war.

The USA had the edge, but it was a fine edge. Spy planes became the business of, what was then commonly known (to those 'inside'), as 'Groom Lake.'

Most interested parties guessed that the Air Force were developing innovative high-speed, high-flying advanced aircraft technology. The U2 was featured in 'Jane's' Defence round-up. Well, if 'Jane's' knew about it then so did the Soviets!

All of this spy-plane malarkey was short lived, as it was not long before satellites flying overhead could do the job faster, better and what was most important; could continually deliver accurate imagery. Why risk a pilot's life when a machine can do the job?

'The Blackbird' spy plane was, once 'official', eventually hung out to dry by the military, rapidly followed by the Hollywood Technicolor inspired conspiracy theorists.

However, there were those who simply would not let the secrets go. If spy-planes were not on the menu, then it had to be pieces of flying saucer debris from Roswell that was now rousing fresh interest. And these pieces were all stored up in hangers on part of so-called Area 51, the region supposedly known as; 'Groom Lake.' It was all there, together with a bunch of aliens that the government kept secret.

And the myth becomes a legend, before becoming mainstream belief, philosophy and even in some cases a religion!

The Roswell event horizon took place due to USAF incompetence and inability to control the media. Everyone was suddenly a UFO hunter in their spare time.

As it was, after a few years, interest in UFOs dipped, until that was the 1970s, when a certain guy (allegedly working for the government), blew-the-whistle and came out with a number of detailed accounts of how he worked with others, to reverse-engineer captured alien space crafts. He had seen artefacts that had allegedly been reclaimed after the previous notorious Roswell incident.

Back in 1953 the same or similar Roswell scenario was once again repeated; when the Air Force somehow got lucky and managed to down a saucer-shaped craft whilst taking a number of 'aliens' captive.

It had been the original whistle-blower who first worked on the downed craft who once more 'blew the whistle.' Having released to the media what he believed was the truth, he suddenly disappeared; never to be seen or heard of again. An occurrence that did nothing more than multiply the numbers of interested people across the globe, motivating them to sit up and take notice of what was going on.

The 'Great Awakening.'

In fact, the man's unaccounted for disappearance only served to inspire a new generation of avid and often fanatical UFO hunters.

Clearly the government had to rapidly respond to the whistle-blowing event/s; to ensure such sensitive information never hit the streets again. Hence, the insidious covert mind-control programme was launched under the appealing and euphemistic code: 'Majestic.' The primary programme's aim being to ensure that people working for the government, or on government projects, kept their mouths tightly shut.

As it was, this new-found-classified- reverse-engineering-whistle-blowing-information was never released and made public. Regardless, hundreds of curious tourist still visited the empty and barren Roswell location.

Ironically, the Rachel tourist enclave, had absolutely not even a tenuous connection with aliens or alien visitation what-so-ever.

Outside of the distant Roswell strewn debris mystery, and the 1953 crash, not one single alien or UFO account concerning Rachel existed in any official or unofficial files. Yet, popular culture talked-up this once quiet enclave, into what became the most known and talked about secret military base in the world, so-called Area 51.

Old, long-since filed away Roswell interviews were resurrected and looked over, and in some cases re-opened. Further-more, new witness came out of the woodwork and even more interviews were conducted by the fresh breed of enthusiastic Ufologists. And at the same time business in Rachel came good.

Now it had seen better days.

53

Gracie Lin at the Rachel Diner

Gracie Lin looked about with an expression that said - *'someone get me a coffee.'* No one obliged.

"What! So, have you been following us?" Diana Rogers was more than in a state of utter confusion. One moment she was fighting a couple of guys for her life, for a vague set of reasons she had already forgotten. The next she is confronted by an out of place ghostly apparition, a cruel spectre - Cruella de Ville, was the comparable character that sprung into Diana's shaken and tremulous imagination.

Gracie Lin Jones was more than content to play such a star part.

Diana reflected - *'sometimes everything gets a little too much and you have to allow the cork to pop!'* She continued repeating a 'popping cork mantra,' one designed to maintain a person's sanity. In her mind she visualised yelping and pleading black and white Dalmatian puppies, all jumping up at her whilst avoiding the spike-like high-heels of - *'she who would have you skinned alive.'* A smug - *'I am in control'* expression across her cruel and unforgiving black and white lips.

"What the fuck are you doing here?" The tension broke.

"Tut tut, such manners Diana. Has that cousin of mine got to you yet? Or perhaps yes! That's it, she 'has' got to and at you. I can just imagine these last few lonely nights the pair of you together as a team. Girls in one bunk, guys in another. Oh, so very cosy. Where is she anyway?"

"Never you mind!" Duncan appeared from lying down and raised his head a little only to note a camera lens pointed towards him. Curious.

The scruffy, hippy of a guy, eye-balled the film

recording device. Bud Always-Jones noted his interest and sat down beside him.

The pair immediately 'clicked.'

"You're going to ask me I imagine, how I found you hiding out here in the middle of no place? Oh yes, and I heard some very disturbing reports on the airwaves as we were driving up here. Something about terror attacks and my cousin? At last she is making a stand against the establishment... Good for her! If she were a man, she would have balls."

"Women can have balls, the metaphoric type." As ever Duncan was clowning around. Something Gracie Lin did not care for.

"I don't know any more than that," Diana cut in. "Just that we were set upon by a couple of big ugly guys, just fifteen-minutes ago. I have no idea where they are now, but they may be back with reinforcements. We are not safe here, none of us are."

"How exciting! Be glad you have a member of the 'Press Corp,' here at your disposal, with camera operator to hand. If that is he can tear himself away from your boyfriend over there." Gracie was as sarcastic as ever.

Duncan sat up, the sudden thought of him being Diana's boyfriend appealed to his male libido. Whilst Bud positioned himself with his camera mounted on his shoulder, he was ready to record anything that was about to go down.

"You see Diana the answers to your questions are contained right here in this Chinese made tin piece of junk. She motioned to the camera. Not the camera man.

"This is as good as it gets ladies, let me tell you." Bud was referring glibly to the camera, but his thoughts were elsewhere.

"Open up the viewing window for me Bud."

He responded accordingly and held the mini screen open at Gracie Lin's eye-level. You see Diana dearest I captured you here in the lens, you have been my prisoner and I have been able to follow you wherever you have been."

Diana had no idea what the crazy women was talking about.

"Take a look for yourself it's like looking in a mirror…"

Diana carefully peeped into the small aperture and saw what was the diner, her current surroundings and environment. Then to her surprise there appeared a feint silhouette, which, if you gently moved the screen and tilted it around, a dark, almost foreboding shape could just be discerned.

"You see that is you Diana, from when we filmed your interview at that ghastly award ceremony, with those ridiculous dirty old men all dressed up in stupid uniforms."

Diana said nothing but inwardly tended to agree with the sentiment.

"I am sorry, I have no idea what you are talking about."

"What she's saying is," Bud butted in, "we have been following you since you left Iowa. I should know cos I have been made to tag along to do the driving."

Gracie scowled at her operative, as if he had no right to an opinion of his own.

"The camera Diana," Gracie continued, "it's the lens to the world, my world. Whoever's image I have captured I can see into their lives. I know what they see, hear, feel, taste and touch. It's like magic."

"It 'is' magic if you're askin' me! Black magic!" Once again Budd added his unwelcome opinion.

Gracie snapped the camera viewing window closed. Diana was none the wiser, but for everyone's sake, she acted as if she understood and was accepting of the bizarre suggestion.

All this time the old couple had been cowering behind the diner's dusty counter. Scattered all over the floor were knives and forks, broken plates, cups, pots and pans, all clear evidence of some form of struggle. Hillary began to sweep up while Clint went to look at the camera which had now been returned to Bud.

"I knows about this." The old man began to explain. "They did it awhile back. 'Remote something or other viewing' they called it. CIA, they wanted to look at Soviet secrets so they got people with so-called special abilities, and sat them in rooms with coffee and cigarettes and pens and paper and got them to think about and write down what they thought they saw."

"Yes I am sure!" Gracie, not being the centre of attention, was dismissive as usual. Unless something truly of importance was about to be said by her alone, she displayed no what-so-ever interest in whatever anyone else had to say.

Diana remained lost in thought, silent whilst the guys, now apparently best of friends, were sitting at their own table, probably chatting about the next big football game.

"I should know young lady because I was one of them guys. Not here, but back down south where we, Hillary and me, used to live. Before here, but then I volunteered again. 'Remote Viewing,' yes that's what they began to call it. Had college kids messing with stuff, telepathy and all. Holding up cards and you had to guess the number or picture. Ass-holes most of them, just kids. Seeing things that aint there and drawing pictures of aliens, and Soviet planes, and tanks and missiles and stuff. We were paid a few bucks. Then they wanted people to stare into mirrors to see what they could on the other side. Foolish people if you ask me, but I needed the dollars, so I went along and saw some mighty strange happenings... For instance, two big high buildings in New York tumbling down, dust, confusion, all hell breaking loose ..."

* * * * *

"I heard that Skunk Works have a tunnel leading to Edwards Air Force Base down in California." Bud kicked off the conversation.

The two guys had found out of sell-by dated cokes in

an old beaten up vending machine out back. Despite the fact that a half mile on up the highway the 'Little Ale Inn' was open and serving all manner of food and drink. No one wanted to risk being rundown by the half-crazed men who had previously attacked them. Duncan sat next to Bud outside on the swing-out porch. He felt relaxed with Bud, and although he hadn't noticed it, his speech difficulty appeared to have almost totally dried up over the past few hours. Both men figured if any more security guys were going to come back, they, Duncan and Bud, would make their last stand there and then, outside in the hot sun and not cowering in the darker recesses of the diner. As it was, the Five Star security team had headed back to wherever it was they came from, to lick their wounds and to await further orders and the return of their boss, who could then decide what to do next.

"You know where they test out new planes and all." Bud was trying to enlighten Duncan concerning a not so recent air show he had attended on Edwards Air Force Base. All four hundred square miles of it. A facility which employed some two-thousand civilians and military personnel. This base was however not one the government denied existed. The aircraft were all there to see. Right up close, you could even sit in the pilot's seat of America's latest fighter planes.

"Oh, so that's where the thirty-billion budget deficit goes eh?" Duncan was not so behind when it came to a wide range of conspiracy-based ideas and data concerning secret military projects. He was already a believer, as were all the Magnetronic Research Unit team. Apart from that was Thelma. She was a hard and fast scientist so seeing for her was always believing. Duncan on the other hand certainly did not require conversion, and unquestionably not a baptism by fire either.

"They say 'they' have experimental craft fifty-years in advance of what they have now." Bud was in a sense trying to out-do Duncan. It was a kind of psychological game of ping pong, played in order to determine the pecking order. Or, more likely, in the carnal sense which alpha male gets to mate with the females of the pride!?

"But if they have that now then it's not fifty- years in advance because it's here, now right?"

Touché, Duncan had the camera man on the ropes.

"The Fish Project' is one example, a plan to develop saucer-shaped aircraft." Bud quickly enjoined.

"Which are flying today right?"

"I don't know," Bud responded. "Well I guess they might be and that is the explanation for all the sightings seen around the planet." He swilled back most of the coke, which despite its expired sell-by date, was still palatable.

"By the time they're on display at Edwards then, for all the world to see, they become the white face of a thirty-billion-dollar black world."

"Like it goes from black to grey to white right."

The two guys were playing the same tune.

"Anti-gravity, that's one," Bud was looking for check-mate. "They have them already, but they're black-black-black and so so so secret. Sooner or later they will end up being white as snow and we will all know and accept them as a method of public transport and for military use of course. It's the world's war machines that drive technology, not cures for cancer."

Bud was certainly right on that count.

"Man, the future is the language of nature, organics, that's what will be next, they will grow aircraft, not build them!" Duncan was uncertain where that ambiguous statement came from? Probably deep in the recesses of his mainly, underused brain.

Duncan possessed many skills and talents which were normally locked away. Unfortunately, he was too timid to bring what he knew into the light of day and on the table of academic scrutiny.

"But it's all down to classification," Bud rambled on. "Misinformation and denial. That's what Roswell was all about. Giving out the wrong information to the wrong people at the wrong time. Like they wanted people to know, cos it demonstrated to the Soviets we had something they didn't have. But at the same time, in domestic terms, it had to be kept secret. If, whatever it was, was disclosed, then the Soviets would have discounted the notion. So, by keeping it secret you kept the Soviets guessing for longer, wondering if you had it or not.

"Yeah sure, I can live with that: white, grey and black projects, which are never acknowledged and no comments are ever made about them. I mean why do they need a runway six-miles long?" Duncan enquired, having recently read a related article in National Geographic Magazine on the design and development of U2 and other USAF experimental aircraft.

"Why do they need a bombing range the size of Switzerland?" Bud smugly retorted.

Duncan was suitably clued up on military aviation, magnificent flying machines and conspiracies in general.

Nevertheless, he had never anticipated the team and project would end up being where they were at this moment in time. Embroiled in what was, on the surface anyhow, beginning to be a genuine mystery. Other than it was all just meat for the conspiracy theorist's table.

No more, no less.

"I saw the documentary on Fox, you know the one about the guy on the quad-bike who rides around scouting the hills around here, looking for old mine-shafts, and evidence of UFO activity, and shit like that."

Duncan pondered. He had seen the YouTube content Bud was referring to.

"Has to be a back door someplace, there's always a back entrance, it's like written in stone." Bud emphatically pronounced.

"There is, south-west down on Mercury, route 369!"

A man of oriental appearance had slipped unseen onto the swing-out, and without invitation or introduction he joined the two young men, who were embroiled in their own conspiratorial soup.

"How much secrecy do they need?" The oriental stranger further interjected.

"Hi, err who for Christ's sake are you?"

Bud Always-Jones was alarmed that a man could creep up on them and take them unawares so easily. He immediately looked about for some kind of weapon which he could potentially use to defend himself. Duncan, slower to react, stumbled trying to get up out of his place. Spilling his coke on the way and falling to the floorboards like a stone.

"Its OK! OK! Let me help…"

The oriental stranger offered a hand and Duncan, his pride hurt, but nothing else, righted himself and rejected the helping hand.

"OK it's OK, the men who were here earlier, they have gone, a while back. Left along the highway northbound."

Duncan and Bud let out long tired exhalations.

"How do you know? I mean how long have you been here?" Bud questioned

"What are you doing here?" Asked the now lisp-free Duncan.

"Where the fuck did you come from? That's what he's trying to say." Bud was more precise.

"I think I can answer that for you gentlemen. Clint stood in the doorway of the diner, he appeared to completely fill the frame as he looked down at two of the three confused people sitting on his swing-out. "Meet Motto Kyoto from Japan. This here is err, um… Duncan and, yes, what was your name son?" Clint and Bud had not been formerly introduced.

"Bud."

"I guess none of us have been properly introduced to one another."

The newcomer Mr Kyoto was slight and lean compared to Bud. His greying hair was long and wispy, flowing below his neck line, whilst his dress was that of a hiker, with back-pack and sturdy boots.

The oriental man and Clint sat together in the furthest corner of the diner and spoke for some time. They apparently had a great deal of catching up to do.

It was, so it appeared a simple coincidence that the oriental man Mr Kyoto had turned up just when the Five Star heavies had high-tailed it up the dusty road. A most welcome development as far as Diana and the others were concerned.

Gracie though remained aloof, hidden away from the others, as she was, in the back of the diner and smoking an increasing number of cigarettes, which annoyed Hillary immensely.

After a while the oriental man and Clint concluded their conversation and whilst Clint continued with his chores, for his part, Mr Kyoto rejoined the two younger men.

"It was posted somewhere on the internet." The oriental man broke into Duncan and Buds friendly analytical conversation. "Facebook probably. I found a recently established link concerning Rachel Jones, you know? The little girl who passed away from a series of cancer related problems all those years back."

Duncan and Bud had no clue as to who Rachel Jones was and of her passing away.

"It's apparently some kind of an anniversary. Seventy-years prior. The entire family and others were all prematurely taken by cancer connected diseases. The Federal Government never compensated any of them. Yep, so, the mail box shrine was set up so as to ensure her memory was never forgotten."

Mr Kyoto continued, his soft melodic voice possessed a soothing effect in all those within ear-shot. Mr Kyoto continued to captivate his audience. "I went up to the crossroads and Black Mail Box the other day, whilst I was there I fixed the spot up a little."

What Kyoto failed to say was just 'how' he managed to get up there. It would take a fit man at least three-days to walk the distance from the diner to the shrine and back.

Few people knew or understood the significance of the 'Black Mail Box' up in the hills, hidden away along the tree line. The MRU team members and the others at the diner, were certainly clueless as to the true purpose of the iconic attraction.

"Someone, the oriental man continued, has created another touching memorial up along the trail. A new addition, a big heart-shaped image made of stones and pine-cones which looks very similar to a typical big-eyed grey alien."

Mr Kyoto had been pleased to note the 'Black Mail Box' was still there and as a gesture wrote a short note to the aliens and posted it through the slot of the unusual facility. He had no clue as to if the letters were ever collected by US mail. Rather he suspected that there were other organisations that might gather the mail up along the pine tree trail.

"Other than the mail box, the main monument to little Rachel is of course the entire enclave of Rachel Nevada. A living testimony and memorial to a brave girl and her family."

Mr Kyoto continued with a potted history of the locale.

"Much of the post-war community of Rachel is all but still there: the research centre, the library, gas station and a couple of diners. One being this place - 'Hillary's and Clint's Joint.' The other places, the diner on 33 and gift emporium, are respectively run by the Carter family and before them the Kennedy's.

In the UFO research centre the radioactive monitoring equipment is still there, where it was left by the Atomic Energy Commission, who erected a number of Nissan huts on the site a few years after the cessation of the second world war. The current research centre still makes use of one of the huts as its base. This gaggle of rundown huts supposedly marked the furthest extent of radioactive fall-out and pollution from the non-existent nuclear testing ground, way beyond the mountains to the south-west, hidden away on land that is to this day still designated as ultra-top secret."

Apparently, Motto Kyoto had recently been reminded of Rachel when one day he had tried to view the general Nevadan region on Google Earth. It so happened that for some fortunate serendipitous reason, there had been a glitch in the satellite selection protocol and agreed censorship process.

On this rare occasion, what was normally off-limits to the general public and blotted out by the censors, quite unexpectedly appeared, revealed to any interested on-lookers; the 'Area' known the world over as '51.'

Once saved to hard drive the images were Mr Kyoto's to keep. He could zoom in and pan around the seemingly innocuous formation of over-large hangers. Close-up he could see vehicles and even personnel. Caught in the lower corner of the image a commercial aircraft could be seen mid-take-off from the lengthy Groom Lake runway. On the north side of the runway a significant-looking air-traffic control tower was highly visible. He could also see from one particular single frame an extensive concrete landing pad with two choppers parked up. The base appeared to be crisscrossed with made-up hard roads, like so many strings of pearls.

What appeared to be busses, were lined up by one hanger entrance way, and people were, although frozen in time, disembarking the vehicles. He speculated as to just where these people were headed.

Empowered and enthralled by what he had seen, he decided to take concrete action and pay the area a return visit. He was, as it happened, heading out to Vegas on vacation. Travelling not from his native Japan, but from Canada, where he had emigrated some years before.

His family was now all but grown up and sadly he was a now a widower. His wife dying coincidently of cancer some years before. Now alone in the world he wanted nothing more than to let, whatever hair he had left, down. He would, for one last time, throw the dice and spend some hard-saved retirement money on the tables of Las

Vegas.

But then he decided no. No, something inside of him told him not to waste his precious time or money on gambling. But rather he should follow his heart and real passion which was and always would be rock climbing. The challenge of which, as far as he was concerned, was now becoming increasingly physically difficult. However, over the last few years he had hauled himself up some pretty daunting and ball-busting peaks. What he really wanted to negotiate now was 'Freedom Ridge,' a high-spot overlooking what was known as so-called Area 51.

54

Thelma En Route to Rachel

The miles dragged by; Thelma's arm was seriously aching from holding up a service issue revolver under the Colonel's chin. On several occasions he had pleaded with her, for both their sakes, to put the gun down.

To no avail.

Now he decided to take a harder more pragmatic approach toward the lady with the gun.

"Come on then professor, what exactly do you know and recall concerning the past few days, but won't let on? Do you feel any compulsive urges? As if you were or have been forced to enact things which are totally out of your character... Do you? Do you remember anything much of that first night? Do you?"

"Not much is how much Colonel, not much, but enough, something..."

"And nothing!"

Thelma was uncertain what he the Colonel was implying.

"Nothing? You saw nothing, exactly as I wanted it. You saw nothing other than that which I wanted you to see. And I am guessing you saw everything I wanted you to see."

"And me? Ask me what I saw, and I'm not saying." Frank interjected.

"Well, I don't need your version of events football-Jock! But I may call upon you as a witness later on!" The Colonel was abrupt with Frank as his ears were still ringing from the double blow the former college boy had served on him. A lucky punch according to the Colonel, he would get his revenge very shortly.

Once more Thelma was more than slightly confused by what she now considered was the Colonel's form of 'double-treble-speak.'

"OK let's say you were sitting outside one minute and the next minute you were in a holding cell, bound and gagged, where time itself stopped still. One-day, two-days, three- days-four. Could you of survived anymore?"

Thelma felt increasingly under pressure, the sensation of being 'crushed' came over her.

Regardless, the Colonel continued his onslaught. "Duct tape over your mouth because you screamed so much half of Nevada could hear you…"

"I can vouch for that!" The up to now almost silent Air Force medic-come-driver added.

Then there were your questions, so many questions we had to put you to sleep for a while… And then someone gave you a shot in the arm."

The woman who was in all possibility a relative of Thelma's added - "Cousin Thelma, I gave you that shot, The Good Doctor' handed me the vial and I followed my orders and under you went."

Thelma thought to herself; 'The Good Doctor?' Who in God's name was that? What sort of a name is 'The Good Doctor?' She felt a strong desire to eke out some form of revenge on those people with peculiar names who had previously assaulted her and held her and her colleagues captive. Fortunately, Thelma was able to channel that aggression by pressing the loaded gun even harder into the Colonel's vulnerable exposed throat.

"Oh! I like that! Spirited eh? I like a woman with spirit, balls you might say! But relax, what you need to understand is that you both, you and the Jock here, as with your buddies, are still under my control. All I need to do is speak two little words and you will react, strongly and violently. I guess however you will probably turn and shoot me first, then your buddy Frank here, then your so-called relative and maybe lastly yourself."

Thelma remained bewildered yet at the same time implacable towards the vulnerable Colonel.

Regardless, the Colonel, unsettled by Thelma's

fortitude and determination, continued his rhetoric: "Oh so much blood. Just like that movie - 'Pulp Fiction' I love that flick, they ruin the upholstery of the car, brains splattered all over. And this is a government owned vehicle entrusted to me so I had better take it back spotless," the Colonel continued, "so I had better keep quiet, make sure all hell doesn't break lose. But wait, I know what you are thinking. You think you are free, don't you? But I have worked something interesting out."

"And what might that be?" Thelma responded darkly.

"Your pineal gland, you know, that little walnut in your head. That's why you are still experiencing pain. And because of that you think you can get out of my control? Truth is no, you can't!"

Thelma no longer had any idea what the truth was. Obviously, as a woman of science, biologically, not spiritually speaking, she knew everything there was to know concerning the pineal gland, but she had no idea as to the context in which the tiny non-functioning gland had been introduced into the brusque conversation, and more so why the clearly crazy Colonel was talking about it.

"Why? You see I know what you are thinking. Because I put the idea concerning your so-called 'third eye' in your head in the first place. It's just another layer of the onion. I thought something slightly 'New Age' might appeal to you and your comrades."

Thelma had little or no interest in what was commonly known as the 'New Age,' she was a scientist first and foremost and had no time for looking at the world in an alternative and abstract manner.

"I could see, back at the press conference," the Colonel continued his tirade, "there is so much conflict buried deep in your psyche. Tell the world the truth, tell them about the little voices, tell them about the top-secret stealth fighter jet that flew over you at tree-top level. You remember that don't you?"

Thelma threw her conscious mind open to grab whatever scraps of recollection she possessed. Yes, the noise, it was the noises she recalled: jets, choppers, vehicles, men, shouting - '*drop your weapons, get down on the ground. Drop it! Drop it!'*

The Colonel had Thelma on the ropes, she was clearly at breaking point.

"And later," the verbal onslaught appeared unstoppable, "remember we took a ride to the hanger? You saw that beautiful Blackbird, and how you wanted to fly away in it, to break out of your encrusted pineal gland and have your eyes and senses prised open. But they remained shut. I took you around the hanger, your buddies were quick to leave but you lingered, and you saw what?"

Once more Thelma felt at breaking point. Regardless the Colonel continued. "The flashing orange warning lights, the floodlights that came on. Then back in the far corner of the cavernous hanger, more flashing illuminations and the burning smell of scorched electrons being earthed."

Thelma could vaguely picture the scene.

"Then you saw them, didn't you? The source of the voices. Little guys, three of them, big oval heads and almond-shaped eyes. And they miraculously made a telepathic link to you, only you, Professor Jones from little old Iowa. Despite years of our scientists trying to communicate with them, you suddenly come along and you understand what they are saying to you, not us, not to the world!"

Thelma felt nauseous and bewildered.

"What if I tell you, the lights, the crackling electricity and the little people, now this is rich, wait for it - they were no more than a holographic projection."

The Colonel ranted.

"It's kids, a bunch of kids doing trick-or-treating, last Halloween. One of the officers on the base filmed them on his camera against a green screen, well just a green wall to be precise. He let me have the images, we created the 3D effect in our labs. Then ran them through a projector and edited in a few choice lines, and there you

265

have the real live alien show. Including the voices speaking into your head. No special effect expense spared here. It was and is a monumental fake. Just like all the other fakes and mistakes made by UFO hunters and abductees. Together with scientific so-called alien autopsies. Fake! Fake! Fake!" The Colonel laughed ironically, he had just, metaphorically speaking, let a big cat out of a small bag. Thelma meanwhile was looking confused and dejected. That feeling you get when you realise you have been screwed over and that there is little or nothing you can do about it.

The Colonel meanwhile pushed on anyway. He sensed Thelma was about to tumble and crack, just as he hoped.

"You must remember the 'Dreamland Lounge' and the sweet cocktails we shared together? I am more of beer man myself, but always open to exceptions. Well, would you mind if I told you there is no 'Dreamland Lounge' on the base? Not anymore. Once there were trailer parks on the site, back in the 1950s, but they're all gone now. Too many workers living in them got cancer, kids were being born incomplete, if you know what I mean. It was worse than C8 contamination. So, it was all levelled and now 'Paradise' is a hard landing pad, where choppers sit. And of course, a platform for drone operations."

The Colonel reflected, "you know what else 'Dreamland' is? No? Well I am going to let you know - it's an Air Traffic Control handle. The 'Ranch' is another. 'Dreamland' is no longer an actual solid place, but it is the open space above and in all our heads. The 'no-fly-zone' that'll get you shot down if you come too close."

The mismatched travelers in the Air Force Lincoln listening to the Colonel made no comment. Frank was confused as ever and he supposed he also must have tagged along to visit this hanger the Colonel had alluded to. And therefore, probably went to have a drink in the cocktail lounge. Not that he could recall one single second of the nonexistent experience. He was however curious as to what C8 contamination was. Maybe he would look it up when he got back home?

Home?

Meanwhile, the Air Force medic-come-driver reaffirmed in her head that Colonel Kernel was a dangerous raving lunatic, or very very clever. As she kept her eyes dutifully on the dusty road, she suddenly felt the desperate need to take a pee, but then had second thoughts. It was wild out there, wild and dusty, and she really hated snakes and spiders and any other desert dwelling creatures.

"You see Professor Jones," the military man in his best dress-uniform carried on. "Nothing you saw, heard, felt, smelt, touched or tasted was real. It was all put there by me. I made your dream, I created your little guys, the voices in your head, pleading with you. It was me and me alone!"

Thelma had no answers for this megalomaniac of a man, and therefore no response to make. She could not prove or disprove the existence of the 'Dreamland' cocktail lounge, little grey aliens, top-secret jet fighters, nothing. There was no longer a rationale to be had. There was no validation to the story, no justification, no evidence either way. Reality had shrunk away whilst no one was looking, possibly never to return.

"Oh and by the way, we know absolutely everything about you and your work at the university, the Magnetronic Research Unit. We know where you were born, everything about your family, mom and dad, brothers and sisters, even your goddamn shoe size, and when you first menstruated. Never mind your sexual preferences. I can and have accessed every phone call, text message and email you have ever made. I know about all the papers you have written for your research work. We know just about what you had for breakfast!"

For a moment Thelma felt as if she, as a human being, was rapidly fading, withering away and another person was being constructed in her place, built out of the shell of the former presence.

Inwardly the Colonel was playing. The number of times he had been through this exercise. Breaking a person down to his or her lowest common denominator, only to rebuild them. The new person would become an asset. A non-thinking sub-human whose only purpose was to serve the cause, whatever the cause maybe.

One relatively new spin-off aspect of the Mega 1-90 project was the marketing of trained assassins to foreign powers and governments. They, 'Der gute Doktor' and his team, could manufacture exportable human resources, assets, to serve and obey. The Saudi Arabians had already taken receipt of three such persons. Under the guise of being military advisors, they had already expertly physically dispatched a substantial number of enemies of the state (including a high-profile journalist), who were seeking to undermine the Saudi dynasty.

Airwoman Jones suddenly pulled over. They had reached and over-shot the almost invisible community of Rachel. Blink and it's gone, behind you, left as a former recollection in the perilous past. To her right was a surprising ten or more-foot effigy of a silver- grey alien, standing as he was, sentinel over the gift-shop-come-research-centre. A little further on she could see a long colourful mural depicting all kinds of iconic and stereo-typical extraterrestrial space-man imagery together with strange flying phenomena: such as saucers, little greys, reptilians, beams of light lifting humans up into the belly of a mother ship. All mythological-hype mostly created by the creative yet controlled minds of the dumbing down movie industry. She rapidly disappeared behind the bill-board to relieve herself.

However, not having been to the enclave of Rachel before, and now having emptied her bladder, Airwoman Jones had no idea where to park. But parking issues were the least of their worries and concerns. There were at this time only a couple of other cars parked up, both hired saloons, one with New Mexico plates and the other with Nevada plates.

55

Mr Kyoto

Mr Kyoto had settled down and felt more comfortable with the circumstances surrounding this unexpected visit. He spoke clearly and precisely but still held onto traces of a colourful oriental accent.

"It is like East and West Berlin back in the day. 'Check Point Charlie.' I crossed over the divide. They were outside looking in, or was it us in the west who were on the outside? So-called freedom of speech one side, secret police ruled dictatorship the other. Like Groom Lake here, outside Free America, inside a Nazi-style dictatorship. You know like the East German 'Stasi.' 'The Shield and Sword of the Party.' Notice, not protectors of the people! But spies to catch the people before they think for themselves." He continued holding court.

"No one talks because of fear. Neither here today, or how it was back in former East Germany. Everyone is controlled. Oaths are taken, and must be adhered to, under the ominous sting of death. You know, most workers on the Groom Lake site are lower-level Freemasons, that is what I heard. You see, so they're already bonded by oath. Under the 'Masonic curse,' which is for them a sure sentence of death."

The Japanese stranger looked thirsty and went to reach for the remaining half-full coke bottle, when suddenly the bottle splintered into a thousand shards, and liquid flew into the air a millionth of a second before the muffled report of a gun was heard.

Instinctively, the three men sitting on the swing-out porch dropped to the floor regardless of glass and spilt drink, as a diner window shattered.

Diana and Gracie Lin, leapt towards the old service counter and tried to take cover as best they could, just as a further shot blew out the mirrored back panel of the counter. The elderly Clinton couple stooped down and got behind one of the tatty worn out seating booths.

"Bud, do something!" Gracie Lin was concerned over her plastic Quaint out-fit, she would rather not roll about the dirty un-swept wooden floor.

"Who is shooting at us?" Diana demanded.

A distant indistinct voice came from outside,

"ome t han up!"

Diana was the first one to put three and five together to make a 'Fibonacci' eight.

"It's clearly the security guards. They have come back for more of our medicine." The young woman sounded remarkably confident and controlled.

"Or perhaps revenge?" The old man Clint was now standing tall behind a booth. "They won't kill us, well I hope not, it's off their patch, private, they have no jurisdiction here in town."

At that very moment a dusty Camo' green Air Force plated Lincoln Continental swept around the back, kicking up a sand storm, before pulling up parallel to the swing-out porch. Bud and Duncan, now covered by an earthy red dust, fell into the diner entrance and deftly rolled over to the more protective rear of the rarely open eating house, both men landing up at the back of the customer seating area. The Japanese man, Motto Kyoto, followed in their eddying glass-strewn wake.

At the same time a further bullet hit Bud's camera, which he had been nursing out on the swing-out porch. The video device exploded, as the rifle's lead bullet passed through it and into the door frame beyond.

Meanwhile yet another round hit the side window of the Lincoln skimming between Thelma in the back and the Air Force Woman, who was still sitting calmly in the driving seat. Frank rolled out of the front passenger door, fearing for his life. Whilst the Colonel took his cue and swiftly grabbed the service pistol from out of Thelma's grasp, before bailing out himself.

In a moment of perplexity fuelled by anger, the Colonel almost lost control. He understandably contemplated squeezing the trigger of his newly acquired weapon which was pointing in the direction of his erstwhile hostage taker - Thelma Jones. Except, for some strange inexplicable reason, he couldn't compel himself to do so. No matter how hard he tried. Rather, he levelled the gun out toward the open landscape and pulled the trigger. But nothing happened. Just a series of dull 'click,' 'click' 'clicks.'

Regardless, and without further thought, the still fit, (despite his desk-bound job) and highly trained sharp shooting Colonel, tried again, aiming once more out into the endless desert scrub.

Again: 'click,' 'click,' 'click.'

"Colonel, quick come inside." It was the voice of the medic Airwoman Jones.

"It's not loaded."

"Not what?"

"Loaded? You didn't tell me to load the gun, you specifically said: 'bring it!' Simply just bring the gun! There must have been one round in the spout, which was the one fired by Thelma Jones in the auditorium."

"Jesus! Are you saying I have had this gun barrel sticking in my neck for over two-hours and the gun is not even loaded?"

There was no response from Airwoman Jones, as yet another projectile smashed through the flimsy wooden walls of the decrepit, termite ridden diner.

56

Captain Kruger

Captain Kruger of Five Star Security, the firm awarded with a billion-dollar government contract to protect US military interests around the globe, flicked on cruise control and relaxed back. He enjoyed his job, which was to keep government property off-limits to those who, for whatever reason, wanted to break down the physical and psychological barriers encompassing the off-limit areas he patrolled. There were some vacuous people who, for whatever motive, wanted to wander around as if they personally owned the real-estate! Then there were those who would stop at nothing to find out exactly what was going on behind closed government doors - the conspiracy 'geeks.'

The stupidity of the human race never ceased to amuse Kruger.

However, what really stuck in his throat and what he found most annoying, was the fact that he had no authority or legal jurisdiction outside of the perimeter wire fence; not out there in the public domain. A 'geek' could stand right by a gatehouse and other than asking politely, there was no way security could legally move them along. The Sheriff would need to be called in to do that.

But there again he neither had any authority inside the perimeter fence line. Other than that was to capture people who had busted into the facility. He could hunt them down like hounds chasing a rabbit.

His jurisdiction then amounted to not much more than the width of the wire fence, it may have been very long, but it certainly was not very wide.

Of course, he and his men could take prisoners down to the gatehouse holding pens, whilst they also enjoyed access to their own drone wing parked up on 'Paradise' hard stand.

His men could of course detain or shoot trespassers. But officially they were not permitted to collect a body or bodies that had been shot. Neither were they permitted to take a body, or person, who had been apprehended off base. If a person was detained on base, they could be held indefinitely, or until the Sheriff's department collected them. Then and only then they were dealt with by the judiciary. Which was an impossible outcome, as a person could not trespass on land which in principle did not exist.

Sometimes weeks would go by and no one came even as far as the 'Black Mail Box.'

Business was slow and easy and that was how Kruger preferred matters.

The Air Force military policeman manning the Groom Lake gate, may as well have been a robot for all that he had to do. Which was: to now and then, prevent someone driving right up to the gate and try talk their way into the government restricted location that officially did not exist. If an inquisitive smart-ass UFO spotter managed to get through the gate, they would have to face a walk of some thirty-miles before they reached any facility, one that was not actually there. A thirty-mile walk under the Nevada sun spelt at least death by dehydration. Or, if you were lucky a quicker demise was to get bitten by a snake.

Other than 'geeks,' serious journalists and inquisitive foreigners needed to be kept at bay. As were would-be Russian, North Korean and Chinese spies, who would now and then stand outside the perimeter wire dressed like tourists. All they really wanted to do was to go stand by the numerous warning signs to take 'selfies' to show the folks back home how courageous they had been.

Some months back a Chinese wedding party came up from Vegas and got hitched by the Black Mail Box. Then had photos takes by the perimeter wire, adjacent to the signs that spelt out: *'death by violent means.'* There was never any accounting for what the new liberated Chinaman would do.

Other than the 'Black Mail Box' gimmick and the

gatehouse, there was little or nothing to be seen on this eastern side of the so-called non-existent Area 51. The other three sides to the square were defined by nothing other than often snow-capped mountains. There were no longer any vantage points left from where any, even determined individual, could view the non-existent secret base from.

Apart from one. And that was the original 'high spot.' A place where tourists used to be taken to, just for the view. 'Freedom Ridge' as it was called, was once accessible by bus and offered a spectacular panoramic view of the entire Groom Lake facility, for anyone to see. Now it was off-limits.

Fanatics desperate to see UFOs or other inexplicable flying objects, would hunker down on the ridge all day long to catch a glimpse of what were normally ordinary unmarked 727s, managed by Five Star Security, aircraft that ferried workers onto and away from the restricted area. No one (and this was on record) in the entire history of the facility had ever seen any unaccounted-for aircraft, flying in, or flying out, during the night or daylight hours. Neither had anyone ever recorded having seen a UFO.

And they never would.

Kruger was fully convinced of the fact that the sterile arid landmass some people designated as so-called Area 51 was all a total myth. An urban legend that popular culture had made mainstream. People get hold of small ideas and hearsay and the myth becomes a legend, then joins up with mainstream history. Because this is what people want. Magic and mystery. They want to believe lead can be turned into gold. The want to believe there are fairies, pots of treasure over the rainbow, and the luck of the Irish.

The bigger the lie the more people invest in it.

Thanks to the Roswell incident millions of Americans now believed in the existence of extraterrestrial life. More than those who believed in Jesus being the Son of God. And not exclusively little grey men. But now the true 'geeks,' who made their money writing books about the subject, were saying there were perhaps forty, fifty or even eighty different kinds of aliens who were inhabiting or visiting the planet. And these same people made irrational claims and other outrageously wild and assumptive statements, without so much as a morsel of evidence to support the notion. No one had ever truly, really, seen an alien of any description.

A person need only to go take a cynical look down in Rachel at the Alien Gift Emporium and they would quickly see someone is making big bucks out of the UFO phenomena, and former Captain K. Kruger was pissed because it was not, he who was making a killing. He was on the front line after all. Yet no one ever gave him a dime to keep his mouth closed or reward him for doing a great job. They just assumed he was a patriot and would honour the oath he had made when he was brought in as security chief.

* * * * *

If there was not enough bull-shit floating around, the Federal Government, once-upon-a-time, decided to draw up a committee of ass-holes to? Well, Kruger did not know exactly what Majestic 12 (MJ-12) was all about, no one did. But President Harry S. Truman back in 1947, after the Roswell debacle, was curious concerning all these tales of aliens. They were after all in the movies and featured in comic books.

So, there had to be some credence, some substance to all the other-worldly notions floating around.

The net result of the former government study being - 'these so-called alien encounters were reported back as bogus and no more than a hoax.' As were the doctored images of US government officials (and the president), standing next to large oval-headed extraterrestrials. The real big million-dollar question on everyone's minds was - 'do they have dicks?'

On paper, Fiver Star Securities covered the perimeter security of a piece of wasteland real estate the size of a small country. However, Kruger knew, as did a very few others in the Pentagon, that given the resources available it was impossible to police the entire hundreds of miles long boundary. It was, in truth, ultimately the mountains that formed a natural barrier to the restricted area, where only the most foolish of individuals would dare to tread. The mountain faces were sheer, and unassailable.

In real terms, the Groom Lake gatehouse was not much more than a show piece. And as for 'Freedom Ridge' it was eventually acquired by the Federal Government and, as previously alluded to - unceremoniously closed down by way of blocking the road up with rocks and boulders.

The 'Camo dudes' were real however, and they were up there somewhere, unseen by unwelcome snooping visitors. Their actual positions were logged daily. Now however, rather than six-teams of two operating, there were, due to spending cuts, in actuality just two team of two.

As for the Five Star pick-up patrols, they were more frequent and visible. Their aim was to intercept drivers, mainly in four by fours, to make certain they kept to the public trails.

The entire vast base relied on one main factor in keeping people out and that was fear…

* * * * *

Captain Kruger snapped out of his malaise. He had given too much lee-way to his men in the field. He hated to think what they must have been up to further along the road at the Rachel Diner. Common sense determined he should call his hounds off and let them go to their homes and families. Afterall, natural daylight had all but gone, the sun ducking behind the mountain ridge.

He made the call. Thankfully his 'goons' had already backed off and left the diner as fast as they could.

57

Principal J. Jones in Vegas

Principal J. Jones Junior was horrified and quickly went into the nearest store and purchased a summer beach hat, which he pulled tight over his balding head. Added to the new disguise were a pair of fake 'Ray Ban' shades, which he glued to his face, despite the fact that the evening was drawing in.

He apparently was now a suspect who was wanted for questioning by the FBI, regarding the recent Las Vegas terrorist atrocity. Concerning the nature of which he was now fully cognisant. His prodigy and number one science department head, was seen in news print, holding a gun aloft in a threatening manner. In one edition it depicted a man next to her in military uniform. He, the Principal of Iowa State University had no idea Thelma Jones harbored any jihadist Islamic tendencies. It seemed impossible and unreal. Apparently, the newspapers: (which incidentally were owned by just two parent companies, one being - Ford News Corporation.' And the other: 'Allied Nixon Syndication), had now coordinated their news reportage arrangements in order to present a unified statement ensuring all publications, local or national, ran the same almost identical story lines.

58

Ms Celia Jones, Iowa State University

As fortune had it, Ms Celia Jones, Secretary to the Principal of Iowa State University, took Professor Thelma Jones' desperate call. In order to communicate with her faculty, the professor had cautiously used the old pay-phone mounted on the wall at the back of the diner to call the university switch board. Having first filled it up with quarters and dimes.

It was clear to Ms Jones that the professor out in the field was evidently under duress. Although Thelma did not reveal a great deal to her concerning the current situation, she and the other MRU team members were in.

Ms Jones had after all seen the news reports and was surprised to hear that Professor Thelma Jones, a woman who she had known for a number of years and held in high esteem was a covert Islamic-fundamentalist-come-potential-car-bombing-terrorist. Which is how the national press had painted her.

Besides that, Ms Celia Jones was no longer interested in the goings on at the State University. Whereas, one scandal maybe dealt with without too much trouble, two or more outrages was and is an impossibility to handle. Or so she surmised.

She was of course referring to the recently posted university Facebook pages, devoted to the Principal and an unknown female sexual participant. The clip was thankfully over very quickly, a few seconds, but long enough to see a pelvis thrust against buttocks. She should have known, having been the; 'friend with benefits' lover to the principle, for what seemed to be half of her life. Now she was busy smashing just about everything she could find of his. Later she was planning to let herself into his apartment with her personal key, and using sharp scissors she would then slice up all his clothes, his bedding and other personal effects.

For all she knew, this sudden unannounced disappearance of his to Las Vegas, only proved further that he was engaged in some form of torrid affair with this unknown woman, his new porn-star-fuck-buddy. A Las Vegas wedding and a Mexican divorce sprung to her mind.

As far as the report Thelma Jones offered up to the now former faculty secretary was concerned, the Magnetronic Research Unit had hit a snag. In as much as they had been detained for trespassing on US Government land and that they had been locked up for at least two-days whilst their stories were checked out. Now they were free to go and would carry on with the next stage of their expedition. At present they were fine and hanging out in a small town called Rachel in Nevada. Oh, and as for the newspapers and TV reports, it was all just a misunderstanding that they were sorting out. And of course, she, the Iowa University Professor, was not an extremist, but as ever a pragmatic, level-headed scientist first and foremost.

59

Back at the Diner

Thankfully, the random shooting bout had abated. Just as it had started up, it stopped. In the distance a vehicle's lights flashed across the diner as whoever was shooting at them left in a hurry.

"OK" Thelma, letting out a tired lungful of air, reported to her colleagues. "So, I have called the faculty, reported all is OK and nothing to worry about just a big misunderstanding. However, seems as if Principal Jones has a few problems."

Gracie Lin spluttered and then suppressed what was an obvious attack of mirth. Evidently none of the folks gathered had looked on Facebook recently. And why or how could they? Two out of their four phones were ground to dust on the diner floor and the other two were out of bounds, just in case someone tried to send them another creepy message.

"You could have had us all killed out there medic! What the hell!?" The Colonel was fuming. His fanciful desire for the young female Air Force medic was rapidly falling away, of which she was totally thankful for.

"You must have used the gun, maybe down on the range," the Airwoman conjectured. "You were sharpening up say, and let five rounds go, forgetting the handgun took six. Left one in the chamber. Very dangerous. Bad practice sir, if you forgive the critical comments."

The sheepish Colonel let the issue go. She, the medic was quite correct in her assumption. However, it was done and no longer relevant to their dire situation.

He, the Colonel, was in deep shit, it was the end of his career: dishonorable discharge, loss of pension rights, maybe even the electric chair for committing treason. Never mind what was in store for the motley bunch who had somehow coincidentally gathered in the old diner. Half of them he had never set eyes on before, but he quickly tried to gain an insight into all of their psychological mind-frames. He was anxious to know who or what he was up against. Fortunately, the Thelma Jones woman had calmed down. Now she no longer had a piece at her disposal, she was far more amiable and relaxed. For now, that was.

"Trouble is we have no means of defending ourselves." The Colonel continued. "If there is still anyone out there, they might be knocking on the back door again pretty soon."

However, now the pick-up had driven off, the shots had ceased. Regardless, everyone remained in a prone position, just to make sure they were not making themselves easy targets.

"Aint no shooters out there now, general, I can assure you of that." The old man spoke up with commanding authority from the back of the diner.

"It's Colonel, Colonel Kernel, to be precise."

"You're kidding me! Clint broke out in a smile. Kernel, that's your name huh?"

It wasn't the first time that people had made fun of his name. The Colonel was wishing he wasn't a Colonel and that perhaps he should ditch his uniform and dog tags and pretend he was a dumb tourist?

"It's the Five Star people," the old man continued, "they're making a point that's all. Once it gets real dark, they'll be gone higher up for the night patrols."

The Colonel was fully aware of the Five Star Security modus operandi. Technically he was their boss and supposedly held the authority either side of the wire line.

"This is so, I saw them the last time I was here." The strange Japanese hiker was almost flat to the floor like a rug.

"And who might you be?" The Colonel addressed the Japanese man, who was first in line of the new faces who were strangers to him. "Are you one of the Magnetronic team?"

Mr Kyoto had no idea what the American military officer was talking about, and so he kept quiet.

"Allow me, err General sir - Gracie Lin Jones, independent press journalist and television presenter." The conniving journalist held out a limp right hand in the direction of the military man, but could not quite reach him as she was on the wrong side of a table and four chairs. Gracie was purring inside; she had always liked a man in uniform. Regardless, she was already contemplating ways in which she might be able to use this high-ranking military man to her advantage.

"That's Colonel by the way, I am not a General as yet, and the way things are going I never will be." The Colonel had dealt with too many press people to be either impressed or phased by them.

"Maybe we need to get better acquainted with one another," The old man Clint interjected. "I mean if they're gonna come shoot us down, then I for one wants to know who I am fighting with."

The Colonel agreed, then turned to Thelma as if to garner her support in the matter. "How about you Miss Jones? Seems to me we are all here because of you and your team."

Thelma did not quite see the situation in the same light. It was hardly her fault that the team had been imprisoned, drugged up and held against their collective will for at least two-nights. However, she felt to sound off one at a time would be positive and helpful.

The Colonel slowly stood and pressed himself flat against a wall. "Well, I am a General apparently, United States Air Force, here on official classified government business. With an empty gun."

"Me?" The Airwoman directed her right hand to her left shoulder as if she were in same way swearing an oath of allegiance. "Medic Reagan Jones, also United States Air Force, seconded to the General, I mean Colonel here, paid to be goofed around with, and have to put up with sexual harassment at Nellis and from my boss the Colonel here."

The Colonel winced and felt embarrassed with the suggestion of impropriety. "By the way I am Thelma Jones' cousin several times removed."

"OK Thelma Jones here," Thelma was still unsure whether she was related to Reagan or not. "Professor at Iowa State University, head of the Magnetronic Research Unit funded by the science faculty to prove my theory that the earth's magnetic fields are influenced by human psyche and behaviour. And my team..." Thelma went on to introduced Diana Rogers: still looking good, if not tousled and unkempt. Duncan Dunkerley, still looking terrible and disheveled. Frank Blake, football quarterback for the 'Hawkeyes' Iowa State. Just looking as, he normally did.

"I guess I don't need any introduction." Gracie's ego was above all of these childish - 'hi and howdedoody' games.

"Bud here," the camera operator gave those gathered an understated wave. "Bud Always-Jones, hey and I reckon I am Thelma's cousin as well as Gracie Lin, here and the other lady Reagan, on either her mother's or father's side. And I am a camera operator, well I was until someone shot my camera up. My hobbies back home are making amateur porn movies and basically screwing around. But I am interested in UFOs and all that conspiracy shit as well."

He appeared quite unashamed with regard to his hobbies and leisure time activities.

"And let me introduce Mr Motto Kyoto, a guest here from Canada but originally from Japan." The old man Clint thought he should introduce the strange oriental gentlemen that, prior to this time, clearly no one knew. Kyoto stood up unsteadily and gave a low bow.

"As Clint said, I am here as a guest, on vacation from Canada where I now live, and I have come here for several reasons. One is the death of the little girl Rachel

Jones."

Thelma looked up quizzically, wondering if Mr Kyoto and the little girl were related? As everyone else just about seemed to be.

"And what else Mr Kyoto?" Thelma politely enquired.

"Second reason to mark the sad occasion of my honourable ancestor's death. Relatives, grandparents to be precise, died in the Hiroshima bomb blast, August 6th 1945. One- hundred and forty-thousand died that day on Broad Island alone."

A moment passed, perhaps reflective of a collective shame. A shudder cut through Airwoman Reagan Jones, regardless of her lowly rank and pay scale she was all too aware of just what was stored underground around fifty-miles from where they were standing.

"And I want the USA to remember each of their deaths."

"Mr Kyoto thank you..." The old man was moved. "And you know me, Clint Clinton and my wife Hillary. We moved up here from down south to find our pot of gold over the rainbow, and well we didn't find much before the UFO boom of the 70s through to the 80s. But now everyone: the Russians, the Chinese, in the UK and France, even Mexico has their own Roswell and so-called Area 51. Business aint so thriving."

"Which does not exist!" The Colonel chimed like a brainwashed bell.

"The hell it don't!" Bud bounced back. Not that he was an expert in such matters.

"Not officially!" The Airwoman medic piped up.

Frank became animated at the sound of her voice. Fluffy clouds momentarily filled his sky and petals fell from the ceiling.

"Official or not, we're all still in a mess." The Colonel countered Bud's naive comment. Pragmatic as ever, Thelma thought - 'food.' She felt ravenous and drained.

"Any chance of a take out?" Apparently, she wasn't the only one feeling exhausted and famished: Frank,

Duncan and now Bud's mouths were anticipating Pizza to go.

60

Principal Jones in Vegas

Principal Jones wandered around like a misplaced conventional traditionalist. He had no idea where to start to look for Gracie Jones. Vegas is a huge town, lit by a million lights, turning night into day. Thousands of casually dressed tourists walking up and down the streets and malls. Whilst he was dressed and looked like an east-coast banker wearing a stupid hat.

Undoubtedly of course he would do the obvious: call the office, speak to faithful Celia, she would update him and then contact Professor Jones, who might be able to shed some light on the newspaper headline matter. Then, once discovering their location, he could go see how they, the Magnetronic Research Unit, were progressing, which would all be under the pretext of encouraging them. Evidently, he had no idea that Thelma had already called Celia, a fourth cousin of hers, and had given her a full explanation of the circumstances surrounding the frontpage headlines, which were now thankfully going to be yesterday's old news, once night fell completely and a new dawn was upon them.

* * * * *

Principal Jones made the call to his office, and as anticipated, even though it was out of normal working hours, the ever-faithful Celia Jones picked up. She had not as yet cleared all of her desk so he was lucky to catch her. For the most part the now betrayed woman kept her composure as she listened to her boss (soon to become former employer, as she had already written, but not tendered her resignation), come up with a catalogue of miserable bland excuses for his likeness being portrayed in local and national press. Clearly, he was not an Islamic terrorist leader and the FBI merely wanted him for routine questioning.

Celia Jones then confronted her former boss with regard to the images on Facebook of him in a compromising position, copulating with a female who was clearly a hooker. Principal Jones was naturally in shock. He quickly retorted that it was undoubtedly an error on someone else's part, and, or there was, some form of a conspiracy taking place against him. Yes, it was the other managers at the university, it was a coup, that's what it was, a smear campaign set against him.

Added into the mix, to create further substantiation and substance to his pitiful justifications, he deliberated over his scandalous fellow academic board members and campus managers. Pointing out, as he eagerly did, just about everything heinous and illegal they had collectively done, or had even thought about doing, or ever were about to do in the future. Pointing the finger of blame was an art he had long since mastered.

Ironically, on this singular occasion, he was in many respects justified in condemning some of his fellow board members, and, as it would later transpire, he would discover exactly how he was being used and manipulated by other fellow 'Shriner' lodge members.

Subsequently, and much to her chagrin, Celia erroneously thought, that she had the Principal under her control, and it had been like that for some time. She was of course fully aware of his rabid sexual needs and desires, and had always hoped, in a foolhardy sort of way, that she was sufficient to fulfil his every whim and fancy. But obviously not. The seventy-five second video clip was evident to that.

The incriminating images of which (quite by chance), had now found their way, as these things do, onto a global web site known as 'Porn-Club.' A site for amateur porn movie makers, of which Bud Always-Jones not surprisingly was a contributor, and had made sure the content had been posted on the site.

The next few audible moments that followed the final part of the phone conversation between loyal Celia and licentious Principal Jones, was akin to the sound of a human head being torn from its shoulders and chewed up, before being spat out.

Thankfully, the university phone system somehow automatically ended the call before the hand-piece had been ripped out of the wall, smashed to pieces and pitched into the trash.

The last words spoken by Celia amounted to: 'rot-in-hell-you-son-of-a-bitching-bastard!" Followed by a more composed ending, as one might expect from a professional such as Celia, who simply confirmed the location of Thelma Jones, as being seventy-to-eighty-miles north of Las Vegas, in a small enclave named 'Rachel' up along route 33, the Extraterrestrial Highway. Which, it transpired, was a two-hundred-dollar cab fare from Vegas, that naturally the faculty was going to have to pay for.

61

Back at the Diner

Back at the Diner Thelma stretched out her leg, her right leg, and smoothed out the material of her borrowed military issue combat-style pants.

Suddenly an astounding eureka moment crept up on her, and, like a swinging baseball bat, metaphorically clubbed her right around the head. An unexpected realisation suddenly returned to her. And that was, she had broken her leg. Now however she was perfectly healed.

A miracle?

Had she dreamt it?

Did the medics make a mistake and plaster her up for no good reason?

Or, had the healing process emanated from some other out-of-this-world source?

Regardless of all the arguments for or against, Thelma was inclined to think that out-of-this world intervention was the strongest contender for the - 'who healed Thelma's leg contest.'

Her low-energy fractured bones, were healed. And it had taken place right up there.   Where?

There? Somewhere out there, in a place that she hardly recalled visiting.

Made whole by a 'power.' Could that possibly be electro-magnetic-energy?

And that same energy source, the existence of which she was now convinced of, had somehow communicated with her. More to the point, the audible requests stored in her brain were an obvious plea for help. And that was something the skeptical United States Air Force personnel could not deny.

Thelma screamed out a garbled revelation. Whilst the

Colonel cupped his hands over his ears. He was sick of joining in such puerile debates. He stood upright as a man facing the firing squad and his immanent execution.

Whereas, an opposing response duly came from Airwoman Reagan Jones regarding the veracity of Thelma's statement. As a medic she was naturally both responsive, understanding and generally sympathetic.

Clearly, Thelma required further evidence confirming the, her, revelation, and so with Airwoman Reagan Jones encouragement she dropped her military pants, as she had previously done, and allowed all those gathered to look at the formerly broken limb; which demonstrated no evidence of muscle weakening, or traces of plaster residue. Zero evidence of having existed. No chaff marks even where the plaster should have rubbed. Nothing.

But what she did have was cannula bruising around a vein on her forearm, marks which her other three companions also wore like battle scars.

62

Principal J. Jones arrives in Rachel.

It was dark by the time Principal J. Jones Junior M.A. arrived at the 'Little Ale Inn.' Situated in Rachel Nevada. He paid the cab driver, who looked longingly for a large tip but was going to be disappointed on that score. As it was, fortunately, the driver had not recognised his fare from the numerous newspaper reports concerning the circumstances that had culminated with the defamed Principal hiding out in the middle of a no particular place on the planet.

Looking for?

Redemption? The cabby was a turban- sporting Indian, arising from some exotic nationality, with little or no grasp of the English language. And so, none the wiser on all counts. Principal Jones eventually gave him a $5 bill as a tip, and grabbing his overnight cabin bag, strode into the 'Little Ale Inn.' It was empty apart from a bar-keep. Who greeted him with indifference

"You best take care sir," the man hesitantly warned, "been some shootin' here today. Not that there aint nothing unusual about shootin' I mean we are on the edge of a gargantuan bombing range, so you would expect to hear gun fire from time to time. But this was small arms."

The Principal had little interest in 'small' arms fire, or 'small talk,' for that matter and politely asked for a room for the night. At which the man, being a drab weather-beaten middle-aged individual, no doubt set in his ways and not about to make much effort over anything, looked around the place in jest. "We aint got no accommodation here sir, this is a bar and diner. You need to go back to Vegas if you want a room for the night."

"I have just come up from Vegas, cost me two-hundred and more bucks."

"Sir forgive me, that's a lot of money, I would have collected you for fifty."

"So, no room at the Alien Inn eh?"

"Nope!" The pun eluded the red-neck.

"Anywhere else in town?"

"You can try the Clinton's joint, but he aint been open for some months now. And I think whoever was doing the shootin' was shootin' at his place. It's just across the street there."

Principal Jones took his leave and crossed the dusty street, lit by one single shorting-out street lamp. He noted on the way the dusty parked up vehicles in the central reservation, opposite, what appeared to be, a derelict wooden shack. Above the swing out porch a sign creaked and grated in the light breeze. The paint having long-since peeled away, leaving a single letter: C' intact.

Rounding the swing-out porch he could not help but notice another parked sedan, sprayed up in green and judging by the numerous decals stuck along the sides, it was an Air Force vehicle, the body work of which as with everything else, was covered in dust.

Taking the few steps up to the porch he was unexpectedly confronted by his prodigy, and somewhat distant relative - Professor Thelma Jones.

63

Former Captain K. K. Kruger arrives at Rachel

Former Captain K. K. Kruger turned into park outside the shabby, dilapidated diner, located in Rachel Nevada. Just as he had done so many times before in the past, when life was sweet and everyone prospered. His brakes screeched as he nosed toward the swing-out porch, only to discover his way was blocked by a green Air Force Lincoln. He immediately knew who had likely seconded such a mode of transport. It had to be Colonel Kernel, without shadow of doubt. Ass-wipe! What the F.K. was he doing here?

Kruger had already been in contact with his men, the two operatives he had sent to keep an eye on the 'geeks.' Tough guys they were, professional people, grown men, who apparently had had the crap beaten out of them by two women! It was hardly credible. So, the same two Five Star employees, thinking they were taking the initiative, smashed the cell phones belonging to the women. Which consequently meant that if he, Kruger, had a mind to call those same ladies or message them even, he would not be able to do so due to the fact they no longer had possession and use of their own cell phones!

What was even more incredible was the fact that these same two security guards, had later on, high-tailed it back into the scrub and set up a sniper's Camo' den, whereupon they had commenced shooting the old diner up, with a view to making those inside crap themselves and come out with hands held high.

Shit kickers! God damn ass-holes.

However, now was not the time to start complex investigations. There would be complaints no doubt. He would be cautioned for sure. There maybe be sanctions as a repercussion of this incident. Five Star might be dropped from their contract, he would lose his pension rights, consequently there would be no more money coming in and he would lose his house, car, quad-bike, the boat, his open top sports and all the other status symbols that proved the American dream was alive and real and even attainable by lowly South African immigrants.

All the more reason he thought to push forward with his TV idea, even if it only made local cable TV channels, it would still be a money spinner. Now he potentially had a celebrity on board: the 'geek' lady, the smart one whose picture was on every news paper's front page, both local and national. Reports of her brandishing a pistol were all over social media, TV stations and radio bands as well. All he needed now to complete his future plans, was the magic snake-bite potion used by 'The 'Good Old Doctor' to make mesmerism happen.

One word from him and Thelma Jones would be hypnotized. Then she would undertake any dumb-ass daredevil feat of stupidity you could imagine: high-wire walking from office buildings, swimming with sharks, jumping into a pit of vipers! Together with the fresh-faced football playing Jock, the college guy. He would make a perfect partner opposite the smart 'geek.' Then to add to the glamour - the pretty one with the sexy body. She would add some spice to the mix. As for the dumb 'hippy kid?' He wasn't so sure about his role as yet. Maybe he would end-up being the fall guy, the clown, the clumsy goon. It was all there, the ingredients to make the cake, now he just needed to bake it!

Kruger scrambled out of the pick-up driver's door and leapt up the swing-out porch, only to run straight into the back of Principal J. Jones Junior, minus his sun hat and eye apparel.

"Hey, watch out!"

Kruger stumbled rearward. A surprised Thelma moved to make more room for both men. Naturally, she immediately recognized the incongruous Principal Jones, even, as he was, out of context.

The second man? She had no idea who he was, he went unrecognised. Despite the fact he had been the one who previously apprehended her, and the other three Research Unit team members, just a few days before.

"We were about to order pizza; can we get it at that place across the main drag?" Duncan was even more ravenously hungry.

Meanwhile, Clint and Hillary, who had not seen the diner so full in months, with the mention of food, used that as an excuse to get going and clear the place up. Diana, in unison, pulled up her sleeves, whilst Bud and Duncan swept the floors and rearranged the tables and chairs.

Gracie sat and smoked yet another cigarette, intrigued as she was by the appearance of the second gate-crasher. A handsome man, apparently called Kruger. But then again, she was thoroughly dismayed, and somewhat taken aback by the appearance of her nemesis, Principal Jones, a man whose reputation she had ruined, and who she knew full-well was mightily pissed with her.

Fortunately, Principal Jones had not as yet, noticed her black and white check shaped form hunched up in the shadows of the backroom.

For a moment a wave of misplaced congeniality washed over the room. It was a strange sensation, generated between an odd group of disassociated people, all gathered for a reason, and Thelma for one wanted to know why?

64

The Truth Serum

The 'Good Doctor' had been awake for forty- eight hours. Perhaps longer. Now he wanted to sleep, but he also felt the need to somehow, interject, as far as the current situation was concerned.

With regard to the high-ranking Air Force personnel headquartered at Groom Lake, he, 'Der gute Doktor was privy to much of their classified information that daily passed through the numerous functioning departments that constituted the Groom Lake facility. He carried high-level clearance that gained him access to all the non-existent workshop and offices below ground level. Not bad for a son of an immigrant, he mused to himself.

As far as his crowd-control techniques were concerned, the rotating workforce thankfully left an almost invisible foot-print, and there was only limited security interaction required between the multifaceted work stations and offices.

His main area of involvement with respect to the facility, in conjunction with Colonel Kernel, was to pacify those workers who came to the base and to ensure they kept focused on their work and thought of nothing else whilst on station. And when they were not at their posts, they would be simple patriotic Americans, living the dream.

It was true to say that, without the input of the 'Der gute Doktor' and his team, there would be no core psycho-hypnotic-inner-security at the base. Other than a somewhat ineffectual system of verbal college honour codes, constructed around nationalistic pride that pervaded across the military cohort and civilian workers alike.

Salute the flag twice a day keeps you being a patriotic

American.

Consequently he, as well as other high-ranking officials, were kept informed as to what was actually going on under their feet, below ground level at Groom Lake. The source of this intelligence was the Groom Lake project departmental heads. They classified, rubber stamped, and documented all relevant and factual information, before sending it through to the Pentagon. Who then, subject to current political trends and fashions, either forwarded the same intelligence back to the Air Force, or stored it away under lock and key for at least seventy-years, for future generations to ponder over its relevance.

Here however hung a curious irony: Pentagon officials, and other agencies, had no clearance to enter onto the Groom Lake base, let alone go to the 'below-ground' levels. Not even the president was permitted to walk in and take a look around.

The Pentagon and Department of Defence therefore manufactured details, derived from information given over by Groom Lake project departmental heads, of pending and current assignments taking place on the base. This was all done in order to inveigle other officials, in particular Congressional Finance Committees, as to what was going on at the so-called Area 51 base. Which of course did not exist. No one ever enquired concerning where the information source originally came from.

There was, as it happened, a colossal disparity between what was going on (which was something that no one knew), and what people were officially informed as to what was going on.

The listings of bogus activities ran into hundreds of catalogued pages, which no one ever contemplated viewing.

And here was the rub: as previously stated, project managers informed the Pentagon and other interested agencies, as to the progress they were making with their particular tasks. The Pentagon then repackaged that information and sent it back to the same various project leaders and departments to re-inform them as to the projects that were live and imminently about to take place.

This all of course equated to absolutely nothing ever getting done, or being real. And if it were not real then you could not see it, hear it, touch it, smell it or even taste it.

A further and more pressing irony was the fact that the very man who was employed by the Air Force (therefore the government), to deliver information to the press and public alike, a man who was in the thick of creating bogus paper trails and broadcasting reams of fake-news and misinformation out to the world, was the same man, it had been disclosed, every curious journalist was looking for, as he was now apparently a wanted traitor and potential agent provocateur.

Colonel Kernel (although he was more or less unaware of his dire situation), was now, according to outside press sources, a leading terror suspect and Russian double agent. Who, according to journalists, had led a poor defenceless female university professor astray! Probably having raped her first.

All America loved to hate the Benedict Arnold character.

* * * * *

The Good Doctors' G40 clearance was seven-grades above Colonel Kernel's pay scale. Although that wage differential was never an issue between them. He had rightly felt they had for some time enjoyed a professional relationship, based on mutual trust and a certain amount of honour; rather than the size of their respective pay-packets.

Whatever the status of their working affiliation, it was considerably more amiable than say, his relationship with Kruger of Five Star Securities. Regardless of the fact that he, Kruger, shared with the Doctor some common, mutual, but tenuous, connections. Mainly, let it be said, of a political nature, being as they were both proponents and supporters of national socialistic ideology.

As an outmoded political movement, in the modern era it was not what people thought it was.

Beyond ideology finesse and political association, Kruger was as crude in his civilian life, as he was in his approach to his job. Whereas 'Der gute Doktor was a more refined and cultured fellow, a lover of Wagner, fine wines and good traditional French food (when he could get it). As it was, 'cuisine' around the Nellis base kitchens, was not a word the incumbent chefs understood. As a culinary consequence he usually had his meals sent down to him on Level 2.

* * * * *

Regarding the situation to hand: as it stood as far as 'Der gute Doktor' was concerned, the CIA censored and redacted reports filtering through were not too unfavorable as far as the - soon-to-be demoted and court-martialed Colonel was concerned. Yes, he was now a wanted man, and, as an enemy agent, was to be arrested on sight by any and all Air Force detachments of the Military Police. If he stepped one foot on any part of the Groom Lake facility he was as good as dead. Outside of the highly classified and restricted non-existent complex, he was wanted for questioning by the FBI, the CIA, Homeland Security, the Sheriff's department and also the Marines all who wanted to question him concerning the issuing of an emergency code, which emptied a guard detachment and left McCarran International Airport vulnerable and exposed. If the Russians or Chinese had attacked the civilian facility, they would have been defenceless.

The clearly complicit Airwoman Reagan Jones, driver of a Lincoln Continental vehicle taken illegally from the Nellis base motor pool, was also under investigation.

Although she was only wanted for questioning, as no charges had as yet been levelled at her.

Admittedly the Colonel did have the right and clearance to draw from the motor pool, and she was only carrying out 'his' unruly orders.

Regardless, she was also wanted for questioning concerning the aiding and abetting of the discharging of a fire-arm.

However, as far as 'Der gute Doktor 'was concerned, he could clearly see a dilemma and obvious anomaly on the horizon. A particularly outcome he had often suggested might take place, would take place, which he had predicted on many occasions, which was, according to him, a disaster waiting to happen.

The FBI and all other related agencies, including the Sheriff's department, wanted access to personnel at Groom Lake for questioning. On the contrary, as Groom Lake and all of its project staff and departments, did not officially exist. Therefore, it was impossible for the FBI and other agencies, to obtain court orders and warrants to enter the highly classified facility, as there was no base or facility to enter.

A fact that the CIA and the Pentagon continually stipulated - 'Area 51 is not there.' The official line was there was no official line, as such a place on earth did not exist.

This despite the fact that the existence of the wider facility had previously been verified; on one singular occasion, just after the phony Vietnam conflict.

Since then this ping-pong propaganda game continued for years. Misinformation, closely followed by disinformation, and so forth. Now when it suited them, the CIA and certain sections of the USAF 'black operations' programmes (that did not exist either for obvious reasons), were emphatic concerning the non-existence of the wider facility based around Groom Lake.

On the one hand the restricted areas that did not exist were in reality fully functioning and working establishments churning out top-secret weaponry and future fighter command designs. These projects it appeared, were common knowledge, as far as conspiracy theorists were concerned. Ask any defence expert and they would tell you that these days all the secret military weapons programmes came out of, and were now being developed at the 'Skunk Works' down in California. Which was attached and connected to The Edwards Air Force base. America's future weaponry was now in the hands of private corporations, which greatly upset the die-hard patriots. When all said and done, Edwards was-white-white-white. Whereas Groom Lake was still very much: black-black- black.

* * * * *

Regardless of what was, or was not, being developed elsewhere, there still existed the argument over the legal status and jurisdiction of the non-existent Groom Lake facility. All of which would make access even more impossible for any other or all enforcement agencies, due to the fact that there would or could be programmes running on the site which were highly classified and were not to be made public under any circumstances.

A restriction precedent that went way up to presidential status. What this meant was only the very top echelons of the CIA and USAF could arrest Colonel Kernel and his driver, and only if they came on to the non-existent Groom Lake base. Whereas, anyone else looking for them, on the very same area of restricted ground, had no rights of access and therefore no jurisdiction or power to arrest them.

The case had already been listed for a Supreme Court hearing, in front of nine judges no less. At which, and whereupon, the FBI were taking on the CIA and Pentagon, who were likewise taking on Homeland Security who were, as if it mattered, taking on the Lincoln County Sheriff's department. All to establish authority and jurisdiction in the matter.

* * * * *

As far as Professor Thelma Jones and the Research Unit crew were concerned, The Las Vegas Police department wanted her for public order offences and the FBI and Homeland Security wanted to question her regarding a terrorist plot to set off a bomb in the main Vegas strip. A notion that was unsubstantiated on all counts. There had to be a scapegoat however and someone had to take all the punches.

Frank, although unnamed in all press reportage, was also apparently wanted for questioning. And unfortunately for him he had coined the name throughout the press of: 'Fatwah Frank!' Who apparently, as there was a gap in his education (he was on tour playing football), the media assumed and stated that he was actually in Syria during that period attending an 'SISI' backed terrorist training-camp Frank did not even possess a passport! Despite the fact that apparently the FBI had picked up a bunch of passports at the scene, one of them being his! These other passport carrying men were obviously part of his terrorist network and fortunately the Vegas police had shot several of the heinous foreign men dead. As for Duncan and Diana no warrants or fingers of suspicion or accusation were pointed in their direction as the authorities did not know they existed.

* * * * *

Kruger, for his part, had nothing whatsoever to do with any of the bizarre occurrences that had just taken place. He was squeaky clean, and there appeared to be no connection between him and other alledged parties involved. Other than of course his willful act of stealing information from classified files, and recording CCTV video tape which were also classified and marked - 'eyes only.' There was also some vague notion, from an unknown source, that he may have illegally executed upwards of a dozen people who had trespassed on government land and ignored all warnings, yet still refused to give themselves up. Inside the compound that was 'doing your job.' Outside it was plain murder.

* * * * *

As far as the FBI were concerned there was nothing in their files to do with Bud Always-Jones. Although at this juncture they had no evidence of his existence and the fact that he had broken numerous laws including: breaking and entering, theft, slander, libel, peddling pornographic images of young women believed to be under the age of consent.

* * * * *

Gracie Lin Jones was clear on all counts, as there was no knowledge of her or her involvement in the situation to hand. If the police had picked her up, they might have thought she was some kind of bizarre Vegas hooker.

* * * * *

With regards to Principal J. Jones Junior, there was nothing much on him. Other than his indiscretion in the bedroom, and misuse of university funds to procure a helicopter for his own personal use. And the fact he had hundreds of images on his computer of both naked boys and girls under the age of consent Again information not as yet known by, or of use to, the FBI or other agencies.

* * * * *

What was more unimpressive was the fact that no single agency had any idea where any of these fugitives and others party to them, were currently hiding, and what significance there was in their involvement with one another.

Furthermore, no one knew or could pin-point the source of the intelligence regarding the matter that was being fed to the press and government agencies.

* * * * *

'Der gute Doktor' was on a mercy mission. Intel' had come up through the Groom Lake gatehouse, via Five Star Securities, that there had been a shoot-out, and a group of people were hold up back down in Rachel at the old diner.

Early speculation suggested that maybe it was a gang related incident? After all this was Las Vegas and in a town that never slept, anything was possible.

The Lincoln County Sheriff had been up to investigate and taken a ride into the country as far as the tree-line and the strange 'Black Mail Box.' Only to find nothing unusual along the trail. No one around, not even Five Star Security pick-up trucks.

Down in the town the gift-shop and research centre had experienced an unusual influx of day-trippers. These days very few excursions to so-called Area 51 were run out of Vegas for tourists, outings which included lunch at the 'Little Ale Inn,' before a run up to the 'Black Box' to leave a note for Peter and Paul the extraterrestrials. Plus, a photo opportunity to have pictures taken against a sign which said: *'If you cross this line, we will use deadly force to prevent you from coming any further or even living any further!'* Or words to that effect.

Given there was only a peaceful bunch of tourists present, aimlessly wandering around Rachel, the Sheriff eventually went back to Vegas to help out with road blocks and directing traffic with the Highway Patrol. Apparently there had been some form of terrorist attack in Vegas whilst he was cruising about Lincoln County.

What the Sheriff didn't know was that the assault on the old diner took place after he left Rachel, and the perpetrators of that assault were Five Star Security operatives.

However, there was always the possibility that whatever happened at Rachel had some connection to what had gone down at the press conference in Vegas. Lots of theories were floating around, everyone was suddenly an amateur detective. There had been some kind of incident for sure, of that it was certain.

Carlos, the guy at the Rachel gas station was telling everyone who stopped by that a couple of Five Star security dudes, having completed their shift, somehow got into an altercation at the back of the old diner and apparently had gotten their asses kicked by a couple of crazy-wild ladies!

This singular small piece of almost meaningless information rang a not so unusual bell for the middle-aged 'Good Doctor.'

The speculative hearsay kept on coming. Someone had mentioned that one of the kick-ass women, had super-human strength. It was then, at that point, clear to 'The Good Doctor,' by process of deduction, that these female topics of speculative rumour, were probably his latest test bed subjects under the influence of his Mega 1-90 programme. One of his latest and best control programmes to date.

Naturally, he could make a guess as to who at least one of these women were, and was also aware that Colonel Kernel had made a concerted effort to coerce one or more of these young individuals back to Groom Lake base, where further tests could be carried out.

Given a sketchy description of the two ladies concerned one was clearly Diana Rogers, upon who he had, just a few days before, snatched control of her vulnerable mind.

Of the second, apparently older woman, he knew nothing of.

It would have been fascinating to follow this development up. However, that would take time and that was something he did not have.

Although, he made an educated guess as to who just might be partially involved in this particular fracas, and the name - former Captain Kruger came up trumps.

Either way, they were, one or both, in the party of the so-called, 'geeks' that Kruger and Colonel Kernel had helped experiment upon, those nights before.

'Der gute Doktor' reminded himself of exactly what the programme was they had introduced into the group who found themselves under arrest and were being interrogated by the crude but effective Kruger.

The targets, so he recalled, had initially undergone a complete wiping of their conscience minds, through a specific and proven drug regime.

The subjects then went through a period of sensory deprivation followed by audio and visual stimulation. Together with a tortuous near-death experience, designed to draw out some of those aspects of their lives they feared the most.

This was all carried out before that was, being reactivated, using hypnotic techniques, linked up to a psychological control programme trigger. In the first instance the activation code was set as the name of a classic Shakespearian play: 'Midsummer Night's Dream.'

This initial control directive was applied as a form of closed-joke between himself and the Colonel. They wanted to see how their subjects would react to this particular nonsensical manipulation process. One that was duly followed by the far more responsive and longer lasting programme encoded as - 'Orion's Belt.' Which unfortunately, it was more than probable that the after effects of the 'Orion's Belt' command could last years, perhaps indefinitely.

As it was, and to complicate the issue, when analyzing the responses made by the target group as a result of the control regime (in his estimation anyway), the mind-bending 'Good Doctor' suspected some form of pollution or meddlesome distortion had taken place concerning the original commands given. What he meant by this was: if a command is given over (say for instance in the body of a text message), which is similar, but not exactly the same as commands already given, it can and would affect the outcome. Commands issued were supposed to be precise and accurate to the full-stop.

There was of course no evidence that this was the case. Who would want to do such a thing? And for what logical gain would they have by doing as much? Whatever the motivation, 'Der gute Doktor' had, what should be the perfect litmus test to hand. One which would most certainly reveal the truth of the matter, and he was going to put those checks and balances into effect immediately.

65

The Party Begins

The atmosphere in the old diner was now heavy with fear, loathing and more so suspicion. Anyone entering would sense the downright depressive feelings of abject hatred floating around. Old Clint could do little about it, only brew coffee and avoid breathing in Gracie Lin's tobacco smoke.

Blood sugar levels were declining all round.

Naturally the Research Unit team sat together, for now, with the Principal, who was longing to get Gracie Lin alone, so he could confront her over the break in and theft of his documentation.

With a view to ending her miserable life.

Of course, he had no actual proof it was her, but it was highly likely that was the case. Every now and then he felt for his carry-on case to caress the comforting snout of his fully loaded sidearm.

Colonel Kernel sat with his driver - Airwoman Reagan Jones, Air Force medic. His empty hand-gun lodged on one of the tables, aimlessly pointing into empty space as if it were about to be used in a dangerous game of Russian roulette.

Kruger sat with Gracie Lin Jones, they actually seemed to be getting along. His holstered side-arm could not be seen, being as it was, strapped to his lower left leg. A habit he had picked up when once, many years before, he had been seconded to a 'special unit' of the South African Police Force, back in Cape Town.

Duncan and Bud Always-Jones sat with Motto Kyoto and talked about every aspect of Japanese martial arts any one could imagine. Whilst Clint and Hillary further busied themselves in their empty and smashed kitchen. Still harboring a vague hope that they might one day re-open the diner, once that was, they fixed up the bullet holes in the walls.

No decision had been made regarding take-out Pizza. Bud, using his cell phone called up the 'Little Ale Inn,' to see if they offered a take-out service. The response being negative, due to the fact their kitchens were closed due to a lack of through trade. And furthermore, there was only the one bar-keep, being himself, and he was rushed off his feet serving Billy and Bobby the Johnson twins, who were truckers en route to someplace else along Highway 1776.

When all said and done Vegas was the closest outpost of civilization that would most certainly furnish them with pizza and a hundred other dishes. But that was a minimum two-hour haul and maybe the end of the world would have arrived by the time anyone got back.

Duncan meanwhile feigned fainting due to lack of food and liquid. At which point there appeared a shaft of headlamp lights, as, what appeared to be a military ambulance, swung around by the now vehicle-infested swing-out porch. The lights flickered and dimmed as two white-coat wearing men walked through the door fully armed with a gastronomic feast. The two men were clearly (as was Reagan Jones), medics, and were wearing Air Force insignia. Both men acknowledged their colleague, the Airwoman, by means of polite nods of recognition in her general direction. Following right behind the duo, came the Jesus-like 'loaves and fishes' figure of 'The Good Doctor,' who personally carried in a crate of beers, followed by cokes and wine, together with four bottles of Jim Beam whisky. Next came his camera, a tripod, his medical bag, and a briefcase stuffed with what was probably classified documentation.

Immediately, as if someone had lit a torch, not only did the gloomy dun coloured diner spring to life, but also the people sitting around it's tables became animated. Even the flickering street lamp out on the road suddenly glowed and shone like a beacon in a stormy night.

"Courtesy of United States Air Force people, come and

get it!" 'The Good Doctor' bellowed out as loud as he could.

Clint and Hillary, being host and hostess, organised the rationing out of both food and drink. Duncan and the boys necked a Bud each and were soon onto their second. Kruger, like Gracie went for whisky mixed with coke. Colonel Kernel took himself a beer, whilst the medic Reagan Jones stuck to straight coke. Concerning which, 'The Good Doctor' duly noted. Thelma and Diana took to the wine, whilst the Japanese tourist Mr Kyoto went for neat Jim Beam. The Principal also went for wine and drained his glass in one swallow.

Food a plenty: pizza, Chinese, corn dogs, coleslaw, fries, enough to go around. Only 'Der gute Doktor' and his two medics initially declined to partake in the epicurean extravaganza laid out before them. Suddenly, loud music kicked in as Duncan flipped a dime into the slot of the wall mounted juke box and Michael Jackson sang 'Thriller', to seemingly everyone's delight...

* * * * *

Time stood still for a couple of hours. Colonel Kernel, as with most men, ever the sexual predator, managed to sweet-talk his attractive medic-come-driver Reagan to sip at a full tumbler of good old Jim Beam. All that was missing was the ice, but no one cared. None of the gathered group had any notion as to what the night had to offer.

Meanwhile, Frank also kept his longing eyes on the pretty medic Reagan Jones. Whilst Principal Jones' face remained thunderously dark and foreboding, his skewer-like eyes piercing Gracie Lin's very soul.

Gracie Lin Jones, for her part, had not once moved position or even used the bathroom, as if some compelling force kept her pinned down in her seat. She was generally amiable, still dressed in her black and white plastic get-up. A form and style which, in some curious manner, attracted the regimented Kruger, who himself always appeared to be dressed for the parade ground. Gracie Lin had always liked a man in a uniform, or so she mused, and felt safe chatting to the security guy Kruger. But all the while she could feel the burning glare of the Principal on her back. A vengeful man whose life she had just ruined.

Thelma meanwhile drew ever-closer to Diana, but felt increasingly despondent as if she was being deliberately distant, not as she normally was with her. Something about Diana had changed, all past forms of intimacy between them had somehow been shattered. Or, that was how Thelma assessed the developing situation.

As if to compensate for any possible pending act of rejection, Thelma, now and then threw a casual and fleeting look toward Colonel Kernel, who, as with any typical man, failed to notice the advancing glances. He however, as did Frank, rather turned his attention to the medic Airwoman Reagan Jones.

Meanwhile drowning in the party atmosphere, 'Der gute Doktor' gradually crept out of his normally impenetrable shell, and even went to the lengths of slipping off his white lab coat to reveal a drab knitted button-front jersey beneath. Once up and animated he made a concerted effort to engage everyone in light banter, and was, at all times charming and polite. His two accompanying Air Force medics, having so far neither drank or eaten, went out to smoke on the swing-out porch, this time grabbing a clutch of beers on the way. They appeared content to waste the evening away.

It was around this time (as darkness had fully encompassed the small town of Rachel Nevada), when Thelma's vision inexplicably began to haze over. Her eyes could no longer focus.

As if in perfect harmony, one by one, all those gathered, who had in particular, imbibed a goodly amount of the 'Jim Beam,' began to lose their sight.

The Doctor's previously concocted additive that had laced the whisky, the wine and beer, did not take long to begin to work.

All had partaken of the magic potion.

All besides Clint and Hillary, who being exhausted, had already retired to the back of the diner and up into the attic bedroom. That left, 'Der gute Doktor' alone, as being the only one now still in complete control of his faculties. Everyone gradually lost their eye sight, (albeit temporarily). Diana, Duncan, Frank, Gracie Lin, Bud Always-Jones, Motto Kyoto the Japanese tourist, Principal J. Jones Junior, Reagan Jones, The Colonel and even Kruger. Once their collective vision had darkened all they could perceive between them were great swaths of bright illumination and colours, as each member of the group entered into their own personal 'Dreamland,' and were duly swept away by those matters in their lives they had in the past buried deep in their personal sub-consciousness train of thought.

The Colonel, who was propped against a wall, still wearing his once immaculate dress uniform, whilst chewing on a slice of now cold pizza, was last to go under, and he knew perfectly well as he did so, what exactly was going down. Half of what remained of his perfect mind was still at the moment fully cognitive.

'Der gute Doktor' had got them.

"Check mate!" the Colonel cried out.

A perfect scenario, so the Colonel contemplated: wipe everyone out; use them as slaves, assets, circus performers, do whatever you want with them - clone them, render them down in boiling water, skin them alive. God only knew what was possible.

Problem solved.

The Colonel clawed through his fragmented sense of what was right and what was wrong. He posed the burning question - how did 'The Good Doctor' know who was here at the diner? The food, the booze, all from the mess hall up in Nellis proper.

More than a two-hour return drive.

How did he know about what went down previously in

Vegas?

The TV news no doubt.

He already knew concerning the attack on the diner. He was aware regarding Kruger using 'his' command codes to inveigle himself and the Doctor, and everyone else!

The Colonel continued to weigh up the situation - were Clint and Hillary part of the deception?

Perhaps they were the obvious solution? Or, perhaps they, as was everyone else involved, mere plants? Trained actors dropped into the convoluted scenario all ready to play out their own simplistic roles.

Paranoia was rapidly taking a hold of the Colonel's wavering mind.

Could it be that the events of the day would be simply washed away?

Everything that had taken place might just be spun out to dry by the media. Forgotten and thankfully expunged from yesterday's news, as if nothing untoward had taken place.

Now it was waiting to become the substance of what conspiracy theories are always made of - conjecture and supposition.

The press conference debacle, would go down on-par with all the other alledged terror attacks on US soil. If, that was, there were ever, past or present, any 'real' terror attacks? He, the Colonel doubted it. He knew enough now to understand how the system worked.   Other than today, at this moment in time he didn't care to dwell on such heinous and devious matters.

9/11 had started it all.

Not only started, but also ended. There were no more rules.

And now someone else, not him, Kernel K. Colonel, soon to be K. Kernel deceased, would be breaking and spinning the latest news to the media.

Because of what?

Because a bunch of not much more than high-school

kids had seen a fuck-off triangular shaped jet fighter at low-level that not even the Russians knew America had up their collective mighty military complex sleeves. A jet that could bomb the crap out of Beijing or Moscow and be back for the sports results.

And that was it, once he no longer served any meaningful purpose his body, along with many others before him, would be taken down to Yucca Lake nuclear waste depository to add to the toxic pollution that was already there.

* * * * *

'Such stuff as dreams are made on and our little life is rounded with a sleep.' Those were the last words Thelma heard for what may have been a lifetime, or just a second.

* * * * *

The 'Good Old' Doctor had drugged them, all of them and felt very pleased with the outcome. Admittedly his medics out on the swing-out porch over-looking the vastness of the Nevadan desert, were not supposed to be party to the event. As it was, he would have to deal with them another time and wipe their collective mind's clean. How he longed for the device the 'Men in Black' used to render the memories of innocent on-lookers, and passersby, blank.

Science fiction often as not becomes scientific fact.

Wiping every memory clean was a mere precaution, just in case someone said something to someone and they mentioned something to someone else and the entire house of straw came tumbling down.

No one could be trusted to keep quiet.

For the Doctor it was going to be one great big grandiose experiment. He was not dealing on this occasion, as he did daily, with the masses of level one workers he kept reined in.

No.

This was of far more complex and one trial and test he had not undertaken before. Whereas it was an incredible accomplishment to take total control of one person's mind, a dozen or more simultaneously, that was something else.

Yes, he had already, long-ago, proved to himself it was possible to inveigle thousands of people gathered together in one place at one time. Sports games and music concerts being the classic examples of learnt and transferred behaviour patterns. People were quick to mimic one another, in order to be conventional, thus conforming, and therefore to become acceptable. The loner on the other hand was harder to tame.

Independence.

Knowing their own minds, straying from the well-trodden path, entering through the narrow gate, not the wide one.

What 'Der gute Doktor' was aiming for in the long-term, what he had in mind, and what his lords and masters, those who paid the bills, the mighty Military Industrial Complex, required of him, was to assess the possibility of if a small squad of soldiers could be of one accord and share the same controlled mind. That being the case then they surely would fight in unison? Each individual would become aware of the other's movements. There would be no battle ground errors. No need for a hierarchy in the chain of command, as each member would be a squad leader in their own right. One mind one body. A shared unified consciousness that would eliminate fear above all emotions.

According to the plan, upon entering a given conflict, troops would be administered a drug cocktail which made them relentless in pursuant of their objectives. Only when the mission was totally completed would they withdraw. Captured troops, those with boots-on-the-ground would have a suicide option, prior to enemy capture and inevitable interrogation and torture.

317

They had it, the technology was there, but so were the Russians, the Chinese and of course the North Koreans. Each enemy of the USA had perfected a similar project. Exoskeleton suits that enabled a soldier to run for miles carrying impossible weights, at speeds that could overhaul a fleeting cheetah, were already on the production line and awaiting field tests.

Where on US soil were, they being fabricated? Naturally down on one of the lower-levels of Groom Lake.

It so happened that they, the Doctor's mysterious benefactors, had agreed that very afternoon to press on and continue funding the 'Super Soldier' project, which was essential and vital to the continued security of the USA.

An experimental project signified as part of the overall Mega 1-90 venture. Thus, making him, the 'Doctor,' and his extensive team, to a greater extent, virtually indispensable.

The programme was now beyond science fiction.

* * * * *

'The Shadow Cabinet,' also known as the 'Dark State', the clandestine group of corporate monsters and psychopathic individuals, who actually ran the United States of America, Europe and the 'free world.' Men who were living luxurious lives in unknown locations around the globe, probably hidden deep underground, were not privy to all of 'The Good Doctor's' work. There was one super-classified project that had surprisingly been running for three generations seemingly without anyone's knowledge.

No.

Not quite without anyone's knowledge. Only now, the real fruit was ripe and ready to be plucked and demonstrated to the entire world. This one singular event would change life on planet earth forever.

* * * * *

Out there in the real world, to those who knew him or of him, 'Der gute Doktor' was apparently a leading pharmaceutical clinician, who ran a lab outside Los Angeles. (A place in reality he had not visited for the last five- years.) The lab brought pencils and paper and had a janitor empty the waste bins. In other words, it was a CIA come Pentagon come black ops' front, one that soaked-up money. Of which thirty-million dollars annually was moved across from the Federal Reserve to pay for bogus military operations, which of course simply did not exist.

Lost in paperwork.

Whereas, the 'real work' really did, and always had, taken place down on Groom Lake Nevada. Where he, 'Der gute Doktor worked on the Mega 1-90 programme and had been doing so for many years, just like his father had before him.

Meanwhile, as of now, as far as his current target group were concerned, 'Der gute Doktor' was about to issue a command code which would invariably pass the group into the second phase of the process. However, what he did next was unfathomable.

Looking at an inviting, almost full bottle of Jim Beam, he took the neck and swallowed back a great belly-full of the forty-percent proof alcoholic beverage.

If the Doctor, who never usually drank alcohol, could have seen his likeness in a mirror, he would have been shocked. On entering his blood stream, the booze drained his face of blood to make him appear even paler than usual. His eyes turned red and his forehead popped out drops of sweat. He immediately felt sick and dizzy.

His Jim Beam concoction was the basic carrier to transfer the chemical ingredients he had created, orally, into the subject's, in this case, blood stream via the stomach. A quicker more efficient resolution would have been to inject each person individually. But to do so would have involved them all agreeing to and accepting the risks and dangers of the exercise.

Therefore, having issued the next command code (which was classified), the entire group, he hoped, would inevitably pass into the second phase of the process.

'Der gute Doktor' tried to pretend the three fingers of Jim Beam he gulped back would be of no consequence, apart from him feeling slightly inebriated.

For good measure and as a boost to his flagging bravado, he took yet another swallow, as if to cancel the previous draft out. On the drinking scale he was behind the others and so now wanted to play catch-up.

The only problem being he had not given himself the verbal command code that the others had originally received once 'high' on the chemical constituent of the liquor they had all partaken in.

In other words, he had no idea how or if the command code he had previously ministered to the group would affect 'his' overall progression in the experiment. This made him, in one sense, one step behind the others and he may not be able to keep control of the event if he himself were out of control. He therefore resigned himself to basically going along with the flow of the already soon to be out of control experiment.

Whilst still 'compos mentis' yet lagging behind the others, he still had a chance to usher in the 'truth or dare' section of the process. Whereupon each of the target group members would, if he was correct in his estimation, open up and share with the wider group, exactly what they knew about any subject matter that was relevant to what had happened over the past thirty-six or so hours. Or, so he hoped.

It was confession time and, if nothing else 'Der gute Doktor' would, as anticipated, glean some important Intel' from each and every member of the group. Or, it may end up being him who opened up the worm can of 'his' life, thus letting all his little hidden secrets out.

As it was, he suspected not all the people gathered

were who he thought they were. He also wanted to know just what motivated them and why and how they found themselves in the circumstances they were currently in. Above all he had to find out how much 'classified information' each one of his subjects might hold in their tenuous memories. And, to gain the answers to the questions he required information on, he was more than happy to take wider, more drastic action, to readily garner what he required to know.

'Der gute Doktor' was now on uncharted territory and therefore felt his two little medic helpers should make themselves scarce, in order for them not to witness what may or may not happen next. Whatever the outcome it would be classified. However, having thrown back a half-bottle of good old American fighting juice, the medics decided to take what remained of the liquor bottle and go find even more of the same at the 'Little Ale Inn.' And maybe some good old Nevadan prime rump steak. By that they meant women!

Consequently, the Air Force medics made themselves scarce, whilst 'The Good Doctor,' feeling a little giddy, set up a hi-end video camera, which he had brought with him, along with a range of other interesting implements, to record the session. He turned to the group and enquired: "what time do we have?" None of the MRU team could answer him as none of their watches still remained in working order.

Bud Always-Jones was naturally curious and was keen to take a close-up look through the video camera lens. The Doctor, cut him plenty of slack. After all, if he was interested in video cameras he might come in useful later on. 'Der gute Doktor' had no idea at this juncture that Bud was a news cameraman in his own right.

The Doctor, having posed the question concerning the time once again, he waited momentarily before he looked through the video camera lens to correlate the time code.

The Colonel suddenly responded in a typical military fashion: "21.11 precisely."

"OK 09.11 p.m. the Doctor replied. All was now good to go and the candidates were invited up to where the video camera was situated.

First up to play the game was the seemingly eager Thelma Jones. She stood confidently before the rolling video camera trained in her direction.

'The Good Doctor,' upon visually examining Thelma, immediately noticed that her vision was beginning to return, as she displayed the usual physical signs he would expect to witness as being apparent in someone being dosed with his experimental Sodium Pentethol, come Dimethyltryptamine, come Amphetamine, come LSD, plus substances unknown, based concoction. One he had recently personally perfected.

There was a certain amount of twitching and convulsing clearly apparent in Thelma's demeanor. Also, she demonstrated signs of increasingly prolonged periods of maintaining blank expressions whilst gazing aimlessly into space. After a few tense moments and feeling unsteady on her feet Thelma began to speak.

"I am and have been researching some important environmental issues and had some time ago written a paper on the subject of polar magnetism, which the Principal of the Iowa State University, assisted me with. Who was by the way related to me; a distant cousin, in fact. After I completed the paper, he wanted to take ownership of my far-reaching research work and extensive articles. In exchange he promised me my own laboratory to work in, and staff to help continue my studies and to expand upon my, what I felt were, critical discoveries…"

"I was only a student at the time," she continued, "when he first took me into his office and jokingly persuaded me to sit on his lap, whilst he stroked my thigh. After a few minutes his hand slid inside of my thigh and he then tried to push one of his fingers into me. I pulled away and ran out. He was angry with me and ignored me for some time. I felt defiled, dirty, as if it were my fault and I had done something wrong. At the time I had not even kissed a guy, let alone have a man's hand between my legs. It put me off men, then and forever. He did not touch me like that again. But for years after he made my life difficult with his suggestive comments and inferred that if I did not ultimately comply to his wishes then the research work, I was engaged in would cease as he would turn off the funding taps, leaving my team and I high and dry. Altogether he made my life more than difficult, impossible even. He was always trying to control and manipulate me. Until one day he actually discovered something for himself pertaining to some old ideas relating to alchemy and Francis Bacon, who attended the court of Queen Elizabeth the first of England. Of who it is said is, or was, *the 'father of science' and the 'mystery schools.'*

Principal Jones traced the Jones family history way back and discovered there was a part of the extensive family tree that was related to and connected with the English aristocracy.

The Jones family were present in the English court and acted as ambassadors for the Prince of Wales who was related to Henry the Eighth. Of course, the Jones dynasty eventually left Britain with the Pilgrim Fathers to settle in the New World. However, they took all of their occult knowledge with them.

Principal Jones is obsessed with the notion of alchemy and wanted to resurrect and re-enact some of his ancestor's ritualistic magic. Here there lies a paradox, in as much as the Jones family were dedicated Christians, with ties to the Plymouth Brethren. A strict Calvinistic inspired religious cult. Whereas, on the other side, they were blatant practitioners of 'black magic' and the occult in general. How could these two disparate disciplines run concurrently?" Thelma began to waiver, as if she were a balloon about to burst.

"However," she continued, "it did and has been doing since the Pilgrim Fathers and their Masonic brotherhood set foot on the soil of the New World."

Thelma suddenly collapsed on the wooden floor and immediately Airwoman Jones scrambled up to assist her flagging cousin.

"Let her sit, someone water now quick." 'The Good Doctor' was quick to react and produced a bottle of still-water.

The others present failed to move.

Everyone was elsewhere and nowhere, sitting or standing in bewilderment, gazing into the air, as if they were attentively watching a movie drift by before their eyes.

Colours flashed around the room, or so they imagined.

Sounds amplified about them, so they thought.

The redolence of cold pizza seeped from the walls, as if the past were bleeding gastronomic memories into the room. Shards of gold and silver rained from the ceiling, bathing all present in a golden shower of ritualistic purification.

Suddenly, and without prompting Principal J. Jones Junior M.A. interjected. However, before he dutifully stood to his feet, his hand once more went down into his carry-on luggage, to feel the secure presence of his hand-gun. Which he increasingly felt a desire to use, but temporarily removed the notion from his mind, as if he were waiting for the right opportune moment to engage the weapon.

"It's about the government," he firmly interjected. Talking as if he were no stranger to the camera and being interviewed. "Over the years, they were always looking for answers, they always wanted to get ahead. Yes, Francis Bacon possessed magical powers, that's why everyone admired him and that's how he gained more and more control and influence in the Elizabethan court. Because you know it is really the people who actually hold onto the power. The others, the kings and queens, are no more than an illusion. The rulers have tricked people into thinking they hold secrets and can control nature or even god. But they can't."

Principal Jones paused unsteadily for effect.

"There are so many secrets in the Jones family. For instance, every male member of the family is forcibly brought into Freemasonry. They have no choice in the matter. All must learn and understand the craft. If you decline? Then you are not a Jones.

Once however, you have progressed up and along the Masonic degrees you are then expected to join the 'Shriners' and pretend you are, along with the others, social benefactors who do nothing other than good deeds all day long. There is nothing that could be further than the truth. I know, I am one of them!"

At that crucial and most significant point, Kruger suddenly left Gracie Lin's side and faced the lurching Principal Jones. Gracie took the opportunity to leave for the bathroom whilst the murderous Principal Jones was otherwise engaged with his tales of Freemasons and 'Shriners.'

"Steady brother." Kruger held out a hand, which the Principal took and shook.

"Steady, you're in danger of bringing down a curse upon yourself" Kruger advised caution. Not wanting to expose the fact to those present that he, as was just about every man who worked on the Groom Lake facility was, also a fully-fledged Mason.

"Hey just wait a minute." The Colonel suddenly emerged from the wall he had been crawling up, tall and full of confidence. "Just hang on Kruger, you aint no Mason and that's for certain!"

Kruger momentarily forgot the Principal and moved to face-off with the Colonel.

"More like a Clansman! You know KKK?!"

It was true enough, even Kruger's initials were designated as KKK! Whilst in South Africa he was a vocal supporter of the apartheid movement, of which he made no excuses over. Once he had arrived in the USA there was ample scope for him to become involved in the white supremacy movement, where a man could freely express his political and racial views.

Colour and racial prejudice was and always had been at the root of Kruger's dislike of the Colonel. He just could not cope with the notion that a man of mixed-race could be telling 'him' what to do.

"What are you all saying here?" Bud Always-Jones, having become disinterested in the camera, left to further demolish another bottle of Bud, whilst feeling more than inebriated, if not totally high. He also needed the restroom, but felt prior to using the 'can' he had to confess, as a Jones, his own tentative involvement with Freemasonry. He eventually decided against it, as a wave of rainbow colours swept over the former camera man and prompted him to begin talking in an outlandish form of gibberish. Addressing not those gathered, but rather a lowly broken bar-stool.

The Colonel meanwhile, having sufficiently provoked Kruger, tried to assemble his own thoughts and add something constructive to the conversation: "OK." You may hate me for my colour… But what was the question again?"

He had forgotten how the conversation had drifted around to issues of race and supremacy, and thought it better to act in a less contentious manner. Paranoia was creeping in further and he wanted to slip like a slimy snail retreating back into his introverted, yet safe fragile shell.

As for 'The Good Doctor,' he was desperate to once and for all set the record straight and to be the one who finally possessed all the obtuse answers to the questions they, including himself, were all asking.

"But in practice it did not work." A small voice sounded off.

Regardless of the question and its origin, 'Der gute Doktor' tried to continue, but was unexpectedly cut off as the quiet Japanese tourist thought he should clarify his position to all those present, and began to expound some principles of his own. "That is why some seven-hundred tests, yes, seven-hundred, lucky number, but not for Japanese people. They are unlucky people." The slight, yet razor-sharp oriental, as with the others, was reaching a high-point in his individual quasi-hallucinogenic experience.

"Experiments" he continued, "were carried out on the Nevada testing range. It was nothing to do with perfecting nuclear warheads, nothing, no nothing. I know because my ancestors were there, when the bomb dropped." Mr Kyoto's face distorted, his entire appearance was dramatically altering.

Regardless, of his painfully contorted expression the Japanese man continued with his assessment. "Because the so-called scientists, thought that the more exposure the heavy-metal lead has to nuclear fission, hah! Yes, the more likely it was to do just that. Just what they wanted, to change its molecular make-up, like grubs in a jar that undergo metamorphosis and change into butterflies.

They set up the Nevada testing ground where it is today, because it was adjacent to the old lead mines. Miles of tunnels that stretch under Groom Lake and beyond; huge caverns like European cathedrals. And all the waste and dross from the mining heaped up into pyramid-shaped mountains until eventually they used the white lime-stone amalgam to lay down the banjo shaped runway. Six-miles of it, millions of tons of rock waste. Everyone believes it to be naturally occurring salt-pans. What stone was left was used to make the concrete to cast the walls and floors of what emerged as potential below ground cities."

Bud for one was more than curious concerning how this diminutive oriental man knew all of these facts? The substance of many investigative conspiracy theorists as seen on the internet. Truths he personally and readily accepted.

Motto Kyoto continued as if he were primed with jet-fuel. "They moved from Los Alamos. Perfect. These mines, 'Hi Ho Hi Ho,' were stripped naked and I don't know anything more."

The Japanese man drew his knees up and buried his face in his hands as if praying to the gods of his ancestors in heaven above.

Now it was Thelma's turn once more as she rallied herself. "Only it was the 'Shriners' who funded my Magnetronic Research Unit project. I don't know why, what their motive might have been, but I think they were people who had another agenda on top of what I was doing. I never felt in control of any of my projects. I always had to answer to someone else."

Thelma had struggled back on her feet and felt better for her brief time-out period. Reagan Jones carefully helped perch her back down on a chair. Looking at Thelma, the Airwoman imagined her as being a multi-colored parrot locked in a cage, her feathers having being plucked. She longed to fly but could not achieve lift-off velocity.

Meanwhile, the Doctor's video camera, having been left to its own devices, was now aimed at the opposite wall. All notions of duly recording the session by now had fallen apart, until Bud rose once more to the occasion.

Diana Rogers suddenly stood up, as if she were about to engage in a kindergarten 'show and tell,' she proceeded in a managed and controlled way to address those gathered.

"I only worked in Thelma's lab I didn't know anything about the Principal and what he was trying to do. I knew I was in love with Thelma however. I could not help it. I did not want to date guys. I don't know why because they all came after me. I was a sex-object and no one, until I met Thelma, accepted me for what I am."

Her brief statement was to those gathered profound and unexpected. Frank looked surprised, as to a certain extent so did Thelma. Diana had, previously, in a sense, 'come out,' and Thelma was at the time glad that she had, as she shared common feelings of lack of acceptance by those around her, for simply being the people who they really were.

As if to strike back, Frank Blake off-camera piped up,

with a managed yet defensive edge to his tone of voice.

As if he actually didn't care or give a damn.

"My life revolves around football, field and track events. Like all the other guys I have been chasing Diana. So, I have wet dreams about her, or did." Hurting Frank was about to throw his retaliatory blow. "Recently however, since we have been on this expedition, I have changed my mind about her." Frank emphatically sat down even further away from the prying lens of the still rolling camera.

Duncan Dunkerley, who was laying prone across a bench seat towards the back of the diner was too busy hallucinating. First, he saw snakes, big ugly suckers that crawled down the walls one after another and he was defenceless against their perpetual onslaught. Left to right, right to left, some tin soldiers had come in the room and he wanted to stand up to attention but couldn't not muster the strength to do so.

Eventually whilst all was quiet, he spoke out, clearly minus his usual lisping drawl. "Nothing to report. I mean I kind of just go along with the flow and see you know where it takes me. I am still hungry though."

Bud Always-Jones unclipped the camera from the tripod and, still rolling, came to Duncan's side. He began to nurse Duncan as if he were a frightened child. He rocked the limp body of Duncan Dunkerley back and forth.

"I don't know why I tag along with her." He, Bud, was clearly referring to Gracie Lin. She treats me like I was her bitch or something. Bud do this Bud do that, all the time. I even steal for her. I broke into the Principal's office at the university for her and downloaded all his files on a memory stick. She has them now, she has it all. Man let me tell you, she's a goddamn evil black witch man and that I am sure. She can see stuff that you or me can't. I don't know how she does it or what or why she does it. Like it's a thing with her, exercising power over other people for no good or real reason."

Bud paused, "Look at me, I'm a mess!" His eyes began to well up with tears that had been long buried beneath the dry ground of his empty soul. He continued to talk off-cam,' whilst the lens was still focused on Duncan.

"So, I can't get a lady of my own. Like that's how I got into this porn game. Thought it would be a way to meet girls. And it is. But they don't want you for you, they just want you for money. So, I never made anything out of it. All that Porntube content. You end up paying the performers, whilst the director-come-camera-operator gets jack-shit, maybe a B.J. If he's lucky. But like hey, man, unless you have a massive 'shlong' you don't ever get to fuck the ladies. Porn mongers only want to see the big cocks, not small ones, they literally never get a look in!"

Gracie Lin Jones, who was far from feeling her normal self, but was still able to be lucid, cut across her lackey-come-side-kick. "Shut the fuck up Bud you dill-weed!"

Having returned from the rest room, she now positioned herself next to 'The Good Doctor,' as if she were the main act of the night.

The Doctor retrieved the camera from the two emotional boys, and re-mounted it on the tripod, before framing the flamboyant retro-clad woman. Who she actually was he was anxious to discover?

Gracie Lin of course was more than comfortable with having a camera shoved in her face. "Why am I here?" Was her opening statement. "You ask me why I am here?" She glared around the room with her back now to the camera. "You asking me why I am here?"

Gracie continued in earnest. "Isn't it obvious? I am here because I am. I am who I am and no one else. I won't allow myself to belong to anyone…

None of you.

Right from when I was a kid, I would not allow myself to be ruled over. You have no idea what it is like, belonging to this huge family that runs an entire State of the mother-fuckin' Union. Iowa. Why Iowa? Bread basket of America. They own it all. The agriculture, the industry, the farm lands, the banks, the schools, hospitals and universities, everything in the State of Iowa is owned by the Jones family. Every other person I meet is my goddamn cousin. It's getting overcrowded by the Jones plague. So, I stepped out and they condemn me. I lost my status because I am not back home getting knocked up every shit-kicking year to produce yet another Jesus-Christ-Super-Star-Jones. So, I kick out on my own and they spurn me. I am alone and they spurn me for that. But I have found a power that consoles me. I need money, money will show them I can be and am independent. Then they will come back to me when I have the gold! Yes, I know about the gold, the 'Shriner's' gold, this is why they funded this minuscule Magnetronic Research Unit expedition, to get hold of the gold. Nothing to do with measuring the earth's magnetic field and polar shifts. Christ is everyone so fuckin' dumb around here? I have seen some of the papers, the theories, his and her ideas." Gracie Lin pointed first towards the wilting Principal and then back to Thelma. Her claw-like accusatorial digit was akin to that of a wizen old hag. Thelma felt a shiver up her spine. Whilst the former Captain Kruger sat bolt upright and was fully attentive to what was being said. Gold for the South African ex-patriot was a key trigger to garner his attention.

Gracie continued… "I know all about it. The grand plan. Not complete as yet, I still needed to grab more information for them. The others, his fellow conspirators, don't trust him." She gestured towards the Principal. "They needed leverage as a precaution, just in case he ever went freelance. They know his weakness - sex. So, having had to 'B.J.' all his old freakish buddies, you know, just to let me get acquainted with them all, they just had to leave their mark on me, to keep me on a tight leash as it were, to remind me of their power and influence." Gracie quite unexpectedly pulled up her right sleeve and turning her forearm up, she thrust the limb in front of the camera lens.

The moment passed, no one saw what she had visually demonstrated, not even the Doctor caught sight of what was probably a tattoo. Or, so the Principal surmised.

"Then I had to screw him, the so-called Principal here." She looked directly into the dark blood-shot eyes of the Principal. "He was easy, a push-over, literally. I fucked him just to find out what he knows. I now know who he is. He knows that. He deserves to be brought down; he knows that. I brought him down. He knows that as well. I remember, I know, he thinks I don't. Because I was just a kid man, a baby more or less. And he did stuff, not just to me, but others in the family. Maybe boys and girls. And no one, the adults, they did not care, it was accepted. I thought that their religion was against that kind of kid molestation stuff, but it was just plain evil. But they let it go, they let them fiddle with us and do stuff."

The air crackled electrifyingly with a whole range of mixed emotions. It was deathly hush hush silent one minute, then as loud as the county fair on a Friday night the next.

Gracie continued… "Whilst he was screwing me, just a few days ago, in his big luxury apartment bed, all I could think of was the fact that he had been there, in me, before, when I was a kid, I remember it all graphically. All I wanted to do whilst he was riding me was, right there and then, rip his goddamn throat out. And I would have done, other than I needed him to point me the way to the rich stuff. You know - Dorothy and the gold brick road. Off to see the wizard of OZ. The wizard of gold bars. OZ means ounces. Lots of them. All I had to do was to kill the wicked witches. And I thought I had done that, but they the wicked witches of the east and the west were not really the problem. It was her:"

Gracie now pointed the same imaginary wizen old finger once more towards Thelma, whose blood pressure had gone through the ceiling, as her heart pumped erratically for the sake of precious oxygenated air.

Gracie, becoming exhausted, due to her prolonged

332

rant, was now thankfully calming down. "But it was her all the time. The fairy Godmother, Thelma Jones, the lady I trusted was the real wicked witch. And I wanted her power. I wanted to be accepted as she was, I wanted to be the successful professor, to be sent off to university, rather than forced to marry some wimpy Jones boy who worked in a shit-hole of a Jones bank. So, I looked for it, I looked for the power. I needed a 'demon,' or 'daemon' to guide me and energies me, and I found it all in 'Mary Quant.' I went retro and found the sixties fashion icon and modelled myself on her until I actually became her. She was my idol, she is me, I am her, my alter-ego, my 'daemon' who I let teach me how to take power and control over others, so that one day I could and would exact my revenge upon them all."

Astounded, 'Der gute Doktor' stood up. He never imagined that his latest little peculiar experiment would produce such a wild and vivid effect.

* * * * *

Sodium Pentethol had always been the bench-mark chemical, used in lie-detection tests which, once administered, normally released people to tell the actual truth concerning a particular set of circumstances. This old process was usually connected to some form of lie-detection test. Whatever it was, the Doctor now had at his disposal, it would end the use and requirement of prehistoric lie-detectors, and the need for the ingestion of crude toxic chemicals.

Clearly moved and shaken by what he had heard so far, the Principal felt he had to respond to the serious accusations levelled at him by some of those present.

Consequently, Principal (soon to be fired), once again checked the status of his precious hand-gun.

"Everything in life is inconsistent, a paradox, a duality. They hated me, but at the same time they needed me." As he spoke perspiration trickled down his forehead before dripping down his back causing him to shiver. "They needed me to do what was necessary, but they did not want to do it themselves, because it was unsavory. They lived and acted as if it were a revulsion, this indulgence of mine. They condemned it, but condoned it, when it came to those 'special gatherings,' those certain nights of the year when they all had to re-affirm their vows to ensure the continuation of the dynasty, the sacred blood-line which dates back a long long way. Back to when they were in Britain, as the ruling 'Druids' who worshipped the sun the moon and the four seasons. They brought all of that with them. All under the guise of branching out to a New World Orderliness, where freedom of speech and freedom of religion was the directive of the day.

Then the Freemasons took a hold.

These days no male Jones can avoid being brought into the fold. And if you didn't comply, then they put the squeeze on you until you basically have no more fight left. And then you die dishonorably. If nothing else your widow gets looked after.

For you however, it's not your loving devoted family that's your first and foremost priority. Rather, it's the lodge members, the sacred societies with secrets to conceal.

The 'Shriners' infiltrated the Masons and took over their communities. Like a creeping cancer they permeated every level of society and every section of the neighborhood. You are a 'Shriner' first, husband and father second. You follow a particular life-style and adhere to a strict code of conduct."

Whilst orating, all the former Principal could envision was a gun, his loaded gun. He imagined its cold ruthless metal held tightly in his palm; the barrel aimed at Gracie Lin.

"They all knew about my little whims, there again I was needed, and it suited their purposes. So, they made sure I was looked after, the job as Principal of Iowa State, mysteriously fell into my lap. I could carry on doing whatever I wanted to do without impunity. So long as they could use me when they required. They even sent me my own 'personal spy' to watch over me. Keep me, as best they could, on the straight and narrow. Of course, she was a Jones family member, Ms Celia Jones acting as my secretary. I've known all along."

Suddenly the former Principal turned toward Gracie Lin, who was contemplating keeping a low profile.

"Now they have sent me another dog, another treacherous Jones female, this time to ruin me and rob me."

An uncomfortable protracted silence pervaded the musty atmosphere, as if everyone was expecting something to happen. Be that as it may, it was getting late, people were already tired and jaded due to the events of the day.

'Der gute Doktor' quietly sniggered to himself when he contemplated the notion of going to 'Dreamland' cocktail lounge and ordering a couple of Area 51 specials. He naturally would be bar-keep and he could mix a hell of a drink that would blow your mind and fry your brain pan!

As it was the amphetamine content of the drug cocktail that had been administered to all parties managed to keep everyone a little more alert than they perhaps might have been.

Suddenly, just as matters were coming to a cessation, the Principal decided to continue his shocking tale of sexual abuse, and who knew what else?

'Der gute Doktor' kept up his observations, just about everything being said was of great interest to him. Be that as it may, his 'big' leading question to himself was: *'how was it none of the target group present were readily or obviously judgmental of one another's conduct or behaviour?'* There seemed to be no condemnation present in the room, shock, revulsion yes, but no condemnation. Which, in terms of human behaviour, was utterly out of character.

"I am not actually an M.A. I don't actually possess any academic qualifications," the Principal continued with his confession. "And so I have to be careful what I say and who I say it to. I have to make certain my back is always covered. Ms Jones sees to that. By the way, where is she? Why isn't she here?"

'Der gute Doktor' was not surprised by such a confused questioning reaction from the Principal. He clearly had lost all sense of any existent time-line and environmental awareness.

The target group were now well into their respective journeys and were experiencing bouts of fear and paranoia. Reality was increasingly becoming warped and blurred, contradiction followed contradiction. At this point of the psychological voyage the individual minds of the target group had to be split into two disparate compartments, each demonstrating opposing characteristics. This was and is how a person could be controlled. One half of the person would be in say: reality 'A' and the other half would be represented by: reality 'B'.

The Principal continued in what appeared to be a highly confused manner. "Sorry Thelma, the entire MRU project was a set-up. We sent you out there to look for psychic phenomena and electro-magnetic activity, whereas all the time 'they,' the mad men who funded your little jaunt, were looking for a certain type of hi-grade lead deposit."

Thelma was initially aghast, her jaw dropped, then stoicism took over and she bit her quivering lip. Why did it not surprise her? Nothing had changed, she had been out manoeuvred by others and used once again by this vile manipulative man, if you could call him a man.

"You and your team needed to be directed to Rachel, like a bull by its nose." The Principal tried to win Thelma back, but the situation had gone too far. Regardless, he continued. "You, me, all of us have been hoodwinked into thinking we were doing something of importance to mankind, but it all ended up being a mere pig circus."

The former bogus Principal collapsed hard on a chair, head in hands, sweating and short of breath, all signs of the drug cocktail doing its work.

Meanwhile Mr Kyoto, in a world of his own making, momentarily pulled his thoughts back together and decided to try back-up some of what the Principal was trying to say.

"Let me complete his story, this man, the Principal, whoever he is. I can complete his story." Mr Kyoto was back from holding his head on, and seemed to have gathered a second-wind.

He had tried to make himself comfortable and waited for the drug, he had been administered against his will, to lose its effect. He had previously considered pumping his own stomach out, but then curiosity took the better of him and he decided to stay with it. He desperately wanted to see what was going to happen next and relished the idea of witnessing whatever the outcome might be. The gambler inside of him figured, by the tell-tale presence of a hand-gun (the Colonel's, with an empty chamber), laid on the round table close to the service counter, that they, everyone present, would eventually kill one another.

Which, under the circumstance, did not really matter to him. He was a stranger to (almost), them all, and his original reason and motive for being where he was at this present moment in time was supposedly to take his own life, a notion that was no longer on his bucket list.

"He is, or was," Mr Kyoto continued, "talking about the alchemists who have throughout history tried to turn heavy metals into gold. They are still trying back in Russia, China, France, India, any country which possesses nuclear weaponry, they have all thought along those lines. And it was there up on the test range," he pointed south-west, "that they built a lead wall to 'soak up' radiation. The theory being: lead would continue to suck in extra molecules until the nature of the substance actually changed. You see, my research, the documents I read, once they had become declassified anyone could figure it

337

all out, if you only took the time to do so."

"And how is it you know so much Mr?" Kruger, who had been silent for much of the time, was now totally convinced he was in a mental home and everyone present, apart from the woman Gracie Lin Jones, were insane patients. His head was spinning, throat was dry and his back and feet tingled in a strange and erratic manner.

"Kyoto, Motto Kyoto at your service."

"Well how do you know? You aint one of those goddamn tourist monkeys that I am paid to keep off government property, are you?"

"No, not exactly, I am, or was a physicist working in Canada. However, now retired, but physics still remains a hobby and interest of mine. Oh, and by the way I saw a documentary about alchemy, it was on Fox."

Kruger quickly lost interest. However, he also had noticed the weapon sitting on the table close to the service counter. And for no particular reason he removed his own gun from its holstered position on his left leg and lay it flat next to what was the Colonel's empty piece.

Mr Motto Kyoto continued regardless of Kruger's lack of interest. "It was secret of course. But the very people who could or would police such revelations, were the ones who were determined to control and benefit from the process. The men at the top, as the Principal alluded to, were all 'Shriners.' I know, they are everywhere, in Canada, Japan, Australia, the UK, Russia and China, the world over. And they keep records, thousands of them, dating way back…"

Now, no one in particular was taking any notice of the camera, or the observations and comments of others. Despite that fact, the Japanese man continued his quasi-scientifically based analysis.

"You see the proceeds from the gold yield would be managed by them and sold into the open market. To reach their goal they increased the number of tests and the detonation activities went up and up.

As a society with secrets they needed to know

everything concerning nuclear fission and how to transform one substance into another more valuable commodity. Before the then Soviets could work it all out. As they always eventually did. Because behind the scenes in the so-called 'arms race' both super-power factions shared common intelligence.

A 'cold war' kept the balance of power on an equal footing. And the 'Shriners' were on both sides of the Iron Curtain.

Every military power on the planet scrambled to do all they could to further the: 'lead into gold' project. Aptly called: 'Plan 666' by some, or 'Golden Fleece' by others." The big idea being - the more the lead deposits were exposed to external radiation, the quicker the gold would 'hatch.'

The longer-term aim being to deposit the bullion in a 'Shriner' controlled global financial system. One that would afford the 'Shriners' total control of the stock and gold bullion markets.

Some, a few, financiers were vaguely aware of what was going on. So, they tried to stabilize and protect the existing markets and financial system. But ultimately their fears were unfounded. Because, although the lead- to-gold metamorphosis worked theoretically, it certainly did not in practice.

To alter the atomic structure, it would take exposure to hundreds of underground blasts for the nature of lead's atomic make-up to change. Ironically some lead was turned into gold all right: 'Fool's Gold' - Iron Pyrite with a radioactive signature that would remain 'hot' for a thousand years." Mr Kyoto felt he was wasting his breath. He slipped in the comment concerning Iron Pyrite to gauge whether or not anyone was paying attention. They weren't.

The Principal thankfully remained in a state of blissful-hypnotic-somnambulant trance.

Meanwhile, the effervescent, Reagan Jones took her turn on the stand and the atmosphere lightened up.

"Hi everyone, I am a United States Air Force paramedic and have been for some years. I was born back in Iowa. Like the other Jones girls here, I wanted to get out. Get out as soon as I was able and so that is what I did, at eighteen-years old I enlisted and trained as a medic and was at Anderson before being posted to Edwards. All I know about my kin is what other relatives, cousins mainly, said about the family as a whole. How, as a female, I was expected to stay at home with my older and younger sisters, and meet and marry some boy from the family and have his children. I was destined to be no more than a housewife changing nappies. But I wanted to see the world. After I left home my parent's cut me off from the family, which I am glad they did, because, when I was younger, on several instances my uncles and older cousins messed about with me. First it was playful, nothing much. I must have been seven maybe. Then it got more serious and on a couple of occasions I went to a sleep-over with my cousins and after lights-out there were men who came into the room. It was a big bedroom, all the Jones families had big houses. Some of the other girls were taken out of the room, some stayed. I stayed and someone came to try and get under my Eiderdown with me. He felt under my tee-shirt and his hands were all over me. I saw it was one of my older boy-cousins. He was trying to kiss me and feel between my legs. I struggled a little and ran out of the room and found the restroom and I locked myself in there. Sometime later I was made to go to another birthday party, to the same house, where my uncle lived. He was something to do with the administration of the State. This time there were older men there. Maybe men who were not cousins or uncles? Maybe? Maybe not. They tried the same things. Later I asked one of my cousins what happened to her, she said she was interfered with by two men that night and to forget it. But I couldn't.

Then one of my cousins got pregnant real young. Maybe eleven or twelve and they took her away to have the baby. I never saw her or the baby again."

Gracie and Thelma felt slightly uncomfortable listening to their new-found cousin. There still existed in both of them, feint traces of repressed memories, unasked for recollections, that were being brought to the surface. They had both heard these and similar kinds of tragic stories before, many times over.

"So, I got out." Reagan continued. "Then when I was fully trained by the Air Force, and been on some combat missions in Afghanistan, Iraq and other places, I was approached off-base one day by a man, a civilian, I guess. He said he knew about my past and the family I was born into and asked if I wanted to serve my country? I said of course I did. He introduced me to some other people. They were CIA recruiters. Usually they recruited out of universities, the military or from existing government posts. They wanted people with my tough exterior resilience, and I could best serve my country by keeping an eye on certain people in the Air Force who they thought were a potential threat to national security and interest.

Or, so they said.

They also told me my classified work would be highly sensitive and dangerous, and it may involve getting close to people, men, high-ranking officers. I was to check them out, see if they talked in their sleep, or spoke out of turn in their dreams. See what I could dig up, and report back. As naive as I was, I did not realise at first that it may have, and did, involve having relations with officers."

"Yes, and go on..." 'Der gute Doktor' echoed everyone's surprise and shock regarding what was being conveyed.

"A lot of men on the bases I went to treated women like objects and thought they could harass them in the work place. Senior officers declined to take any notice of what was going on around them, and they did little or nothing to stop the open forms of stalking and abusive pestering that many Airwomen endured. I was OK, tough, often seen as a challenge, sport to some of the fly-boys.

As it was, I already had a definite agenda to mix it with the higher-ranking officers. And so, I looked at it in different terms, I was not vulnerable and powerless like some of the other enlisted women on the bases."

The Air Force Woman looked accusingly toward Colonel Kernel. "My current assignment is him!" Reagan gestured towards Colonel Kernel. "I have been seconded to his Intel unit for a few months and have opened an interesting file on him.

Higher-ranking officers, the 'top-brass' in the Pentagon feel he may in the future be a security breach. Their biggest fear is if he retires and goes off-base to write his memoirs, which may open a big can of worms. They want to make sure whichever way, and if he does go off-base they will then plot some way to get rid of him."

The Colonel kept very still and very quiet. Nothing of what he was hearing troubled him, he knew the process and procedures, he helped to write the manual.

Then again, he was terrified shit-less and wanted to get out of the crap-ass outfit he was in before it got too late.

Suddenly, Thelma broke across the interview. "You were wearing some kind of a vacation sports shirt, or tee, and short pants with golfing shoes. I remember that." She was referring to the Colonel and what had previously taken place. Waves of recollection kept on washing up on her shore-line as her mind began to slowly recover.

The Air Force Woman took the centre ground once more and continued her tale.

"However, the Colonel already knows what happens to men or women when they are no longer of use, and become liabilities. They disappear into Yucca Lake never to be seen or heard of again."

Reagan Jones had learnt how to act, or put on an act, she was a skilled dramatic operator. "He has sent men to their death, and now I feel he may feel a deep-seated guilt regarding his actions. So, I was told to go along with whatever he does, watch his back and report to them if and when applicable."

"Who is 'them' and 'they' Reagan?" Diana had said very little regarding the strange confessional session they were involved in.

"Well, I, I don't know, I mean I can't tell. They have coded identities; I am not supposed to say."

"You can now, you can because of the truth serum, the Sodium Pentethol derivative. You cannot fight it, it draws everything out of you, you cannot fight it ... you cannot fight it..."

'The Good Doctor's' hypnotic voice and words sent The Airwoman's head reeling. Regardless she tried to continue. "I don't know any of them, never meet them, but they all had coded identities: one was known to me as Harry S. Truman. Another was Dwight D. Eisenhower, then another Franklin, Franklin D. Roosevelt. Then outside of the higher-ranks I only know Colonel Kernel here, and 'The Good Doctor.' Who, and he is not aware of this, or privy to what I am about to say. I have also been seconded to watch. And I have been officially made part of his Mega 1-90 project as a kind of snoop ...

'The Good Doctor's' eyes grew large in wonderment. He always thought he knew his superiors, whoever they were, but suddenly he realised that he did not. He was profoundly shocked. For a brief moment his world crashed in on him.

Only for an instant.

Air Force Woman Reagan Jones, now a self-confessed undercover agent, carried on. "My practical day-to-day role is simple: although I am billeted up at Nellis, I take the first plane ride in from McCarran to Groom Lake. And then in hanger-bay 5, level 1, I check people in as they come onto the farm. I need to search them for anything they are not permitted to bring on board such as cell-phones, video cameras and any other recording devices. There are others working the line, not just me, we check people out. Sometimes I send them to see the 'Doc,' if I think they need a shot or a treatment session. That is my other job, to administer medication to any one of the subjects that come through the programme."

Both 'Der gute Doktor' and Colonel Kernel were fully aware of some of the Airwoman's duties. As it was the Colonel was regretting trying to date Reagan Jones, she may have been more than a handful, a viper at the breast, a woman that he perhaps could not manage or control.

"I initially had no idea what the overall work was or is on the Groom Lake testing ground." Reagan continued in a labored fashion. "I know Edwards in California is a white air base. Whereas Groom Lake was once ultra-black. Now the Groom Lake base is grey. It holds former black projects that, for whatever reasons are no longer one-hundred percent black, neither top-secret or classified."

Of this, only the Colonel and 'Der gute Doktor' had any real inclination as to what the Airwoman was relating.

However, the Japanese tourist, come physicist, Motto Kyoto was having a few of his former conceptions and conspiratorial theories readily confirmed.

The Airwoman pressed on. "I am also aware that there is a large part of the facility dedicated to experimentation concerning mind control, psychic powers and reading, telepathy and related pseudo sciences. All under the authority of these two men here." She gestured towards the Doctor and the Colonel.

"The levels below level 2, what do you know of what takes place there?" The good Doctor had previously held the Airwoman in high-regard and was pleased with her work ethic and performance, as one of his more reliable assistants. As it was with these new revelations, he felt more than mildly disappointed and slightly perturbed by the thought that he was being spied upon. Yes, the Airwoman was only a conduit, but this still made him uneasy in her presence. As if to try and outrank her, he had asked her a highly poignant question. To which she responded as best she could. "Nothing, I only know level 1. and 2. where myself, you, and the Colonel work. I do know, from what the Colonel has already told me is that he does not venture below level 2. For what reason I am uncertain."

The Colonel swallowed back at the thought, of lower levels, as if he were afflicted by some form of clinging claustrophobia.

"However, at Nellis," she continued, "they all say there is a bunker store down there, filled with nuclear weaponry, a thousand defunct warheads, which for the most part are being dismantled as part of an on-going treaty fulfilment with the former Soviet Union. But others say it is a store house for the next, fourth generation of tactical nuclear battlefield weaponry. Small is better is what everyone is saying."

All this time Gracie Lin was acting in a subdued manner and was still trying as best she could to keep a low-profile. *'Dangerous talk cost lives,'* is what she thought to herself. Here she was listening to what was clearly highly classified information and she had no recording instrumentation to soak all the Intel' up. It was, so she consoled herself, a good thing she possessed, an almost perfect, didactic, one-hundred-percent memory recall.

At last the Airwoman, feeling jaded and brain numb, concluded. "As far as conventional weapons are concerned, what were formerly one-thousand-pound bombs are now two-fifty pounds, which means less air-load, which means more destructive power, hitting more targets, and a quicker, particularly on-deck, turn around. But that's all talk from Nellis, not from me here."

'Der gute Doktor' was so far pleased with the way the overall process had unfolded. No extreme reactions, yet! Open and honest confessions. No startling revelations, well a few, particularly surrounding the representatives of the Jones dynasty. There was clearly some form of hereditary ancestral abuse endemic throughout the entire family. The root cause of which currently remained a mystery.

It was now the turn of former Captain K. K. Kruger to take the floor. 'Der gute Doktor' had his reservations regarding Kruger, and supposed the former Captain would not be compliant. As it was, he was only too keen to stand up and relate whatever it was he needed to rid himself of.

"It goes way back to South Africa," he opened with his usual strong South African accent, despite the years he had lived in America he still hung onto many of his native Afrikaans pronunciations. "The ANCA. I was always against this. It had been shown all over Africa that the blacks can't govern themselves." He took a slow, tired look toward the Colonel, being as he was African American, he figured he should temper his opinions accordingly. "They're too lazy. And way too corrupt. I had seen my own family broken apart, my father murdered and sister raped by gangs of marauding coloureds, armed with machetes and knives. They just wanted to kill white folk, white people who for a hundred-years or more had put bread on their table. It was white folk who created a thriving economy, making South Africa rich.

So, I was a Captain. Regular soldier in the army, but like others we saw the writing on the wall. The army did not want white men anymore. But they still wanted them to train the blacks, teach them how to shoot the white folk and each other at the same time! But they did not want white soldiers around anymore. They had ship out to become mercenaries and fight for money. Africa is a big continent and there are plenty of lucrative conflicts going on. Before we left SA, we had to set up local militias, squads of armed men to patrol and police the township areas to make sure rival factions did not wipe each other out. Then in the hinterland we had to protect the few farmers that decided to stay behind in the hope that the political climate would eventually change.

More and more farmers and their families were brutally murdered. It's called genocide if white folks kill the blacks, or ethnic cleansing. However, if a black kills white folks it's called *'claiming back what is rightfully theirs.'*

Anyhow, one particular time our Intel' told us some fugitives from the law were hiding in one of the smaller townships. The police did nothing as usual. They were corrupt, paid off to keep out of it. So, on one night two-squads of our men entered into a small township and we found where the gang was holed up and we went in killing about twelve-men. Unfortunately, they were not just armed men in the building, but women and children too. Nine women and eleven children to be precise. All were killed, caught in the cross fire of a shoot-out.

So, those of us who stood for preserving the law, were now fugitives from that law. We left, my mother and older sister cleared out too, went northeast. We left the farm, my father's birth place and homeland. I went west and up to the Belgium Congo where they wanted ex-military men to act as paid mercenaries. I did that for six-months.

Whilst serving in one particular militia group I met an American guy, ex-special operations. He said he could get me to the USA. He said he knew some people in New York who had a contract with the Pentagon to provide security for a number of Air Force and Naval bases. He reckoned he could get me in there. I was sick, sick of sleeping in the jungle and getting bitten by a thousand insects every night. And the killing all around me was killing me. I wanted out. He got me out, he also got my mother and sister out. They had been keeping a low-profile in Zimbabwe, which was at the time not much better than South Africa was, as far as white farmers were concerned."

Everyone appeared moved by Kruger's tale, delivered straight from the heart. In particular Gracie Lin who was clearly besotted by the rugged former South African.

"So, we all had visas, special visas from the State Department and we were reunited once again, my family and me in New York."

* * * * *

'The Good Doctor' had all he wanted for the moment. The people were tired as he was, despite the amphetamines they had been dosed with. Now it was come-down time, as most of those gathered had reached the pinnacle of their secret journey into truth and voracity.

What was in particular interesting to him, the clinician observed, was the fact that despite some similar life circumstances, each one of his target group members seemed to have experienced their own 'individual journey.' Each one unique, each experience personal to the individual.

* * * * *

The 'Good Doctor' could now 'see.' For the first time in his long career of 'fucking' people's minds up, he was actually experiencing the effects of the drugs he had sometimes indiscriminately apportioned out to others. Suddenly he blossomed, he bloomed, the welcome bud opened to be fertilized by the pollen-carrying bee of truth. He knew and understood for the first time in his life the certainty of who he was and what he did and exactly what he had done in the past.

He sensed a new birth, his long-awaited delivery into the city of new beginnings. Here was his Jerusalem, brought to him by way of his Megatronic spirit-self. His new found atomic senses were a compound of classic and vicarious progressive Biblical thought, entwined together with New Age spiritual sequencing.

Now the people, all of the gathered throng were here, the party of twelve, signifying the months of the year, the signs of the zodiac, the number of doubting disciples Jesus had to contend with. The dozen, all sitting under the same blossoming almond tree and watching the spirit beings ascended and descended the ladder that Jacob had seen in his dream.

A short-lived vision.

The 'Good Doctor' asked himself if it were possible to

'hack' each person's individual dream? Had he been able to penetrate the pineal gland, what would he have seen? Was it possible to infinitely layer dream on top of dream? Leaving the subject in total spiritual, emotional and physical limbo, as if memory were nothing more than a cream and Jell-O sponge cake.

Could he construct a totally unreal situation, whereupon an individual under his influence and control, could have their memories reconstructed to the extent that nothing about them were real? Could reality be totally deconstructed and then reconstructed again, to create a totally unreal world?

Was he deconstructing himself?

"How many are there?"

"How many are there what?" Gracie Lin had snapped out of her besotted condition to raise a serious, but somewhat obscure question. "I mean aliens? How many types of alien are there?" The question was valid, perhaps, but not one 'Der gute Doktor' could answer, or even respond to.

"I read somewhere over eighty. Can that be possible?" Bud, considered himself an aficionado concerning such matters as how many alien species there were visiting the earth?

"There's no such thing dear lady! Kruger addressed Gracie Lin. Believe me I know, and I should know, I have been here, around Groom Lake for years, never seen nothing no how, or nowhere, or what, why, when or how, nothing that was remotely alien, flying or on the ground." Kruger was ever the sceptic. "But I will tell you," he continued, "they're doing something up there, something they pay me to make sure no one comes in to take a look at. It's an irony eh, you keep people out and I keep them in!" He addressed the Colonel, who was still crawling up his own wall, which to him was a mountain face.

"Indeed." 'Der gute Doktor' interjected, "But what would you say my dear Colonel? What would you say if I told to that every time you have seen aliens up in Hangar

2. they weren't simple digital projections? Like you said to the woman here driving back from Vegas." He pointed somewhat indifferently towards Thelma. To the Doctor she was a mere inconsequential guinea pig worthy of nothing more than an object of experimentation.

"The trespassers you played host to a couple or three nights before. You showed them the inside of the hanger, the Blackbird, U2 and other recon' aircraft. That was what they used to construct here. But before our time. You told them, a couple of them, that the images, the three little grey men, were just footage taken one Halloween. A guy from the base here, filming his kids having fun, trick or treating, right eh?"

The Colonel felt uncomfortable, as if he were about to be shot down in flames, not by the enemy but by someone on the same side as him. Nevertheless, he was immediately puzzled by the fact that the Doctor knew what he had previously said to Professor Jones regarding the 'projection' of the images of extra-terrestrials. After all he was not present at the time.

The Doctor continued. "What would you say if I told you that is what I made you believe? That every image you took to be unreal, was in fact actually real. Live, skin and bone." There was an audible intake of breath from across the room.

"You have always told people the images were fake. You enjoyed toying around with human sensibility. Keep everyone guessing until the very culmination of the event. And bang! The genie burst out of the bottle, the Monroe look-alike woman pops out of a surprise birthday cake and sings to a soon to be assassinated president. Meanwhile, the objective of all of this is?"

"To keep people interested in the so-called Area 51." Motto Kyoto cut into the Doctor's speech.

"Meanwhile, the real action is someplace else." The Japanese physicist had been taking everything he was hearing into his analytical thought process, and could clearly see what was going on here. It was bluff and

350

counter bluff.

"But what about my broken leg, and my pants?" Thelma's issue concerning how her leg miraculously mended and how it was the split up the seam of her borrowed pants had been repaired, still evaded her. No one other than Reagan seemed to be interested in cargo pants.

"I slit the side seam, with one of 'The Good Doctor's' scalpels. After you peed. I went to look in my kit-bag. I always carry spare pants and shirts; you sometimes need to. You know in case there is a medical emergency and someone is bleeding alright. Yeah, so I cut open the trouser leg so the plaster cast leg would slide into the leg of the pants."

"Then what?" Thelma continued...

"Then nothing," Reagan responded casually, "you left with the Colonel to go see the lounge bar, and other base facilities."

"You mean to say you conditioned me to think of something as being real when it wasn't so?" The Colonel addressed the Doctor and consequently cut across all the current conversations. "After all these years we have worked together, trusted each other, you go hypnotise me?"

"I would say yes that is the case. It's just how it is." 'Der gute Doktor' tentatively responded. "Everyone, with no exception, is on a certain pay-scale and subject to the full spectrum of 'need to know' Intel.'

The Colonel, as with all the others, was becoming increasingly confused and uncertain regarding the veracity of just about anything and everything that was being said.

Tension mounted, the Colonel's face contorted and twisted, glowed for a while as his blood pressure rose, before settling down again as he repossessed his faculties. His strict and highly disciplined military training enabled him to absorb, analyse and act accordingly.

Suddenly, and quite unexpectedly, Thelma broke into the conversational deadlock, and posed the million-dollar-question: "Why do they call you, The 'Good Doctor?' Doctor?"

The Doctor's head turned in mild surprise, this was the question, for perhaps not obvious reasons, he never wanted anyone to ever ask. Regardless, due to his drugged state of mind he had to respond accordingly.

"I have always been known as: 'Der gute Doktor' for precisely contradictory reasoning. I am good at what I do and that is being bad. Because I am bad. I should then in reality, be 'The Very Bad Doctor.' But there again, the nature of my name is very much dependent on the perspective of the individual enquiry. Objective or subjective or pure conjecture? If I was healing you, I would be - 'The Good Doctor.' If I were injecting toxic waste into your blood stream to kill you then I would be - 'The Bad Doctor.'

But there again I inherited the 'Good Doctor' persona from my father, and more so his father. Both of who worked alongside certain other renowned 'Nazi' (so-called), doctors. One particular inspirational and influential man, known only as the 'White Angel' was just one of the many butchers who experimented, for the advancement of science, on thousands of starving, life-less corpses. Even if they were not dead, they were soon to be dead. Dead even before they died. Their spirits having been unwillingly plucked and dragged screaming out of their physical bodies.

Gracie and Bud-Always, like thirsty dogs, were both lapping up what was being shared.

Having said that, concerning 'The Good Doctor's' ancestral past, there was ever- present an over-riding excuse for what he, as 'Der gute Doktor' had been forced to perform and carry out.

"All experimental atrocities carried out by my father were under a certain amount of duress, pressure which, as it usually does, filtered down from those ruling from above. Coercion was the word, forced to perform certain tasks, all under compulsion, with the Damaclean threat of death for non-compliance hanging over his head."

352

"But he did not have to comply!" Diana somewhat naively blurted out.

The Doctor ignored her outburst then continued wearily. "These were the rules he lived and worked under, edicts issued by the 'Deep State,' 'dark people' of the shadow region, the real rulers of mankind."

Mr Kyoto nodded his head in partial agreement. "I understand, people have been brainwashed to believe and accept as truth the propaganda that has been served up to them for years. The very word 'Nazi' triggers anger, fear, hate, violence and protestation. If you as much showed any sympathy to their cause, the entire world would turn against you."

"I agree, the Colonel enjoined the conversation before Kruger could get a responsive word in.

"Nobody likes a Nazi, despite the fact that now the neo-Nazis-Zionists rule America, Europe and just about every other place else on the map. They won the war - the people who accuse everyone else as being anti-Semitic, they won, the ruling communist neo-fascist elite. And they all live in Washington!"

As if to deliberately commit a mischievous act, the Colonel, possibly out of fear, anger, frustration and spite, yelled out aloud: "Orion's Belt!"

The four team members of the Magnetronic Research Unit immediately reacted. Diana was first to move, she leapt on Frank, who had been keeping himself to himself, and wrapped her hands around his throat attempting to strangle the six-foot tall football player. Who, for some inexplicable reason failed to defend himself against her onslaught, as if he almost gladly wanted to face death at the hands of a women he had been besotted with for years. Diana screamed the scream of the demented soulless 'Banshee,' a mythical creature of Irish fame and fable.

Likewise, the normally quiet and reserved Duncan tried a similar strangulation manoeuvre on his new friend Bud Always-Jones, sending the erstwhile camera operator flying across the seating booth and landing on the contemplative Japanese gentleman - Motto Kyoto.

Thelma, not one to drag her trainers and hold back, launched into Colonel Kernel and tried to wrestle him to the ground. The woman was overloaded with pent-up adrenaline forged anger as she screamed at him with a wolverine howl. Demanding he tell her there and then how her right leg became healed. And to unravel the mystery of the Air Force uniform trouser seam, which had miraculously become repaired.

Naturally the Colonel regretted his irresponsible and reckless manoeuvre and was surprised that just about everyone reacted to the command, whereas it should have only had an effect on the Magnetronic team members.

He did have a motive however, or supposed he did. And that was his need to escape, for the sake of his sanity. Either that or to defuse the prevailing tension and try get everyone settled back down into normality once more.

However, the sudden collective violent outbursts emanating from the previously mesmerized Magnetronic Research Unit team, was, as would be expected, eclipsed by Gracie Lin Jones. Who, in the midst of the prevailing confusion (although not effected by the 'Orion's Belt' command), almost predictably grabbed one of the two pistols balanced on the table in front of her, and, having hold of the un-loaded piece, pointed it towards the struggling spaced-out Principal, who remained prone on the floor, half obscured by the centre column of the same table.

The crazed journalist squeezed back the trigger and 'click', 'click,' 'click!' The chamber was empty. She had selected the gun previously wielded by Thelma, having originally been introduced into the equation by Airwoman Reagan Jones back at the Vegas press conference.

Exasperated by her misfired fortune, Gracie Lin dropped the pistol to the floor, as the figure of the Principal unexpectedly loomed over her writhing form. In part, his impulsive reaction was out of pure anger, perhaps some retaliation, and more so, a sense of hopelessness. He could not continue living in the knowledge that he, the University Principal, was no more. His life was now worthless. His reputation both sullied and shattered, having been all but destroyed by the actions of one singular twisted and revenge-seeking woman. Who, like him, was under the control of others. Her justifiable anger may not have perhaps been solely directed upon him, but on an entire family.

The Jones family.

Subsequently, grasping at what was his own firearm, the former, now dethroned Principal, having already cocked his weapon, accidentally fell backwards with the gun pressed under his protruding chin. The resulting fulmination stopped everyone in their tracks, bringing all actions and reactions to a heart racing halt.

All eyes were now directed towards the frame of the man drifting backwards as if in slow motion. Behind him a large circular red stain blotted against one of the diner partition walls. The empty body gradually collapsed in silence.

At that point the old man Clint appeared. Having come down from his sweltering bed on the upper floor, to see what the commotion was that had disturbed his rest. He saw a man swimming in a pool of blood.

(Bob Dylan played on the now weary Jukebox - 'the Story of the Hurricane'). Simultaneously, the two medics from Nellis appeared at the diner's threshold. They had returned from across the street having found scant diversion at the 'Little Ale In' and had been further alerted by the gun shot. The duo were subsequently both stunned to see the limp body of a man sprawled out under a table. They immediately exercised their dedicated job, but clearly it was all in vain and too late. He was dead.

Reagan Jones was also on the case. Pulling a stained counter cloth from one of the tables she lay the material over the Principal's lifeless body. There was nothing anyone could do for him now, as the back of his head was no longer present. The suicide weapon loaded with death and pain, lay aside the lifeless corps.

"You had better take a look outside" The stunned medic mentioned as an aside. "Out front, you need to see it." He addressed no one in particular.

The shock of the firearm exploding was enough however to begin to sober everyone up.

As he supposed he was the highest-ranking military man present, the Colonel took control of the situation and pushed wolf-girl Thelma to one side (as she had now stopped trying to wrestle with him), and strode with exaggerated yet confident steps, towards the swing-out porch and into the empty darkness of the Rachel's Nevadan night.

Now standing in the middle of the street, illuminated by the single flickering street lamp, looking south-east, he could see a ribbon of light making its way, heading north toward them along Highway 33. Some lights flashed red; others blue. Still more were plain glittering crystal head lamps.

Kruger appeared, his eyes straining to look into the distance. It was without doubt a column of vehicles methodically heading their way. "Jesus H what the hell is that?"

Perhaps the mile-long procession was merely out for a sight-seeing night-time drive? The now dismayed Colonel reasoned.

"If you ask my opinion it's a police column alright, headed toward us here in Rachel. No doubt about it." Kruger was emphatic. "They must have recognised you from the TV and now they are headed for the gatehouse. The Sheriff's department knows where it is and how to get there.

"Hey listen, we have to go, back to the base, lie-low until this all blows over." The overly optimistic Colonel addressed Kruger.

Meanwhile, the Air Force paramedics had followed the Colonel out front.

"What are you going to do with that dead guy? This is

going to be a crime scene soon enough. We can't help you with this one Colonel, we were just doing someone a favour. My buddy and me, we have to get the wagon back to base otherwise our-ass-is-gonna-be-grass come sunup."

"And boy has that Jim Beam got a kick! I mean man I am hallucinating? It's like nothing is real! I feel weird..." The second medic furthered their justification for leaving.

The Colonel understood and appreciated the implication of two medics taking a wagon-load of food to a bunch of crazy fugitives come terrorists, and returning back to base with a stiff in the back of their truck. The police would be on high-alert due to the fictitious terrorist attack and heavily armed SWAT teams would shoot first and justify their actions later. He knew how these people operated.

Without further thought, as the medics sped away heading north, the Colonel ran back into the diner and bellowed out -

"Such stuff as dreams are made on…" and

"Our little life is rounded with a sleep…" "We have got to get out of here quick people."

This particular Shakespearian command code immediately negated any and all previous mesmerizing directives.

The Colonel quickly illustrated the serious nature of his request, and consequences that would occur if they remained where they were. His natural leadership skills came into play, and even his rival Kruger was quick to fall into line.

"So, the cops are on their way?" Kruger emphasized. He then addressed Gracie Lin directly. "Well, I have not had a hand in any of this malarkey."

True enough, Kruger had had no hand in, or involvement with, what had been going on. He could legitimately just drive off into the brush and turn his lights off until morning. However, he now had Gracie to consider. There had been some form of peculiar chemistry exchanged between them. Difficult to describe exactly what, but despite the journalist's strange traits, dress sense and other bizarre attributes (such as trying to ruin a man before aiming to shoot him dead), he intently admired her. In particular her determined, somewhat devious and direct approach to life. She had made him forget about his money-making scheme to manipulate the MRU team into acting in a TV comedy show. He had immediately been, and still was, attracted to her. Her strength and resolve inspired him and was curiously just what he wanted in a woman. Consequently, once outside he gallantly picked her up, and slid her into the passenger seat of his Five Star Security pick-up truck. As he was last to park, he was first out and reversed into the darkened main street. He checked his ankle holster was in place, he had not forgotten to holster his firearm, a weapon he supposed he may need before the night was out.

Before leaving, Kruger once more turned to the Colonel. "I don't have to do any of this you know."

The Colonel understood.

Acknowledging the Colonel, Kruger continued, "we can shunt the body in the back of my truck and then I can take it up to Yucca Lake when I can." That constituted a one-hundred and sixty-mile round trip, that in part followed the perimeter fence, a journey which would not be undertaken anytime soon.

As it was, Yucca Lake could be reached from Groom Lake, but in order to get there, a driver would need to cross some open country ranges, before picking-up the fence line.

An alternative was to head south back down Highway 33, turn west skirting the mountains and keep going along the road forever until there was a small sign on the right, pointing towards an enclave called 'Mercury.' Through this high security gate lay the place where they formerly assembled the bombs that were tested a further thirty-miles in at the foot of the mountain ranges.

What was generally considered to be salt pans,

were in actual fact limestone pits, containing sludge and impurities leftover from the former lead mining operations that had long since closed down. The stagnated dross pans had become highly radioactive and the entire area closed off to everybody, due to high-levels of contamination. No one in their right mind would go near the place under any circumstances.

* * * * *

Duncan and Bud were already on disposal and clean-up duty. The Principal's life-less body, along with his carry-on luggage, the gun, his identification and reputation, everything he had on him, was duly destined to be committed into a toxic waste pit. And no one thought otherwise.

Once loaded, Kruger roared off into the darkness. His destination the Groom Lake gatehouse.

As Kruger was not 'officially' cleared to enter Groom Lake freely and with unfettered access, he was mildly excited concerning the current opportunistic situation. It looked as if at long last, he was going to get inside the facility proper, which was something he had been longing to do for some time. He wanted to know what lay beyond, in those mysterious hangers.

After the Principal's body had been stowed away, Gracie left Bud Always-Jones with a directive to follow on behind her in their hire car. She was tastelessly frothing over with joy at the thought of her nemesis being justly punished, she would never have to think of him again.

Reagan and Thelma had found pails and mops which they used to dutifully clean up the blood and brains spilt over the diner floor. Leaving a bloody mess would not appear favourable as far as the elderly proprietors were concerned.

Bud ran out to the rental car he had driven up from Vegas, and pulling back to the diner, he hustled Duncan and Motto Kyoto into the vehicle, which was already to get going down the highway. He spun the wheel, moved off the central reservation and followed Kruger's tail lights on Highway 33 going north.

Next to back away from the diner came Reagan Jones, accompanied by Thelma Jones, 'The Good and the Bad Doctor,' together with his camera equipment and a briefcase full of papers plus his little bag of medical instruments and a lot of drugs. And finally, but not least - Colonel Kernel, who settled down in the back of the overly familiar Air Force Lincoln. He knew where they were going, as did Reagan Jones.

Lastly Frank hammered the Jeep in reverse, with Diana as his passenger and followed the Lincoln. The second Research Unit jeep was still, or so Frank and the others imagined, parked up at the Vegas convention centre, where 'all this' kicked off.

As for Clint and Hillary (who would do anything for a quiet life), they quickly dressed in sensible clothing and went out back to the old dilapidated garage adjacent to the swing-out porch. Whereupon Clint flung back the broken door, to reveal the gleaming sight of a double-buddy-seat classic Harley Davidson motor cycle. Which, some years back, had been left at the diner for safe-keeping, whilst its owner went up to explore, and with any luck penetrate, the perimeter fence of so-called Area 51.

Chillingly, the man never returned.

It was a while since the old fellow had turned over the engine, yet in a couple of minutes the – 'Born to be Wild' couple were cutting through the cool night air, heading north, easy-riding the wind to their daughter's place outside of Tonopah.

Everyone by now knew that a few miles north of Rachel, there was a left turn off the main road, one which is not marked on any map. This route doubles back, swinging south in the direction you, the driver, have just come from. If a curious tourist was hoping to find the gatehouse for Groom Lake, this is the way they would have to come. Once they reached the famous 'Black Letter Box,' the road splits. Right goes up up up, until the perimeter fence stops you from going any further.

This was the point at which the Five Star Security 'Camo' dudes would get you. Shoot first, ask question later. Like spindle-legged spiders in the brush, that lurk, waiting for something to get caught in their web.

Continuing on from the 'Black Letter Box,' the road carries on until an obvious turning area can be seen in the track. Sensible tourists and UFO freaks alike should turn back at this point. If, however you want to persist and keep on going for several miles, the track, being not so frequently used, appears to come to an abrupt end. Except that it is easily passable if you are driving a 4WD, Quad Bike, or on foot. The trail continues on going right up to the actual security fence.

After following the perimeter wire for a few hundred-yards, eventually the Groom Lake gatehouse comes into view.

The barrier is usually guarded by at least one solitary Air Force Military Police person.

This is where Kruger, with his Five Star Security pass, and the Colonel, with his high-ranking insignia security pass and the remainder of their little party arrived safely, having left Rachel and the pursuing birddog convoy. Which was probably led by the Lincoln County Sheriff's Department.

The gatehouse party had wildly underestimated just how long the trailing column was, and what it actually comprised of.

From the gatehouse nothing could be seen of Rachel or the highway below, which at this point was east, some twenty-five to thirty-miles behind and below them.

Where the police convoy might be at this particular time was pure speculation and conjecture.

Perhaps they carried on north?

The logical way.

If, however, they took the track into the hills to the

gatehouse they could easily become grid-locked and grounded. There were very few passing points and areas where a vehicle could easily turn about. Over and above that the track was pot-holed and often strewn with boulders that had slipped off of the ridges above.

If they did eventually reach the gatehouse, the Groom Lake base was situated a further thirty-miles west across unlit roads and devoid of any directional signs.

You either knew where you were going or didn't.

Getting lost was dangerous and possibly life threatening.

Either way, they, the authorities, whoever they might be, would end up in a position whereupon they would have to decided whether or not to forcibly gain access onto the Groom Lake site. The chances of them finding whoever it was they were looking for however, was a classic needle in a haystack scenario.

Perhaps 'they,' the Sheriff's Department had applied for some form of subpoena or legal writ from the Attorney General's Office? One that would allow the cops legal access.

Or, perhaps not?

A previous judicial enquiry held by the Supreme Court, brought by the Congressional Finance Committee, regarding US military spending on 'Black Operations,' concluded the police and courts had no jurisdiction over the Groom Lake facility, as it did not exist! Therefore, no case could be brought against it, or against any alledged personnel working on the base. (The identities of whom could not be found and no tax records were in existence regarding the same phantom staff.)

And, furthermore, according to the high-level Congressional findings, no access could be granted on to the base, if it were not there in the first place. The 'Deep State' controlled Joint Chiefs of Staff, made certain bases such as Groom Lake and many others like it, remained off limits and out of bounds.

* * * * *

As it was, the illuminated trail of lights down on Highway 33 that were moving toward Rachel, may not have been the police, or CIA, or any other security agency. It might well have merely been a luminous vehicle trail made by some crazy flying circus troupe heading out of Vegas. No one knew for certain. It was all simple assumption, fuelled by the remnants of drug-induced paranoia.

Unfortunately for the band of gypsies seeking refuge for the night, G. I. Joe was on Groom Lake gate duty.

G.I. Joe (AKA Grunt) was a stereo-typical, obedient, strict orders pain-in-the-ass kind of Air Force Military Police person. He was not about to lift and barriers to a Colonel who, according to orders, was not to be permitted onto the base, under any circumstances. If he did try to cross the symbolic white-line, he was to be arrested on the spot. The Colonel took a submissive step backwards as the G.I. nervously fumbled to un-clip his side-arm.

Airwoman Jones intervened, muscled her way forward and stood as tall as she could by the barrier, before pulling out her lanyard. G.I. stepped back, partly in disbelief, partly in shock, choosing to try and ignore the pay and clearance grade disparity between himself and the… she was a woman?! How could this be?

G.I. Joe was clear when it came to dealing with the Colonel, but in the case of Airwoman Jones, he was thrown as to what to do in the circumstances.

The Colonel aside, G.I. was not about to admit any civilians, including Kruger, onto the base. In his view, Five Star Kruger, was technically a civilian and therefore was not permitted access to the military base, in the event that was, the base was under attack from outside forces. (Russians.) Despite the fact there was, at that moment in time, no outside threat to the facility by foreign forces. Regardless it was all too dangerous to have civvies on site.

As for the others in the party? He immediately

recognised the four students (which was how he addressed Thelma et al, as being 'students'). To that end he reminded Kruger and the Colonel he had been on the gate the night Kruger and Air Force security teams had brought the party of four on base.

Other than that G.I. could not bring himself to comment on the strangely dressed Gracie Lin, Bud or the Jap'. Perhaps they were going to a Halloween party or something along those lines?

Except, there was a singular person who G.I. Joe did overlook, one who by now was 'pissed' with what was going on, and that was - 'The Good Doctor.' Who, having crept closer to the military guard, thanks to Airwoman Jones' diversionary tactics, was able to stab a six-inch syringe into the G.I.'s right-thigh.

At which point Kruger had a flash of inspiration and ducked under the barrier heading into the guard house. From there he opened up a channel on the guardhouse radio to the chopper command and control centre, on 'Paradise,' which was also where the Five Star 'Drone Wing' was bunkered down.

The Colonel swiftly read what was going on, and caught G.I. Joe, just before he met the dirt road. Reagan Jones assisted him in throwing the limp body into the driver's seat of the standard issue Air Force Jeep parked behind the gatehouse.

"He'll come round in a few minutes, then you get to do what you like with him." The 'Good Doctor' was beyond any form of compassion as the team drove passed the flimsy wooden barrier and into the night, commencing a journey of some thirty-miles towards the dark shadowy mountains that cloaked Groom Lake.

Kruger picked up the rear and Gracie Lin Jones acquired the wheel of the Five Star pick-up, whilst Kruger took on communications and a note of the audio report coming from the skyward drone that he had dispatched from the 'Paradise' hard-stand drone wing.

The Colonel slapped the G.I.'s face and the gatehouse

man came round. At which point he verbally relieved G.I. Joe of his duty and ordered him to drive back off the base and head for Vegas to have a good time. This the gatehouse soldier did with relish, having already covered half of his twelve-hour shift.

Waving the guard off the Colonel snapped back into some form of reality. In one sense he was happy and relieved, but on the other hand he was realistically considering exactly what his fate might be.

He broke into a heavy drug-induced sweat. Was it possible he had already been discharged from the Air Force? G.I. Joe had stated as much, that he had been - *'relieved of his command due to the seriousness nature of the accusation the press and others had already laid out against him.'* News hungry journalists had already put him on trial and found him guilty.

For a moment he laughed to himself at the irony of the situation. He being a wanted terrorist, and yet here he was heading into America's most top-secret military establishment!

* * * * *

By this time, most if not all of the bizarre effects of the doctor's Mega 1-90 experimental drug cocktail had worn off. The results of which caused just about all of the present party to suffer severe headaches, dehydration and fatigue.

Recollections of the episode down in the old diner were thin, sketchy and vaporous. However, the haunting horror of the image of Principal Jones blowing his brains out now slowly drifted back into everyone's minds.

Gracie Lin, somewhat out of character, began to quietly sob. What had happened to her she was not certain, but whatever it was left her fully convicted of her recent and past behaviour. Particularly relating to her flagrant involvement with the occult. She felt penitent, sorry even, and sought out the comfort and solace of

Kruger's strong arms. He longed to kiss her, and more. But they were once again on the move, driving further toward the dark heart of the Groom Lake facility. More specifically to Hangar 2. where 'Der gute Doktor' ran his dirty three-hundred-million-dollars black programme from.

His experimental activities into the use of mind-altering substances had already mesmerised the entire base, thus making them all, in effect, under his command, control and influence. As if he were some modern day 'Svengali.'

Meanwhile Colonel Kernel was thinking about golf and the driving range. The Dreamland lounge and restaurant, the swimming pool and bowling alley, which were, or so he had recently learnt, all fabrications of his own imagination. Locations manufactured not for his singular benefit alone, but for everyone who lived and worked on the base. They all, to a man, believed and accepted the same distortion of the truth.

The general ambience and prevailing atmosphere of the Groom Lake facility appeared cosy, warm, inviting and welcoming. Whereas, in reality the facility was cold and sterile. Industrially metallic by nature, like some ancient workhouse. A slave pit of indignity and servitude.

* * * * *

Ten minutes down the line and Kruger was being fed intel' from the launched drone. It was not good.

Kruger pulled over on the side of the dark road. Once his lights were dowsed, from his location, he could see nothing other than stars and the approaching vehicles of the others who had left the gatehouse.

Once everyone was present, he verbally relayed the information he had been forwarded from his spy-in-the-sky. Apparently, Rachel was almost surrounded. Vehicle lights ringed the small town. There were so many military and police vehicles in the convoy that it trailed back along

Highway 33, and beyond the reach of the launched drone. More critical was the live-feed that clearly showed a trail of lights beyond Rachel moving north towards the left-spur, that miles further on took you to the very same gatehouse they had just driven away from. The general consensus across the party was that this leading string of vehicles were made up of Lincoln Country Sheriff's Department Officers. Who would have been the only group amongst the collective aggressive military contingent that was aware of just how to reach the gatehouse from the highway.

At a guess the Colonel estimated their ETA on to the base to be around fifty-minutes. Thankfully, by then the fugitive group would be fully ensconced in Hangar 2. or wherever it was Der gute Doktor' had in mind.

Once again, the convoy moved off, but not before Kruger reminded the entire group, the Groom Lake entrance was not the only access to so-called Area 51. Some one-hundred miles south of their current position, on the other side of the mountains, lay the strongly fortified 'Mercury Gate.' Which offered access to any multi-wheeled vehicles that might need to come 'on-base'.

A third highly questionable entrance to Groom Lake was located in the north through Bald Mountain and the old look-out spot at Coyote Summit. However, this route generally remained impassable for any heavy military and standard road vehicles.

Kruger put his foot down.

* * * * *

The Groom Lake facility Air Force Command Centre was at an impasse. Radar as yet showed no inbound air traffic requiring clearance to turn into restricted 'Dreamland' air space, for landing along the Groom Lake runway. Nothing unusual as there were no flights scheduled at this particular time on this particular evening.

Often as not supplies came in by night, and workers by day. The control tower averaged at peak times traffic movements every ten-minutes.

Nothing however had come up from 'JANET' at McCarran airport in Vegas. This was due to the part close down response to the terror attack.

That was in Vegas though.

Ironically the Groom Lake command centre was somewhat isolated as far as what was going on in the outside world was concerned. As the base did not exist, it was not considered as being 'in the loop.' If nuclear war broke out, the workforce could theoretically relocate into the service sub-levels to evade fall-out.

As far as the base was concerned, the Russians probably knew more about the facility than certainly Congress, the Pentagon and the all-powerful American Military Complex did.

As a precaution, triggered by the terrorist threat and what he had seen earlier in the day on the TV, the duty base commander had placed most of the facility on amber alert.

This was unprecedented.

Hence the gatehouse order to deny Colonel Kernel and others access to the base.

Gatehouse duty soldiers, when on amber alert, were required to report their status every ten-minutes. G.I. Joe unfortunately was no longer at his post, but rather some miles down the decline and about to run directly into the Lincoln County Sheriff's Department front lead team of deputies.

As with other United States Air Force bases, The Groom Lake facility barracked a division of troops on site. A military force whose prime objective was to defend US airspace and air base takeoff, landing and refuelling facilities. In the event of any form of attack or aggression by an enemy force, the standard response was an all stations alert and lockdown.

All men to their posts. Defensive positions taken to

maintain the fence line perimeter. All surface to air weaponry to be positioned and primed in preparedness of air attack. As it was, a wing of F35 fighter aircraft were already out of their bunkers and parked up on 'Homey' runway, ready to intercept anything that crossed into 'Dreamland'. The identical action was repeated across inter-linked facilities. Nellis had already doubled the guard after the so-called Las Vegas terror attack.

However, G.I. Joe's tenacity and determination had also been severely underestimated by the Colonel. The brave and dutiful soldier gathered his senses after being 'jabbed' by the bunch of crazy people he had apprehended at his post. And, by the time he had arrived at the 'Black Mail Box,' his mind was sufficiently clear to make him about-turn and proceed at high-speed back to the gatehouse. Whereupon he called in a breach alert, foreign intruders were on the base.

The commander reacted predictably to the intelligence information reported by G.I. Joe, which resulted in the instigation of amber-to-red ... a total base lockdown.

* * * * *

A distressing potential scenario: US military fighting US military on US soil. It was tantamount to civil war.

* * * * *

'Der gute Doktor' naturally had a plan and was not about to waste years of hard and dedicated work only to see it all blown up in some form of wild-west shootout.

* * * * *

Any incursion into 'Dreamland' air space from now on would be met by deadly force. Just like it said on the perimeter fence signs: 'Shoot to kill.'

Stay frosty!

Any offensive force attacking the base may well be dressed in United States military uniforms to confuse the defending troops. 'Shoot on site!'

The base commander summoned his officers and they quickly reminded themselves of protocols regarding such a situation. Orders were clear:

Yes; Shoot to Kill.

There would be no communication lines open from and to the base, as the facility, according to Strategic Command, was not there. Consequently, there was no attack by foreign aggressors, and as a result those stationed at Groom Lake were very much on their own.

* * * * *

G.I Joe's message was a portent of doom, kicking off sirens and triggering flashing warning bulk-head lights. Civilian workers on the night shift (thankfully fewer than the usual employee numbers on-base), aimlessly ran in all directions looking for their emergency assembly point. Panicking like hapless extras in a 1950s black and white horror movie.

As with any work place, the various sections of employees were drilled to collectively assemble outside in designated pre-determined areas.

Busses arrived out of the night to take them in groups to the now cleared in-coming commercial aircraft that would take them back to McCarran in Vegas.

The central air-traffic control tower suddenly became illuminated like a Vegas casino. All-six miles of the Groom Lake runway fired up to light the approach for incoming commercial aircraft which were, according to protocol, en route from Vegas. A ride of around thirty-minutes from take-off to landing. At night these birds flew in fast and low. Six aircraft were already in the air.

* * * * *

Prior to the gyrating lights, general confusion and wailing sirens kicking into life, the now eleven person Rachel diner crew (having eventually reached Groom Lake proper), ditched their vehicles and entered into a key-coded Hangar 2. Level 1 access area. This was one of the entry channels through which the workers had to traverse each and every shift. Each worker was micro-chipped, on the back of the hand. The chip was read and access given. The model was that of any domestic aircraft departure facility around the world. CCTV surveillance kept close watch at all times.

Once in and passed the security systems, the workers shuffled mindlessly along to their workstations. Images of which were similar to Fritz Lang's lethargic 'doppelgangers' taken from his film 'Metropolis.'

Each worker upon completing security checks followed a coloured line which took them onwards to their sub-station. Here the coloured lines spilt into groups. Dependent on their particular role or work skill. And so, the system continued, dividing down and down again, guiding each worker to his or her individual subterranean station placement area.

Now with the emergency signs flashing warnings, it was every man or woman for themselves, as more white-coated lab technicians ran towards the emergency break-out exit doors. A human flow which was stampeding en-masse, in the opposite direction to where 'Der gute Doktor' wanted to guide his hopefully attentive and compliant puppets.

As if nothing else, regardless of the mayhem ebb and flowing about them, Thelma and the others felt safe.

Safe from being arrested for terror offences.

Duncan and Bud were thinking - *'heavy man, heavy!'* Whilst Diana, who had been as usual, unusually quiet for some time, felt something was very wrong. In fact ever since they left Iowa she had felt in the same disapproving and censorious manner concerning the entire project.

Thelma no longer cast a loving glance her way, Frank no longer tried to playfully squeeze her thigh. The expedition had started out as fun, but now it was no more than some weird perverse horror show, the purpose of which she had no inclination. Who were all these people? What did they want? Everyone was aimlessly running around. Whilst every person in the party seemed to be attempting to control someone else. People were running after mere allusions. Chasing, power, fame and even sex. Now there was one dead man. How was that all going to be explained away?

As he was from the outset, Motto Kyoto was drinking in the scene. His analytical physicist's mind longed to look wide-eyed around some of the numerous installations and now obsolete aircraft that were located on Level 1. However, what he took in before him was only a mere fraction of what was soon going to shock him and the others.

'Der gute Doktor' was managing well, despite still remaining under the final remnants of the concoction he had willing imbibed. He was behind time compared to the others by around thirty-minutes. And, possibly with his second exaggerated swallow of the whisky mixture, he had absorbed more than most, but not as much as some others. Gracie Lin being one in particular.

'The Good Doctor,' as any tour guide would, felt he should be offering his guests a guided tour of the entire facility by means of his explanatory discourse - he continued to explain the workers educational range, which varied between Mexican cleaning staff, to university professors and scientists recruited primarily from the USA. "Many scientists, such as myself, more or less live on the base." He paused for effect, as the last of the fleeing workers filtered through the emergency doors and out into the becoming cooler Nevadan night.

"I Have my own bunk down on Level 2."

There was in truth very little to see in Hangar 2. Level 1. Apart from the antiquated and obsolete spy-planes, there was the sprawling 'entrance lounge,' as some of the workers sarcastically labelled the 'cordoned off'' space where workers would wait their turn to go to check in. At this point reception security was run by another division of Five Star. One totally independent from Kruger, his 'Camo dudes' and pick-up crews.

At present Kruger was far too interested in Gracie Lin to be bothered with the hanger and its rusty flying relics. Never mind lounges and security check points. He had seen a similar set-up over at McCarran, where he had previously worked for the Five Star industrial giant.

What he really required more than anything right at this moment in time was someplace he could disappear to with Gracie. She was surprisingly soft and compliant, her mouth inviting and the warmth of her body permeated through the black and white plastic-retro-outfit that 'wore her.' All which added to his singular aching desire to fuck her.

As it was, he had picked up on the fact that the quack doctor had a bunk on a lower level. Consequently, he lingered back from the others, and reached out a comforting arm around Gracie's' waist. As if she were a princess going for a stroll in the park with her consort.

He patiently waited for his moment to act.

On initial entry to Level 2. from above, all that could be seen in the dark hanger space were more old decommissioned 'spy planes.' Developed throughout the decades, all serving with the USAF. Some successfully and others not. These obsolete objects of a cold war were left to remind and impress upon the workers that Groom Lake was actually only an aviation museum. Or so the story went.

To the left of the entrance reception areas, on Level 1, there were several sets of elevators, iron gantry stairs, moving floors and other means of accessing the next lower Level 2 facility. This deeper subterranean area was around four times the floor area of the level above them, and consisted of a multitude of sectioned off work stations.

Here aircraft designers were developing aircraft fifty-years in advance of what was already flying across the world. It was clear to see how aircraft such as the U2 spy-plane began its life in these very hangers, on the aeronautic development and designers drawing tables.

At the rear of the facility, and almost out of sight and rarely noticed, there were three saucer-shaped objects under wraps. Flying craft which may or may have been of an extraterrestrial origin. Except they were more likely to be-crazy-unworkable-flying-disasters. Designs taken from German rocket engineers brought over from Nazi Germany, post the cessation of WWII.

At this level, the 'Good' or perhaps 'Bad' Doctor' was king, as far as those who were involved with chemical weapons development, were concerned. His department worked on a number of inter-connected experimental projects, including: biological armaments expansion, paranormal and psychological phenomena, gazing at goats, scrying, out of body and levitation exercises, spoon bending, automatic writing and every other psychological experiment that could be imagined by mankind.

Also of note was the research into telepathy and artificial intelligence development. Together with cyber research, 'super soldier' creation, anti-gravitation experimentation, DNA screening and selection and cloning trials. All added to the vast and expansive portfolio under the doctor's immediate control. Glued together with a whole host of other, some far-fetched disciplines: including some obscure paranormal and occult research into the principles of alchemy. Including the Thule Society, and many other occult practices, embracing all forms of paganism, voodoo, hexing and cursing.

Here on Level 2. every form of dark art and black magic had been probed into and put to the test. Demons had been summoned, entities best not spoken about had been manifested, devils conjured and spells cast. Just in case, there was even a resident Roman Catholic Priest and team of exorcists on hand should the occasion arise. Every activity linked and tied together, with the one singular solitary aim and purpose - to employ whatever ugly advancements they made against; 'the enemy.'

Every single person working on the base, according to 'The Good Doctor,' was looking to, and was paid to, develop any number of crazed-half-cocked-goony-goofy-military-killing machine-applications.

The pinnacle of the research, the project that attracted most, if not all, the black-money, was the pursuit of cloning and nurturing of laboratory grown 'super soldiers.' Every one of which came with an expendable life.

'Der gute Doktor' continued his narrated tour as the group struggled to keep up with his fast paced, chemical induced diatribe.

"Here, this is where you thought you saw some little aliens eh Colonel?" The Doctor was half in jest, but not so the Colonel, who was more than jaundiced by the fact this jumped-up clinician (supposed friend), had fooled him for some time over the existence of alien life forms housed below ground. Now he simply did not know if they existed or not!

Thelma vaguely recalled the aircraft hangar, and the arcing electrical bolts rising from the gantry that led to the lower levels. It rightly occurred to her that they had accessed the building from another door on their previous visitation.

As far as the other team members were concerned, Duncan, Frank and Diana all recalled briefly looking into the hangar but no more than that. Plus, it had been dark then as it was now, only service lights illuminating the cavernous space.

Meanwhile Motto Kyoto was in his element. He lapped up every word shared between 'Der gute Doktor' and the rest of the group, and took in everything he saw. He thankfully no longer felt he had the desire or stomach to commit Hari Kari on behalf of his ancestors and so buried that thought. In the hope his relatives would forgive him.

Gracie and Kruger were in a world of their own. He frankly did not care what was going on under his feet, aliens or not, he would shoot at them anyway. Gracie Lin for the first time in her life, felt at ease with a man. She realised that Kruger had no need to have stayed at the old diner, he had nothing to answer for or to. Therefore, his current presence was clearly for her benefit alone.

Bud at the present time was feeling lonely as he missed looking through the lens of his camera, and therefore his outlook on life had dramatically altered.

As for the Airwoman and possible femme fatal, Reagan Jones, she was still curious regarding the family connection between herself, Thelma and Gracie Lin. It was highly possible, probable even, that they were indeed connected. However, they just as easily may not have been related. Only DNA testing could or would prove such a fact. An undertaking that they could easily employ in one of the numerous laboratories that by now surrounded them.

Be that as it may, Airwoman Reagan Jones, was intentionally keeping quiet. As far as pay-scale and official grade was concerned she certainly held sway over the Colonel. Kruger didn't even come close; he was basically a civilian. This left 'The Good Doctor,' whose intentions she was uncertain about and wondered exactly what he was going to say and do next. Should she step in and try arresting him? He was definitely breaking his terms of contract. Regardless of what might have been going on outside. Showing civilians around what was a top-secret and classified restricted area was a treasonable offence.

Not forgetting that the entire MRU team had witnessed at close quarters the almost crash-landing of a top-secret TR-3B fighter aircraft. One that almost came down outside Vegas. Which, in the final analysis was the very reason everyone present found themselves where they were!

However, it remained clear that their very presence on this mysterious base was sufficient to lock them away for life. The Colonel had tried to explain the aerial phenomena away to an impatient and jaundiced press corps. But had failed miserably. Potentially setting off what could be a full-scale battle. All because of a top-secret military aircraft that people had seen flying in the night sky. The particular TR-3B in question, was in fact a half-size unmanned drone. There was no weaponry slung underneath its triangular shape.

The TR-3B had originally been designed and developed where they were, in Groom Lake. But had not flown from there as someone high-up emptied the black-money coffers and the project funding went with it to the private sector, to be precise - 'Skunk Works.' They took over the project and initially developed an unmanned drone version. And that was what everyone was seeing out their backyard windows. A dark triangular shape with three glowing lights on the underside, with the ability to move side to side and up and down at ease, before taking off at a lick, as no one had ever seen before. The sound barrier being broken over and over once flying above the ocean.

And, as for the Japanese man, Motto Kyoto? No one knew who he was. Or, what or why he was party to the group? And further more, what exactly was going on with him?

66

Gracie Lin and Kruger

Kruger and Gracie Lin held back, allowing the others to walk on ahead. Eventually the group came to a division in the passageway. He, Kruger, being full of bravado, recklessly followed the yellow line to the left, whilst the others veered to the right.

The passage before them was oddly constructed. It was bright, but had no obvious form or source of visible illumination. The walls were flat with a smooth metallic finish that appeared to alter colours depending on what angle you looked at it. Also, there were no signs of screws or fixings that might suggest how the passage was constructed.

Kruger was desperately looking for an anti-room, a bunk house, or even a janitorial store to creep into, but there were no visible door apertures. Eventually and in desperation, Kruger stopped and pressed Gracie Lin against the wall and began to fervently kiss her moist lips, cupping one hand on her face whilst the other tugged on her hair.

His hand quickly felt for her breasts as she heaved her chest higher to greet the welcome advance. They were rabid, fervent, like two young lovers. Kruger's other exploratory hand pushed between her thighs, which opened wider in response. He continued to kiss down her neck to her throat and she tilted her head back and closed her eyes in wild desire. However, as she opened her eyes in response to Kruger's lustful advances, she saw a most remarkable and terrible sight - a disembodied head floated just besides Kruger's shoulder. The face appeared to shimmer as if it were made of some form of metal. The apparition was human-like other than the forehead protruded out indicating a large cranial capacity. The mouth was small and tight, almost invisible whilst the eyes were black and did not appear to have pupils.

Gracie screamed in horror.

Without further thought she broke from Kruger's passionate embrace and comically ran as best she could with her undergarments holding her back.

As for Kruger, he had no inclination as to what was going on and what he might have done. Consequently, he responded by following Gracie around the passage way and back to where the colour marked paths had split.

At the same time the other party members appeared from the right-hand passageway, where Gracie Lin and Kruger should have followed. Last in line came 'Der gute Doktor' who suppressed an out of character belly laugh. His obvious mirth continued as Kruger appeared.

Meanwhile, Thelma and Reagan embraced the terrified Gracie, who sobbed and cried out in fear and shock.

"It's just a projection!"

"What?" Kruger questioned in a bewildered manner.

"I projected it onto the wall." 'Der gute Doktor' confessed.

"Projected what?" The Colonel was more than keen to hear this, having himself been the unwitting victim of more than one of his fake visual pranks.

"I have explained all this before, the alien projection is to scare unwanted intruders off. A high-tech scarecrow."

"Which is what I saw?" Thelma was also curious.

Kruger was livid and pulled his sidearm from his ankle holster. Everyone reacted calmly by holding their hands up, that was apart from the Doctor. Who, joking apart, wanted to press on.

Gracie shrugged her female counterparts off and lunged at the Doctor, slapping his face uncontrollably. It was Kruger who pulled her off.

"Look what is all this madness?" Thelma was just about at the end of her leash; she had no idea what was going on and or where they were headed.

"Look I am getting out of here..." Kruger turned

holding Gracie by one hand, his gun held tightly in the other. The pair walked back the way they thought they had previously come.

"Going somewhere?" The Doctor interjected. "The base is on lockdown now. You won't be able to get through the hangar doors, and maybe you won't like what you see out there."

"He's right you know; it will be as tight as a drum." The Colonel confirmed.

"The only way is 'down' I am afraid." Concluded the Doctor.

The Colonel was more than nervous, he simply did not take the 'down' option, never, ever. He really did not want to know what was hidden beneath their feet.

67

One way only and that is down

"How did you do that? I mean the projection?" Bud was keen to find out the little idiosyncrasies of the workings of the base.

"Ask him." The Doctor motioned towards the Colonel.

"It's just Halloween pranks Doctor, as you have already told me."

"Or was it?" 'The Good Doctor,' tried to be dramatic.

"Looked real to me, horrible, gross, Ugh! I will never get that image out of my mind." Gracie Lin had by now calmed down, as the group continued on their way down.

Meanwhile, Bud, who was none the wiser, took Reagan aside and began to question her as they walked concerning the TR-3B conceptual programme.

"TR-3B, well, I mean what's the propulsion unit? I mean, you can tell me, we are after all kind of cousins, well I am related to Gracie Lin."

"She gives you a hard time I can see that."

Reagan, ignored the technical question, and demonstrated the fact that she was genuinely concerned for Bud.

Cousin or not.

"She sure does, but let me ask you, I saw on-line in Jane's, they had a silhouette of a triangular craft, 'Ace in the Hole' they called it.

Said it was being built at 'Skunk Works' in California. How come everyone acts so secret, and yet I can, as any one on-line can, read about it?"

It was an interesting and valid question. Albeit one Reagan could not answer.

"Hey cousin Bud, I don't have a clue, I am just a simple medic. You wanna talk about security leaks you need to chat to the Colonel; I am sure he just can't wait to talk shop."

Nothing was further than the truth. As all the Colonel wanted to do was to get everything over with and go home. Although he did not have any where he could call home right now.

The 'The Good Doctor,' Gracie Lin's violent assault on his person behind him, wanted to head towards the nearest elevator. "Now look, I want you to see some interesting geographic anomalies and strange artefacts, revelations that just may change your mind concerning a great many things.

We may come across some reasons why I do not think in a million years any current US Marine Commander is going to launch an attack on Groom Lake. Or forcibly enter any other part of the so-called Area 51 complex. Because last time they got beat."

There was an audible silence, only the sharp intake of astonished breath verified the fact that they were all still alive.

The Colonel looked puzzled... he knew it, aliens, aliens, aliens, here, it had to be. It all made sense, there were visitors from another world here, and it looked like he was about to meet them! He was clearly not as far in the know as he thought. Served him right for not going deeper into the subterranean levels, where clearly all the answers lay.

Diana and Frank exchanged glances, sceptics as they were, hearts leapt and butterflies fluttered around in the stomach.

Reagan Jones looked at Thelma who looked as if she wanted a clipboard and calculator to hand, partly to use as a weapon, and partly as protection to hide behind. Duncan was convinced he was still enjoying the acid trip of a life-time. Mr Kyoto looked smug, as if he knew all along there were aliens and was eagerly expecting this announcement. Which in truth he was.

Gracie Lin turned her attention back to Kruger and took his hand, pressing it into his cheek to comfort her.

The elevator silently arrived and the Doctor shepherded everyone into the spacious metallic box. Everyone felt a jolt as the elevator allowed gravity to suck it down deeper and deeper. A bump and a jolt told everyone they had arrived some hundreds of feet below the surface.

"You see this is what six-hundred trillion dollars can get you in prime real estate." 'Der gute Doktor' was once more the tour guide, like a child in a toy shop. Animated, elevated, a real showman in the most theatrical sense of the word.

As the elevator doors swished open the group were greeted by a spacious waiting area. The space was fabricated using the same metallic-like material as the corridors in the upper levels. The walls were smooth and showing no signs of apertures or portals through which to go on further. Light appeared to radiate from the actual walls rather than by external forms of illumination.

In the centre of the space an 'S' shaped desk drew attention to itself. Inlaid into the desktop were a series of flat-screens that appeared to glow as if they were in some form of 'standby' mode.

To one side away from the main desk there were located a number of sofas, chairs and small side tables, just like any normal office.

Opposite the seating array, a tube appeared, as if it morphed out of the far wall.

The entire company continued to stand by the still open elevator doors, as if waiting to be 'invited' into the room.

Eventually, 'Der gute Doktor' motioned to the tube-like apparition and as the group moved closer, it was clear to see that inside the tube there were in a single row bullet- shaped seating capsules. The small 'train' before them also glowed as did the walls. The configuration was more reminiscent of a carnival ride, one that commenced going round and round before lifting high and low, elevating the rider in a dizzy fairground fashion.

There were no signs of life, or having been life present in the room. Regardless, with some further persuasion from 'Der gute Doktor, each party member found a seat in the 'train' and made themselves as comfortable as possible. Anticipation levels were high, once more reminiscent of a carnival ride prior to commencing the wildest conveyance of a lifetime. As they settled down the environment surrounding them began to melt and fade way, as if dissolving like liver-salts in a tumbler.

And then the vehicle moved at a fantastic rate of acceleration. Thankfully, there seemed to be no resistance to or gravitational influence upon the rapidly moving vehicle. Neither was there any 'G' forces in play. This made the ride easy and comfortable.

After what may have been a minute or perhaps thirty, it was hard to tell, the bullet train abruptly, yet smoothly stopped.

"Welcome to Area 52"

'The Good Doctor,' stood abnormally tall and large before them; the White Wizard whose presence appears in the east out of the early morning sunrise. Yet, paradoxically, still preserving the appearance of a raggedy old scarecrow, who now motioned to the group to vacate their seats.

As they group disembarked, the image of the transportation they had just travelled in abruptly dissolved; whilst to the group's left, a room, the mirror of the space they had just left behind, began to manifest.

Area 52?

No one could speak a word.

The desk and configuration of the chairs appeared to be the same as the space they had just vacated. The only major difference being - behind where the desk was located there opened up a large aperture, at least twelve-feet wide and the same high. A warm golden glow emanated from the opening.

As the curious awe-struck group approached the portal, the space grew wider as a cathedral-like cavern opened up before them. The roof of which was at least one-hundred feet above their heads, and the depth of the void went back into the infinite distance.

What however was most remarkable was the fact that entire volume was or appeared to be covered with or made up of solid gold. The entire company took several steps back and gasped with amazement.

Gracie Lin's dream had come true. She had found her 'rich stuff.'

Kruger's fear of losing his job melted into insignificance.

Bud thought of the latest digital high-end cameras.

Mr Motto Kyoto, felt even more smug, because he was once more right in his thinking.

Regan Jones touched her security lanyard, and wondered to herself whether or not she had jurisdiction here.

Frank rubbed his eyes and fondly looked over to Reagan Jones. His imagination took him running through fields of golden Iowan corn, together with a fair-haired woman, a couple of kids and a crazy over-excited pooch.

Before that was, the image of Principal Jones shooting himself flashed across his wakening mind. As far as the Principal of Iowa State was concerned, Frank remained ambivalent.

Diana essentially felt depressed. Nothing would or could alter the situation. She would never be the same, no one would. All she wanted was to get away, anywhere other than where she was. As far as the Principal's suicide was concerned, well, she really did not possess a strong opinion regarding the matter. It was a mess, it was 'messy.' His demise altered nothing.

Colonel K. Kernel thought about that ranch he had always dreamed of as a kid. Horses roaming the wide-open spaces of Wyoming, a life-time away from where he was actually raised; Kentucky. Where African Americans were still despised and frowned upon.

His mom and dad, who he had not seen recently were

still there. He would change that. He would offer them a new life.

Then the cold light of day struck him. As he remembered he was a wanted terrorist madman who would be shot on site. And that at any time a SWAT team would abseil down from the ceiling and shoot him to pieces with automatic weapons.

Thelma felt anger and disappointment, as she had continually been deceived. The entire world had made a fool of her, she had been used and abused.

This was it.

'If,' and it was a big 'if,' she got out of this unholy mess she would, she would what? Write a book about it all?

Deny her real feelings? Remain unfulfilled, never at peace, never satisfied. Who would or could ever take the burden of her miserable life off of her aching back?

Duncan still thought he was on the best acid trip he had ever undertaken and was loving every colourful minute of it.

Der gute Doktor basically felt elated and victorious. He was about to open up the curtains to a performance that would be the 'Greatest Show on Earth,' and it was not going to be any flying-pig-circus.

The mouths of the gold-diggers began to salivate and dribble, whilst others remained more objective and sober with their thoughts and inner-reactions.

Then, as if the situation could get even more questionably unbelievable, in the centre of the concave golden rock formation, a figure slowly and gradually appeared. The light remained behind the approaching entity, thus placing much of it in shadow.

However, there remained sufficient light to pick out some more obvious details relating to the vaporous being. Each member of the group, not only witnessed the form from a different angle, but rather, according to their own psyche, perceived something uniquely different, but all equally as challenging.

Gracie Lin saw in her fragile mind the same projected apparition she had previously seen along one of the upper-corridors. Was it then simply another projection trick? It might well have been? Did it matter with all this gold around?

Nothing was real.

Now no one in the group could tell fact from fiction, or a truth from a lie.

The figure meanwhile moved cautiously forward.

To the entire group its head appeared overly large. The eyes were deathly black holes, its mouth to Diana appeared to be almost non-existent.

Frank perceived the body which to him was thin, with little or no muscle structure.

To Thelma the arms came across as being extra-long and ungainly.

As Thelma gazed on in awe, a soft, hardly audible voice entered into her mind… repeatedly saying: 'help me … please help me … help me…'

Thelma immediately knew that this was the same repetitive voice she had previously encountered in Hangar 2. Therefore, being the source of her miraculous healing.

For a moment a surge of warm energy washed over her body. She felt, light, as if she were floating through balmy therapeutic air.

Duncan, had given very little thought to anyone or anything. However, he did realise that there was some connection here between himself and the strange, what he took to be a visual projection, or more likely - hallucination, he now perceived before him.

He wanted to move closer to the image, to reach out and touch it, to see if there was any substance to what he was seeing.

The notion of the image before them being a projection became infectious as now, apart from, 'The Good 'Doctor,' who was suddenly noticeably absent, all the other party members: Thelma, the Colonel, Kruger, Motto Kyoto, Bud, Duncan, Diana, Frank, Gracie Lin and

Reagan Jones once more collectively reached out. And as they did each one felt a strange electrify sensation move up along their bodies, followed by a strong sense of relaxation and well-being.

However, only Kruger held back. He was cynical and harbored serious doubts regarding the so-called - 'Good Doctor's' agenda, such as it was. Someone needed to take control and bring all this bull-shit to a realistic conclusion.

Once and for all.

If truth be known, Kruger was totally pissed with the fact that he had been disturbed whilst trying to seduce Gracie Lin. So angry was he, that in order to prove the validity or otherwise of the apparition standing before them, he pulled out his sidearm from its leg holster and discharged two well aimed rounds toward the image.

THE END

Lightning Source UK Ltd.
Milton Keynes UK
UKHW010656270121
377761UK00002B/454

9 781800 316409